BY ALLISON BUCCOLA

The Ascent

Catch Her When She Falls

THE ASCENT

THE
ASCENT

—

A NOVEL

ALLISON BUCCOLA

RANDOM HOUSE
NEW YORK

Random House
An imprint and division of Penguin Random House LLC
1745 Broadway, New York, NY 10019
randomhousebooks.com
penguinrandomhouse.com

LIBRARY OF CONGRESS CATALOGING-IN-PUBLICATION DATA
Names: Buccola, Allison, author.
Title: The ascent : a novel / Allison Buccola.
Description: First edition. | New York, NY : Random House, 2025.
Identifiers: LCCN 2024012644 (print) | LCCN 2024012645 (ebook) |
ISBN 9780593730003 (hardcover ; acid-free paper) | ISBN 9780593730010 (ebook)
Subjects: LCGFT: Thrillers (Fiction) | Novels.
Classification: LCC PS3602.U226 A93 2025 (print) | LCC PS3602.U226 (ebook) |
DDC 813/.6—dc23/eng/20240423
LC record available at https://lccn.loc.gov/2024012644
LC ebook record available at https://lccn.loc.gov/2024012645

Printed in the United States of America on acid-free paper

randomhousebooks.com

1st Printing

First Edition

Book design by Edwin Vazquez

The authorized representative in the EU for
product safety and compliance is Penguin Random House Ireland,
Morrison Chambers, 32 Nassau Street,
Dublin D02 YH68, Ireland.
https://eu-contact.penguin.ie.

For Emma

"This was the best time of my life. And these people were my family."

—Laura Johnston Kohl,
as quoted in *Stories from Jonestown*

THE ASCENT

No one knows what happened to my mother and sister and the rest of The Fifteen. That's the truth, although people like to pretend otherwise. Everyone likes to think they've solved it, that their theory is common sense, everything else fantasy.

"He shot them," my cousin Clara told me over breakfast one morning, a few weeks after I moved in with her family. I was twelve and she was thirteen, and she held my sudden appearance in her home against me. "That's what my mom says."

I focused on my bowl of cereal and tried not to react.

"He buried them in the woods. He's probably on his way to South America right now."

There was no proof—no one ever found Christopher, or bodies, or blood—but no one corrects people like my cousin. People like her are allowed to have their theories, to speak their minds, because they look and act the right way. No one ever reminds them gently *we don't know that*, or exchanges concerned looks when they start speaking. No one jots down each tic or stutter like it might mean something, like it's *something to keep an eye on.*

No one ever calls them crazy.

I, on the other hand, have to watch what I do and say at all times. I grew up under scrutiny, any misstep a cause for concern. The adults in my life—my aunt and uncle, my teachers, my therapist—were always waiting for the other shoe to drop, watching for something to manifest.

I am my mother's daughter, after all. And maybe his, too.

When I married Theo, when we moved in together and set up our house like a home, when the nurse at the hospital placed our daughter, red and writhing, on my chest, I thought I had finally put The Fifteen and my old self behind me. I thought I could keep the past in the past. I thought I could build my own family, a good family, that I could be a good mother.

Lucy, I love you.

Lucy, I'm sorry.

PART ONE

—

SLEEPWALKING

CHAPTER ONE

—

Theo wants to move Lucy upstairs to the third-floor room, but it's not ready yet. It was probably someone's office before we moved in, the walls hunter green, dotted with small nail holes. The thick white paint on the dormer windows cracks in places, old layers exposed. The house is a hundred and fifty years old, a Philadelphia rowhome, and there is lead in the paint, the pipes, everywhere. *She's not going to get lead poisoning,* Theo says every time I mention it. *It's not like she'll be roaming the room licking things. She'll be stuck in her crib.*

He raises the issue again this morning. Lucy squeezes a banana in her fist, smashes it against her tray. I sit beside her, watching. I am so tired that my vision blurs when I turn my head too fast, a sharp pain building in my right temple. She still only sleeps for two-hour stretches, and she needs to be held and rocked and soothed for half an hour every time she wakes.

"She gets up all the time because she smells you," Theo says. He is pacing the kitchen, looking for something. He lifts a stack of mail and scans the counter. "She knows you're right there. She'd sleep better if she were upstairs."

"You'd sleep better, you mean," I say. Theo sleeps downstairs but claims he still wakes whenever she does. He can hear her crying, my footsteps as I cross our room, back and forth. He's already folded his sheet neatly this morning, placed it in the corner of the couch, his pillow resting on top.

He stops moving and shoots me a look that says *that's not fair.* "We'd *all* sleep better," he says. "You can't keep this up, either. It's not healthy."

"I'm fine."

Theo spots his phone on the table behind Lucy's pink-and-turquoise stuffed turtle and grabs it. "I was sleep trained at four months, and I turned out okay. My mom said—"

My chest constricts. I set my coffee down, harder than I mean to. "I don't want to do that."

Theo blinks and looks away, which he thinks doesn't count as rolling his eyes. He tops off his thermos of coffee and sits beside me.

"What do you have planned for today?" he asks. He likes it when I have a plan, when there is order and structure to our day.

"We've got our moms' group this morning," I say, and he nods in approval.

"You should see if some of the other moms want to meet up for playdates. Or even drinks sometime. Moms' night out."

The tightness is returning.

"Maybe," I say.

"Fey and Niko want to get drinks after work." Friends of his from law school. "I'm sure my mom could watch Lucy if you want to come."

"You have fun," I say. "I don't mind staying home." Fey and Niko and Theo mostly gossip about people I don't know or care about: old classmates, colleagues, judges. Fey went to a large law firm after graduation, Niko works in-house for a start-up, and Theo became a public defender, but all three of them still inhabit a shared world that feels foreign to me.

"I just think you could use some time with other adults."

"I'm fine. Really."

Lucy has eaten some of her banana, and the rest is on her face and beneath her high chair. She claps her hands together, *more*, and I stand to get her another. Theo is still watching me, frowning, like he's trying to make sense of me. I've been catching him looking at me that way with growing frequency: leaning in the archway between our kitchen and family room, studying me as I count out blocks for Lucy or bounce her stuffed turtle toward her on the rug. It's like he's realized he had me all wrong. Like he's asking himself: *Who is this person in my house?*

"I can get the banana," he says, and I hold it up, *already done*. I peel it, break it into pieces for Lucy.

"Do you want to take a shower before I head in to work?" he asks.

"That's okay."

"Lee," he says, impatient. "It's fine. Go shower."

I hesitate. Lucy cries if I leave the room without her, a high-pitched, desperate howl.

"*Go*," he says. "I can watch her for five minutes. She's my kid, too."

I go, because this is something we are "working on," and I really am trying to be better, but her cries follow me up the stairs. I turn on the shower, but it doesn't help. I can hear her even with the water running, and the sound cuts through me, a physical pain. Theo isn't doing enough to soothe her. He isn't reassuring her that I'm right upstairs, or telling her I'll be back soon. He's probably not even holding her. I shower as fast as I can, dry myself and dress hastily, and rush back.

Lucy has stopped crying, but only because she has tired herself out. She is whimpering now, her breathing erratic and hitched, and Theo is smiling, pleased with how things have gone.

"See?" he says, handing her back to me. "Isn't that better?"

He gives Lucy a kiss on the top of her head and squeezes my shoulder. "I love you," he says, but the look he gives me—pointed and intentional—makes it feel like a message for someone else. The person I was before Lucy, who he knows is still in there, somewhere, waiting to break free.

"I love you, too," I say.

He leaves, the door clicking shut behind him. At first, his absence is a relief. But then it's quiet, Lucy looking up at me, the digital clock switching from seven forty-two to seven forty-three. Now it's just me and Lucy, the full day stretching out before us.

"All right, sweet girl," I say. Lucy smiles and reaches for my face, her hand gummy. "Let's get you changed."

And so the day begins.

Lucy watches me from the family room rug—Theo's mother's rug, which she "gave" to us but still inspects discreetly when she comes over for our weekly dinner. Lucy is just learning how to sit; she is bolstered by a pillow and leaning on her turtle for support. I pack the stroller, checking and double-checking to make sure we have all the things we need. A blanket for nursing cover, diapers, a spare outfit. The baby carrier, just in case. My phone. My keys. My wallet. For the past seven months, my thoughts have been a series of checklists, routinized procedure, the steps I must take to get from point A to point B. I do not sleep. If something isn't on one of my checklists, it doesn't get done.

My phone buzzes. A text from Theo.

Niko and Fey are going to come over instead. They'll bring food!

I sigh, but respond to the text with a thumbs-up, then drop the phone into the basket beneath the stroller. Theo means well. He's trying to include me. He thinks it would help if I made mom friends, if I arranged coffee dates to "stay in touch" with my co-workers at the Academy of Natural Sciences. He hopes that if I take regular showers, and change out of my sweatpants, and spend increasingly long increments of time away from Lucy, I'll emerge on the other side of this fog, my old self again.

Theo doesn't know about my family.

I told him on an early date, drinking old-fashioneds out of a thermos on the steps of the art museum, that I don't know who my father is. That my mother is a hippie, a little self-involved. I told him I went to live with my aunt when I was a teenager and haven't spoken to my mother in a long time. "Estranged" was the word I used, and it felt good rolling off my tongue, like I could fix the separation whenever I wanted. As soon as I decided it was time.

That must be so hard, Theo said, his eyes glassy and sympathetic.

It's fine, I said, brushing it off. *It's just how it is.*

We had late-into-the-night conversations about cutting off a parent, about setting boundaries, about forgiveness, and there was never a good time to tell him those conversations were based on a part-fiction. So now he thinks what I'm experiencing—*postpartum depression,* he's decided, neat and clinical—is a phase, a hormonal imbalance, something to manage and correct and get through.

I have experienced this before, and it is not depression. It is an untethering. But that's not something Theo will understand.

"Ready, sweet girl?" I ask Lucy.

We walk, navigating the uneven sidewalks, driven up by tree roots. I put in my earphones and settle into the back-and-forth of two podcast hosts discussing the highs and lows of parenting. One has preschoolers and the other has kids in middle and high school, and their struggles—the negotiations, the school politics, the iPads and phones and friends exerting questionable influence—seem so foreign. I can't imagine Lucy as a toddler, an eight-year-old, a preteen, and sometimes my inability to do so makes me uncomfortable, like Lucy isn't meant to reach those ages. I have that thought again now, and I push it aside.

We're at the bakery.

We go here not because it's particularly good or because it's particularly on the way, but because, unlike at most Philadelphia storefronts, there are no stairs leading up to the entrance and it's possible to fit the stroller through the narrow door. I get in line, put in my usual order, and wait. The barista pours cold water over coffee grounds, making slow, careful circles with her wrist. A large clock with exposed gears hangs on the subway-tiled wall behind her: nine-fifteen.

I look toward Lucy in her stroller, and there is someone touching her, a hand on her small, bare foot.

My whole body tightens, adrenaline coursing through me. I grab the stroller handle and the girl beside us—who is in her mid-twenties, maybe—casually lets go. She looks at me, unconcerned, gives me a gap-toothed smile. Her hair is short and uneven, like she took a pair of scissors to it herself. She's too thin: her collarbone protruding, her bony shoulders curved in.

But Lucy is looking back at her and smiling.

Lucy does not smile at strangers. She barely smiles at people she knows, apart from me. She tolerates Theo with a guarded skepticism, as long as I'm still in the room; she screams when Jacqueline, Theo's mother, tries to hold her. But here she is, smiling at this stranger who is covering her face with an unfolded napkin, sticking out her tongue, scrunching her nose.

"She likes you," I say, my grip on the stroller loosening. "She doesn't usually like people."

"Smart girl," she says, squeezing Lucy's foot again, a gesture that's met with laughter, Lucy's delight. "I feel the same way."

The barista calls out *latte*, and the girl slides forward to the counter, takes the drink. She waves goodbye to me and winks at Lucy, and she's gone. The woman who was in front of me in line is looking around, confused. She's approaching the barista, *excuse me*, and the barista is making another drink, and Lucy is becoming unhappy again. I push the stroller back and forth, trying to soothe her as her whines grow louder and more insistent, until at last my drink is called and we are out the door and walking again.

———

Our Mommy and Me group has begun. I sit cross-legged on the gym's springy floor, Lucy on a pink muslin blanket in front of me. We are surrounded by gymnastics equipment, balance beams and blue plastic mats, low-hanging uneven bars, a foam obstacle course. A class for three-year-olds meets immediately after our session, and so we some-times see the mothers in the waiting room through the glass partition, their kids climbing on chairs and pushing their faces against the door.

". . . don't see what's so hard about it," Amanda is saying next to me. I pick at a piece of yellow tape peeling from the mat, realize I'm fidgeting, stop myself. "There's a schedule. I've written it out for her. It's right there on the table where she can't miss it."

Dr. Dana is nodding, a therapist's patient nod. She lifts the water bottle beside her. The plastic crinkles under her grip. Her reddish-brown hair is cut into a sharp bob. I was nervous when I found out this group was being led by a therapist; I worried she'd see right through me. But Dr. Dana has never seen right through anything.

"It can be hard for everyone," Dr. Dana says. "Stepping into these new roles. Sometimes blurring family and caretaker lines—"

"She acts like she's doing me this big *favor*, but it's not a favor if she's not going to do it right."

"I have the same problem with my mom," Winnie says from across the circle. "I swear she's doing it on purpose to make some kind of point."

"Right?" Amanda says. "Thank you."

I picture my mother with a pang of jealousy. In my mind she's holding Mona, who always wanted to be carried, even at five, six. Mona clings to her, burrowing her face into her neck. My mother supports her with one arm and reaches out her other hand for me. Her hands were always rough and calloused, her fingernails cut to a short and practical length, a freckle at the base of her thumb.

This way, Ophelia. Keep up.

"Lee?" Dr. Dana says loudly, like she's repeating herself. "Do you have anything you want to share from this week?"

I realize I'm picking at the tape again and smooth it back down. I go to this group because I like the structure it imposes on my day. I like sitting in a circle, the physical closeness, the feeling that, for forty-five minutes, I am one of the moms. I like for Lucy to see the other babies, although I am not sure she recognizes them from class to class. I do not like sharing.

"We've been okay," I say. When Dr. Dana looks at me like this is not enough, I offer: "Theo wants to move Lucy out of our room, and I'm not sure I'm ready."

"Moving Jackson out of our room was the best decision we ever made," Amanda says.

Maggie nods enthusiastically on my other side. "You need to get her out and start sleep training her," she says. "Seriously, it's a game changer."

I picture Lucy on the third floor. Alone. Terrified I've left her, that I'm not coming back.

"I don't think I'm ready for that."

"I didn't think I was ready, either," says Maggie. "But oh my god, I was."

"These transitions can feel scary," Dr. Dana cuts in, diplomatic. "But often, once you're on the other side, you realize it wasn't so bad."

"I don't want to move her," I say. My tone is off, too short, and I try to correct it. "Her room isn't ready yet."

"And there's nothing wrong with that," Dr. Dana says.

"I just wish Theo would let it go." I tear up and blink, embarrassed. These women in the support group are not really my friends. They're people I see once a week.

"Husbands don't get it," Amanda says.

"I keep having this dream," I say. "I fall asleep with Lucy in my arms, and I wake up, and she's gone. And then I start searching for her, tearing through the sheets, half asleep, until Theo finds me and wakes me up and tells me it's okay, that she's still in her bassinet."

I worry I've said too much.

"Oh, I used to get that dream, too," Maggie says. "It was horrible."

I do not mention the other dream: that I look into Lucy's bassinet and her face is blurred, unrecognizable. *Who is she*, I shout, *where is she*, and Theo says, *right there, right there.* I am always afraid I will trip up and say the wrong thing, a red flag, that it will become painfully obvious I am not fit to be a mother. That Dr. Dana will suggest—and then demand—I seek additional "help." The wheels of the system will start turning, and I will lose Lucy.

"Very common," Dr. Dana says, nodding sagely. "Maybe you could start small? Prepare her room, see how that feels?"

"That's a good idea," I say.

"Did you take your trip to the grocery store?" she asks, and at first I'm not sure what she means. But then I remember the commitment I made last week: a solo errand while Theo stays home with Lucy.

"Oh right," I say. "Yes."

"How did it feel?"

"Good," I lie. I didn't go to the store; I looped the block twice and came back home. Dr. Dana nods and smiles, and the conversation drifts to Maggie, who is preparing for a vacation, their first flight as a family, and then Lauren, who is struggling to remind co-workers that she really is not available on Mondays and Tuesdays unless it's an emergency.

I pull Lucy onto my lap and kiss the top of her head. Her hair, still short and fine. It hasn't grown yet. I feel the weight of her against me, and it calms me, reminds me: *She is here, and she is mine.*

Theo told me on an early date that he wanted to have four kids. *Or five, why not?* he said, only half-joking. He's an only child, the kind who imagined a brood of brothers and sisters for himself, who didn't like the quiet.

Who's going to raise them all? I teased.

At some point they start raising each other, he said, waving it off with a grin. *Simple.*

Theo is good with kids. Relaxed, easy. He talks to them without condescending. He listens to their questions and gives real answers they can understand. He knows when to feign surprise, how to tell a good knock-knock joke, how to react to a bad one. He will be—he is—a good father.

Things don't come as naturally to me. Nothing about motherhood ever seemed simple, or easy, or straightforward, and before I met Theo I wasn't sure I wanted to have children at all. But Theo's enthusiasm was contagious, and he convinced me I could do it. *A new little person in the world*, he said. *Experiencing everything for the first time, and you get to be right there with them.*

When my pregnancy test was positive, it shouldn't have been a surprise. We had been trying for three months, I had missed my period, and that morning the smell of sausage frying on a food truck grill had hit me hard, turning my stomach. I spent the day at the Academy in a state of uncertainty—*mother, not-mother, baby, not-baby*—and rushed home at five. I thought I knew what I wanted the result to be, but when I took the test and saw the blue line, I realized I had been wrong.

Theo came home late that night, flicked on the lights. I was curled up on the couch, staring at the wall.

Why are you sitting in the dark? he asked.

I'm pregnant, I said.

He slid onto the couch behind me and pulled me in toward him.

Hey, he said. *This is good news. Really good news.*

I don't know how to be a mother, I said.

No one does, he told me. *You figure it out as you go along.*

My mother didn't.

You are not your mother. Theo sat up so he could look me in the eyes. *You are kind, and loving, and present. You're going to be the best mom.*

I blinked back tears, his conviction almost enough to convince me. I wanted so badly to believe that he was right, that he knew me better than I knew myself.

We're going to be parents, Theo said. *We're going to build a family together.*

My pregnancy was easy. Theo made me mocktails in the evenings and took my picture every week, and we looked up the various fruits and vegetables that matched the baby in size. We agreed quickly on the name Lucy. Theo liked it because it was his great-aunt's name, and I liked it because it was the name of a character from my favorite childhood book. We read everything we could on pregnancy and labor and the baby's first weeks and attended birthing classes together. We rolled our eyes at the doula/teacher's enthusiasm for essential oils, but also bought some, just in case. We were in it together, a team.

Labor was fast, and Lucy cried right away. *She's got a good set of lungs,* the nurse said, and I looked up and Theo was crying, too, his hand squeezing mine. The nurse placed Lucy on my chest and she blinked her eyes open, a vivid blue. She looked at me like she knew me, something familiar in this new and startling world.

Hi, sweet girl, I said. *I'm your mother.*

The end of an era and the beginning of a new one.

It will be different, I told myself. *It will be okay.*

I walk home from Mommy and Me with Amanda and Winnie. The two of them have a real friendship: They meet at parks in the afternoon, they coordinate music classes and story times and stroller tours at the art museum. But all three of us live in the same general direction, and so sometimes, if diaper changes and feeding and packing line up, I walk with them. When the sidewalk narrows, we walk in single file. When it widens out again, Amanda and Winnie walk next to each other, and I trail behind.

My phone pings with a text from Theo.

How was moms' group?

He checks in more these days. He wants to make sure we are staying busy, active. Engaged.

Good, I type back, and then add: Walking back with Amanda and Winnie. He'll like that; it will put him at ease. Amanda is talking about her mother's inability to follow simple requests again, and Winnie is commiserating, and I am listening until we reach the park and Lucy and I splinter off for home.

I park the stroller next to our front steps and unbuckle Lucy. I unlock the door and set her down on the rug, propping her against a pillow. I drag the stroller up the three stone steps and through the narrow doorframe. Lucy slumps to the side, nearly hitting her head. She is startled, silent at first and then howling. I scoop her up, bouncing and shushing. Getting into the house is a process, and I am so focused on calming Lucy that I almost miss the envelope that has been slipped through our mail slot. Theo's name is written in thick black Sharpie on the front, all capital letters. No address or postmark. It is not sealed.

I pick it up. Lucy grabs for the envelope and I hold it out of her reach. Inside is a glossy photograph, a young boy with a wide grin, proudly showing off a missing tooth. On the back, a message: WHAT IF IT WAS YOUR CHILD?

I wince, pull out my phone and take a picture, text it to Theo.

I'm sorry, he writes back. Try not to touch it too much. I'll bring it to the marshals tomorrow.

Theo has been getting these photographs since he began working on a case I've only heard him refer to as "the kid case." *It's a tough one,* he told me after the arraignment. *What is he accused of?* I asked, and he shook his head, his mouth a grim line. *I don't want to say,* he said. *You don't want to know.* The photographs started soon after.

Theo says these kinds of things happen. Not all the time, but sometimes. Judges and prosecutors receive threats from people they've put away. Defense attorneys receive them from clients who think they haven't done a good job, or victims who think they've done their job too well. *These aren't really even threats,* he told me, trying to calm me down. *They're pictures from someone who doesn't want the victims to be forgotten.*

But they feel like threats to me.

Whoever is sending these knows where we live, I type back. What if they escalate?

Theo sends a quick response: I'm taking care of it.

What if they hurt Lucy?

Ellipses appear and then disappear on my phone. A long pause, and then, finally, a response.

Don't worry. We'll get this resolved.

I put the photo and the envelope in a Ziploc bag and set it on the counter. Lucy is bothered that I am distracted. I try to clear my mind and put on a happy face for her. I lie down on the ground beside her and read her a book about letters, and another about manners, and one about a band of woodland creatures who have lost their way. I keep my voice light and cheery, and Lucy listens, and for once, she is calm.

Theo comes home after Lucy has gone to bed. I hand him the bagged photo, and he puts it into his briefcase.

"This needs to stop," I say.

"I know," he says. "I know. We're taking care of it."

Before I can say more, the front door swings open and Fey and Niko are there, holding pizza and a bottle of wine. They are old friends, the kind of friends Theo thinks shouldn't need to knock.

"Hey you two," Fey says. She searches out Theo first, pushing herself up on her toes to wrap her arms around his neck. Theo squeezes back, a hug that seems to last just a second too long, but—I remind myself—this is how they are. Theo is a toucher, and so is Fey. She finds me next, hugs me a little less enthusiastically. I am not a toucher, and it shows. *Uncross those arms,* Theo used to tell me, joking and not joking, when we were in the early stages of dating. *Open your-self up to the world.*

Niko is through the door next, and he and Theo greet each other with a "hey man," a hand grab, sturdy pats on the back. Niko has a fratty congeniality, and he brings that out in Theo, too. He is Black, wearing a fleece vest with the Harvard shield and overpriced sneakers, looking every bit the tech bro he is.

"Lee," Niko says, hugging me, too. "Thanks for letting us barge in on you like this."

"Of course," I say. "It's good to see you guys."

I usher them to the back patio quickly so they don't wake Lucy. Our patio table wobbles on the uneven bricks, terra-cotta pots lined up behind it. A string of globe lights hangs overhead, giving the patio a soft glow. Fey uncorks the wine.

"How are you?" she asks brightly. "How is Lucy?" She is wearing a tailored jacket, a matte pink lipstick, her hair curled into smooth, blond ringlets. She is from the South—one of the Carolinas, I think, or maybe Georgia—and I have never seen her out of makeup or with her hair mussed. It used to make me self-conscious, but now the gulf between us is so wide it hardly seems to matter.

"Great," I tell her. "We're both great." Fey and Niko don't have children yet—have not started thinking about it, as far as I know—and she's not really interested in what Lucy is up to. I wouldn't have been either, two years ago.

"Are you back at work?"

"Not yet. Soon."

"So nice that the Academy is so flexible with their maternity leave," she says, and I smile in response.

"How have you been?" I ask.

"Great," she says. "Super busy with the Stutton case. Has Theo said anything about it?"

"I don't think so."

"Oh, it's crazy." She launches into a story that is ostensibly for my benefit, about a twenty-year feud between neighbors using their extravagant wealth to spite each other and a judge who finally had enough, and Niko and Theo, who have heard this story before, jump in, asking questions and adding commentary.

"This is exactly why you need to stop representing rich assholes," Theo says, laughing, and Fey rolls her eyes and waves him off.

"Not all of us are bankrolled, you know," she says. She's teasing; they have this back-and-forth about Fey's law firm and Theo's public defender job all the time. "We can't all afford to be 'heroes.'"

The conversation drifts, as I knew it would, to old classmates—someone wrote a firm-wide email that ended up on a legal gossip site, another classmate is getting divorced, another is running for office. I excuse myself to check on Lucy and slide the door shut behind me. I linger by the bottom of the stairs, but Lucy is sleeping soundly.

I turn back toward the glass door. They're laughing, Theo's head thrown back. Niko was Theo's roommate their first year of law school—*the o-bros*, they used to call themselves, which should be embarrassing but they have such a close friendship it's hard to fault them for sometimes being ridiculous. I think being around each other makes them feel like they're twenty-five again, in a walk-up apartment in West Philly.

I try to imagine what that kind of relationship would feel like. Someone who knows you, who knows your past. Doesn't just know it: lived it. Has the same memories, the same associations, the same shorthand.

Lucy is still quiet, and so I fill a water glass for myself and return to the patio. Fey has lit a cigarette. She holds it between two fingers, her nails painted a soft pearl. Niko refills his wine.

"So," he says. "Watch any good shows lately?"

I look at Theo, and he holds out a hand, as if to say *your turn*.

"Not really," I say. "I fall asleep if anything is longer than twenty minutes."

"Oh," Fey says. She swats Niko on the shoulder, excited. "We just started this docuseries on Netflix. About Jacob's Hill? Have you heard of it?"

The ground drops out beneath me.

"Hmm," Theo says, only half paying attention. He has pulled out his phone and is frowning at the screen in concentration.

"What is it?" I ask Fey. I sip my wine and set it on the table, which tips toward me. A part of me has been waiting for this moment, although I had tried to convince myself it wouldn't happen. A "producer" reached out about two years ago: Meghan Kessler, a name with a Twitter account and no production credits. *Not a threat,* I told myself.

"So this cult—"

"Goddamn it," Theo says. "Fucking Haney."

Fey and Niko groan and roll their eyes. I don't know who Haney is—a prosecutor or a judge, maybe—but they clearly do. Theo rises from his chair.

"Sorry," he says. "I have to deal with this."

"Duty calls," says Niko.

Theo ducks inside, sliding the glass door shut behind him, and my whole body loosens. Maybe the topic of conversation will change, the documentary forgotten as abruptly as it was remembered. But Fey leans forward, oblivious, and continues.

"It's about this doomsday cult," she says. "And they were here. Like, right outside Philly. In Strathhaven."

Niko furrows his brow, blinks a few times, a connection forming. I shift in my chair.

"Aren't you from out there?" he asks me.

"Lee is from the Main Line," Fey corrects. The wealthy Philadelphia suburbs that run northwest from the city. A number of their Penn classmates grew up there; many of their colleagues live there now. "Right, Lee?"

I glance back toward the sliding door. I can see the glow of Theo's laptop inside. He's working, preoccupied. Theo does not watch much television, I reassure myself, and when he picks for himself he picks sports, comedies, lighter shows. *I get enough of the heavy stuff at work,* he says. He tries to mask it around Fey and Niko, but he is emotionally invested in his cases, and they take their toll.

"I moved to the Main Line when I was a teenager."

Niko's forehead wrinkles again. He is doing the math.

"They just *disappeared,*" Fey continues. "Vanished. There were no signs of a struggle, but it also didn't look like anyone had *planned* to leave. No one even packed their clothes. They were still there, hanging in the closets. Their toothbrushes were still by the sinks. All the food they had preserved was just left in their root cellar, which—don't you think you'd want to bring some of that with you if you were going somewhere?"

The *drip, drip, drip* of the faucet in the communal kitchen. The countertops wiped down, the wooden floors swept. Bowls and glasses and plates drying on tiered racks. A large pot from last night's stew soaking in the sink. *Hello?* I called out. *Hello?*

"Huh," I say, lifting my glass. I try not to look at Niko.

"The leader of the group had written this, you know, *manifesto,* and had these messianic delusions, so it might have been a ritualized suicide, something like that, but no one ever found them."

I wince, just a little, but Niko is perceptive and I worry he notices. He rubs his chin, but Fey keeps going.

"There were fifteen of them, and it's not like this was in the *wilderness.* The police searched the compound and the forest but never found anything. No clues, no bodies."

Compound. A word the early reports used over and over, conjuring a certain idea: something sinister. Something wrong. Not "residence." Not "home."

"But, on the other hand, it was a big enough group—and four of them were kids—so if they were still out there, you'd think someone would have *seen* them somewhere."

"Maybe they ascended," I say, and Niko tilts his head, but Fey laughs and throws her hands in the air and says: "I mean, *who knows!* It's so weird."

"So *did* you live out that way?" Niko asks. "Before you moved to the Main Line?"

"I did," I say, and I take another sip of wine, this one bigger. I haven't drunk much since Lucy, and the alcohol hits me faster than it used to, a soft unsteadying.

"Close to Strathhaven?" Fey asks.

"In Strathhaven."

Fey sits straight in her chair, crushing the butt of her cigarette with the toe of her ballet flat. This is the most interested she's ever been in me.

"Did you know about them then?" she asks. "Did you ever see them?"

I reassure myself that Fey and Niko will not repeat this conversation. It is, to them, just a conversation about a television series.

"They mostly kept to themselves," I say.

"So you *were* there when they disappeared," Fey says. "It must have been a huge deal."

"It was."

"Do you have your own theory about what happened?"

"I—"

The glass door slides open, and Theo is standing in the doorway, looking at me. I catch my breath.

"She's up," he says.

"Sorry," I say to Fey as I push up from my chair, relief coursing through me. "I've got to . . ."

"Go, go," Fey says, dismissing me with a wave. "But you really need to watch it. Especially if you were *there*. It's so good."

I step back into the house, slip off my shoes, and close the door behind me. Lucy's cries are loud and urgent, and I shout to her that I'm coming. I steady myself as I climb the stairs. I pull Lucy from her bassinet to feed her, and we settle into our rocking chair. She latches, her eyes heavy. I close my eyes, too, and listen. Theo is outside again, and they are talking too loudly, muffled laughs floating up into the room, but at least it sounds like the conversation has shifted. I can only imagine what the documentary has to say. The same sensational content as always, probably: breathless references to Heaven's Gate and Jonestown, the reporters' thinly concealed hope that maybe something like that could happen here, too.

WHOLE CULT VANISHES INTO THIN AIR read one early headline. *Police continue their search for doomsday group operating in Philadelphia suburb.*

The headline was wrong, of course. It wasn't all of us.

I'm still here.

CHAPTER TWO

—

My mother sometimes claimed to have a sixth sense about big, life-changing events: a kind of gut-knowing, an awareness that her world was about to be turned on its head. I never knew whether to believe her, but I certainly didn't inherit that skill.

On the morning of April 4, I woke to a stream of light through the window and the soft scrape of a branch against the glass. This was unusual: for most of my childhood, I had been jarred awake by Mona's elbow in my ribs, the sudden cold of sheets ripped off me, Josephine's heavy stomps across the floor. But Mona had begun sleeping with our mother—she was unwell, again—and Josephine had left a few weeks earlier, and so now I had the room to myself. I lay still for a few moments because, for once, I could.

If I had been paying attention, I would have realized the silence extended beyond my room. Normally, I could hear two-year-old Kai's shrieks of laughter through the thin walls. The bathroom was right across the hallway, and the door slammed loudly against its frame whenever anyone was coming or going. There were seventeen of us on the floor—fifteen once Josephine and her mother had gone—and three bathroom stalls, two showers, a narrow hallway.

I rubbed my eyes, pushed myself up, swung my feet over the side of the bed. When the quiet finally registered, I wondered if I had slept in, if there would be hot water left for me, if maybe it would be wiser to wait.

I slid open the nightstand drawer holding my prized belongings: a ragged stuffed cat I had outgrown but couldn't bring myself to part with, a soft-covered journal. My mother's bracelet, hidden in a torn piece of fabric. She had given it to me on my last birthday, a simple silver chain with a heart pendant. I checked the time on the clock that hung between the two windows and it was not late at all—six-thirty. Instead of alarm, I felt relief I hadn't overslept. I've always wondered what would have happened if I had realized something was wrong then and acted sooner. Maybe, in those early morning hours, I could have found them.

Instead, I grabbed my towel and basket of toiletries and crossed the hallway to the bathroom. On most days, I would have been met by hot, damp air, droplets of water radiating out from the shower stalls across the tile. But that day the floor was dry, the air cool. I set my basket on the narrow bench in the shower cubicle and pulled the curtain shut. The hooks scraped against the bar, a smell like iron rising from the shower drain. I didn't always get hot water, and so I took my time.

I dried myself, dressed. Christopher encouraged plain, simple clothing, no adornment. *Vanity is a weakness,* he said, *a clinging to this world.* I put on a dress my mother had sewn for me, brown and formless and old. She had let out the seams a few months before. *You're getting so big,* she said. I put on a sweater over it, pulled down the sleeves so they covered my bracelet.

I dawdled. I flopped onto my bed, studied the cracks that ran across my ceiling from the residence settling. I imagined one chunk of plaster falling, and then the next, and the next, until the entire ceiling caved in on top of me. I sat up, wrapped my hair in a wet bun, and laced my boots.

The residence walls were covered in scuff marks and dings and dents. A crack from a play fight between River and Echo, four and six, that had gotten out of control. A hole the size of my fist. Animals lived in the walls now; I could hear the sound of something scuffling, the crumble of plaster. It hadn't always been that way. When I was younger, I helped spackle and paint. We brushed down cobwebs before they became a problem.

I knocked on my mother's closed door, and, when she didn't respond, I swung it open, stepped inside. The bed was made, the quilt smoothed. There was a glass of water on the nightstand, next to a book on birds and migratory patterns. A scrap of paper marked her place two-thirds of the way through. Later I would find a note in her handwriting in the margin—*but what about the wind?*—and three dog-eared pages, 27, 87, 93. I ran my thumb over my mother's words so many times in the years that followed, the ink faded.

I felt a pang of uncertainty, a question forming: Was I forgetting something? An early breakfast, a meeting in the common house? There had been more and more meetings recently, long debates on sourcing food that went nowhere. Christopher had final say in what would and would not be put to a vote, and he said we were fine, that he had an answer.

I took the stairwell down to the first floor. The common room was empty, a half-completed botanical puzzle on the coffee table, next to a deck of cards. Mona and I had been playing with them the night before, but not for very long, because Mona wasn't a good sport. She was only six, half my age and still such a child. I caught her peeking at a card before pulling it from the spread and I threw down my hand and called her a baby and told her I wasn't playing with her anymore.

Now the cards were neatly stacked again, the top one bent, just a little. The clock on the wall said seven-fifteen.

I started toward the common house and braced myself for a lecture. My mother would be upset I was late.

The path was thick with new wood chips. It wound through ginkgo trees and honey locust and then forked. To the right was the communal garden, the plastic film of the greenhouse visible through the trees. I had helped prepare the beds the day before. Mona had been with me; she was having a good morning. She climbed to the top of a mulch pile and flopped down, her small body sinking into it. Bark chips caught in her hair, which was already a bird's nest, twisted into knots so tight my mother would need to cut them out. She grabbed a handful of mulch and threw it at me, and I threw one back at her, and Adrienne, who normally would have shot us a look that said *get back to work,* turned her head and let it slide.

Today, I was supposed to help Adrienne build a new fence out of chicken wire stretched around poles. I looked to see if she was already out there in her large-brimmed hat and paisley gloves, working the soil. But the garden was untended, and my stomach twisted again. *They're in the common house,* I told myself. *You've forgotten a meeting. You weren't paying enough attention.*

I continued straight ahead, the common house looming in front of me. Here, the path was stone, lined with hyacinths and golden forsythia and unsettled dirt from the holes Christopher had been digging late at night, every night, all of them filled back in.

I walked up the steps to the heavy wooden door. I pulled it open.

The grandfather clock ticked in the corner, the sound echoing in the common space. Empty chairs formed a circle. The flip chart on the easel, where we wrote out the pros and cons of any proposed change to the way we did things, was turned to a blank sheet. This room connected to the kitchen and dining hall, but there was no clink of silverware against plates or chairs scraping against wood, no buzz of morning conversation.

My stomach lurched.

They're gone, I thought.

But no: They wouldn't leave without me.

"Hello?" I called out, pushing forward into the dark dining hall. The chairs were still turned over on the tables from last night's sweeping. Water dripped in the kitchen. The door to the root cellar gaped open, stone steps leading down into the dark.

"Hello?" I called out again, a tightness taking over my body.

Calm down, I told myself. *There's another explanation.*

There was a time when we left the grounds regularly. We sold goat's milk products and some of our harvest at local farmers markets. We played on the elementary school playground nearby and made occasional visits to the town library. Christopher still encouraged reading then. We made excursions to Walmart for supplies and staples we couldn't produce ourselves. We were not yet self-sufficient. But little by little Christopher had begun insisting that leaving the property was a problem, something to be done infrequently, and then not at all. *We are reaching the end of an era,* he'd say, *and the beginning of a new one, and times of transition are rocky.*

We were supposed to be prepared.

This is no longer a safe place for us, Christopher told us. *They're scared of us, and they're scared of what we stand for. They want to keep us in the dark, asleep.*

Maybe the time had come.

I squeezed my eyes tight. My mother hadn't mentioned anything when she came to my room the night before. Instead, she had talked to me about Mona. *You need to be patient with her. She's younger than you are,* she said, which was true, but also the problem. Once Josephine left, Mona became the closest thing I had to a peer, and the years between us felt like an eternity. And on top of being younger, she was often unwell, too tired to play or work or keep me company. *She idolizes you, you know,* my mother said, and I huffed, a sullen preteen.

That was all she said. I was sure of it. My mother had paused by the door on her way out, like maybe she was about to say something else but changed her mind. *Good night, Ophelia,* she said instead. *Sleep well.* She asked me if I wanted her to turn the light out, and I said no, to leave it on, and she closed the door.

We were supposed to build the garden fence today. We were supposed to have a community meeting tonight. They were here, somewhere. They'd be back. I made myself toast, flipped over one of the chairs, and ate in silence, pushing down my growing alarm. I made and ate a second slice of toast, too, because there was no one to tell me flour was running low.

I peered into every room in the common house, even the dark root cellar, which looked the same, untouched. I walked the property. Both of our vans—large and white and beaten down, older than I was—were still parked in the gravel lot, as they had been all winter. I followed the paths that meandered through the wooded grounds, crossing over the makeshift bridge that cut across the creek, cables wrapped tight around two tree trunks, wooden planks suspended in air. I saw no one.

I slipped through a gap in the fencing that marked the boundary of our lot, my heart pounding. I made my way to the creek, followed it upstream.

"Mom?" I called out, the water soaking the hem of my dress. "Mona?"

I pushed through the brush until I reached the small clearing, the grassy knoll.

"Hello?" I called out.

There was no response.

I pulled my knees into my chest, rocked myself back and forth. *There's an explanation,* I told myself. *They wouldn't leave you. They'll be back at the residence now.*

But when I returned, they still weren't there.

I followed the main path out of the residence to a public trail, the same words on loop in my mind, *they left they left they left,* but they wouldn't have, I told myself. They couldn't have. Not without me. I heard the rustle of wind, birds calling out, and then footsteps. I froze.

A man I didn't know appeared around the bend. He was jogging, feet pounding against the packed dirt, a black Lab on a leash at his side. My heart raced. I thought of Christopher's warnings: *They hate us. They're coming for us. They don't even realize the kinds of atrocities they're capable of.*

The man slowed to a stop, and, when he saw me step backward, pulled his dog in closer.

"She's friendly," he said. He stepped forward. "Are you okay?"

I turned and ran.

I ran until my lungs burned and my legs ached, tripping over unsettled stones and tree roots, branches catching my sweater, the side of my face. I ran until I reached the edge of the forest and a woman's voice cut through the leaves: *Stop.*

"Mom?" I called back. I pushed past branches and blackberry brambles into a neighborhood, a street lined with old houses made of granite and serpentine stone. A woman who looked the same age as my mother played with her toddler son in their front yard, bubbles floating, suspended in the air, a rainbow-colored ball resting a few feet from the curb. She saw me and scooped up the boy with one arm, edged closer to the street.

"Are you lost?" she asked, tentative.

I shook my head and kept walking, blinking back tears.

"Wait," she called after me, and I quickened my pace.

I had it in my head that if I kept walking, I would find them. They had disappeared suddenly, and so they could come back suddenly, too. They couldn't have gone too far. Each time I reached a new street, turned a new corner, I held my breath, hoping this would be the moment I found them.

It never was. I reached the end of the neighborhood and turned onto a street with no sidewalk, just a narrow band of grass and a steep upward slope leading back to the woods. A pickup truck blew past me, close, and I wrapped my sweater tight around myself.

They have to be somewhere, I told myself. *They wouldn't have left me.*

I heard another car approach. It slowed—a police cruiser—and cut me off, pulling onto the grass in front of me.

The door opened, a crack first, and then all the way. I stiffened like a trapped animal, my heart pounding.

A man stepped out. He was uniformed, with a bald, round head and skeptical squint, and he towered over me. He took slow, cautious steps in my direction.

"Are you okay?" he asked. I looked to the sloping incline that separated me from the forest. I wouldn't make it up in time.

"Are you lost?"

I could run back the way I had come. But I knew this man was faster than me, stronger.

"Are you from Jacob's Hill?" he asked. "Do you want me to take you back there?"

"They're gone," I said, my voice barely a whisper.

His eyes widened and his face blanched, and I know, now, the images that must have played through his mind. Bodies laid out in a suburban house in Rancho Santa Fe, faces and torsos covered by a purple cloth, Nike sneakers. The nine hundred dead at Jonestown, a third of them children, defectors shot.

"What happened?" he asked.

"I don't know," I said. "I don't know where they are."

"Come on," he said. "Get in." And I did, because I didn't have any other choice.

We drove, and the officer talked to me like he thought we'd find them on the side of the road somewhere, too. It wasn't until later that I understood he was biding time and collecting information. *Ten-fifty-four at Jacob's Hill,* he said into his radio while I buckled myself into the car. *We need a team out there.*

A digital clock in the dashboard read two fifty-six, which meant they had been gone nine hours at least. More than that if they left in the night. Why had I wasted so much time? Why hadn't I started to look earlier? I could hear my mother's words, her frequent admonition: *You need to pay attention, Ophelia. You need to focus on what's going on around you.*

We turned in to a neighborhood. People clustered at the street corners, checking their watches and shifting their weight. Hope flut-tered in my chest, and I scanned each face carefully, looking for someone familiar.

"School bus must be running late," the officer said, and I swal-lowed back the lump in my throat.

"Can you tell me about them?" he asked. "So I know who we're looking for?"

I described my mother, but not well enough. *Brown hair,* I said. *Tall, thin.* I told him my sister's eyes changed colors depending on her mood. That she had lost two teeth; that a third was loose. I told him Christopher's eyes were light blue, that when he looked at you it felt like he was seeing right through you, that he knew so much about so many things.

"Uh-huh," the officer said, turning left around a bend.

I told him about the Taylors and the Coxes, Adrienne Dagnelle and Patrick Speight. Katrina and her sons, River and Echo. Lottie Dunn, who was older, a grandmother-like figure to us all.

"Did they say anything about leaving?" the officer asked.

"I don't know," I said. I didn't think so, but my mother was right about me: I didn't listen. I didn't pay attention.

"How about Christopher? Did he talk about leaving? About going somewhere?"

The suspicion in his voice raised my hackles and reminded me I shouldn't be in this car. I didn't know this man. He wasn't one of us. *He's closed,* Christopher would have said. *Sleepwalking.*

The radio crackled and I jumped. I gripped the armrest tight, clenched my teeth. A staticky voice said something about a com-pound, no bodies at the scene.

The officer glanced in my direction and then looked away.

"Have they left like this before?"

"They haven't left," I said. "They're here. I just don't know where."

We drove along thick woods, past the middle and high schools, past long driveways that cut into the forest, the houses obscured by trees. Into town. I held my breath and tried not to think about how far we were from my home.

We parked in front of a plain brick building with a flagpole out front.

"What are we doing?" I asked. "Why are we stopping?"

"This is the police station," he said. "We're going to get a few more people to help us."

"I don't want to go in there," I said.

"It's okay," the officer told me. "We're going to get this all figured out."

He stepped out of the car, and I did, too. I thought about running but realized I had nowhere to go. I followed him into the lobby. He held up a key fob beside a gray door, and it clicked open. We stepped through, and the door swung shut behind us, heavy, trapping us in. My chest tightened. The room glowed yellow, strip lights buzzing above us. It was a maze of filing cabinets and cubicles, ringing phones and glowing screens. A copy machine hummed in the corner, a mechanical whir, the printer tray rising and falling to adjust itself. This was all wrong. This was not where I was supposed to be.

A woman in a blouse and slacks rose from her chair. "You must be Ophelia," she said. She had round, red cheeks and heavy eye makeup, shiny and soft pink, eyebrows plucked thin and drawn back on.

"I'm going to leave you here with Leanne," the officer from the car said.

"Sit, sit," the woman said, nodding toward a seat at the end of her desk.

"Where are you going?" I asked.

"Don't worry," the officer said, which I came to understand meant *I'm not going to tell you*.

"We're going to get this all figured out," the woman said, gesturing, again, at the chair.

"I want to go home."

"I know, sweetie, I know," said the woman. The officer left, and the big gray door clicked shut, locked, behind him. "My son likes to play with the hole punch when he comes in. But you're probably a little old for that, aren't you?"

The phone on her desk rang, jarring and urgent, and I blinked back tears.

"How old are you, sweetie?"

I squeezed my eyes shut and told myself this wasn't happening, that any minute I'd wake up in my bed in the residence to the sound of my mother's voice: *You're late, Ophelia.*

"Eight? Nine?"

Keep up, Ophelia.

"I'm twelve," I said, barely above a whisper.

"*Twelve*," the woman said, like that was a positive thing, like she wasn't making a mental note about my size. "Almost a teenager. What's your full name, sweetie?"

"Ophelia Clayborne," I said, and then worried I was saying too much. Christopher wouldn't like it.

"Is there someone we can call for you, Ophelia? A grandparent? An aunt or uncle?"

I bit my lip, staring at the gray door.

"That's okay," she said. "That's okay. What's your mom's name?"

"Sylvie," I said, and she wrote it down on a yellow legal pad.

"Sylvie Clayborne?"

"Sylvie Sorensen."

"S-O-R-E-N-S-E-N," she said, speaking the letters aloud as she wrote them down on the paper. My mother would be upset, too. *You shouldn't be talking to them, Ophelia,* she would say. *You should be here with us. Come find us.*

The woman clicked her pen, rolled open her desk drawer, and pulled out a bag of vanilla creme cookies.

"Max accidentally got two of these from the vending machine the last time he was here," she said. "That's my son. You want them?"

I shook my head, but she opened the bag and placed it on the desk anyway.

"You hang on just a second, sweetie, okay?"

Another officer with a grave expression on his face was waving her over, a thick manila folder in hand. They glanced at me, and then looked away, and I told myself this was my chance. I could run for the door. I could escape. Later I wondered what might have happened if I had. But fear took over—I had nowhere to go, no idea of where to start—and so I stayed in my seat by the desk. A picture of the woman's son was pinned to the cubicle wall: five or six, with wild curls and a wide smile. Next to it was another of the woman and a man, goatee and aviator glasses, on a sandy beach. I looked down to the yellow legal pad on the desk, where the woman had written my mother's name. JACOB's HILL was written in big letters at the top of the page. *Call Armisen Arms and Agent Lansdale,* beneath it. I leaned in to see what else it said.

"Okay, sweetie," the woman said, suddenly at my side. She snatched the notebook up and out of my view. "We're going to get this all figured out, but to do that I need to ask you a few questions. I know they might be hard, but it's important you answer them so we can find your family, okay?"

I nodded.

"Did Christopher ever say or do anything that made you uncomfortable?"

"No," I said, but I said it too fast, or not fast enough. The woman frowned. She leaned in.

"It's okay," she said. "You're safe here. You can tell me what he said."

"He didn't threaten us," I said. "He cares about us. He just wants to make sure we're ready."

CHAPTER THREE

—

Lucy and I are at a playground full of children, chubby toddlers pushing small tractors and ambulances along a low brick wall, three- and four-year-olds clustered on a slide. Lucy is too young for anything here, but she watches the older kids with a quiet fascination, and so this is one of our regular stops. A sticky tube of bubble solution juts out of my backpack. Lucy's turtle jangles from the side of her stroller, clipped onto a small plastic loop.

I felt sick when I woke this morning, partly from the alcohol but more from a lingering sense of dread: *Did Fey and Niko mention the documentary to Theo? Did he put the pieces together?* But Theo did not seem troubled by anything when I finally made my way downstairs. In fact, he seemed more at ease than normal. *That was fun last night,* he said as he poured me a coffee, and I agreed. He did not push sleep training. He did not give me any of his looks.

He asked about my plans for the day, and I told him we might go to the Academy. Just to drop in, say hello. Lucy would love to see the animal dioramas: big cats mounted on tree branches, antelopes frozen beneath them, unaware. The idea of me reconnecting with my old colleagues made Theo so happy, and when I said it, I really meant it.

But we didn't make it to the Academy. We didn't make it anywhere. Today is a Tuesday, and Tuesdays are long and shapeless. I have spoken to three adults since Theo left the house: the barista at Sweets on Pine; the greeter at CVS; an aggressive petition circulator just outside Rittenhouse Square who sensed, rightly, that I didn't actually have anywhere I needed to be. The day will culminate in our weekly dinner with Theo's mother.

I hate Tuesdays.

Lucy grabs her turtle and turns it over in her hands, gnaws on one of its legs. *Niko and Theo talk all the time,* I think, unable to quiet my thoughts. *He's bound to say something at some point.* I remind myself there's nothing for him to say. It's just a television series. All Niko knows is that I lived in Strathhaven. Theo knows that, too.

I try to focus, instead, on the sounds and rhythms of the playground. There are people everywhere. I recognize a few women from previous outings: one in all athletic gear shouting at her son to drop the stick he's wielding as a sword; two others chatting while their toddlers scratch shapes in the dirt. I nurse my tea while Lucy watches a squirrel climb an empty stroller to root for crumbs in the seat.

Past the sparrows hopping and pecking along the rim of the municipal trash can, a girl stretches, arms raised overhead. I feel a jolt of recognition. It's the girl from the coffee shop yesterday, the one who touched Lucy's foot. She has sunglasses on, but it's unmistakably her: her spiked, choppy hair, her too-thin arms. There is a tear along the hem of her shirt, a rash of acne up her cheek. She bends to one side, then the other, and then sits on the low brick wall.

I wonder what she's doing at this playground. No one comes here without children. I watch her, trying not to be too conspicuous. She laughs as one of the toddlers sends a small ambulance flying into her thigh, and then drives it back toward him, making a sound like a siren.

I'm being nosy; it's none of my business. But there's something so incongruous about her, something off about her presence here.

Maybe it's just that she looks like an outsider. This neighborhood is wealthy, the parents all professionals, almost all in their thirties or forties. None of the mothers at the playground look like she does.

But it feels like something more.

She could be a nanny. She was so good with Lucy, after all, so comfortable. It would make sense if she worked with kids. She turns her head, and for a moment it feels as though she's looking straight at me, although her glasses make it impossible to tell. I almost wave but stop myself. We had one fleeting interaction. She won't know who I am. She's probably looking because I'm looking. I avert my eyes.

She stretches again, swaying from side to side, and when enough time has passed, I glance in her direction. I watch to see if she's focused on any particular child. But her attention flits across the playground: first to the tangle of boys on the bridge that connects two structures, then to the baby trying out her first slide. Maybe she's responsible for one of the older children, one of the four- or five-year-olds roaming in a pack along the wire fence that separates the playground from the train track.

Or maybe she's not here with a child. Maybe she's meeting someone, a friend. But she doesn't seem to be paying attention to the playground entrances or looking for a familiar face. She's not looking at a phone, passing time. She's just watching. Her head turns in my direction again, and I look away.

A line of children in bright orange vests passes me. Most of them hold colorful loops attached to a rope; two hold a teacher's hand. When they reach the playground they scatter, diving into the swarms of other children and a maze of playground equipment, a dozen of them and three teachers.

How do they not get lost? I've asked Theo when we've passed one of these lines together. I never noticed them before Lucy, but now I see them all the time, waiting patiently at an intersection, shuffling around the sidewalk.

The vests? Theo suggested. He shrugged, unconcerned. *It works somehow. You never hear about them losing a kid.*

I turn back to the brick wall, and the girl has left. I scan the playground equipment, crane my neck for a better view of the wire fence. I don't see her. I feel a stab of disappointment for no good reason. It's not as though I would have struck up a conversation if she had stuck around longer. But the absence of an explanation bothers me. I don't like not knowing. I hoist Lucy onto my hip, unlock the stroller, and push it forward with one hand. We walk at a faster pace than normal, out of the playground and into the larger park. To our left, the dog park and a stretch of open space, families lounging on picnic blankets, children on scooters. To our right, the street. I catch a glimpse of the girl on the sidewalk, her back to us, walking away. She's alone. I try to follow, but a kickball rolls in front of us, and then Lucy is arching her back, angry about the way she's being held, and by the time she is secured in her stroller and happy again, the girl is gone, swept back into the city.

Lucy goes down for her nap, after forty minutes of rocking and bouncing, rocking and bouncing. I settle on our couch, open my laptop, and pull up the Academy website. I check their job listings, as I always do, scrolling until I see what I'm looking for.

A listing for my position: archivist. Still unfilled.

When people ask what I do, I tell them I am an archivist at the Academy of Natural Sciences, present tense. It is beginning to feel more and more like a lie. But every time I see this posting, I think: *There's still hope.* If I went in tomorrow, told them I was ready, maybe they'd take me back.

Just talk to Raffi, Theo says, like it's simple. *He likes you. They all like you there. And they don't want to have to train someone new.*

There is a half-written email in my drafts folder, an apology, a request for more time. But to send it, I would need to give a specific number. *One month. Three.* It would set a clock in motion, ticking down.

Maybe you could go back part-time. Just a few days a week, Theo tells me, full of solutions.

When I was pregnant, and in those early months with Lucy, I thought I had things under control. I had fears, but so did all the other mothers I talked to. Everything I read told me it was normal. I had anxiety about going back to work, but so did everyone. We enrolled Lucy in daycare a few blocks from the museum. Theo has a few colleagues with kids a little older than Lucy, and so they gave him the full rundown. The places to go and the ones to avoid. *Get on the list early,* they told him, and so we did, before Lucy was even born.

I prepared. I pumped extra, built up a solid freezer supply. I talked to Lucy about the daycare, in case there was a part of her that could understand. We walked past the building, brick with a bright, welcoming blue awning, handprint decals on the windows, shades pulled down, and I told her, *see, there, that's where you'll go, and at the end of the day I'll come back and get you.* I knew leaving Lucy at daycare would be hard—I knew I struggled even to leave her alone with Theo—but I also knew it was something other women worked through. At the time, I still thought I could, too.

On the day I was supposed to go back, I showered with Lucy in her bouncer on our tiled bathroom floor. I blow-dried my hair for the first time in months and put on makeup. A button-down shirt. Stretchy black work pants. I loaded Lucy into her stroller with all the things she would need, dug my purse out of the depths of our front closet—an adult purse, not my diaper bag. I talked to Lucy the whole way there, *we're going to the place we talked about, with your new friends,* my work shoes chafing against my heels, too tight after my pregnancy.

But when we reached the daycare block, and I saw that blue awning and the black-and-yellow pansies in the window planters, I froze. I thought about these women I didn't know taking Lucy into their arms, Lucy who didn't like anyone other than me. This room full of babies, and not enough eyes or hands. She wouldn't have their full attention, not really. How easy it would be for something to happen to her, for someone to take her out of her small wooden cot, to leave the building before anyone noticed. I imagined returning to blank stares, *we thought your husband picked her up early* . . .

I walked right past the line of parents waiting, turned the corner, and released my breath. It was a sunny, clear day, and I took Lucy to the splash grounds a few blocks from the museum, turned her in the stroller so she could watch the older kids dart in and out of the streams of water. I emailed Raffi a short, vague excuse. *Sorry, emergency at home.* I ignored Theo's text asking how drop-off went. Lucy and I walked, traversing the city, and Lucy slept, and I draped the muslin over the stroller to shield the sun but let it droop, just a little, so I could see her.

That was four months ago.

Theo says I'm being *irrational,* and I know that what I'm feeling isn't normal. Fear sneaks up on me, grips me, won't let me go, even though I tell myself other people run errands and go to jobs and leave their children with other people every day, and it's fine, almost every time. But I also know how easily you can lose the ones you love, and how quickly it can happen, without warning. I know what "almost" means. Theo doesn't.

The Academy can wait. The fear will subside soon, and I will get this under control. Lucy will get older; she will be less vulnerable; I will know, in my heart, that it's time.

I'm just not ready yet.

I navigate away from the museum website and open Gmail. Buried in advertisements for baby clothes, newsletters from the Y, and receipts from Kids Play is an email from Meghan Kessler, the documentary producer, the subject: The Fifteen.

Meghan first emailed me two years ago, with a gushing request for an interview. You are an inspiration, she said, and I almost wrote back *How did you find me? Do not contact me again,* but stopped myself in time, realizing how it would look. The fact that she had managed to track me down shouldn't have been that surprising. I changed my name from Ophelia Clayborne to Ophelia Sorensen ten years ago: enough of a change to hide my past from acquaintances and colleagues with Google and a modicum of curiosity, but close enough that my mother could find me if she ever came looking. Which meant that anyone else with enough time and interest could potentially find me, too. I googled Meghan, and she didn't seem to have an audience, so I told myself this wasn't a real thing. I sent back a short response: sorry, not interested. Since then, I have deleted all of her emails without opening them, a part of me hoping that refusing to look would make the whole thing disappear.

That strategy obviously has not worked.

I swallow, hovering my mouse over delete, and then change my mind. This time, I open it.

Hi Ophelia!

Informal. Like we're friends, or I've done something to invite this contact.

I hope this email finds you well! THE FIFTEEN began airing two weeks ago, and since then we have not stopped receiving messages expressing admiration, concern, and sympathy for the young girl who found her way out. I can't imagine the strength and courage it must have taken to go through what you went through at such a young age. I know you've had some reservations about speaking publicly, but I thought it might help to know how much your story means to people. We would love to sit down and talk with you about your experience—then and now—as part of a follow-up episode tying together loose ends. We do not need to show your face and could modify your voice. Let me know— your story is SO important, and I would be honored to help tell it.
xx Meg

My story. Not just an account of what happened at Jacob's Hill, but a narrative that mentions me explicitly, that tells some version of what I went through. My heart pounds as I type out a response:

Did you use my name?

Within seconds, I receive a reply:

No, of course not. We refer to you as "the survivor" throughout. As I said, we are totally willing to work with you to maintain confidentiality.

I stare at Meghan's emails, trying to make sense of them. Without my participation, without my side, what is there to say?

Plenty, apparently.

I open Google and hesitate. I promised myself ten years ago that I would avoid searching for Jacob's Hill or Christopher or the names of old friends and family members. Looking snowballs; things can quickly get out of hand. But searching for Meghan is different; it is a matter of self-preservation. I type in her name. Two years ago, she had a Twitter account, a LinkedIn profile, and a single headshot used for both social media sites. Most of the image results were pictures of other Meghan Kesslers. But now, the results have exploded into interviews, write-ups on the documentary, Reddit threads with fan theories. Professional photographs from news articles, grainy screenshots from interviews, smiling, serious, thoughtful. She's everywhere, and so is the story she's telling.

I delete the email chain, close the laptop. Let her say what she wants; I still have no intention of talking to her. I know what she's thinking: Maybe the key is buried somewhere deep in my subconscious. Maybe I hold the answer to what happened the night they all disappeared. I used to think that, too. In the years following the disappearance, I would comb my memory for clues about that day, for significant details from the weeks leading up to it, something I must have missed. For explanations, for reasons, for the breadcrumbs I knew my mother must have left behind.

I always came up empty-handed, even in those early days, when the memories were fresh and vivid in my mind. Now my memories have calcified, become memories of memories, the real thing lost to time. If I ever had answers, I don't have them anymore.

And if I did know something, it wouldn't be any of Meghan Kessler's business.

A cry from upstairs: hesitant at first, and then demanding. I shout to Lucy that I'm coming, and try to push the documentary and the disappearance and my mother and sister out of my mind. I know what happens when I dwell on the past. It's nothing good.

Theo's mother arrives at eight, her normal time, forty-five minutes after Lucy has gone to bed and an hour and fifteen minutes before she'll likely be up again. Her sleep cycles are unusually short, according to Jacqueline, my moms' group, and the internet. Theo says it's because I coddle her by feeding her every time she stirs, but I can't stomach the alternative.

Jacqueline is holding a bottle of wine: something nice, I'm sure, probably French. She took a trip to the Pays de la Loire region of France last summer, and has not stopped talking about Clos Rougeard Saumur Champigny and Domaine Huet Vouvray and an elaborate cooking class she took in a small countryside château.

"I was surprised Di Bruno's had this," she says, handing the bottle to me.

"I'll open it for us," I say as I start toward the kitchen.

"Is Lucy still up?" she asks, although she must know the answer is no. Jacqueline is always more interested in seeing Theo than Lucy, and I suspect she times her visits so that she can chat with Theo undisturbed. Which is just as well.

"Sleeping for now," I say, holding up my crossed fingers. Jacqueline moves aside Lucy's blanket and my rounded nursing pillow and takes a seat on the couch. Theo has moved his own pillow and sheet to our room for the evening; they'll come back down when his mother is gone.

I pour three glasses of wine and distribute them and then retreat into the kitchen so that Theo and Jacqueline can have some time together. Jacqueline is recounting her day, busy as always. She has a full-time therapy practice, where she specializes in helping battered women. She serves on boards: Mural Arts, Bartram's Garden, the Philadelphia Orchestra. She is an advocate of literacy, in the process of putting together her own foundation.

I mix our salad dressing, check on the tenderloin roasting in the oven, bring the glaze to a boil and let it simmer. Theo tells Jacqueline about his day, the resolution of a conflict he never mentioned to me, a colleague he suspected was mistreating a client.

"Good," Jacqueline says in response. "Better not to be passive in those situations. You can't let those things fester."

In addition to our weekly dinners, Theo and his mother talk almost every day. He gives her a quick call to check in on his way home from work. Theo's father was much older and died not long before Theo and I met. Maybe that amplified Theo's feelings of responsibility toward Jacqueline. I think they've always been close, though. Sometimes I envy it; sometimes it makes me uncomfortable. Their closeness means that Jacqueline doesn't just know the details of Theo's life but the details of my life as well: the fact of my pregnancy almost immediately; the sudden sadness I felt after Lucy's birth, which I shared only reluctantly with Theo in the first place; my fear of what might happen if I let Lucy out of my sight.

It's part of being a family, Theo says when I mention I don't like him sharing these things. *It's normal.*

The sauce is reduced and dinner is out of the oven, and I rest against the counter for a moment, half-wishing for the sound of Lucy's cries so that I'd have an excuse to spend dinner soothing her, pacing and singing, just the two of us. But Lucy will still sleep for another forty-five minutes, and so I set the table and Jacqueline pours herself and Theo another glass of wine and we sit.

"This is wonderful, Ophelia," Jacqueline says. Jacqueline hates the name Jackie and believes that others must have a similar aversion to nicknames, regardless of stated preference.

"Thanks," I say. "How is paint night going?" A fundraising initiative for Mural Arts that Jacqueline has been spearheading.

"Fantastic." She launches into a long string of details. I notice, with a twinge of irritation, that she hasn't asked any questions about Lucy yet. But maybe, I think—reminding myself to be generous—she's already covered this topic with Theo.

"Theodore tells me," she begins, and I cringe because this is never the start to something good, "you're going to be starting back up with the Academy soon."

I glance toward Theo, who nods encouragingly.

"They haven't filled her old position yet," he says.

"I'm thinking about it," I say. "I haven't—"

"It will be *so* good for you," Jacqueline says, her words slow and too bright. "It would be nice to get out of the house."

"We do get out of the house."

"To spend time around other adults," Jacqueline says. "When was the last time the two of you went on a date?"

"Not since Lucy was born," Theo says, like he's just answering her question, but I can tell this is coordinated, something they've discussed in advance.

"Why don't you two pick a date," Jacqueline says, "and I'll baby-sit."

"I don't think she'll go to sleep for other people," I say. "Theo can't even get her down."

"I'll come after she's in bed," Jacqueline says, waving a hand. "I'll bring a book."

I imagine Lucy alone, in her bassinet, crying out. Wondering where I am, why I'm not coming for her. Jacqueline, on the couch, turning one page, then another. *You should be sleep training*, she likes to tell me. *It's well past time.*

"Something sort of funny happened today," I say, to change the subject. "Well, not funny, but—unusual."

"Oh?" Jacqueline says, carving into the asparagus.

"There's this person I keep seeing," I say. "This girl."

As the words come out of my mouth, I realize this is not a story. More of a half-thought, an observation. A feeling.

Jacqueline takes another sip of wine, and Theo waits, uneasily, for me to continue.

"Is it . . . someone you know?" he asks, trying to discern the point. There is nothing unusual, after all, about seeing a person more than once. There are plenty of strangers I see over and over again, people with similar routines, the same paths through the city.

"No," I say. "Just—Lucy and I saw her at the bakery yesterday, and then again today at the playground. But the strange thing was, I don't think she had a kid with her."

"*Is* that strange?" Jacqueline asks, in her practiced, guiding tone.

"Isn't it?" I say. "How much time have you spent at playgrounds by yourself?"

"I mean, if she were a guy, it would be weird," Theo says. He sets down his fork, wipes his hands on his napkin. "But a woman? At a playground? Maybe she just likes being around kids."

"I don't see that many women at playgrounds just watching," I say. "And I spend a lot of time at playgrounds. A lot more than you do."

"Maybe," Jacqueline offers, still using her therapist voice, "she recently found out she's pregnant and wants to see what her life is going to be like. Or maybe she's grieving a loss."

"She looked out of place," I say. "I just noticed, is all."

"Hmm," Jacqueline says.

"I'll clear these plates," Theo says, jumping up, and when he's gone to the kitchen, Jacqueline leans in, like she's about to confide in me.

"Motherhood can be so challenging," she says. "Even under the best of circumstances. And I know you didn't exactly have a role model . . ."

Theo enters the room again, and she leans back and gives me a meaningful look.

"I'm here if you ever need to talk," she says. "That's all I wanted to say."

"Thank you, Jacqueline," I say, doing my best to sound pleasant, grateful. "I appreciate that."

I go upstairs before Jacqueline leaves, ready for sleep. Lucy will be up soon, and then again in a few hours, and then again. But I can hear pieces of Theo and Jacqueline's conversation downstairs, their voices low and serious, and I know they're talking about me.

"She's not well," Jacqueline says. "You can't just ignore it and hope it gets better. It doesn't work that way."

"I don't know what to do," Theo says. "I've talked to her, but she's not thinking straight. She's not—"

"She's not stable," Jacqueline says. "She needs help. Someone other than you."

"I know," Theo says. "I know."

I shut the bedroom door and turn up Lucy's sound machine so I can't hear them. I do not want to see someone. I know where that will lead. I can get through this; I will figure this out. I am a mother who loves her daughter, and I am trying my best.

I lie down. Lucy's bassinet is at the foot of the bed, and I have rearranged my pillows and blankets so that my head is right by hers. Her eyelids flutter as her eyes move beneath them. Her arms jerk and she startles, resettles herself.

Sometimes I look at Lucy and see Mona as a baby, her snub nose and serious expression. I still remember the first time I held her, while my mother was recovering from labor. Adrienne instructed me to sit on a couch in the residence common room. She propped a pillow under my arms and placed Mona down carefully, and the fear I had felt those past twelve hours gave way to a groundswell of joy, relief.

You are her big sister, Adrienne told me, *which is an important job. It's your responsibility to take care of her.*

Mona's face was scrunched, her body small and delicate. *Hi Mona,* I whispered, and her eyes squinted open, a dark gray that would lighten in the weeks that followed.

See? Adrienne said. *She knows you already.*

Lucy jerks again, and this time I am sure she'll wake, but she re-settles herself with a hitched sigh. I reach out and feel her warmth, the rise and fall of her back. I close my eyes. I sleep.

CHAPTER FOUR

—

Twenty years earlier

"Good news," Leanne said to me. She had cleared off the side of her desk and given me sheets of printer paper and a pen for drawing, both to keep me busy and to see what I would do. I had answered the same questions over and over again—from Leanne, from a woman who spoke too fast and didn't blink enough, from someone who introduced himself as *agent,* from someone who introduced herself as *doctor*. "We've been in touch with your aunt. She's coming to get you."

I pictured Adrienne, her dirt-covered overalls and hair in a loose braid, pulling me into a hug, and I burst into tears of relief. *I knew they'd come back,* I thought. *I knew they wouldn't leave me.*

But when the gray door swung open, the woman who entered was not Adrienne or my mother or anyone I had ever seen before. She had white-blond hair and nervous eyes that flitted around the room, finally landing on me. She gripped the handle of her purse and forced herself to smile.

"Are you Ophelia?" she asked. I looked to Leanne, who gave me what was probably meant to be a reassuring nod.

"I'm your aunt," the woman said. "Anne. Did your mother ever mention me?"

My chest tightened. This was all wrong. This wasn't supposed to be happening. This wasn't where I was supposed to be.

The woman pressed her lips together.

"How does this work?" she asked Leanne.

"We may need her to come back to the station and answer some questions, depending on . . ." Leanne's voice trailed off. The woman grimaced, then caught herself.

"Right now, though," Leanne continued, "I think what she needs most is rest."

"Okay," the woman said, nodding. "Okay." And then, addressing me: "Are you ready?"

I shook my head.

"I don't understand," I said to Leanne, the words catching in my throat.

"You're going to stay with your aunt for a little while," Leanne said.

"No," I said. "I'm not. I want to go home."

Leanne and the woman exchanged looks, and Leanne crouched so that she was at my level.

"I know, sweetie," she said. "And we are going to try to get you home as soon as possible. But for now—"

"*No,*" I said again, more forcefully this time. "She's not my aunt. I'm not going with her. I need to go *home.*"

"I hear you, sweetie," Leanne said. "I hear you. But home isn't an option."

Leanne and the woman moved away from me, toward a wall of filing cabinets, talking in low voices. A thought, the thought I'd been trying to keep down all morning, bubbled up again.

They left me.

I closed my eyes and saw Christopher, emerged from a weeklong fast in a darkened room: no food, no light, no contact. His cheeks sunken, the circles under his eyes more pronounced. We all crowded into the common room to hear what he had to say. Mona curled beside my mother on the couch, the seam of one of the cushions split, revealing the foam inside. I sat in front of them, cross-legged on the floor with the other children, Josephine on one side and Echo on the other. Christopher's eyes were closed. His jaw pulsed. Even when—especially when—he was silent, Christopher had the ability to hold a room. A coiled energy radiated out from him: an aura, my mother called it. Wind whistled through the trees outside; Echo, beside me, scraped the heel of his shoe against the wood floor.

Christopher's eyes blinked open, and I placed a hand, instinctively, on Echo's small leg. My mother pressed her palm against my shoulder, willing me to be still.

They are coming for us, Christopher said. *Soon.*

He scanned the room, making deliberate eye contact with each of us in turn.

Some of us are still not ready, he said, and I could swear, when he said it, he was looking straight at me. *Some of us, even here, are sleeping.*

His gaze broke, and I let out my breath, hoping I wasn't too loud, hoping no one else had noticed.

When the time comes, he asked, *will you be ready?*

No, I told myself, shifting on the seat of the plastic police station chair. No. They wouldn't leave me. And besides, nothing had happened. No one had come. I pushed the memory down again. This was all some kind of mistake.

"Okay, Ophelia," Leanne said, her tone too cheerful, too light. "Ready to go?"

Leanne came to the parking lot with Anne and me like a chaperone, both to make me feel more comfortable, probably, and to make sure I didn't run.

"This is us," Anne said, gesturing toward a black SUV. I stood beside it, numb. Leanne opened the door for me and waited for me to climb in.

"We are going to do everything we can to find your family," she said. "If you think of anything, you give me a call, okay?"

She gave me her card, and then lingered.

"It's going to be okay," she told me, nodding as she said it, maybe reassuring herself as much as anyone. "We're going to get this figured out."

I mumbled in response, and she gave me a tight smile before closing the car door.

"Have you . . ." Anne started, glancing in my direction and then quickly looking away. "Have you been in a car before?"

I nodded, although, apart from the ride to the police station that morning, it had been a long time.

"That's good," she said, and then she pressed her lips together. She twisted in her seat to back out of the parking space, and I jumped at her sudden movement, her hand on my seat.

"It's okay," she said. "I'm not going to—" Her voice broke off. "Jesus," she said, and then: "Sorry." She blinked and wiped at her eyes.

I watched through the window as the town passed by—the post office, Fairbrother's Hardware, the gas station and deli. We drove along the woods and kept going, faster and faster, out of Strathhaven and onto a highway thick with traffic.

"I have two daughters," she said, breaking the silence. "Your cousins. They're—how old are you, Ophelia?"

"Twelve," I whispered.

"That's right around Clara's age," she said. "Clara just turned thirteen. And Rachel is nine."

"My sister is six," I said, and Anne drew in a sharp breath.

"What's her name?" she asked.

"Mona."

"Mona," she repeated, and we fell into silence again. Her hands tightened and relaxed around the steering wheel. I could feel the distance building, each mile a mile farther from home. The seatbelt dug into my neck. Anne clicked on the left turn signal, navigating around a truck spewing exhaust.

"Do you have any favorite foods?" she asked. "Anything you'd like me to pick up?"

I straightened in my seat. Without the truck obscuring my view, I could see an old, boxy white van just ahead.

"I'll be going to the grocery store tomorrow, so if you think of anything."

The back bumper was bent, the left taillight broken. My pulse quickened.

"Or foods you don't like? Anything I should avoid?"

The license plate was different, and it was only one van. But license plates can be changed, and the other van could have been nearby. The gap between us narrowed, the van slowing. Three car lengths, two.

"Can we go faster?" I said.

"What's that, honey?"

A blue sedan pulled into our lane and tapped its brakes.

"That van," I said. "It's—"

The van pulled off at the exit, and we barreled ahead, flying past it.

"That's them," I said. "That was their van."

"Honey—"

"We have to go back," I said. "They're looking for me. They're trying to find me."

"That's not—"

"We have to go back," I said again, louder this time. I pulled at the door handle. It didn't give. I slammed my hand against the tempered glass. "We have to go *back*."

But Anne kept driving forward, the wrong direction, away. I reached for the steering wheel and yanked, and the car lurched to the side. The minivan to our right swerved and blared its horn. Anne pushed me, hard, back into my seat, and pulled off to the side of the highway. She was breathing heavily, her eyes darting between me and the road, frightened.

"You can't do that," she said in a low, quiet voice, once she had recovered enough to speak again. "That's not safe."

They were gone, too far for us to catch them now. We hadn't acted fast enough. We had let them get away again. I couldn't hold it back anymore. I started to cry.

"It was them," I said, wrapping my arms around my knees. "That was them."

"Okay, honey," she said. She looked at me like I was a feral animal. "We'll call the officers when we get home."

We finished the drive in silence.

CHAPTER FIVE

—

Today we have a doctor's appointment. Lucy is small, and Dr. Mann is "not concerned" but told us we should come in for an extra weight check anyway.

Is something wrong? I asked at our last appointment, when Dr. Mann finally pulled up Lucy's growth chart on the computer screen and scrunched her forehead.

No, no, she said. *I'm sure she's fine. But why don't you come in again in a month, just in case?*

Just in case what?

She stood and made a face at Lucy, then shone the otoscope in her eye. Lucy squirmed, unhappy.

We just want to be sure she's gaining, she said. *That's all.*

I have spent the last month googling why Lucy might not be growing. Thyroid issues and gastrointestinal problems, genetic abnormalities. *Did Dr. Mann say she was concerned about any of those things?* Theo asked, as I read a few of the possibilities out loud to him. *She's not* not *growing, she's just on the low end of the weight chart. There's always someone on the low end. That's why it's a distribution.*

But now we are here in the waiting room, with its soft yellow walls, a rainbow painted on one side of the room, a tree on the other, its sponge-painted leaves spotted with small squares of Velcro. Two sisters stick foam apples onto the branches, working together at first and then fighting over the basket. Beside us, a girl with a messy braid scribbles red crayon on a printout of Elmo. I try to imagine Lucy with hair long enough to braid like that, focused on drawings of her own. I remind myself it doesn't mean anything that I can't.

I think of the boy in the photograph slipped through our door. I push him out of my head.

A nurse calls us back and tells me to strip Lucy down for her measurements. Lucy is cold and miserable. She clings to my shirt when I try to place her on the small plastic scale, stretching my collar, revealing red patches of skin climbing up my back and over my shoulder.

"It's okay," I tell Lucy, prying her off me and adjusting my shirt, self-conscious. "I'm right here. It will only take a minute." The nurse looks at the number on the scale, types something into the computer.

"Is it okay?" I ask. "Does everything look okay?"

"Dr. Mann will be right in to talk to you," the nurse says, which can't be good. If the numbers looked fine, she would tell me.

I dress Lucy, and we wait. The sheet of paper on the table crinkles beneath me. Lucy stands on my knees, with my help, bobbing up and down, testing her weight. I hold her, and my eyes drift from sign to sign in the room. How to read to your child. The importance of limiting screen time. Developmental stages and early red flags. A thought occurs to me: *What if they think the problem is you?* Lucy eats all the time. She nurses and devours finger foods and yogurt and oatmeal. But the doctors don't know that.

I picture a call to CPS. Home checks. Assessments. Background checks.

I think of the way Theo watches me now, looking for signs.

Is she a good mother?

Dr. Mann knocks at the door and then swings it open. She says hello to Lucy, who does not smile in return, and sits down at the computer. She wiggles the mouse to bring the monitor to life and then squints at the numbers.

"Well," she says finally. "They're not great."

"What does that mean?" I ask.

"She's probably just small," she says. She looks at me. "You're small."

"So is she okay?" I ask.

"We'll keep an eye on it," she says, and she gives me a printout with a list of high-calorie foods on it, feeding suggestions. "Why don't you come back next month?"

I leave Dr. Mann's office feeling agitated. I text Theo: Dr says we should keep an eye on it, and he texts back: I told you it would be fine. Theo thinks that everything will work itself out because, for him, everything always has.

The city is loud today as we walk back to our house: the pulse of jackhammers breaking concrete; the streets backed up, cars honking in frustration. There is a man gesturing wildly one block ahead of us, pacing like the tigers Lucy likes to watch at the zoo. We cross to the other side of the street before we reach him, but I can still see the largest words on his cardboard sign, IMPLANT and HYBRID CHILDREN and ESTABLISHMENT. Behind us, one-half of a telephone argument, a woman shouting: "What the fuck were you thinking? No, no, I'm not done . . ."

The throbbing pain in my right temple returns.

In spite of, or maybe because of, the chaos, Lucy falls asleep in her stroller. Her head slumps down against her chest, and I push it back gently, rest it against the cushioned side of her seat. Lucy will not stay asleep if I try to transition her from stroller to crib, and so I steer us toward the park by our house, set the stroller beside a shaded bench, and take a seat.

I grab my phone from the stroller basket. I tell myself no good will come of searching for what might be wrong with Lucy. *You already know what it says*, I remind myself. Instead, I check the Academy's job listings, looking for *archivist*.

I can't find it. My stomach turns. I've waited too long.

I rub at my eyes until my vision is bleary, refresh the page, try to search another way. But the listing is gone. They've filled my position. They've replaced me with someone new.

Theo's voice in my head: *You're jumping to conclusions. Just talk to them. I'm sure they'd love to hear from you.*

I start a new email to Raffi: Hope you've been well. I've missed you all! And then, like always, I freeze. Lucy's foot, which protrudes from under the blanket, twitches. She is stirring; she'll want to move soon. I put my phone away. I stand, stretch. Unlock the stroller brake.

We walk, and I hope that the motion will clear my head, but I'm stuck in a loop: *You waited too long. You missed your chance. You fucked it up.* But I always knew, deep down, that I wasn't going back, didn't I? That the job listing wasn't for me, that they weren't waiting. It's been too long.

I think about how disappointed Theo will be, how frustrated. *But there are other jobs,* I remind myself. *I can work somewhere else. I can find something new. When we're ready.*

They won't take you, a voice in my head responds. *No one else is going to want you. Not if they know who you really are.*

Lucy is fully awake now, blinking back at me.

"It's fine," I tell her, trying to project a calmness. "Everything is fine."

But I am distracted, thinking of Meghan and the docuseries, *a national phenomenon,* one write-up said. I step into the street without really looking, and a bike swings around us, narrowly missing. A car blares its horn, and Lucy startles, begins to cry.

"Shh shh shh," I say, walking and trying to soothe her at the same time, unlatching the turtle from its hook and handing it to her, pulling a chewed-up book out of the stroller basket, then a prized car. And so it is not until we are right in front of our house, slowing to a stop, that I see the girl from the coffee shop, sitting on the cast-iron bench beside our front steps.

She is folded into a ball, her knees pulled in, arms wrapped around them. She is scratching at her forearm, and I can see that her fingernails are uneven and bitten down, mascara smudged beneath her eyes.

My first thought is of the boy in the picture. Is this his mother? Is she the one who has been sending Theo these pictures?

My second thought: *Is she here to hurt us?*

She looks up at us and releases her legs, like she's been waiting and is relieved that we've finally arrived. I consider pretending I haven't seen her, passing by like we don't live here, like we have somewhere else to be. *A coincidence,* I tell myself, *nothing to worry about,* but even so I park Lucy's stroller on the other side of the steps, away from her, while I fish my keys out of my bag.

"Ophelia?" she says.

"Sorry," I say, reaching for Lucy's stroller handle. "Do we know each other?"

She smiles. "It's been a long time."

"I'm—" I unlock Lucy's stroller, ready to run. "I'm really sorry, but I don't—"

"Mona," she says, and she stands from her perch on the bench. "I'm Mona. I'm your sister."

PART TWO

—

THE
AWAKENING

CHAPTER SIX

—

I study her, looking for the Mona I remember from twenty years ago. She wears a thick layer of foundation, partially concealing a smattering of freckles. Her nose is pointed and a little crooked, not a child's snub nose. Her smile is different, too. Mona had an overbite and two bottom teeth that turned inward. But those were baby teeth. A child's face. Her eyes are the same: green flecked with gold.

Is it her? I ask myself. *Is it really her?*

It is jarring to have this woman in front of me and not know. Mona is a part of me, her face in my earliest memories. I picture her as a baby, wrapped in a cotton blanket, a tiny knit hat on her bald head. At three, an earthworm wriggling in the palm of her hand. At six, curled into my lap, turning her face up to see me. *What are we doing here, Fee-ah?*

The woman standing in front of me shifts her weight, self-conscious. I've been staring. The side of her mouth twitches.

It has to be her. I want so badly to believe it. *Why would she lie?*

"Sorry," I say. "I'm just—I don't know what to say."

"I shouldn't have surprised you like this." Her voice is raspy, a smoker's voice. "I wasn't sure how else—"

"No," I say. "I'm—I just can't believe it's you."

She is real, here, standing by my front steps. My sister.

She steps forward, her arms outstretched, an awkward motion. I hesitate but then catch myself. This is what I want. This is what I've always wanted. I pull her into a hug. Her frame beneath my hands is sharp and fragile. A stranger's body.

But of course she feels unfamiliar. It's been twenty years, and she's not a child anymore.

"I know this must be weird," Mona says, like she's reading my mind, and I shake my head.

"It's a lot." I laugh, wiping away tears. "It's a lot to process."

I don't know what to say, how to be. This is not like I imagined. In my mind, our reunion has always been uncomplicated, joyful, easy. Mona and my mother appear together, young and happy, and it's like no time has passed at all. A fantasy, I know.

"Where is Mom?" I ask. Mona looks stricken, and my stomach turns.

In the stroller beside me, Lucy begins to fuss. She strains against the stroller straps. She needs to come out or keep moving.

"Do you want to walk with us?" I ask.

Mona nods, one side of her mouth rising into a half-smile. Her cheek dimples, just like when she was young.

"Yes," she says. "I'd like that very much."

We fall into step beside each other, silent. I take her in out of the corner of my eye, her tiny frame. Mona was small and often "not well," a catch-all term because Christopher did not believe in doctors and diagnoses. She was slower than the other children, often tired, needing to be carried. Bedridden for days or weeks at a time. I remember my mother being *worried*—not just from time to time but a constant state, a part of who she was.

Her feet scuff the ground as she walks, a lazy, reluctant gait, and suddenly I am ten again and Mona is four and we are helping build a stone pathway leading up to the common house. I see it as clearly as if it happened yesterday. Christopher gave the younger children buckets to fill wheelbarrows with sand, and River and Echo worked diligently, their attention focused on their small metal trowels. Josephine and I carried stones from the barn to the common house and sorted them into piles.

My mother looked happy that day. She was working beside Adrienne and Terese, the three of them digging into the old dirt path, and she was laughing. I hadn't seen her laugh in a long time. Her hair was pulled up off her neck, and her face looked bright, alive. Then Mona threw herself on the ground, sprawled like a rag doll, limbs splayed. I saw her first, before my mother did. *I'm too tired*, she said. *I don't want to do it.*

I turned to see my mother, still laughing, driving her shovel into the ground.

You can help me, I told her, and I hoisted her onto my back. Together we smoothed the fill sand along the path and tamped it down, then matched the stones to one another like a jigsaw puzzle—the right shape, the right thickness. Mona helped me deliberate—*not there, there*—and when we finished, the path felt like ours, each stone in the place we had chosen. My mother brought us food from the dining hall for a picnic—thick slices of wheat bread with raspberry jam, goat's milk cheese. I split dandelion stems with my fingernail and thread them together, making a crown for each of us.

My beautiful girls, my mother said. I leaned into her, and her hair smelled like peppermint. *I love you both so much.*

I blink, returning to the present, this woman—Mona—beside me. Lucy holds her stuffed turtle, gnawing on its colorful patchwork leg. I look at Mona's hair, bleached white-blond and brittle, but this close I can see the dark roots beneath. *My sister.* By the time we reach the river trail, I am asking myself how I missed it, how I possibly could have failed to recognize her at the coffee shop, the playground.

It all makes sense now, the way she caught my attention, the way she stood out.

Of course it's her. Of course.

Lucy rattles her turtle, a small bell ringing in its belly. She is studying Mona, too, her blue eyes large and curious. She senses this is someone important.

"What happened to Mom?" I ask, quietly, breaking the silence. Mona's hand flutters to her head, and in my mind I see Mona at six, knotting her hair between two fingers. It's not long enough to twist now, and her arm falls back to her side.

"She passed away," she says. "A few years ago. It was very sudden."

My world tilts on its axis again.

"I'm sorry," I say, like this is Mona's loss and not my own.

Mona twists her mouth, looks at me.

"I'm fine," I say, although I'm not sure it's true. Mona is here and my mother is gone and I feel like I am falling, anticipating an impact that hasn't yet hit. "I lost her a long time ago."

The Schuylkill River flows beside us, the highway running along the other bank loud and jammed with cars. We are surrounded by people—joggers, bikers, students on their way to class—but no one notices us. No one pays attention. I have found my sister and lost my mother, and to them it's just like any other day.

"Where did you go?" I ask. "Where have you been?"

Mona purses her lips, gives me a tight shake of her head. "I can't."

I don't understand, but I am scared to push. I can see that this question has put her on edge. She has a nervous, animal energy now, like she's ready to run at any moment. If I say the wrong thing, I'll lose her.

"She's beautiful," Mona says, changing the subject, looking at Lucy. Lucy slams the turtle against her seat, the bell jingling.

"I think she's showing off for you."

Mona smiles and waves her fingers, and Lucy beams, delighted. She's like a different child around Mona. My sister, her aunt.

"How did you find me?"

"Luck," she says. "I saw you at that coffee shop."

A fluke encounter. Five minutes, in and out. If Lucy had fussed more or less that morning, we wouldn't have crossed paths. We might never have found each other.

"Why didn't you say something?" I ask.

"I wanted to be sure," Mona says. "It seemed too good to be true."

"Do you live nearby?"

She shakes her head, *no*, sucks on her bottom lip.

"I'm surprised you recognized me," I say. "I was only twelve when you left."

The words are like picking at an old wound, *you left you left why did you leave me*, but I push the feeling down. None of this is Mona's fault.

"It's the way you hold yourself," she says. "You hold yourself like Mom."

A sadness courses through me. This is too much, all at once. I stop, grip the handle of Lucy's stroller.

"Are you okay?" Mona asks. "Should we go back?"

"I'm fine. I just need a minute."

She waits, quiet, as I steady myself, count my breaths. When I'm able to go again, we walk in silence, neither of us sure what to say.

A familiar refrain plays in my head: *They chose her they left you they chose her they left you.* Mona was special, my mother used to say. *A special, special girl.* Christopher saw it, too. He paid little attention to me, except when I was misbehaving, but Mona was different. *A light in the darkness*, he called her. *A gift from God.*

"My husband doesn't know," I say abruptly. "No one in my life knows about . . . everything that happened."

I expect her to ask why, but instead she nods and keeps walking, like she understands. She lived it, too, or something similar.

Lucy throws her turtle over the side of the stroller. It hangs from its chain, but she can't pull it back. Mona reaches for it, places it in Lucy's hands.

"You looked familiar to me, too," I say. "At the coffee shop."

"You don't have to lie."

"I'm not," I say. "I think I recognized you without knowing it."

She laughs, runs a hand through her short hair. "It's fine," she says. "I'm not offended. It's been twenty years. I know I've changed a lot."

"No, really," I insist. "You stood out to me. I noticed you."

It's true: I *did* notice her in the coffee shop, and then again at the playground. I brought her up at dinner for a reason. I cross paths every day with dozens—maybe hundreds—of people. I must see plenty of them more than once, but most of them aren't even a blip on my radar. This was different. *A knowing,* my mother would have called it.

"Where are you living?" I ask.

"Here and there." A thin, bearded man walks toward us, a muscular dog on a leash beside him. Mona tenses, uneasy. "I've been patching things together, mostly."

It's not a full answer, and her discomfort is palpable.

"Is Lucy your only child?" she asks, changing the subject. The question makes me uncomfortable, although I can't pinpoint why.

"She's our first," I say. "Theo—my husband—wants a lot of kids, but we'll see."

She said *Lucy.* That's what it is: Have I mentioned Lucy's name? I don't remember saying it, but I forget so much these days, and I find myself talking to Lucy without even realizing, a stream of one-sided chatter. *Look, Lucy, look. A bird. A wind chime. Ready, Lucy? Red, Lucy. A dog, Lucy, woof woof.* Of course I've said her name in front of Mona. Of course there's a reason she knows.

"Do you have children?" I ask.

Mona scratches the back of her hand. "Not yet."

Out of nowhere, Lucy howls, her small face bright red. Her pacifier has fallen into the crevice of her seat. I fumble for it, but I know this cry: There's no soothing her. She arches her back, fighting against the stroller straps. I unbuckle her and hold her close, hoping it will calm her temporarily. We are making a scene.

"Sorry," I say to Mona, and then: "Lucy, it's okay. It's okay, Lucy." This doesn't work. It never works. Lucy cries more than the other babies in my moms' group. They used to cry like this, too, but they stopped. Lucy didn't. *No one hears the cries as loudly as you do,* I remind myself, Dr. Dana's gentle mantra. But I'm not sure it's true. Two college students in backpacks look at us and then away. A woman in a navy peacoat turns her head to stare. *You're imagining things,* I tell myself. *No one cares except for you.*

But Mona seems uncomfortable as well. She is scanning the path like she's looking for someone. Her eyes fix on the underpass ahead.

"We might have to head back," I say over Lucy's cries. "Do you want to—"

"I should go," she says.

"What's your phone number?" I fumble for my phone in the stroller basket, a motion that upsets Lucy even more.

"I don't have one," she says.

"Should I give you mine?"

"I'll come back," she says. "I'll find you."

"How about tomorrow?" I am bouncing and Lucy is screaming and we need to go, but I can't leave with this uncertainty. I need to know I'll see her again.

"I don't think—" she starts, looking past me. "I'll come back," she says again, and then she breaks off from us, her pace rushed, urgent. I feel a sudden dread that I've done something wrong. I try to stay calm, for Lucy's sake. I shush her, *it's okay,* and she keeps crying, and the two of us start toward home.

CHAPTER SEVEN

—

Lower Merion, Pennsylvania
Twenty years earlier

"Girls," my aunt called as we stepped into the foyer, her voice reverberating in the massive space. The ceilings were two stories high, an ornate chandelier hanging at the center, a rounded staircase leading up to the second floor. But the space was almost empty, furnished with only an upholstered chair that I came to learn no one ever sat in, a small table, a periwinkle flower vase with large silk flowers. "Peter. Ophelia is here."

My uncle appeared from an arched doorway, looking tidy and maintained, like everything else in this house. His hair was cut short, his light blue polo pressed.

"Good to meet you, Ophelia," he said, holding out his hand as if for a handshake. Anne gave him a look, like they had discussed this and he had gotten it wrong. Anne, I'd learn, was an analyzer, a worrier, a let's-plan-for-everything type of person. Peter ignored her look, instead glancing toward the second floor. Two heads peered over the wooden railing. My cousins, Rachel and Clara.

Rachel, the younger of the two, had stringy blond hair and a plain, freckled face. She gnawed on her thumbnail, hewing close to her sister's side—a worrier like her mother. She wouldn't meet my eyes. Clara, on the other hand, stared straight at me, her brown hair pulled back in a high, ribboned ponytail.

"Girls," Anne said, her voice tight. "Why don't you come down and meet your cousin?"

Rachel looked to Clara for a cue. Clara didn't move at first, her eyes running over me, sizing me up, *no*. But once enough time had passed to establish that she was not taking orders from her mother, she started slowly down the stairs. Rachel trailed nervously behind.

"I'm sorry about your family," Clara said.

"They'll be back soon," I mumbled.

She gave me a look like she was embarrassed for me.

"Why don't I show you around," Anne said, clapping her hands together, "and then we can have some dinner. Peter, did you order the pizza?"

"What do *you* think happened, Ophelia?" Clara asked.

"Come on," my aunt said, cutting her off. "I'll give you a tour."

Anne pointed out the master bedroom, the study, the girls' rooms. Clara's room was soft ivory, and Rachel's room was baby-doll pink, with a lop-eared rabbit chewing lettuce in a wire crate in the corner. "That's Lucky," Anne told me. She showed me the bathroom the girls shared—"You'll share it, too, of course," she added quickly, nervously—the linen closet, and finally, at the end of a long hall covered in school pictures and family portraits, my room.

"Here it is!" Anne said. "I hope it's okay. There's a guest suite in the basement, too, but there's a door down there, and . . ."

She left the thought unfinished, a dozen different possibilities swirling: *And it might be frightening for you, being so far away from everyone. But there is a door down there, and we don't want you to escape. But there is a door, and we don't want you letting anyone in.*

"This is nice," I said. "Thank you." The room was part guest room, part craft-supply storage, furnished with a bed covered in throw pillows and a wooden dresser covered in scrapbooks, piles of patterned paper, baskets of stamps and ink pads and scissors with crimped blades.

How are they going to find you here? I thought to myself. This was not where I was supposed to be, miles from my home, in this strange house with strange people. The heat kicked on, the soft whine of air forced through the pipes breaking the house's unnatural silence. The walls were too thick to hear any chirps or rustles from outside. I thought of Mona, out there without me, wondering where I am.

What are we doing here, Fee-ah?

Anne palmed the crafting scissors and crossed her arms, trying to be discreet. "I know it's been a long day. If you want to take a shower, the bathroom is right there, and pizza will be here soon."

My mother will know, I told myself. *She'll do what it takes to get back to me. This is her sister's house, after all. She'll put the pieces together. Any minute she'll be here, looking.*

"I think I just need to go to bed," I said. I rolled up the sleeves of my sweater, suddenly hot, and Anne's eyes fixed on my wrist. I pulled my sleeves back down.

"Is that your mother's?" she asked, meaning my bracelet.

"She gave it to me," I said defensively.

"I didn't realize she still had it," Anne said. "I gave it to her. I didn't know she took it with her."

She stepped forward, and I drew back, worried she might try to reclaim it.

"It's okay," Anne said, seeing my discomfort and giving me space. "It's yours now. When did she give it to you?"

"A month ago," I said, barely a whisper, "for my birthday," and Anne's face twisted, like she was trying not to cry.

"Oh," she said. "Well, I—" She blinked again, pulled herself together. "I'll be right downstairs if you need anything, okay?"

"Thanks," I said. She left, and I turned out the lights. I pictured Mona, curled up beside me, sleep-heavy and warm. That past month, Mona had been having night terrors. I'd sit beside her when they happened, pull her into me, her heart racing like a bird's. Her small body drenched in sweat, shaking.

It's just a dream, I'd tell her. *You're having a nightmare.*

He's right there. He's in the doorway.

You're okay, I'd say, over and over until I could hear her breathing slow, feel her body going slack. *Everything is going to be okay.*

I pulled the sheets over me and repeated those words to myself. Then I turned to the window, and waited.

I must have eventually drifted off to sleep, because I woke to a tap on the windowpane. *Let us in, Ophelia.* I sat up in bed, looked out into the dark. *You're hearing things,* I told myself. *You're on the second floor. No one is out there.*

But then I heard it again. A sharp, distinctive crack, a pebble hitting the glass.

Someone was here.

I was ready.

I raced downstairs and was about to run out into the yard when Anne spotted me. She was in the living room, lit by a single standing lamp, her eyes red and cheeks slicked with tears. She rose from the couch, wiped her face with her hand.

"Where are you going?" she asked. Not stern or threatening, just a question.

"I heard something," I said. "I think it's them."

As soon as the words came out of my mouth, I regretted them. I was sure she was going to send me back to my room, dead-bolt the door, call the police. But instead she tightened her robe around her waist, slipped on her shoes, nodded to where she had put mine.

"Come on," she said. "Let's see what's going on."

———

Anne grabbed a flashlight from the kitchen drawer, and we stepped out onto the porch together. She cast the beam from side to side, illuminating only an old oak tree and a line of bushes.

"Sylvie?" she called out. "Is that you?"

No response. She nodded for me to follow, and so I did. We looped the house, pausing every so often to listen: for voices, breathing, any sign of life.

"Were you and my mom close?" I asked. I rubbed the bracelet's silver chain between my thumb and forefinger. My eyes were adjusting some, and now I could see the rolling backyard, the gentle slope into a dark wall of woods.

"Sometimes we were," Anne said, looking out at the tree line. "Not always."

"Were you close when she left?" I asked.

She looked me over, like she was debating whether to tell me the truth. "No," she said. And then I heard it: a rustle, the crack of a twig. I knew Anne heard it, too, because her eyes shot toward the woods.

"Mom," I shouted, and Anne called out: "Who's there?"

"Do you think it's her?" I asked, and Anne shook her head but started toward the woods, the beam of the flashlight bouncing in front of her.

"Hello?" she said. "It's Anne and Ophelia. We just want . . ."

She didn't finish that sentence, because what could she say? The sound of running water grew louder, a creek somewhere nearby. The flashlight lit the line of trees, one by one, but there was no one behind them, only empty forest. "Sylvie, if it's you, come talk to us. Please."

She put her hand over her mouth and closed her eyes, like she might start crying, and then turned back to the house. Her hand dropped, like she saw something, and so I turned to look in the same direction. But I only saw the house, its massive silhouette, most of the windows dark except a light in the kitchen and another shining through the basement door window.

"She's not out here," Anne said, with a finality that surprised me. We had both heard something in the woods.

"You heard it, too," I said. She shook her head, resolute.

"Come on back to the house," she said. "I'll make you a hot chocolate, and we can both get some sleep."

"We need to keep looking," I said. "She's here."

Anne shook her head. "No. She's not. If she wants to be found, we'll find her. But that's not going to happen tonight."

I followed Anne back into the house because I knew she was right. My mother *was* hiding, but not from me.

Next time, I'd come alone.

CHAPTER EIGHT

—

I wake to a rustle at the foot of my bed, Lucy grumbling in her bassinet, soft at first, growing louder. She's unhappy, hungry, as though I didn't just feed her two hours ago, and two hours before that. Her cries always escalate so fast, like she's worried this time will be different from all the rest. Like this time, I'll decide not to come.

"I'm up," I tell her. "I'm right here."

I lift her from her bassinet and bring her into bed with me. My room is dark, like always, heavy curtains drawn to block the city glare. The bedsheets are tangled, a pile of laundry by the door. Lucy's dresser is on the third floor, and so we do not use it. Instead, her clothes and blankets and bibs are in baskets scattered across our bedroom. Theo takes big, performative steps around them whenever he comes up to fetch something, a reminder that he's been ousted from his room. "Replaced," he sometimes says, with mock hurt that probably masks something real, but I do not have the energy for that conversation.

He came home late last night, after Lucy and I were in bed. Theo's workload ebbs and flows; it always has. He went back to work two weeks after Lucy was born and started putting in long hours again nearly right away, a fight at the time. *The world doesn't stop because we had a baby*, he told me. *It does though*, I wanted to say. *It did.*

But last night, I was grateful for his absence. I had been worrying about how I would tell him about my sister, what I would say, and then it turned out I didn't need to say anything at all. But he's back now, and awake, moving around downstairs. I picture him folding his blanket, shuffling to the kitchen. The ice machine in our fridge grinds noisily.

I don't know how I'm going to explain this.

Theo knows I have a younger sister, and that I have not talked to her in a long time. A ripple effect of my estrangement with my mother, a sensitive subject, one I don't like to discuss. He believes I chose to live with my aunt as a teenager, and left Mona—who was much younger than me—with our flighty, irresponsible mother. He believes I feel guilt, regret, shame over this decision, which is why I don't have a relationship with Mona now. It's a story he's cobbled together for himself, based on my half-truths and omissions and therapeutic concepts he learned from his mother, and I've never corrected him. It's a story that serves us both well.

But now she's here—the real Mona—and Theo is going to find out the truth.

Lucy jerks her head away, *done,* and I change her into a woodland-themed onesie covered in burnt-orange foxes and forest-green vines.

Theo, I've been lying to you.

If it were only the disappearance, he might understand. Something traumatic happened to me as a child. I was a victim; I lost my family. The secrecy would bother him, but he'd come to terms with it in time. He works with clients who have been through trauma; he understands the different ways people cope. He knows it is not always straightforward or rational, that it is sometimes self-defeating.

I trade out my milk-soaked nursing pads for clean ones. I grab a sweatshirt off the top of the laundry pile, faintly sour, like everything I own.

He might understand the disappearance, but he won't understand the years that followed. If you google *Ophelia Sorensen*—the

Ophelia he met four years ago, the Ophelia he married—you get very few results. Ophelia Sorensen sprang into existence as a graduate student. She has a LinkedIn page, a couple of publications on library science, a mention on the Academy of Natural Sciences' blog. She is a private person, a person who has never had social media, a person who has never been at the center of anything.

I splash water on my face in the bathroom, pull my hair into a loose ponytail.

If you google Ophelia Clayborne, the girl who lost her family at Jacob's Hill, you get something very different.

I'm sorry, Theo. I thought you'd realize I wasn't good enough. I thought you'd leave and take our daughter.

I hoist Lucy onto my hip. She pulls at the neck of my shirt, her fingers grazing the red raised skin. I told Theo the burn scars were from an accident when I was younger; my mother left me alone when she shouldn't have.

It's true enough.

Lucy smiles at me, her sweet, barely toothed smile.

Was I wrong? Will you stay?

Theo has brewed coffee. He leans heavily against the kitchen counter, circles under his eyes.

"Morning, ladies."

I wonder if he has slept at all.

"What time did you get in?"

"I don't even want to say." He leans his head from side to side, stretching his neck. "Too late."

"Is it the kid case?" I ask, setting Lucy in her high chair. He flinches. He's bothered by the case but tries not to let it show. He doesn't think it's fair to the client. *Everyone deserves representation,* he says when people ask him politely or not-so-politely about being a public defender. *Everyone needs someone in their corner, especially when they're up against the state.*

He's about to shake his head, change the subject, but something makes him change his mind. It must be really bad. "It's pretty ugly."

"You can tell me about it."

He glances at Lucy.

"No," he says. "I can't. I'm just ready for it to be over."

"I'm sorry."

I pull a loaf of bread from the drawer and butter from the fridge, consider talking to him about Mona this evening, instead. He's under so much stress already.

You're making excuses, I tell myself, dropping two slices in the toaster. *It's not going to get easier.*

Theo rolls his shoulders, steadying himself for the day ahead. He pours his coffee into a thermos, not a mug. He won't be here for long.

"What's on tap for the two of you today?"

"We might . . ." I start. *Grocery shopping, playground, baby music class.* Easy, neutral answers, answers he'll like. But I can't ignore this; it isn't just going away. "We might see my sister, actually."

"Your sister?"

Lucy bangs on her tray, and I realize she's lost her pacifier. I crouch to peer beneath the table; it's come to rest behind one of the wooden legs.

"Mona," I say, like that's what he's asking. I rinse the pacifier in the sink.

"Yeah," he says. "I remember. You're in touch with her?"

"We reconnected," I say. The toast pops up.

"That's great. How?"

I butter the toast, cut it into strips for Lucy.

"Lee, the toast can wait."

"It's done." I place the strips on her tray and sit. "Yesterday. She showed up here, after Lucy's doctor appointment." *Truth.*

"Here, like at our house?"

"I don't think she had my phone number. She must have found our address online." *Part truth.*

"That's big," he says. He lowers himself into the chair beside me, studying me carefully. "Your sister. How are you feeling about it?"

A Jacqueline question.

"Good," I say. "I feel like this could be really good. For all of us."

He nods, takes this in.

"How long has it been?"

"I don't know exactly." *Lie.* "Years."

He leans back in his chair, casts a discreet glance at the clock. He needs to leave, but he's postponing.

"Did she seem good? What's she been up to?"

"She just moved here," I say. "To the city."

It doesn't answer his question, but he lets it slide. "Does she live close by?"

"I don't think so."

He squints at me, confused.

"I'm not sure she's totally settled yet."

Another glance at the clock.

"I hate to do this."

"Go," I say. "It's fine."

"I have a hearing," he says apologetically. "But I want to hear all about this tonight."

"Sure," I say. Lucy throws a strip of toast on the floor and looks at me expectantly, *pick it up.* "I mean, there's not that much to tell."

"Of course there is!" he says, standing. "She's your *sister.* This is a big deal." He kisses Lucy on the top of her head, gives my shoulder a squeeze.

"I love you," he says.

"Love you, too," I say, and he walks out the door, and I exhale.

On most Thursday mornings, Lucy and I attend a baby music class. It's in the Italian Market, a forty-minute walk away, and we spend forty-five minutes sitting on a round, colorful rug, shaking rattles and singing along with kid-friendly covers of pop hits. Lucy naps on the way back, and that's our morning, filled. It is something I look forward to, a bright spot in the week, but this morning we skip it. Mona might come back, and I want to be here when she does.

I read Lucy her books and give her a bath and let her roll from side to side on my bed. She tries to scrunch herself forward like a worm. Maybe she is close to crawling, after all. I talk to her, describing objects in the room—*pillow, isn't it soft? soft pillow*—repeating words and phrases like Dr. Dana is always telling us to do, *twenty-one thousand words a day!*, like we're counting. But I am distracted, and Lucy knows it.

I am waiting for a knock at the door.

It's time for Lucy's nap. I feed her and rock her until her eyelids are too heavy to stay open, and then five minutes longer just in case. I set her down, gently, in her bassinet, and she twitches but doesn't wake, and I sneak downstairs.

There is one window in the front of our house, beside our front door. The blinds are drawn, like always, to keep people from looking in. *You don't want to invite trouble,* Jacqueline says, meaning thieves, but the bigger concern for me is the neighbors. They don't need to know if I'm in the kitchen or the family room; if Lucy is sleeping or awake or unhappy; if I have showered; if I am rested; if I seem well. But now, I open them. Sunlight pours in, and I step back and watch the comings and goings on my street: Deborah, who has lived on this block for twenty years, taking her small Pomeranian out for a walk. Our across-the-street neighbor fielding what looks like an acrimonious phone call on his front steps. A young man with a baseball cap delivering groceries. Two women from a cleaning service with brooms and large garbage bags and a vacuum cleaner. No Mona, not yet.

She will come back, I tell myself. *She has to.*

I need a distraction. I open my computer, pull up the Academy website. Still no job listing. I stare at the screen for a moment, debating, and then google *Mona Clayborne.*

It's different than before. I'm not digging up the past this time. She came to find me.

But it doesn't matter anyway. There is nothing about her online. Her name was not released in the early reports on the disappearance, and the rest of her life has been lived in private, off the grid.

And that means Meghan Kessler has not used her name in the documentary, either. At least not yet.

I listen for Lucy but don't hear anything. I turn on Netflix, scroll down, and there it is, *The Fifteen,* under Top 10 TV Shows. *She's not using my name,* I remind myself. *There's nothing to connect me to it.*

Yet. Even if Meghan is willing to keep my identity a secret, that doesn't mean other news outlets will be as discreet.

My chest tightens, and I click on the show, and suddenly Jacob's Hill fills my screen, familiar and foreign at the same time. A yellow house with a red-tile roof, ropy vines climbing the exterior, hollowed-out windows. The stone path I helped build.

It's still there, I realize. *This is recent footage.*

And then Meghan is on the screen, too, walking down my old paths, stopping to examine a brass wind chime that still hangs from one of the trees. Black-framed glasses, hair pulled up in a practical way. She grew up in a neighboring town, she says in a voice-over, right here in Delaware County. She slips in an accented word—more *woo-ter* than *wah-ter*—which is intentional, I'm sure. There's no way she talks like that in Brooklyn, or wherever she lives now. She tells us she grew up with the story of the disappearance. To her, it was like a fairy tale, Christopher the pied-piper, leading children away. She and her friends used to break into the property in high school, with their cigarettes and pilfered bottles of liquor, daring each other to *go farther,* and I feel a surge of anger, protectiveness, *not yours. Mine.*

She shows a picture of Christopher from his time as an adjunct at Swarthmore. He's lecturing to a captivated audience, his hand extended, his eyes wide. His dark, curly hair is unruly. He's striking, a study in contradictions. Slim, but with an obvious strength to him: He was already building, already preparing the land. He has a heavy-set jaw and square face, but the rest of his features are almost feminine: high cheekbones, thick lashes, eyes jarringly light in color. I remember people focusing on his appearance at the time of the disappearance, *doesn't he even* look *like a lunatic?* But without context, he might have been beautiful.

The screen cuts away from Christopher, taking us back to the late nineties, setting the scene. I fast-forward through the montage of Tamagotchis and Furbies, boxy computers and AOL home screens. A *Newsweek* cover with "THE DAY THE WORLD CRASHES" in big, bold font, another magazine cover featuring a lit bomb labeled: YEAR 2000. Marshall Applewhite's face frozen in perpetual surprise, shots of bunkers filled with Campbell's soup and canned vegetables and pumpkin purée. I stop when the footage switches back to Jacob's Hill, this time the interior of the residence, a close-up on stick figures drawn on the wall. Forest's or Echo's handiwork, most likely.

"Only one survivor," Meghan is saying. "A young girl who, for some reason, was left behind. We were the same age—twelve—when it happened, and maybe that's part of the reason why I've never been able to let this story go. A part of me saw myself in these run-down hallways, alone in this empty space."

I turn it off, disturbed, and then realize the show now appears under "Recently Watched." I panic, and then google how to make it disappear.

People are watching this. *Lots* of people. I grab my computer and search for Jacob's Hill.

There are many results, most of which seem to postdate the documentary. Articles about the disappearance, about the lingering impact on Strathhaven, about the sociology of cults. I click on one of the first ones, a thought piece on the language used by high-control groups and the sway words can have over us. The designation of *insiders* and *outsiders*, Christopher's use of *opened* and *closed* to create an "us versus them" mentality. Another article asks: Why do we love cults so much? We are curious, this author says, about what drives normal people—people just like us—to fall under someone's spell. To give up everything, to choose a new life, a new existence, a new reality to pursue. We want to know what makes a seemingly normal life go so entirely off the rails: What are the warning signs we should be looking for? The article's tone is dismissive and condescending, almost glib. *How could some people*, it seems to ask, *get it so wrong? Why don't they see clearly, like we do?*

I feel a familiar agitation. There's a reason I stopped looking. I know it's not good for me.

But this is different. If I want to be able to protect myself, I need to know what's happening.

I open the next result, a Reddit thread.

tyrantintraining: I think we can all guess what happened to the doomsday cult that disappeared without a trace . . .

rustyroad26: Yeah, the only real mystery here is whether *Christopher* is still alive. True believer who killed himself to hop on the comet, too, or con-man who took everyone's money, killed them, and started over with a new identity?

Wrong, I think to myself. *Wrong wrong wrong.* I know the truth. I know they survived, because I know Mona survived.

The thread is one of many, part of a subreddit devoted to the documentary. I navigate to the list of recent threads, find one called "The Survivor."

kelleybeeee: That poor little girl. How could they leave her behind?

tyrantintraining: Uh, pretty sure she's the lucky one . . .

There is a heavy thud outside the door, the crunch of breaking glass, a woman's voice, cursing. I look to the window and see someone I don't recognize, a woman my age in an Eagles sweatshirt, looking frustrated. She hoists a moving box from the sidewalk, leans back awkwardly to support its weight.

I open the front door, peek outside.

"Need help?" I ask.

She looks up in surprise and shakes her head.

"Thanks," she says. "We're good. This one is supposed to be helping me." She nods toward a preteen boy on his phone, a thick mop of hair falling into his eyes.

"I *am* helping," he says.

"Put that away," she tells him.

"Okay," I say. "I'm Lee, if you need anything."

She gives me a tight smile, a terse head nod, uses her back to push open her front door. I return to my couch.

> **wherethebodies:** Did they interview her for the documentary? She's out there somewhere, and she knows what happened . . .
> **loobylooby:** Does she?
> **wherethebodies:** Yeah obviously. She was THERE.
> **rustyroad26:** I don't think anyone knows where she is.
> **tyrantintraining:** Untrue. wanttobelieve82 tracked her down. There's an old thread here.

My body goes cold. I know it's possible to find me; Meghan Kessler found me, after all. My identity is not a witness-protection-level secret, but it also hasn't been easily accessible public information.

Maybe now, it is.

It could be bullshit, I tell myself. *It's the internet. People make things up all the time.*

On the older thread, iwanttobelieve82 painstakingly describes his process for "unearthing" the survivor. He found police files that mention my old name—Ophelia Clayborne—and my mother, Sylvie Sorensen. A Delayed Report of Live Birth filed by my aunt twelve years after the fact. A smattering of hits online—a paper co-authored with one of my college professors at Pitt, news articles from Pittsburgh. And then, nothing.

> **iwanttobelieve82:** I almost gave up at that point. I looked for an obit and didn't find one, checked online death records. And then I realized Pennsylvania requires public notice for name changes. I searched old newspaper archives from around that time, and, sure enough, Ophelia Clayborne becomes Ophelia Sorensen, taking on her mother's name.

A few years ago, Ophelia Sorensen becomes Ophelia Burton through marriage. Ophelia and Theo Burton own a house together in Philadelphia, and the address and purchase price are available online.

mercinarymandible: Dude. Nice work.

iwanttobelieve82 posts my address—not just Philadelphia, or my neighborhood, but everything, down to the street number. I am half-expecting a photograph of me feeding Lucy on a park bench, oblivious, exposed, vulnerable. I search for other threads that use my current name, but there is nothing, so far. I set an alert on Reddit for any future mentions of my current or former names, and then a Google alert, too.

loobylooby: Theories for why they left her behind?

dramallama8903: sleeper cell

rustyroad26: Most likely imo it was a suicide pact and she hid or someone concealed her.

tyrantintraining: Or could be she was a black sheep, didn't submit to Christopher, challenged group norms? Groups like this foster very black and white thinking. Doesn't matter that she's family, or a child. If she's rejecting the group mentality, she's the enemy and needs to be cast out.

loobylooby: Maybe they left her behind to spread the word? Didn't Heaven's Gate do that?

rustyroad26: If that's what she's supposed to be doing, she's not doing a very good job. 😬

fanofthekoolaid: Seems pretty clear she was working with Christopher in some way

dramallama8903: maybe she's the one who got rid of the bodies?

mercinarymandible: 🔥 🔥 🔥

rustyroad26: 😩 😩 😩

I slam my computer shut. *This is not about you, not really,* I remind myself. *This is a story they're making up for themselves. It's not true. It has nothing to do with you.*

I have built a new life for myself. I am Theo's wife. I am Lucy's mother.

I am Mona's sister.

Theo is happy, light, when he walks in the door. His phone is pinched between his ear and his shoulder. He sets his briefcase by the secretary desk.

"That's great news, man," he says, holding a finger up toward me, *one minute*. "We did it. I told you you could do it."

He hangs his jacket on its hook. "Keep me posted, okay?" He sets his phone on the desk and gives Lucy a kiss on the top of her head.

"Good day?" I ask.

"You remember Sam Grady?" One of Theo's former clients, a twenty-one-year-old who has been in and out of trouble since he was twelve. "He got his GED."

"That's amazing," I say, as Lucy bats at my face with her palm. "Good for him."

"It's just good to get some positive news for once." He runs his hands down his face. Theo cares about his clients in a way some of his colleagues have warned will lead to burnout fast. He listens to them, finds out their family situations, their backgrounds, their struggles. He goes the extra mile. "How were things here? Did you see your sister again?"

"No," I say, trying to sound neutral, but something in my tone gives me away.

"When's that going to happen?"

"I'm not sure," I say. I shuffle into the kitchen so he can't see my face, but he follows.

"Are you going to set something up?"

"I don't *know*, Theo," I say, wishing, more than anything, he would just drop it. I have spent all day thinking about Mona, worrying about whether or not she'll return. I don't need Theo's judgment on top of it. "It's not really up to me."

"Sure it is," he says, so confident he has the answers. "Just text her, see if she wants to get coffee tomorrow."

"It's not that easy."

"It *is* that easy. If you want it to be. She sought you out. She *wants* to reconnect. But if you don't follow up . . ."

"Okay," I say to end the conversation, but Theo doesn't stop.

"You can't keep pushing everyone away. It's not healthy."

"We have a new neighbor," I say, changing the subject. "She was moving in today."

"Okay," Theo says, still frowning.

"I went over to introduce myself."

"What's her name?" he asks.

"I don't remember."

A look.

"She might not have said. She's around our age, though. A little older than us, I guess. She's got a teenage son."

"Okay," Theo says, and I get the distinct impression he is not satisfied, just tired. "Well, that's great. Nice to have someone else our age on the block. Maybe the two of you will hit it off."

"Maybe," I say, happy to pretend if it ends this conversation. "Dinner is just about ready."

This is just a rough patch, I remind myself as I creep into our room, careful not to wake Lucy. I peer into her bassinet, her face dimly lit by the light from downstairs. Theo is still moving around down there; shuffling papers, responding to emails. *Things have not always been this strained between us, and they will not stay this way,* I tell myself. *We will figure this out.*

I try to remember the early days, when everything about Theo was new and exciting, when nothing was zero-sum, when there was no real weight to any of our conflicts. The first time we met was at the Academy. One of Theo's bar associations had rented out some of our space for a cocktail party, and so he was there, dressed in a sports coat alongside fifty or so other lawyers. Normally, I would have steered clear of that kind of event, but my key card had fallen out of my pocket earlier that day and I was searching for it before heading home. I tried to be discreet, sticking to the periphery of the gathering as I retraced my steps. It was loud in the hall, polite chatter bouncing off the glass displays. A tortoise—one of the Academy's live animals trotted out for the event—slowly chewed a head of lettuce in the corner. One of the animal handlers weaved through the crowd with Betsy the ball python wrapped around his neck.

An older man—clearly a gesticulator, his hands waving wildly as he recounted another lawyer's courtroom gaffe—stepped backward to avoid the snake, nearly bumping into me. I stepped back to avoid him and instead crashed into someone else. Something cold and wet soaked into the back of my blouse. I turned and saw Theo, holding a half-empty cup of wine.

"I'm so sorry," I said, and he shook his head, grinning, an open, playful smile.

"Why are *you* apologizing?" he said. "You're the one with wine all over you. Here, let me help with that."

He pressed his cocktail napkin against the small of my back, and I felt a jolt at his touch. He was attractive in a way I usually found unnerving. He reminded me of the boys my cousins dated in high school, lacrosse players with easy smiles and clean skin, who never questioned the space they took up, who either ignored me entirely or gave me a wide berth. He laughed, shrugged. "Well, that didn't do much. Let me grab some more."

"No," I said, flushing. I shouldn't have even been there. "It's fine. I'm fine. I'm just heading home."

"You work here?" he asked.

"Yeah, I—"

A girl appeared—Fey, I know now—and rested her head possessively against his shoulder.

"Helen is pissed," she said. Her roommate, I'd later learn, who had been in an on-again, off-again relationship with Theo for the past year.

"Helen will be fine," Theo said. "Fey, have you met . . ."

"Lee," I filled in. Fey straightened and extended her hand, her nails perfectly manicured.

"You're not a lawyer," she said, not a question.

"And thank god for that," Theo said, winking at me. "Lee actually taxidermied all these animals." He swept his hand around the hall.

"I'm an archivist," I said. "I was just looking for—"

"And!" Theo said, his eyes glinting playfully, "she's going to show us one of the museum's secret collections. Something the other guests never get to see."

"I—"

"Oh, come on," Theo said, and his enthusiasm was contagious. "I know there must be some good stuff in storage. Monkeys riding goats? Little Victorian rabbits dressed in suits?"

"You know your Walter Potter," I said with a laugh.

"I try to know a little bit about everything," Theo said. "Just enough to ask informed questions."

"Theo," Fey said, rolling her eyes. "Our resident dilettante."

"You never know when you're going to need to have a conversation with a mysterious taxidermist," he said, holding up his hands.

We didn't see any of the museum's secret collections that day— I only found my key later, shoved into the corner of the elevator floor. But I soon realized that Theo hadn't really been kidding. On our dates, Theo would strike up conversations with waiters and find his way back into the kitchen, getting samples of new dishes and recommendations from the chef. When we saw performances at the Kimmel Center, we lingered afterward to chat with the conductor and a handful of the performers—people Theo likely knew through his mother's service on the board, I'd eventually realize. He navigated the world with the confidence that he belonged everywhere, that all doors were open to him, that nothing bad could ever happen. Under his wing, a part of me started to believe that I belonged, too. And I think he liked being the one to show me that world, to bring me out of my shell. *I've never met anyone like you before*, he used to tell me. I took that to mean all sorts of things at the time, but now I think he was probably saying: *You don't belong here. Let me help.*

Everything changed when Lucy was born, of course. It's funny how the same things that attract you to a person can be the things that push you apart. The same confidence I used to love now terrifies me; he doesn't know to be vigilant. He doesn't know how badly Lucy needs to be protected. And while before I was a project—someone he could help, save, improve—my regression, my inability to snap back after Lucy was born, is a problem. Theo can't be the savior if I can't be saved.

We are not the only ones going through this, I remind myself. I hear it in my moms' group, on my parenting podcasts, read about it in think pieces on motherhood. The first year is hard; everyone agrees on that. It scrapes at vulnerabilities you never even knew existed; it pits you against each other. But people grow, they move beyond.

The light downstairs flicks off, and Theo's footsteps stop, his sound machine switching on. We'll get through this; I know we will.

I hope Theo knows that, too.

CHAPTER NINE

On Friday mornings, Lucy and I normally loop the park by our house. We start at the community garden. It's fenced and kept locked, but we can usually slip in behind someone with a plot and a key. I tell Lucy the names of the flowers and vegetables, hold her close enough to smell them, watch to make sure she doesn't grab any in her fist. I tell her someday soon we'll get our own plot, with sweet peas and heads of kale and spinach, purple hyacinths and pink and yellow tulips. At Jacob's Hill, my mother and I planted bulbs together every fall and watched them bloom in the spring.

I know it's important to stick with a routine. It's not good for me or Lucy to spend all day cooped up in the house, stacking blocks and knocking them over, watching the numbers on the clock. But it's not forever: just until Mona comes back. I don't want to miss her.

Lucy is irritable; she is picking up on my nerves. I've made her lots of food—toast with ricotta spread on top, sweet potatoes mixed with coconut milk—but she doesn't want to eat. Instead, she fusses and cries. I play a song on my phone about dinosaurs stomping, pull her out of her chair and bounce her around the kitchen to get her to laugh. We play it five times, and ten minutes pass, and then she is unhappy again.

"I'm sorry," I say. "We have to wait for Aunt Mona. She's coming to see us."

There's a knock at the door. My heart leaps. *Finally.* I run to open it.

But the woman standing on the other side is not Mona. It's my new neighbor, holding two cups of coffee from Rival Bros.

"Hi," she says. "I'm Andi."

My heart drops, but I try to keep a polite smile on my face.

"Sorry if I didn't make the best impression yesterday," she says, holding out one of the cups. "I hate moving."

"Oh, I get it," I say. Lucy shouts from the kitchen, and Andi cranes her neck to see her.

"Aww, who's this?" she asks, and I gesture for her to follow me inside.

"This is Lucy," I say, pulling her out of her chair. "She's seven months old."

"Oh, I miss when Des was this age," she says. "I mean, you couldn't pay me enough to go back to it, but *god* they're so cute. Sleeping?"

"No," I say.

"It gets better. Des does nothing but sleep now."

"Where are you moving from?" I wipe off the ricotta that has made it onto Lucy's hands but not into her mouth.

"Oh, not far," she says. "Just Fairmount. Divorce."

"I'm sorry."

"Thanks," she says. "It sucks."

There's something refreshing about her frank manner, and I'm about to ask her if she wants to sit down when my phone pings. A notification from Reddit, a new mention of my name.

dramallama8903: oh man, if you want to know more about ophelia clayborne, you need to see this . . .

"Lucy and I need to get ready for an appointment," I say. "But—"

"Oh, totally, sorry for barging in on you," she says.

"Not at all!" I say. "I'm glad we got the chance to officially meet."

"Des babysits, by the way," she says. "He's a real sweetheart, if you can manage to pry his phone out of his hands."

"Good to know," I say, pretending to file this information away for later.

I shut the door behind her and click on the link. TikTok opens on my phone, and a woman's face pops onto my screen.

Not just a woman. My cousin. Clara. She's made-up, her face contoured, her hair in soft, relaxed curls. In the background, a beautiful kitchen, children's artwork on the walls.

You all know me, she says, *and you know I'm an open book. Motherhood, marriage, I tell it like it is, and you've all been with me on my journey. But one thing I haven't really spoken about before is my own childhood, and I wasn't sure I was going to bring this up here, but I feel like I have to.*

She blinks, like she might start crying.

My cousin is the "survivor" from Jacob's Hill, and she came to live with us after the disappearance. I was thirteen, and it was a difficult adjustment for all of us, but we did our best to welcome her into our lives.

She grimaces, shakes her head.

It didn't go well, she says. *There's something very wrong with her. I think—*

She purses her lips together, like she's debating whether or not to say it.

I think she was involved in whatever happened that night.

CHAPTER TEN

—

Anne made breakfast most mornings, and the morning after I arrived at the Richardson house was a pancake day. I came downstairs and saw that Anne had pulled an extra chair up to the table to accommodate me.

"I don't like pancakes anymore," Clara said as my aunt set the plate down on the table.

"You don't have to like them," Anne said. "You do have to sit with us."

Clara sat across from me, glittery eye shadow swiped across each eye. Rachel, beside her, cast sidelong glances in my direction when she thought I wasn't paying attention.

"Are you going to school with us?" Clara asked.

"Not yet," Anne answered for me. I would not realize for another few years the legal wrangling she had to do to give me an identity. I had no birth certificate, no Social Security number, no medical records, no witnesses to my birth. I saw only glimpses of how these problems were resolved: Anne in the kitchen chopping vegetables with the phone wedged between her ear and shoulder, *yes, I'll wait.*

"I don't go to school," I said.

"Well," Anne said, stabbing a pancake for Clara and dropping it pointedly onto her plate. "That might change. But for a little while, you'll be staying home with me."

"Why don't you go to school?" Rachel asked, her eyes wide.

"It's a waste of time," I said. "You don't learn anything real."

"I don't know about that," said Anne. "Does anyone want strawberries?"

You're lucky, my mother had told me. This was when we still had sheep, and we were washing the wool in giant tubs, side by side. My mother placed her hand on mine—I was doing it wrong, felting the wool—and she showed me what it should look like, a loose clump. *Other children are locked inside for seven hours a day, and the only thing they learn is how to sit still and take orders. They won't be ready. You will be.*

"What do you think we *should* be learning?" Clara asked.

"How to support ourselves," I said. "How to grow food, how to trap it, how to preserve it. How to protect ourselves."

"Why do we need to learn that?" Rachel asked, gnawing at her cuticle.

"For when we're on our own," I said. "What are you going to do when there are no more grocery stores and you can't just flip a switch to get electricity or turn on a faucet to get water?"

Rachel stared back at me, horrified.

"Girls," Anne said. "Clara, if you're not eating, go get dressed."

"I thought I was supposed to sit at the table."

"Go."

Anne waited as Clara stalked off, then turned back to me. She looked like she was straining for something to say.

"You'll have to give me some help in the garden," she said finally. "I have the opposite of a green thumb."

"I won't be here that long," I said.

After breakfast, I dressed and braided my hair and clasped my mother's bracelet around my wrist. *Our secret,* she had told me when she gave it to me, and I liked to keep it on me during the day, squirreled away in my pocket where I could brush my fingers against the cold metal, or hidden under the long sleeves of my dress.

Something I had just begun to understand about my mother was that she liked to have those kinds of secrets—her own small rebellions—especially when Christopher's attention was focused elsewhere. I remember weeding the garden with her one morning, and her hair was down, which was unusual; she typically wore it in a braid. It was hot; sweat dripped between my shoulder blades, and I could almost feel the itch of her thick hair against her neck. When she couldn't stand it anymore, she twisted her hair back, and I saw it: an earring fashioned out of a fishhook, the skin around it red and irritated, a small, pearl-colored bead hanging on the end.

What did you do? I asked, my chest tightening.

Oh, she said, touching a hand to her ear like she had forgotten. *I've always loved earrings.* Like she was a child, like she didn't know what would happen.

At the time, I thought it was a stupid mistake. How could she be so impulsive, so foolish? But eventually I realized she did know, and she did it anyway: to prove to herself that she could, maybe, or to get his attention, his anger better than nothing at all.

I rubbed the chain between my fingers and looked out the guest room window, hoping for movement. Nothing. I turned and there was Clara, standing in my doorway. For all I knew, she might have been standing there a long time. Her face was pinched, her arms crossed over her chest.

"I saw pictures of Jacob's Hill," she said. "It was in the news."

"Oh," I said, unsure of how to respond.

"Pictures of Christopher, too," she said. "He looks like a psychopath."

"He's not."

Clara sat on the foot of my bed cautiously. "So was your mom, like . . . one of his wives?"

"No," I said. "More like a student. He's a teacher."

"Is he your father?"

"He was like a father to all of us," I said.

My child, Christopher would say. *My children. My flock.*

Clara raised her eyebrows but didn't respond. Instead, she tugged at the cuffs on her jacket, her fingernails a dark, sparkly purple. When she raised her eyes to meet mine again, her face was neutral, her voice softened. "So what did he teach you?"

"All kinds of things."

She looked genuinely interested, and I didn't yet know better, and so I told her he showed us how to insulate a building to conserve energy; how to build turbines and create power using the water on our land. How to build a snare; how to raise our own livestock; how to butcher our own meat.

"What kinds of animals?"

"Goats, sometimes. Rabbits and chickens, mostly."

"Like Lucky?"

"Sort of," I said. "We don't name them, and they live in hutches outside, not in the residence."

"How did you do it?" she asked, leaning in. And so I told her: You hit it on the head, right behind the ears, with a rod or a heavy piece of wood. You hang it by its feet to drain the blood, cut along its belly and legs and pull off the skin. Her eyes widened.

"Sorry," I said. "Is that not what you were asking?"

"No, no," she said. "I want to know."

"You've never butchered anything before?" I asked.

She scoffed, then caught herself, softened again. "No."

I asked what school was like, what she did all day.

"Pretty boring," she said. "Not that much." She liked art class, though, she said, and when I told her I liked drawing, too, she went to her room and brought back a sketch pad, detailed flowers and butterflies filling every inch of the pages.

"Those are beautiful," I said, and she smiled, and I thought, in that moment, that maybe I had made a friend.

———

Two officers stopped by later that day. The woman who didn't blink enough and a man I hadn't seen before, both in suits. Anne told them to make themselves comfortable in the living room. An upright piano that no one played stood in the corner, with decorative porcelain cottages on top. The officers both took a seat on the floral couch, and I perched on the stiff, tufted armchair. Anne brought out glasses of water, set them down on coasters. She lingered in the archway, watching, and I got the sense the officers didn't want her there, but she stayed anyway, a gesture I appreciated even then.

"We have a few more questions for you," the woman explained, pulling out a notepad.

"I told you everything yesterday."

"We know, and you did a great job," the man said, smiling, the friendlier of the two. "But it could help to go back through it, see if there's anything we missed the first time."

"I don't know anything else," I said.

"Sometimes people surprise themselves with what they know," the woman said. The words themselves were not unkind, but I could tell by the way she said them she thought I was hiding something. "Let's start with the night before. You went to bed—when?"

"I went to my room at eight," I said. "Maybe eight-thirty."

"Do you always go to bed so early?" she asked.

"No," I said. "I wasn't sleeping. I just wanted some time to myself."

"Why?"

I shrugged.

"Was something bothering you, Ophelia?" the man asked.

"No," I said. I was unwilling to tell these strangers the petty truth: that I was frustrated by my younger sister, that the last thing I had said to her had been cruel. "I just wanted to read my book."

The woman's eyes reminded me of fish eyes, large and bulging. The man leaned back against the couch, pretending to settle in although it wasn't comfortable, acting like this was just a casual chat.

"My son's a big reader, too," he said, his smile broadening. "So eight, eight-thirty, that was the last time you saw anyone? Before the disappearance?"

"No," I said. "My mother came in to tell me good night."

The woman wrote something in her notebook, and the man leaned forward again, resting his forearms on his knees.

"What did she say?"

"I don't know," I said. "Normal things."

"Normal things like what?" the woman asked.

I squeezed my eyes shut. I hadn't known at the time how important those words would be. I hadn't known to pay attention, to commit them to memory. I remembered her sitting on the side of my bed, reaching for my arm. I remembered jerking away.

"She said she loved me," I said, and I could see the concern flash across both their faces. "She always did. That wasn't—it wasn't strange. I love you, sleep well, see you in the morning."

"She said that?" the woman asked. "I'll see you in the morning."

"Yes?" I said. "I think so. She always said that."

"Did she say it that night?"

I pursed my lips, hesitated.

"She's not sure," Anne said, stepping into the room so she was beside my chair, arms crossed over her chest. "She said that already."

I expected this to get a reaction, pushback, *we're not talking to you*, but instead the man nodded, sat back again, asked gently: "When do you think she left your room?"

"I don't know," I said. "Maybe nine-thirty?"

The woman nodded and wrote it down. My aunt took a seat in the other armchair, crossed one leg over the other, standing guard.

"But I don't know that for sure," I said. "It could have been earlier or later. I'm not sure."

"And that was the last time you saw anyone?" the man asked.

"Yes," I said, nodding my head, relieved to have a question I could answer.

"Did you hear anyone else on the second floor?" he asked. "While you were reading, or while you were falling asleep?"

"I heard Terese putting Kai down at some point. They're in the room next to me, and he takes a long time to settle."

"So you can hear a lot from your room," the woman said.

"The walls are pretty thin."

"Did you wake up at all during the night?"

"No," I said. "I told you that yesterday."

"Sometimes people forget things," she said. "You didn't wake up to go to the bathroom, or to drink some water, or . . ."

"No," I said. "I told you, I didn't wake up at all."

"Is that normal for you?" the man asked. "To sleep straight through the night, even with everyone coming and going?"

"I'm not sure," I said. I thought about the bathroom door slamming against its frame, Kai's muffled cries, the adults shuffling to bed after a late-night bonfire. Christopher's shovel, hitting rock as he dug his holes around the residence. *We need to be ready.* I thought about our route through the woods, up the creek and through the brush, to the clearing. *Keep up, Ophelia.* I pushed the thought aside. It wasn't what they were asking, and I went to the clearing myself. There was no one there.

"But that night, you're saying you slept all the way through," the woman said.

"I'm sorry," Anne said, holding out her hand to stop me from talking. "Are these questions, or is this an interrogation?"

"We're just trying to figure out what happened," the woman said, her tone short.

"We all want to find them," Anne said. "But Ophelia has been through a lot, so unless you have any *new* questions for her . . ."

"Ophelia," the man said, leaning toward me again. "What we are trying to understand is how fifteen people could up and leave without you hearing anything. That seems strange, doesn't it?"

"I don't know what happened," I said.

"If you saw something," the woman said, "you won't be in trouble. You can tell us."

"I didn't see anything."

"But if—"

"She said she didn't see anything," Anne said, cutting her off. "I think she's done for now, officers."

"We all want the same thing here," the man said.

"What I want," Anne said, "is for my niece to get some rest. If she thinks of anything else, we will be sure to let you know."

"We will need to talk to her again," the woman said.

"Of course," said Anne. "But not today."

She showed the officers to the door, her hands shaking, her mouth drawn. She turned to look at me, and I could tell she was replaying the officers' questions in her mind. *You must have seen something. You must know.* She opened her mouth, and I thought she was going to ask, but instead she said: "I'm going to make myself a sandwich. Do you want one?"

"No," I said. "I'm going up to my room." And I went upstairs and closed the door.

I was wrong about Clara being a friend, of course. Anne made dinner that night, from the neat, Styrofoam packages of chicken stacked in the fridge. Clara wasn't there—*at a friend's house,* Anne told me when I asked—and Rachel looked more distraught than normal, her eyes red from crying. Anne seemed nervous and distracted, sometimes watching me for too long, sometimes avoiding my gaze altogether.

"How was your day today?" Peter asked, carving into his dinner, oblivious to the tension.

"The police were here," she said.

"Have they found anything new?" he asked.

"No," she said. "They just wanted to talk to Ophelia again. To see if she remembered anything new."

"Hmm," Peter said.

"I wonder if we maybe need a lawyer."

Rachel looked close to bursting into tears, and Peter squinted, surprised.

"Why?"

"Just if—" Anne looked at me and then looked down, catching herself. "We can talk about this later. I just wondered, is all."

After dinner, I helped Anne with the dishes.

"Clara told me," she said, over the spray of water. "What you said about Lucky."

The room shifted, my head buzzing.

"What you . . . said you'd do to him."

"I don't know what—"

"She said you described how you'd kill him in graphic detail," she said quickly, not looking at me. "I don't—"

"No," I said. "I mean, she asked. I told her I had butchered rabbits, and she asked me how I did it."

Anne looked at me, unsure of what to believe, the same look she had given me when the police officers left. A look like I might be a monster.

"She asked," I said, "so I told her how it worked. That's all."

"Okay," Anne said. But that night Lucky's cage moved from Rachel's room into Anne and Peter's room, just in case.

CHAPTER ELEVEN

—

Theo putters around our kitchen, making pancakes for the three of us. He measures out the flour and the sugar with an old law school mug, heats the oil on a skillet on the stove.

Tell him, I think to myself. With Mona's return, and the documentary, and Clara's desperate bids for attention on TikTok, it's only a matter of time before he finds out on his own. It will be better if he hears it from me.

"You remember I was telling you about Jameson?" he says, looking back at me from the stove, the batter sizzling behind him. Jameson, one of his clients, is schizophrenic, and more often than not untreated. "I got him into mental health court," he says. "He'll get a lot more support there. We were feeling hopeful, but just got confirmation." He flips the pancakes. "He's lucky I was the one assigned to his case," he says. "Can you imagine Kurt taking the time? Or Donovan?"

Theo, the hero.

Stop, I tell myself. *Be generous.* This is a real victory, and why shouldn't he take pride in it? These wins matter, and they happen so infrequently on the criminal defense side of things. And he's right: Donovan wouldn't have taken the time.

"That's great," I say. I shouldn't spoil the moment. I'll tell him later.

"Voilà," he says. "Perfect." He scoops the pancake onto a plate for Lucy, cuts it into strips. "What do you say we do something as a family today? We should go somewhere. Anywhere you want."

I hesitate. What I want is to be at home, available, in case Mona comes back.

"It'll be nice," he says, softer. He knows something is wrong, even if he doesn't know what it is. "It'll be good to get out of the house."

I look toward the door. I know that Mona can't really expect me to stay here, waiting, until she decides to show up. If she returns and we are not home, she'll come back another time.

Maybe, I think. *And who knows how long that will take?*

Theo senses my hesitation, and his good mood shifts. "Please," he says, more seriously this time. "I think some time together would be good for us."

"Okay," I say, attempting a smile, trying not to imagine Mona showing up, knocking, no response. "Sure, yeah. That sounds good."

"What about the Academy?" Theo says. "I know you've wanted to take Lucy there."

I feel a tug of hesitation but give in. "Sure," I say. "Let's go."

The doors to the Academy slide open, and I see a familiar face, Sherrie, behind the front desk.

"Lee!" Sherrie says, rising from her seat and wrapping me in a warm hug. "You're back! And look at that baby!"

Sherrie is a grandmother many times over. She loves children, and babies especially. She crouches down to see Lucy in her stroller, her face close.

"What a cutie," she says, brushing Lucy's arm with her finger. "What's your name?"

"Lucy," I say, feeling a twinge of guilt that I haven't sent pictures or updates, not even Lucy's name. Sherrie was someone I saw multiple days a week for years—not a friend, exactly, but a part of my life. We'd chat when I was coming in and out of the building about which of her children lived nearby, which ones depended on her for childcare, where she liked to take the kids in the city. She recommended long walks and pineapple and spicy foods to induce labor. "She's seven months old."

"How is that possible?" Sherrie says. She straightens herself, smiles at Theo, who gives her a warm smile back.

"I hope you're taking good care of the two of them," Sherrie says.

"I'm doing my best," Theo tells her.

In the elevator, he rubs my back, and I lean my head against his shoulder.

"See? Everyone loves you here," he says.

I have not told him yet that my position has been filled: another omission, but one that now seems small compared to the rest. I close my eyes, breathe in and out. I need to come clean about all of it. Someday soon, Mona will meet him and let something slip about our past, or Meghan Kessler will change her mind about my privacy, or another reporter with fewer scruples will swoop in, and it will all come out. It will be better if Theo hears the truth from me.

The elevator door opens, and we step into the dark hallway. We loop around the exhibits to the Serengeti Plains diorama, where a mounted zebra grazes next to gazelles and impalas, frozen in time and place. I point out each animal to Lucy, telling her their names and where they came from.

"Some of these exhibits," Theo says to Lucy, as if she can understand, "are over a hundred years old, and your mom helps make sure they'll last another hundred years. Each one is like a little time capsule, a glimpse into the past."

I feel a swell of pride. When we first started dating, Theo confessed that he had spent a lot of time at the Academy as a child but really only liked the dinosaurs: the Deinonychus statue and the Tyrannosaurus rex skeleton, the Elasmosaurus hanging from the ceiling. *The rest of it is kind of creepy,* he said. *Like a mausoleum.*

The dioramas are my favorite part, I told him. *They're like windows into a different era.*

We walk the floor slowly, Lucy transfixed by the pride of lions, the towering gorilla. We were in the process of restoring them when I left, and it was part of my job to research the materials used in their habitats—the silk ferns, the marble berries, the living moss and sticks and stones—so we could find the best way to bring them back to life without damaging them. Dish soap for the animal pelts. Synthetic saliva for the wax leaves.

Someone else's job now. But there will be other opportunities, I tell myself. Theo puts his arm around my waist, and I lean into him. "I'm glad we're doing this," he says, and I agree. It's just a rough patch we've been going through, that's all. Babies change relationships, but the pieces can come back together again, even stronger than before.

"We can talk about it if you want," he continues, his voice low, like he doesn't want to disturb the quiet in the hall.

"About what?"

"Your sister."

I pull away, turn to look at him.

"She searches you out a few days ago, and then . . . nothing? You've barely mentioned her since then, and it's obviously bothering you. I don't know what happened, Lee, but you can talk to me about it. I want to know what's going on."

I realize, with alarm, that my eyes are filling with tears. I can't stop it.

"She hasn't talked to me since that day," I say. "I must have said the wrong thing."

Theo's expression morphs into one of understanding. "Maybe she just needs a little time?"

I shake my head. "I keep replaying our conversation in my head, trying to figure out where I went wrong. But I don't know what happened."

"She sought you out," he says. "That's a big step. She obviously wants to repair the relationship."

"It's been such a long time. Maybe I'm not the person she thought I was going to be. Maybe she doesn't like me."

He pulls me in again, rests his head on mine. "Not possible," he says.

I could tell him right now. I could explain everything, the disappearance, what came after, and maybe it will all go like this. Maybe it will be okay after all. But then Lucy begins to fuss and squirm in her stroller, her unhappy grunts escalating. She needs to be changed.

I'll tell him soon.

"We'll be right back," I say.

Lucy and I take the elevator to the third floor, where the bathroom is. The elevator doors slide open, and I catch a glimpse of wavy brown hair. I freeze.

Clara.

The doors begin to close again, and I recover, push forward. I only saw her for a moment, not long enough to know if it's really her, and now she's turned the corner, out of view. Clara lives around here, or at least she used to, so it's possible.

Lucy squirms, unhappy we are not moving forward. I push and pull the stroller, small rolls back and forth, hoping that will satisfy her long enough that Clara will be gone by the time we turn the corner.

If it's really her. Maybe it's someone else who looks similar.

The last time I saw Clara was at my aunt's funeral. My aunt died of cancer, a few years after her diagnosis. She held on long enough to see the birth of Clara's son. He was a newborn, sleeping snugly in his detachable car seat. Clara had rested a thin blanket over the carrier to block out the light, and while she welcomed guests and accepted condolences I pulled back the corner of the blanket, just a little, to see his face. Before she passed away, my aunt told me she saw some of my mother in him, *in his eyes,* and I wanted to see for myself.

Lucy kicks her legs, her frustration growing, not fooled by the stroller's repetitive motion. We edge toward the corner, and I hold my breath, worried Clara will still be there, that she'll see me. I don't want a scene, not here, not with Theo so close by.

That day at the funeral, Clara had seen me looking at her son. *What do you think you're doing?* she shouted, rushing back toward us, panicked. *Don't touch him. Get away from him.* I had backed away immediately, bumping into the neatly arranged rows of chairs, apologizing profusely, trying to explain.

We turn the corner, and my cousin isn't there. There's another brunette with a similar build, a three-year-old tugging at her hand, probably the woman I saw. I breathe a sigh of relief. *Okay,* I tell myself. *Everything is okay.* I am letting things get to me; I am overreacting. I park the stroller in the hallway and push open the bathroom door, strap Lucy into the pull-down changing table. My hands are shaking so badly I nearly drop the wipes.

Calm down, I will myself. *It wasn't her.*

I check my appearance in the water-spattered mirror, wash one hand at a time while I hold Lucy with the other. She tugs at my shirt collar, and I pull it back to conceal the red skin.

It wasn't her, but it could have been. She's in the city somewhere; it's only luck that our paths have not crossed since the funeral. Maybe it's only a matter of time, another minefield to navigate. I strap Lucy into her stroller, put in my AirPods, and pull up Clara's TikTok account.

Police didn't look that closely at my cousin, Clara says to the camera as she twists her hair up into a bun, like this is just a casual chat, *because she was twelve at the time of the disappearance. Just a kid, so how could she have possibly been involved? But her father was a cult leader, and she was much more capable and much less stable than the police realized. She was not a normal twelve-year-old girl.*

I don't notice Theo, walking toward us from the elevator bank, until he is standing right in front of me. "There you two are," he says, and I drop my phone in the stroller basket, try to remove my AirPods without him noticing. But he sees, gives me a curious look.

"What are you watching?"

"Just a stupid video," I say. "It's nothing."

I can't tell him. I can't risk it. I know what happens when people find out about the disappearance; I have seen the mental shift happen time and time again. I become a victim to be pitied or a freak to be avoided.

I can't handle seeing that change in Theo, too.

"Should we see if Lucy can pet some turtles?" Theo asks, gesturing down the hallway.

I nod and do my best to smile, Clara's words at my aunt's funeral echoing in my mind, the things she told the guests who came to her aid as I rose and rushed out of the church, my face burning. *She shouldn't be here. She's fucking crazy. Do you know about the fire? Do you know what she did?*

CHAPTER TWELVE

—

Twenty years earlier

The early days at the Richardson house rolled into one another, one following the next with nothing to differentiate them. No new leads, no information, no sightings of my mother or sister or the rest of them.

"It doesn't make sense," I heard my aunt saying into the phone when she thought I wasn't listening. "People don't just disappear."

I overheard other snippets of conversation, too: my aunt's no-nonsense tone: *No comment. No, she's a child. Please leave us alone.* As with her efforts to build me an identity, document by document, I only appreciated later how much work she did to protect me. She held off the reporters, funneled information between me and the police.

She also held off the family of members of Jacob's Hill. A few of them tried to contact me, but she turned them away. She told me when they reached out, and she said it was my choice but she didn't think it would be a good idea. "They're upset," she said. "Just like you. But they're also looking for someone to blame. They'll take any target they can get."

I only spoke to one of them, and only once. Nobody else was home, and the phone rang. I answered in the same way my cousins always did: "Richardson residence." I heard a woman's voice on the other line, shaky, thin. Pained. *Ophelia?* she said, and when I didn't respond: *What happened that night? What did you see? I know you saw something, Ophelia, what did you see?*

I slammed the phone back into the receiver and never picked up again without checking caller ID first.

It was spring when I went to live with my aunt and her family, and Anne decided there was no point in enrolling me in school that far into the year. Better to start in the fall, she told me. A fresh start, a new beginning. *I won't still be here in the fall,* I thought. I didn't say it this time, though, too familiar with the look she would give me in response, faking a shared hope. It had been weeks, and they had not returned.

Anne homeschooled me instead, which meant working together on math and composition and science and social studies in the mornings, and freedom in the afternoon. That's when Anne ran errands, and I lingered in the house, mostly in the office on the desktop computer that was always on, the whir and grind of its console constant background noise. I hadn't used a computer before but figured it out quickly. Clara let her AIM account run even when she wasn't home, collecting messages. She got upset if anyone logged her off, so I left it on in the background, turning down the volume so I didn't have to hear the sound of doors opening and closing and new message chimes.

I wasn't interested in talking to anyone. All I wanted was information about my family.

Anne tried hard to protect me from news and stories about Jacob's Hill. If a segment about the disappearance came on the TV or the radio, she'd rush to turn it off. Newspapers that mentioned Jacob's Hill were thrown into the trash. "You don't need to see that," she said.

But Anne was naïve about how much information was accessible online, and so I read it all there. Write-ups on Christopher that mostly seemed to pull facts from the same handful of places. In some, Christopher was said to be forty-one, in others he was forty-three. He was from upstate New York originally, an engineer-turned-philosopher who taught as an adjunct at Swarthmore College. Mentally ill, they agreed. Police found magnets buried around the property in carefully spaced holes. They weren't sure of their purpose, but I knew: They were to block the devices FBI agents were using to listen to us. There were interviews with family members: Amy Price, Katrina's sister and River and Echo's aunt. Gregory Dunn, Lottie Dunn's adult son. Elise Dagnelle, Adrienne's sister. Pictures of them at press conferences, looking into the camera and asking the police to keep looking, begging their family members to come home.

The news reports online all used the same words to describe our living conditions—dirty, cramped, monastic—like they were copying one another. The Fifteen were "more educated than you might think," they said. The members had left behind promising lives when they went to live at Jacob's Hill. A few attempted to offer an explanation, citing a sociologist who studied high-control groups, or a psychologist specializing in narcissistic personalities. As if my mother, a student, had the same reasons as Adrienne, an environmentalist who had spent ten years working on organic farms. As if either of them had the same reasons as Lottie Dunn, who had lost her husband of forty years, or Patrick Speight, who spent the first twenty years of his life afraid to speak. As if there was a simple answer, one you could find by looking at Christopher, rather than looking at them, the whole of their lives.

None of the reporters had any real information to offer about what had happened, but that didn't stop them from speculating. Christopher was working on a "manifesto," the news reports said, a term they used instead of "book" to encourage associations with the Unabomber. The book detailed what Christopher believed to be the four stages of enlightenment: sleepwalking, an awakening, resistance, and ascent.

Law enforcement officers were still searching but feared the worst. The "computer use rule" in the Richardson house was that the office door had to stay open, but I could always hear Anne as she came up the stairs, which gave me plenty of time to close out of the articles and switch to something permitted. She'd peek her head in, ask how things were going.

"Fine," I'd say, and she wanted to believe me, so she did.

By that point, Officer Leanne had helped me retrieve a few of my belongings from Jacob's Hill, not that there were many. My clothes, which Anne had folded and placed in a trunk in the depths of my closet. My books, and the book my mother had been reading. My quilt, which my mother had sewn for me when I was a baby, pieced together out of clothing she had brought with her but gradually stopped wearing, denim and velvet and flannel. One square was made from fuzzy gray cotton, from the sweatshirt of a boy she had been friends with in college.

He was in love with me, she confided in me once. *He was a musician, always playing guitar. He wrote a few songs for me, with my name in them.*

Another made of soft green corduroy, from the jacket she had been wearing the first time she stepped into Christopher's classroom.

My mother came to Jacob's Hill already pregnant with me. In the last picture I have of her, a picture from her freshman year of college, you can see her body changing, her stomach rounded, her hand resting protectively on her abdomen. I remember Adrienne's gentle ribbing about that. There was a barn raising when they all first arrived at Jacob's Hill, marking the beginning of their new life together, and everyone participated except my mother. *I was nine months pregnant,* my mother would laugh. *I could barely waddle.* I was the first of a new generation, the children of Jacob's Hill.

I kept that quilt wrapped around me in the computer room, which was always kept at sixty-eight degrees. I scoured websites and chat rooms where people talked about homesteading, self-sufficiency, the fragility of civilization, holding out hope that I might find some clue there, something to lead me to them.

I was on a website about cyber threats when I heard Anne's familiar footsteps. I closed out of it quickly.

"Knock knock," she said, leaning in the doorway. "Everything good up here?"

"Yep," I said, giving her a smile.

An instant message popped up on the screen, a message sent to Clara's username but not for Clara:

iamtheway: OPHELIA

"I'm making popcorn downstairs," Anne said, not noticing. "Thanks," I said. "I'll be down in a little bit."

iamtheway: OPHELIA ARE YOU THERE?

I minimized the window and tried to make sense of what I had read. Someone knew who and where I was, that I'd see Clara's messages, that this was a way to contact me. I looked out the window to the backyard. Empty.

"I've been thinking," Anne said. "About your name."

I glanced toward the screen. The rectangle on the menu bar blinked blue; another message.

"Maybe when we file your birth certificate, we should put it down as Ophelia Sorensen. Instead of Clayborne."

"What?" I said. My mind was racing. *Ophelia.* Could it be the police? A reporter? *They'll try to get you to talk, any way they can,* Anne had told me. *You can't trust them.*

"Just because—" Anne bit her lip, afraid of saying the wrong thing. "Well, because Sorensen is your mother's name."

"I don't know," I said, glancing out the window again. Was it my imagination, or did I see movement? How did they know I'd be here, me and not Clara?

"I thought it might be good for you to have that connection to her," Anne said. "And—"

"No," I said. "My name is Ophelia Clayborne."

"Okay," Anne said, nodding. "Right. Of course. Sorry."

I waited until she left, until I heard her footsteps retreating down the stairs, to pull up the message. There were two more: OPHELIA, YOU NEED TO ANSWER ME. And: WE DON'T HAVE MUCH TIME.

Who is this? I typed back. A minute passed, and then another, and I thought I had missed my chance.

But then, finally, a response.

iamtheway: IS THIS OPHELIA?
Yes, I wrote back. Who is this?
iamtheway: CHRISTOPHER. WE'VE BEEN LOOKING FOR YOU.

I swallowed, unsure of what to think. Where are you? I wrote.

iamtheway: YOU WEREN'T READY BEFORE. YOU WERE TOO WEAK, TOO ATTACHED TO THIS WORLD. BUT WE'VE BEEN WATCHING YOU, AND IT'S TIME.
I'm awake now, I wrote back. I'm ready.

CHAPTER THIRTEEN

—

Jackson has hit a sleep regression. This is despite Amanda's rigid adherence to schedules—naps every hour as a newborn, and then every hour-and-a-half, and now a strict two-three-four plan (two hours awake, nap, three hours awake, nap, four hours awake, bedtime). She is recounting the foods she has fed him over the past week—yogurt, pureed beans, strips of salmon—nothing spicy, all organic, but even so, she wonders if the sleep troubles could be related to a change in diet. Fish was a new addition; could the fish have disagreed with his stomach? There are head nods around the circle. Some of the other babies have regressed, too, even the ones that, like Jackson, have been dutifully sleeping through the night since eight weeks old. Lucy's sleep, of course, is unchanged; you cannot regress if you have not progressed.

"I've tried everything," Amanda says, near tears. "I don't know what to do."

I pick at the blue tape on the floor, scrape the gummy residue on the back with my fingernail. It is Monday, and Mona still has not returned.

Amanda looks to Dr. Dana, hopeful she'll have the one trick she has yet to try. I wonder what Dr. Dana thinks of her—of all of us, really, this circle of women turning to her for answers. She takes a swig from her plastic water bottle.

"Sleep regressions often happen during developmental leaps," she tells Amanda. She sweeps her gaze to include the rest of us, too: This is good for us all to know. "There's so much happening at this stage—language development, motor development. They're pulling themselves up in their cribs, exploring their worlds."

I shouldn't be here. I should be at home, waiting, just in case. But when I suggested to Theo that maybe we'd skip moms' group this morning, his whole mood changed, concern darkening his face. *You should go,* he told me. *You and Lucy need community. It's good for you.* And so I'm here, "getting community," and Mona is god-knows-where.

"He's been rocking on his hands and knees," Amanda says, some pride returning to her voice. "He's about to take off at any moment."

I need to be honest with myself: I'm not just here because of Theo. I know, in my heart, that if she hasn't come back yet, it's because she's not coming. I said the wrong thing. I disappointed her, or scared her away.

The sharp pain in my temple has returned, a ringing in my ears. Dr. Dana raises her eyebrows knowingly at Amanda, and Amanda adjusts Jackson into a crawling position. He rocks back to seated, grabs a rattle toy with colorful balls inside.

"Oscar just started sleeping again, but it was a *battle.* I can give you the contact info for the sleep consultant we used," Winnie offers from across the circle. "She is *amazing.*"

"Thank you," Amanda says, nodding intently. "I feel like I'm losing my mind."

"We've all been there," Dr. Dana says.

I can't focus. My mind is drifting, replaying the times I have seen them before—or the times I thought I saw them, anyway. My mother in the stands at my graduation, her long, loose braid. There one moment, and gone the next. Kai, in the baby seat of a shopping cart in a Pittsburgh grocery store, kicking his feet against the cart's wire body.

And now Mona, on the bench beside my front steps, waiting for me and Lucy to come home.

She was real, I tell myself. *Lucy saw her, too. Lucy* liked *her.* I talked to her, touched her. I did not feel manic. I did not feel out of control.

"Do you think it might be teething?" Lauren asks. "How many teeth does he have?"

But I have not had a full night's sleep since Lucy was born—have not slept for longer than four hours at a time, and it's usually more like two. And on top of that, there have been the pictures and Lucy's weight checks and the goddamned documentary.

"He has been drooling," Amanda says.

Stop, I tell myself. *She is real. You saw her. Lucy saw her.*

Dr. Dana is saying something else, but I can't focus on the words. The room smells like plastic and mildew, colonies of mold probably growing beneath these blue springy mats, spreading across the floor.

"Peanut butter!" Winnie says. "She gave him peanut butter."

"How did she do it?" Maggie asks, and Winnie looks at her, momentarily confused.

"I mean, did she mix it into oatmeal, or . . ."

"Puffs."

"Oh, we've gotten those from Trader Joe's," Maggie says. "They're really good."

It's possible, of course, the whole thing was a hoax. I think about the Reddit thread: Plenty of people know who I am, thanks to the documentary and online commentary. They know where I live. "Mona" could have been someone playing a trick on me, a fan of the documentary who got too wrapped up in the story. Maybe she realized on our walk together that this wasn't just a game to me, that this was cruel, that she had taken it too far.

"Did he have a reaction?" Dr. Dana asks. She squints, blinks, rubs her glasses on her shirt.

"No," Winnie says. "It's the principle of the thing. It wasn't her decision to make."

I felt something when I saw her, though. There was a recognition, a knowing. I *knew* her.

"—need to find a new nanny now," Winnie is saying. She tucks a strand of hair behind her ear, sniffs nervously.

Mona is real. She was telling the truth; she had to be. No one would lie about something like that.

"So if anyone knows of someone . . ."

I replay our short walk in my head, trying to pinpoint a comment that might have given offense, a misstep.

"Lee?" Dr. Dana says.

"We've been good," I say, forcing a smile.

"Any challenges this week? Any victories?"

"No," I say. She purses her lips, disappointed, and I correct myself. "Well, okay. I've been missing my family."

Dr. Dana's water bottle crinkles. "They're not in the area?"

"No," I say.

"That's hard," she says. "That's something a lot of us can relate to."

There are sympathetic head nods around the circle.

"I know," I say, and then, because I think I'm supposed to: "Being here really helps, though."

"I'm so glad," Dr. Dana says, and she moves on.

CHAPTER FOURTEEN

—

I left a note for Anne in my bedroom after everyone had gone to bed. *Thank you for everything. Don't worry about me. I'm with my family.* She'd report my disappearance, of course; she had to. Officer Leanne would add me to their list of missing people, but they wouldn't find me, just like they hadn't found the others.

I made my bed neatly, pulling the comforter up over the pillows. I grabbed my old dress from the drawer and my sweater from the closet. I'd leave everything else behind.

Christopher told me in his messages they'd be at the playground near the Richardsons' at one A.M. They wouldn't stay long, and so I couldn't be late. This was my chance.

I cracked my door open, just a sliver, and listened, holding the dress and the sweater in a bundle against my chest. All I could hear was the rattle of air through the vents. Everyone was asleep. I stepped out into the hallway, crept past Rachel's and Clara's closed doors. My heart was pounding so hard I could almost hear it, and I was certain Anne would hear it, too, that my nervous energy would wake her.

If someone wakes up, I reminded myself, *I'm just getting a glass of water. That's all.*

But I have never been a good liar, and I knew they'd see right through me: my shaking voice, my eyes that wouldn't meet theirs. And it was important I be on time. I had to show Christopher I was committed. That I was ready for whatever lay ahead.

Mercifully, Anne's door stayed closed.

I took the stairs carefully, avoiding the one that creaked. I walked softly to the alarm panel by the front door. Peter sometimes turned the system on at night, which could be a problem. I thought I could turn it off on my own but wasn't sure. I checked the glowing screen: inactive. *Good,* I thought, taking it as a sign. *This is working. I'm doing the right thing.*

I slipped on my shoes but didn't leave through the front door. I worried the dead bolt's click would wake Anne and Peter. It was the type of sound they'd be listening for subconsciously; *someone going, someone coming, something wrong.* Better to leave through the basement. And besides, I needed a flashlight.

I stopped in the kitchen. I kept the light off, willing my eyes to adjust to the dark. I could see the shadows of the high-backed chairs, the outlines of the counter, the silhouette of pots and pans hanging from a rack above the island. I opened the drawer where I knew Anne kept a flashlight, fumbled to find it. My fingers touched on pens, erasers, a pencil sharpener, the handle of a screwdriver, but nothing with the heft of a flashlight. I slid open the next drawer. Upstairs, a floorboard groaned under someone's weight. I held my breath, listened. Slow, sleepy footsteps; someone getting up to use the bathroom. I tried to remember if I had closed my door behind me. I wasn't sure.

They won't notice, I told myself. But what if I was wrong? They'd see the empty bed, the note on my dresser. I needed to leave now, flashlight or no flashlight. I crossed the tile floor, trying to walk carefully, but each step felt clunky, too loud. Any moment, I was sure, the lights would flick on, *what are you doing, Ophelia?* I couldn't let them stop me. I opened the basement door and steadied myself on the railing, counted the steps, *ten, eleven, twelve.* I reached for the dangling string at the bottom of the stairs, pulled, and a bare bulb flickered on, illuminating the space. Peter had a workbench down there, a hammer and saws and screwdrivers hanging on wire loops in a pegboard. I scanned the wall quickly, looking for an extra flashlight, a lantern, something I could use. No luck.

A door at the back of the basement led outside, to the backyard. The doorknob turned easily, unlocked. I wondered if Anne and Peter knew it was open; it was the type of mistake Anne didn't usually make. I pushed the thought aside and stepped out into the night air, cold and wet, closing the door behind me.

It's happening, I told myself. *I'm going home.*

Outside, I allowed myself to fully picture it. Headlights, and then the van rolling into view. The door opening, my mother and Mona inside. My mother taking me into her arms, kissing the top of my head, her peppermint smell. Mona burrowing into my side. *We would never leave you behind.*

I took a few steps and glanced back at the house. Only the basement light was on, the other rooms dark, the family sleeping. I stripped out of my T-shirt and sweatpants and slid on my dress. I left the shirt and pants folded neatly for Anne to find. Now I needed to get to the park, only a few streets away. I shuffled down the sloped hill, toward the line of trees I knew was waiting. I squinted, looking for black on gray, holding my hands out in front of me. I felt uneven ground beneath my feet, and then a tree root, and then bark on my fingertips. In the distance, I could see a porch light, left on like a beacon. Past that house was the road, which would be easier to follow, and after that the park wasn't far. I started walking faster, more self-assured. Too self-assured. I hit the dried-up creek bed without realizing it, and my right foot landed wrong on a rock, my ankle twisting. I fell, pain shooting up my leg.

You can't stop, I told myself. They wouldn't wait forever, and this might be my only chance. I knew I'd never find them on my own. I pushed myself up and navigated through the rest of the tree line, slow, careful steps across the stone. *I'm coming,* I thought. *I'll be there soon*. Like they could hear me somehow, or sense I was on my way. *Wait for me. Please.*

I gave the house with a lit porch light a wide berth, favoring my left foot as I traversed their side yard. I found the street and followed the curving road north. I worried that any second I might hear an engine, a car approaching behind me, its headlights shining in my direction, exposing me. *There shouldn't be anyone out here,* I reassured myself. *Not at this hour.* The houses here were set on big lots, few and far between. A few had lights on—not many, just enough to let would-be burglars know these houses were occupied. Farther up, the road was lined with streetlamps, guiding the way to the park.

I was so close. My heart pounded with anticipation, hope. When I reached the clearing, I could make out the outlines of playground equipment: three empty swings on a metal frame, a small platform with a slide. No movement, no sign anyone else was there. I took a seat on one of the park benches, my ankle pulsing.

"Mom?" I called out. "Christopher? Hello?"

No response.

They'll be here, I assured myself. *I just need to wait.*

Behind me, a twig snapped. I stood, placing too much weight on my ankle, and grimaced.

"Hello?" I shouted out again. "I'm right here. I'm ready."

A cough, and then the sound of feet shuffling and a bark of laughter, high-pitched and adolescent.

"We're ba-ack," said a male voice. A flashlight switched on, blinding me first, and then swinging up to show two teenaged boys. The one holding the flashlight laughed until the boy beside him shoved him, sending him stumbling to the side.

"That wasn't the plan, dipshit," he whispered loudly.

The flashlight beam swung until it hit on Clara, standing with her arms crossed beside them.

"I told you," she said. "She's brainwashed." She wouldn't look at me, and I wonder, now, if she sensed she had gone too far. But she was never one to back down. "I'm living with a fucking Manson girl."

"I knew it wasn't really him," I mumbled, cold and alone, my ankle roaring with pain. Clara finally looked at me, a look halfway between pity and contempt.

"Then what are you doing out here?"

CHAPTER FIFTEEN

—

Chicken thighs and thinly sliced potatoes roast in the oven. I am scrubbing down the countertops, although they are clean already, vein-streaked marble shining, while Theo and his mother chat in the next room.

"It's a cycle," Jacqueline is saying. "It's hard to break."

I finish my first glass of wine and pour a second. I wash a plastic mixing bowl, the hot water stinging my hands. The sink is a farmhouse sink, large, *great for entertaining,* the realtor told us when she took us through this house. *Look at these appliances,* she said, *brand-new, top of the line.* And the kitchen is beautiful: original wood floors, emerald-green cabinetry, convection oven carefully crafted to look antique. A far cry from the kitchen at Jacob's Hill, which was industrial, practical, everything built to feed a dozen, two dozen people. A tile floor, easy to wash. I open my compact pantry and think of the stone steps down to the root cellar, filled with salted meats, braided strands of garlic and onion, carrots and beets and radishes packed in sand. All of it still there on the day of the disappearance, none of it touched.

I dry the bowl slowly, deliberately, stalling. I can almost hear the *drip, drip, drip* of the sink, the sour smell from the pipes.

I hang my washcloth on the oven handle, lean against the counter, take another sip of my wine. Allow myself to wonder what the police did with all the food in the root cellar, if it's still there, rotting. It was meant to last a long time but not forever.

Jacqueline laughs from the other room, asks Theo: "How is Niko doing? And how is that *Fey*?" She emphasizes Fey's name, like always; Jacqueline likes to make it clear how partial she is to Theo's successful, pulled-together friend.

I do not know how I'm going to make it through this dinner.

The timer buzzes, and I pull the baking tray from the oven. *Only an hour*, I tell myself. *Then you can go to bed.*

There is a knock at the door.

I hear a rustle, Jacqueline and Theo standing.

"A little late for visitors," Jacqueline says.

I slip off my oven mitts, drop them in the drawer.

"Probably Amazon," Theo says, crossing the family room. "It's amazing how much stuff one tiny person needs."

"*Needs* is a strong word," Jacqueline says. "We didn't have all these things. They're profiting off of—"

The door swings open, and I brace myself for nothing, for Theo's polite *thank you*, his annoyed *no, sorry, now's not a good time.*

"I'm looking for Lee."

It's her.

"Is she—"

"Mona," I say, rushing for the door. Theo turns to me, surprised. He does not like to be caught off guard. "This is my sister," I say. "Mona."

"Sorry," Mona says. It's raining, and small beads of water cling to the tips of her hair. Her eyeliner streaks beneath her eyes. "Is this a bad time?" She avoids Theo's eyes and Jacqueline's questioning stare.

"No," I say, ushering her in. "Don't be ridiculous. This is perfect. We were just about to have dinner, and there's plenty—"

"Ophelia's *sister*," Jacqueline says. She edges closer, looking Mona up and down with undisguised curiosity. Mona crosses her arms over herself, her jacket soaked through.

"Mona just moved back to the area," I say. I'm not sure how much Theo has told his mother about her, but I assume it's everything he knows.

"What an unexpected surprise," Jacqueline says.

"Mona," Theo says. He shifts gears. "It's nice to meet you. Lee's told us a lot about you."

She looks to me for confirmation, and I give a small shake of my head, *he still doesn't know.*

"I don't want to interrupt anything," she says. She glances back toward the door, like she's looking for an escape route.

"Don't be silly," Jacqueline says. "Come on in. Make yourself at home."

Mona gives Jacqueline a cautious smile.

"Do you want some dry clothes?" I ask.

"I'm okay," she says, although she's drenched, her shirt sticking to her.

"No, really," I say. "Come upstairs with me. I'll get you some sweatpants."

She takes off her boots. They are caked in thick mud; it looks like clay. She peels the socks from her feet, follows me to the second floor.

"Bathroom's right there," I say, careful to keep my voice low. I slip into my bedroom, where Lucy is sleeping soundly in her bassinet. She has rolled herself onto her stomach, her knees tucked beneath her, her turtle pulled close. I tiptoe across the floor, avoiding the spots that creak, grab a pair of pre-pregnancy sweatpants and a T-shirt from my bottom drawer. Lucy sighs but doesn't wake.

I pad softly across my room and hand the clothes to Mona, then leave her to change. Theo and his mother are suspiciously quiet as I return downstairs, the silence of two people cut off mid-gossip.

"You didn't mention she was coming," Theo says.

"I didn't know," I say. "Is it a problem?"

"Of course not," he says.

Your mother is here all the time, I want to say. I shouldn't need to defend myself. *Fey and Niko barely even knock.*

"We have plenty of room for one more."

Theo gives me a look.

"Lee, it's *fine*," he says. "I just wondered if you knew."

"I think it's so wonderful that you and your sister are reconnecting," Jacqueline says. "An opportunity to repair old childhood wounds."

"Let's not turn this into a therapy session," Theo says, light but pointed, and I'm thankful for his pushback.

A floorboard creaks above us. It sounds like it's coming from my bedroom. I think of Lucy in her bassinet and rush to the stairs. But I am only halfway up when Mona emerges from my room, wearing the sweatpants I gave her, rolled at the waistband, and a zip-up hoodie she must have grabbed from my floor.

"Sorry," she mouths. She tiptoes down the stairs with exaggerated caution. "I didn't realize Lucy was in there. I just grabbed a sweatshirt. I hope that's okay."

"Of course!" I say, willing myself to calm down. "Absolutely fine. And it sounds like she's still sleeping. So that's good!" Too much, my anxiety ringing through.

Theo and Jacqueline exchange a look—*see how overprotective she is*—and just like that, they're aligned again. I try to tamp down my nerves.

"Should we eat?" I say. "The food is ready."

Dinner begins uncomfortably. An awkward shuffle as Mona sits in Theo's regular seat.

"Oh," she says, noticing. "Is this your chair?"

"Sit, sit," Theo says. He sits beside me, across from his mother. "No assigned seats here."

Jacqueline studies Mona, clocking each nervous scratch, each glance around the room. I can see it in her smug micro-nods: She already thinks she has Mona figured out. So confident in her ability to read people, to size them up, to slot them into the place they belong.

"It is so nice," she says, "to *finally* meet a member of Ophelia's family."

A jab, but luckily Theo recognizes it. He doesn't always.

"Mom," he says, a warning tone.

"I'm so happy to be here," Mona says without looking up. She cuts her chicken into smaller and smaller pieces.

"Where are you living?" Jacqueline asks. "Are you in this neighborhood?"

She obviously can't afford to live in this neighborhood, and Jacqueline knows it.

"I'm not really—" Mona's eyes flit toward me, and then back down. "I'm not settled yet."

"Where were you before?" Theo asks. He finishes off his glass of wine, pours us all more.

Mona looks at me, her shoulders stiffening, and I feel a surge of guilt for putting her in this position.

"I did some traveling," she says.

"Good for you," Jacqueline says. "It's so important to see the world as a young person, when you have nothing but time and flexibility. And then . . ." She laughs, amusing herself, takes another sip of wine. "You get to do it all again as an *older* person, when your child is finally out of the house. I was just in France, in the Pays de la Loire region—"

"Where did you travel, Mona?" Theo asks, cutting his mother off.

"Lots of places," she says, almost a mumble.

"In the U.S.? Europe? South America?"

She shifts uncomfortably.

"Is this an interrogation?" I ask. I smile, try to keep my voice light.

Theo grins, holds up his hands, *you caught me.* "Just trying to live vicariously," he says. "It might be a long time before I'm on an international flight again."

"That doesn't have to be true," Jacqueline says. "We took you to

Switzerland when you were nine months old, and it was *wonderful*. I thought you might ski before you could even walk."

"Well," Theo says. He seems to sense my tension, chalks it up to his mother, squeezes my knee. "We don't have any trips lined up for the time being."

Mona sets down her silverware. I'm not sure she's actually eaten anything.

"What do you do, Theo?" she asks.

"I'm a public defender."

"Theodore has always had such a big heart," Jacqueline says, a little tipsy. "He cares *so much* about others." I cringe, but Mona does not seem bothered by Jacqueline's fawning.

"That's important work," Mona says. "Everyone needs someone on their side."

"That's what Theo always says," I say.

"What do you do, Mona?" Jacqueline asks.

Mona picks up her silverware again, pushes her chicken around her plate. "This and that," she says. "Whatever needs done."

I shift in my chair, uncomfortable with how this is going, and Theo looks at Mona. He's noticed the evasiveness of this response.

"Are you working now?" he asks.

She hesitates, an answer in itself.

"What's your skill set?" Jacqueline asks. "Maybe we could get you set up with something."

"I'm not—"

"Do you have a college degree?"

Mona shakes her head.

"How about experience waitressing? Cleaning? Are you—"

"I'm fine," Mona says. "Really. I appreciate it, but I'm figuring it out."

"Well, you let us know," Jacqueline says, nodding decisively. "Ophelia's family is our family. We are happy to help."

Mona nods, clearly overwhelmed. I stand, my chair scraping against the wood floor. Jacqueline winces.

"I'm going to do some dishes," I say. Normally this is Theo's job at our weekly dinner: I cook and he cleans after, an equitable division of labor.

"Can I help?" Mona asks.

"I would love that."

"Do you want—" Theo begins, but I shake my head and he acquiesces. Mona follows me into the kitchen as Jacqueline launches into more stories from their time in Switzerland, trapping Theo at the table.

"Sorry," I say, quietly, once we're alone. "They can be a lot."

"You have nothing to apologize for," Mona says. "I'm the intruder here." She smiles like it's a joke, but I sense the worry underneath.

"I'm so happy to have you back," I say. "Really. You don't know how much this means to me."

Mona lifts her hand to her head then drops it down, that nervous tic. I can almost see her knotted locks of hair.

"I was starting to worry—" I begin.

"Oh, there it is," Jacqueline says. I turn, and she is standing in the kitchen archway, looking back and forth between Mona and me.

"Do you need something, Jacqueline?" I ask.

"No, no," she says, waving her hand at my misunderstanding. "The family resemblance. I've been looking for it all evening and wasn't able to see it, but now I do."

Normally this type of comment from Jacqueline would irritate me, but the idea of a family resemblance fills me with warmth. *My sister.*

"You think we look alike?" Mona says, leaning against the counter.

"Oh yes," Jacqueline says. She is three glasses of wine in and not slurring, exactly, but her words are looser. "Although it's hard to pinpoint—your facial structure, maybe? Theodore?"

Theo has come up behind her and is standing in the archway now, too, his arms crossed over his chest.

"What do you think? What's the resemblance?"

He looks at us, at my face first, and then Mona's.

"I'm not sure I see it," he says.

"It's something," Jacqueline says. "I didn't see it at first, either, but it's definitely there."

Theo squints at Mona again, and I think he's about to say something when Lucy's cry emanates from upstairs. It's that time.

"I'll be right back," I say, mostly to Mona. She squeezes my arm.

"Thank you for dinner," she says.

"Stay." *You can't go yet*, I want to say. *Not until we have a plan to meet. Not until I have a way to contact you.* "I'll be right back down."

She shakes her head. "I should get going."

"Can we meet up tomorrow?"

"I'll come back," she says. She gives me a reassuring smile. "I promise."

CHAPTER SIXTEEN

—

"It was nice meeting your sister last night," Theo says, pouring two mugs of coffee. We did not have a chance to discuss her reappearance last night; by the time Lucy went down again, Jacqueline had gone home and Theo had set up his bed on the couch.

"I'm glad she came by," I say. An understatement. Lucy is eating blueberry and cinnamon purée; it is smeared in dark blue streaks across her face. She pounds on her tray, proud of her handiwork.

Theo hands me my coffee and sits beside us.

"How much . . ." he starts. He's being careful with his phrasing, trying not to give offense. I brace myself. "How long has it been since the two of you last saw each other?"

"A long time."

He squints. He wanted something more specific, but he's not going to push. Lucy claps, purée splattering.

"How much do you know about her life now? What she's been up to?"

I stand to get a paper towel, turning so he can't see my face.

"Enough."

"Okay," Theo says, and for a moment I think he's going to let this go. But then: "Did you notice how evasive she was when I asked her questions?"

"Not especially." I wet the paper towel in the sink.

"I don't think she answered any of them. Like, *any* of them. She wouldn't say where she lives now, or where she lived before, or what she does for money."

"It was a dinner conversation, Theo," I say, turning off the sink. "Not a trial."

"You really didn't notice?"

"It can be hard to stay on track around your mother," I say. "She likes to jump in. Tell her own stories."

Theo raises his eyebrows, *that wasn't it*, and I duck to wipe the splatter off the floor.

"Do *you* know the answer to any of those questions? Has she told you?"

"We're just reconnecting. It's been a long time."

"That's pretty basic information."

I throw away the paper towel, sit back in my chair.

"You and your mom come on strong. She was probably nervous."

"Where does she *live*, Lee? With friends? By herself? In Passyunk? In Kensington?"

"I don't know where this is coming from," I say, now fully defensive. "I thought you were happy I was reconnecting with my sister."

"I was," Theo says. "I am. But last night—something seemed really *off*."

"It's all very new," I say. "Of course it's going to be a little awkward."

Theo looks at me, like he's trying to figure out if I really don't see it, too. "That wasn't it."

I shift in my seat. If he knew our past, if he knew where she was coming from, all the pieces would fall into place. This would all make sense.

But then I think about Clara's videos: *I knew from the beginning there was something wrong with her, and I was right.*

I think about the fire.

"I don't know what you're talking about," I say, pushing up from the table. "She didn't seem off to me."

"I'm not trying to be critical." He watches me as I pace the kitchen, from the counter to the fridge and back again, all nervous energy. "But did you see her eyes?"

"What about them?"

"Her pupils? The way she was scratching her arms?"

I don't respond.

"This?" Theo scratches his head, a crude and exaggerated impression.

Not scratching, I want to say. *Twisting her hair, an old nervous habit.*

"What about it?"

"I think she's an addict."

He sits back in his seat, waits for my reaction. *No,* I want to say, *you're wrong, there's so much you don't know,* but I can't do that, can't explain without giving too much away, and so instead I say: "That's ridiculous."

"I work with people like her all the time, Lee. I have a good sense for these things."

"People like her."

Theo runs his hands over his face.

"I'm not trying to start a fight here. All I'm saying is, she shows up out of the blue, after years of no contact, and suddenly wants to reconnect? She probably found out about your situation and now she wants something."

"What's my 'situation'?"

He sighs, shakes his head like I'm being purposefully obtuse, then gestures around the kitchen. "This. Your life. She realized you had *money,* Lee."

"She hasn't asked for anything."

"Yet," he says. "She hasn't asked you yet."

"So what if she does ask for something? She's my *sister,* Theo."

He holds up his hands, a mock surrender. "What I'm saying is you should be careful around her. You don't really know anything about her."

"I know plenty."

"Addiction changes people. I see it all the time."

I unlatch Lucy's tray from her high chair, run it under the tap. Theo waits.

"So you don't want me to see her," I say. "Is that it?"

He gives me a look like I'm overreacting, twisting his words. "I'm saying you should go into this—*reunion*—with your eyes open."

Lucy babbles at us from her chair, *ba ba ba,* still buckled in. Theo looks at her, and then at me.

"And maybe it's a good idea to keep some distance between her and Lucy? Just until we get to know her better?"

"She's my *sister*. You can't ask me not to see her."

"And I'm *not* asking that. If you want to get coffee or drinks or whatever with her, fine. Great. But I don't want Lucy there."

"You know I can't do that."

"You need to figure that out." His tone is harsh now, his patience gone. "You have me. You have my mother. We have the resources to hire someone. You can leave the house without Lucy. She's seven months old. It's *fine.*"

"It's not that easy," I say. I am close to tears, but I won't let that happen. "It's not something I can turn on and off."

"So *see* someone," Theo says. He's almost shouting now, and Lucy is agitated, upset by the tension. I unbuckle her, hold her close. "This is tearing us apart, Lee. You have to see that, right? You need to *do* something to fix this."

"I *am* doing something," I say. What Theo doesn't realize is that Mona is the answer. The way to heal, to move forward. I know it. I can feel it.

"What?" he demands. "What are you doing?"

"I'm figuring it out."

He gives me a stony glare.

"I hope that's true," he says. "Not just for our sake. For Lucy's."

I would never do anything that would hurt Lucy, I want to say. *Everything*

I do is for her, to keep her safe. Instead, I'm silent. Theo glances at the clock, *time for work.* He rises, gives Lucy a kiss on the head, looks at me until I meet his eyes.

"I just want you to be careful," he says. "Please."

I hold back my tears until he closes the door.

CHAPTER SEVENTEEN

—

Days pass without word from Mona, but I tell myself this is fine, normal, what she does. *She'll be back,* I tell myself. *On her own time.* Today is our moms' group, a good distraction. Lucy and I arrive early, and I stake out a spot on the waiting-room side of the plexiglass. Lucy watches from her stroller as a cluster of four-year-olds bounce across the trampoline, and I slip my phone out of my pocket. There are new notifications this morning, new alerts triggered by my name.

> **loobylooby:** Ophelia Clayborne is a confirmed sociopath.
>
> **dramallama8903:** called it.
>
> **wherethebodies:** WTF

Clara has posted a new TikTok. I slip in my AirPods and open the link, and her face fills my phone screen. She's walking, the pale yellow brick of a renovated warehouse behind her.

I've been hesitant to share details, she says, *but I think I need to get into it. We need to talk about the rabbit.*

"Is that Clara Matthews?" Maggie asks from behind me. I flinch and slip my phone into my pocket, but she does not seem to notice my discomfort. "I *love* her," she says. "She's so real about parenting."

"I haven't watched that much of her," I say, my whole body buzzing.

"My sister was actually in a music class with her when their kids were babies," Winnie says from across the room, and the spotlight is redirected toward her, Maggie peppering her with questions, *where does she live, what's she like in real life, does her skin actually look that good or is it just a filter.* I am only half-listening to Winnie's answers, my mind stuck in a loop, *the rabbit the rabbit the rabbit.*

"All right, ladies," Dr. Dana says, arriving with her oversized purse and her plastic water bottle just as the four-year-olds begin to spill out of the gym. A slim woman in gray and black athleisure enters behind her. "We've got a special guest today. Sophie is a certified nutritionist, and she's going to walk us through balanced diets and meal plans."

"Oh, I've been looking forward to this class," Amanda says.

We follow Dr. Dana and Sophie through the plexiglass door and take our seats on the springy mat. My phone buzzes in my pocket, another alert, and then another.

The rabbit the rabbit the rabbit.

"I *love* this age group," Sophie says from her spot beside Dr. Dana. "Now that our littles are transitioning to more and more solids, it's *so* important to establish a good routine and a healthy relationship with food from the get-go."

I didn't do anything to Lucky.

"Colors are key," she says, rifling through her bag for handouts, passing a stack to Amanda. "I like to use something called the rainbow method to make sure I'm hitting all the crucial nutrients."

Lucky was Rachel's pet, and I would never have done anything to hurt Lucky or Rachel, despite the rumors that circulated at school before I ever stepped foot on campus, rumors I never managed to shake.

"Now I recommend pureeing your own meat, which—I know— might not look too appetizing to our adult eyes, but, trust me, your littles will love it. I have some printable recipes on my website . . ."

In the days after Clara's prank—which is what everyone called the incident at the playground except my aunt—I rarely left my room. Clara avoided me entirely, and my uncle and Rachel shuffled past me when we did cross paths, uncomfortable and unsure of what to say. Only Anne still made eye contact when she came to my room, bringing up breakfast and lunch and dinner, taking the barely touched plates from the top of my dresser. *I'm sorry*, she told me. *What Clara did was extremely cruel.*

My phone buzzes again, and my mind wanders to what people might be saying online. *Brainwashed. Psychopath. Daughter of a cult leader. What did you expect?* I know what happens now; I've heard it all and worse, whispered in the middle school hallways, scrawled across my locker.

Rabbit killer. Psycho. Freak.

"Do you have a scale you recommend?" Amanda asks from beside me. "For measuring out the portions?"

After the playground, my aunt forced Clara to apologize. She grounded her for weeks; she took away her AIM privileges. She began taking Clara to see a therapist of her own, to "help with this adjustment period."

But I knew it wouldn't be enough.

"So I also want to address a big problem I know a lot of you will be facing," Sophie says. "I call it 'the beige food trap.'"

I didn't do anything to Lucky. What I did was thaw prepackaged meat from the freezer and leave it arranged on Clara's pillow one night after she had fallen asleep. It was chicken, not rabbit, although I counted on Clara not being able to tell the difference, and I was right. A dead animal slaughtered by someone, but not by me, a fact my therapist assured my aunt and uncle was very important. I laid a butcher's knife beside the meat, along with Lucky's half-chewed toilet paper roll, and I woke the next morning to Clara's screams.

"What about the pouches of purée you can get from the grocery store?" Lauren asks. "Are those okay, or—"

"They're fine," Sophie says. "In a pinch."

"Excuse me," I say. I scoop up Lucy from her blanket and carry her with me to the bathroom in the back of the gym. I flip on the fluorescent light, lock the door. The noise from the fan blocks out the chatter outside. There's a diaper genie in the corner, but it doesn't fully conceal the smell. An air purifying spray and wipes sit on the back of the toilet; a Paw Patrol potty seat hangs on the wall. Lucy and I sit on the toilet lid, and I hold her against me, close my eyes, focus on her weight, real, tangible.

The thought like a mantra: *She is here, and she is mine.*

The night after the rabbit incident, I heard my aunt and uncle at the kitchen table, long after they thought I had gone to bed.

Is it safe to keep her here? my uncle asked, and my aunt's pause brought a lump to my throat. *We don't know—*

This isn't a choice, Anne said, cutting him off. *She's Sylvie's daughter. We need to think about Rachel and Clara.*

I am thinking about Rachel and Clara.

She—

I'm not discussing this, she said. Her chair scraped across the floor, and I scrambled back toward the stairs before she caught me listening. *I won't talk about this. She is ours now. We are responsible for her. She's staying.*

My aunt never wavered on that decision. I don't know what would have happened to me if she hadn't taken me in, if she hadn't been kind in a world where so many people are not, if she hadn't stuck with me despite my efforts—and there were many, over the years—to push her away.

Tears spring to my eyes, and I force myself to focus on the present, on Lucy, on now. *It will be okay,* I tell myself. *It's going to be okay.*

Lucy and I are walking back through Rittenhouse, almost through the park, when I spot Mona sitting on a bench. She's wearing sunglasses and an oversized sweatshirt despite today's unseasonable warmth. Her legs are pulled in; she picks at a scab on her knuckle.

"Mona?" I say, quietly so as not to startle her. She's lost in her thoughts; she doesn't hear me at first. I repeat her name, a little louder.

She hears me this time, jumps. She turns toward me and Lucy, and she doesn't look happy to see us. Close up, I see her face is caked with foundation. Her lip, split and swollen, like she's been hit in the jaw.

I hear Theo's voice in my head: *You don't know anything about this person.*

What I do know—the only thing that matters—is that she is my sister, and she needs help.

"Lee," she says, her expression morphing. She smiles, or tries to, winces. "Where are you coming from?"

"What happened?" I ask.

"It's nothing." She lifts her hand to pull at her hair, or to scratch her scalp, and her sleeve droops. There's a bruise on her wrist, the black-and-blue imprint of someone's grip. For a moment, I see her as a child again, dark bruises climbing her arms and legs.

"It doesn't look like nothing."

"I fell," she says, bringing her arm back down. "Want to go for a walk?"

Mona keeps pace at my side, lost in her thoughts, and I am lost in mine. I am thinking of the time we almost left, together. I came back from the woods, and Mona was sleeping in our bed, and my mother was gripping a large sack. Her eyes were red and puffy from crying, her cheeks wet. She pulled my dresses from the closet and stuffed them in with a rough carelessness she would have scolded me for.

"Mom," I said. "What are you doing?"

"We're leaving," she said. She looked back at Mona, who was beginning to stir.

"What?" I asked. "Where?"

"I don't know." She grabbed shoes from the bottom of the closet, the neatly stacked pile of blankets and quilts. Mona was fully awake now and confused, frightened.

"What are you *doing?*" I asked, louder, and Mona joined in, crying, a high-pitched whine, telling her to stop.

My mother froze, shook her head, jarred from her state. She doubled back, checking the bag, the closet, running her hands down her face. She sank onto the mattress, and Mona and I crawled beside her, and I burrowed my face into her side.

"It's just time," she said. "It's time." Her face contorted, her lips pulling, and she started to cry, which made me cry, too. She put her arms around both of us, pulling us in. "It'll be the three of us. An adventure."

"No," I said through my tears. "I don't want to go."

"No," Mona echoed. "No."

Jacob's Hill was our home; the only place we had ever known. This was where we had notched our heights into the wood beams of the barn; where Adrienne had taught us how to tell the difference between oaks and ginkgoes and magnolias and how to find the best branches for a tree fort; where I had watched Mona and River and Echo take their first steps. Where Kai would be taking his soon.

My mother's shoulders sagged, her eyes closed in resignation. "Tomorrow," she said. "We're leaving tomorrow."

Mona and I head to the river path, which is full of people taking advantage of the warm weather: joggers and bikers and friends cutting out of work for a slow, meandering lunch break. We walk to the end of Boathouse Row, passing the line of Tudor and Victorian rowing clubs that host regattas in the spring, before turning back toward home. On our last walk, I wondered if Mona was watching for someone. On this walk, I am sure she is. She glances around us, nervous and edgy, studying each cluster of people passing by.

I wish I knew who she's looking for, what she's been through. I don't know how she's been surviving since she left our family, who she might have fallen in with.

"You can tell me," I say. "If something is wrong. If there's anything I can do—"

"I'm fine," she says again, shutting down the conversation.

Lucy drifts to sleep in her stroller, her head lolling. I drape a swaddle over her and notice Mona watching me, tracking my movements.

"I always knew you'd be a good mother," she says. I'm not sure if anyone has ever called me that before.

"Why?" I ask, and she shrugs, crossing her arms over herself.

"You always looked out for me."

"Not always," I say. I think of Adrienne: *It's your responsibility to take care of her.* I think of all the ways I failed.

"Enough," she says, and then: "What's it like?" She nods in Lucy's direction. "Are you happy?"

"I don't think that's the right way to think about it," I say. "She's everything to me. But I don't know how to do this."

"No one does."

A constant refrain at Mommy and Me: *We are all figuring it out. We are all doing fine. We are all trying our best.* "I don't know if I have that internal blueprint."

Mona nods, seeming to understand instantly.

"You had Anne," she says.

I hesitate. I didn't realize Mona knew about our aunt. But of course she would have googled me, just like I googled her. When I don't respond, she asks: "What was she like? What was it like living with her?"

"Anne was a good aunt," I say. An understatement: I'm not sure what I would have done without her. "She took care of me, and I know it wasn't—*I* wasn't always easy."

The art museum looms beside us, ionic columns and soft yellow stone. A two-year-old in a Spider-Man hat and red gloves toddles ahead of us, alongside his mother. He stoops to pick up a leaf, turns it over in his hand.

"We have cousins," I say, although maybe she knows this already, too. "They live right around here."

"Do you see them?"

"No," I say, and Mona does not push for an explanation.

I think of our family: Adrienne, with her dirt-caked hands, Kai and Echo and Forest, boys who would be grown men by now. Christopher.

"When did you last see . . ." I begin. Mona purses her lips and shakes her head, and I let the question drop. In the sun, her bruising is more visible, green-black beneath her foundation.

"Come stay with us," I say. It comes out of my mouth as soon as I think it, before I can second-guess the decision. Mona raises her eyebrows, then shakes her head.

"I can't."

"Of course you can," I say. We're approaching a bend in the path, a blind corner. The toddler in front of us pockets his leaf, bends down to grab another. "We have a spare room. On the third floor. It's no trouble at all."

A bell chimes, and a bike shoots around the bend. The toddler startles, stumbles into the bike's path instead of away. I gasp and his mother grabs him, just in time.

"Jesus," I say, shaken, and Mona squeezes my arm, dirt in the beds of her fingernails.

I think she is about to change the subject, to let the offer drop, but instead, she asks, "Would Theo be okay with that? Me staying with you, I mean?"

No.

"Yes," I say. "Absolutely. Family is the most important thing to him."

"I don't know . . ." she says. It's better than *I can't*. Her resistance is giving way.

"Stay with us," I say. "As long as you need. It would be great to have you around."

"I wouldn't want to be a freeloader," Mona says. "I could help around the house. With Lucy."

Theo's words: *Keep some distance.*

"Yes," I say. "That would be great."

"Okay," Mona says. She nods her head, bringing herself around to the idea. "Okay, if you're sure."

"Absolutely."

She smiles—a full smile, one that shows her teeth.

"Okay then," she says. "Let's do this."

"Do you want to get your things?" I ask. "I can help."

"No," Mona says, quick, nervous, and I worry again that I've overstepped somehow. "That's okay."

"Or I could meet you somewhere later."

"I don't have much," she says. "I'll bring it by in a few hours."

"Great," I say, and the smile returns to her face.

"Great," she repeats. I feel a giddy rush of excitement. My sister is here, and she is coming to live with us.

We never left Jacob's Hill, of course. That next day at breakfast Christopher sat beside my mother again, their shoulders close, an inch apart. She reached for her fork, and he placed his hand on hers, gently. He leaned in to tell her something, words I couldn't hear, and she nodded, straightened, her resolve weakening. Or maybe that's all she had wanted in the first place: for Christopher to sit beside her again. I watched it happen, could see the plans fade from her mind, and what I felt, in that moment, was relief.

Three hours after our walk, Mona shows up with a rucksack. Nothing else. The straps are worn and one of its buckles has been ripped off so it no longer closes all the way.

"You haven't changed your mind, have you?" she asks. I shake my head, *of course not,* usher her in.

"Where's Lucy?" she asks, sliding the bag off her shoulders.

"Napping," I say. "She'll be up soon."

Mona sets her bag by the door, and it sags open. I see the glint of something shiny inside. She crouches down to adjust it.

"Do you mind—could I have some water?" she asks.

"Oh sure," I say. "I'll show you where everything is. This is your home now, too. Make yourself comfortable."

I give her a quick tour of the kitchen—cups, plates, forks, and knives—tell her she can help herself to anything. "And let me know if there's anything you like or don't like," I say, "and I'll add it to the grocery list."

Mona opens the fridge door, studies its contents. She runs her hand along the marble countertop, picks up the clay sugar pot and examines it, returns it to its place.

"I'm easy," she says. "I'll eat anything."

"I think Theo should be home at a normal time tonight. Maybe six, six-thirty?" I try to say this calmly, try not to think about what Theo's reaction will be when he comes home to a new houseguest. *He'll adjust,* I tell myself. *She's my sister. She needs a place to stay, and we have a room.*

"How about I show you upstairs?" I lift her bag from beside the door, trying to be helpful, a good host, but she startles and grabs it back from me.

"Sorry," I say. "I didn't mean—"

"It's fine," she says. She smiles, but it looks forced, like she's trying to compensate for her strange reaction. "I can carry it."

You don't know what she's been through, I remind myself. *You don't know what kind of trauma she's carrying with her.*

She follows me up the stairs. "It's a Trinity," I say. "Built in the 1870s. You see a lot of these around here—one room on each floor, stacked on top of each other. So this is our bedroom here, and your bedroom—"

I gesture at the thick, wooden door, held shut with an old latch. I push the latch and the door swings outward, revealing a staircase even steeper than the first, winding up into the dark.

Mona whistled. "This is supposed to be Lucy's room?"

"It's just how these old houses are built," I say, hearing echoes of Theo in my explanation. "Families have been making this work for generations."

I take hold of the metal bar bolted to the wall in lieu of a railing. "But she'll be in our room for a while longer, so . . ."

Mona follows me, steadying herself against the plaster.

"It's hard to imagine going up and down these with an infant," she says.

I see it every time I climb these stairs: a missed step, a foot slipping, my body pitching forward. *I'd hold on to her,* I tell myself. *I'd protect her.* I try not to picture what would happen if I let go.

I flip on the light. It's dusty up here; a thick, unused smell filling the space. We've been using the room for storage. Stacks of cardboard boxes and old picture frames are lined up against the walls, and piles of paper and books sit on top of the dresser we built up here for Lucy before she was born, before we realized how long it would be before she would use this room. Most of the stuff belongs to Theo. Only one of the boxes is mine, a small collection of items from my aunt's house I've never been able to sort through.

"I'll clear this out," I say. "I've been meaning to, anyway."

"Oh no," she says. "Don't worry about it. There's plenty of room."

"We have an air mattress for now," I say. "And blankets and pillows. I can get some actual furniture—"

"No," Mona says. "Don't do that. An air mattress is perfect."

"I'm sorry it's not—"

"It's great," Mona says. "Really. I can't thank you enough."

She throws her arms around me, catching me by surprise. "Thank you."

Downstairs, Lucy wakes and calls out.

"I should—"

"I'll get her," Mona offers, and she is already halfway down the stairs before I can tell her *no, Lucy won't like that, it has to be me.* I follow her as she pushes open my bedroom door, greets Lucy with a wide smile.

"Hi there, Lu," she says, and Lucy beams. "I'm going to be staying here with you for a little while." She pulls Lucy from the bassinet, balances her on her hip. "I think we're going to become good friends."

Lucy is delighted. I have never seen her so calm with another person. *This is it,* I think. *We can help each other. This is the way forward.*

Theo will come to see that, too. In time.

CHAPTER EIGHTEEN

—

It's just me and Lucy in the family room when Theo comes through the front door. Mona is upstairs. Sleeping, I think; she told me she needed to rest. I can only imagine how long this day has been for her.

"My favorite girls," Theo says as he sets down his briefcase, hangs his jacket on the hook. "Good day?"

"There's—" *There's something I need to tell you,* I am about to say, when I hear Mona on the staircase behind me. Theo's eyebrows lift in surprise.

"Thank you so much for letting me stay," Mona says. She has changed into sweatpants and a bulky sweatshirt, her hands lost in its baggy sleeves. Her face has been washed clean. "You have no idea how much it means to me."

Theo's eyes meet mine, his face frozen in a neutral expression. "Stay?"

"The third-floor room," I say. "We're not using it, and—"

"It's Lucy's room. Lucy is supposed to be in there."

"But she's not."

Understanding flashes across Mona's face as she realizes Theo didn't know about our arrangement. "I'm sorry," she says. She is backing up the stairs, like she is about to grab her things and go. "I thought—"

"It's *fine*," I say, just as Theo says: "She *should* be in there." He looks back to Mona and winces as he registers the bruising on her face.

"I don't want to cause any trouble," Mona says.

"You're not," I say.

Theo sighs, rolls his shoulders. "You're Lee's family," he says. "If you need a place to stay, we'll figure it out."

"Thank you," I say, but Theo won't meet my eyes.

"I'm taking a shower," he says. He slides past Mona on the stairs, and Mona looks at me, eyes wide.

"It's fine," I say. "Don't worry about it. It's your room, for as long as you want it."

Mona retreats to her room and does not come back down for dinner. Sleeping, maybe, or giving us space. Theo's anger radiates off him in waves.

"Theo, I—"

"Stop." He won't look at me. He carves at his food, knife scraping against the porcelain plate.

"I just—"

He sets down his knife and fork. "Do you want to do this now?" he asks, glancing toward Lucy in her high chair. "Really?"

"She's in trouble," I say. "You saw her face."

"Do you know who did that to her?" Theo asks.

I shake my head.

"Did you ask?"

"I'm not—"

"Is someone *looking* for her? Are they going to follow her *here*?"

"It's not like that," I say.

"You don't know *what* it's like," Theo says. "You don't know anything about her, or what she's mixed up in, or why she showed up here out of the blue, after all this time."

"I know enough."

Theo looks at me, incredulous.

"All this talk," he says, his voice low, "about threats to Lucy. Choking hazards. Drawstrings. Uncovered outlets and sharp corners and sleep training and daycare and god forbid she's left alone with me or my mother for thirty minutes, and then this? This?" He shakes his head. "I don't understand this, Lee."

"Theo."

"I don't understand you."

"I'm—"

He holds up his hand.

"I can't handle any more of your excuses tonight. Not tonight."

He rinses his plate and crosses the family room, puts on his jacket.

"What are you doing?" I ask. "Where are you going?"

"I need a walk."

"We should discuss this."

He walks out the door and slams it shut behind him.

When I go upstairs, I pause by Mona's stairwell. I hear movement and consider rapping on the door, asking if she wants to talk. *You don't have to do this alone*, I could tell her. *You can tell me. I can keep you safe.*

The thought is fleeting. She's not ready, and I want to respect that. I want her to feel comfortable here; I want her to know she can set boundaries and they will be respected. She can open up in her own time.

I lie beside Lucy, replaying Theo's departure in my mind. I am doing the right thing, I tell myself, but I can't shake my guilt. It's my fault Theo doesn't understand. And maybe my reluctance to pry into Mona's past isn't all selfless. There's a part of me that's afraid to hear what she will say when she finally does open up. What has she been through these past twenty years? What did Christopher become after they left?

Christopher had a manic intensity in those final months. He was so sure we were about to be under siege, by local police or federal agents, the strong arm of the state. He really believed the end of life as we knew it was near. I remember his fists, pounding against the wood table in the dining hall, rattling plates and glasses and silverware, the din of conversation coming to a standstill. I remember him waiting, an uncomfortable silence filling the room.

None of you is ready, he said. *Not a single one of you. When they come for us, and they're coming for us soon, they'll tear you apart.*

Christopher, Adrienne said, beginning to rise from her seat.

No, he said.

You don't—

No, he said again, and this time he threw the chair he had been sitting on across the room, the leg splintering against the wall. Mona began to cry, and I pulled her into me, did my best to quiet her.

He wasn't always that way. Not even always at the end, although then it was more frequent. He really did think he was protecting us; really did want to save us from the outside world and from ourselves. *Christopher has the gift of insight,* my mother used to tell me. *He can look at a person and see who they are, what they're afraid of, what they need, all in an instant. He chose each of us specifically because he knew we could make Jacob's Hill better, and he knew Jacob's Hill could make us better, too.*

Of course, he didn't actually choose me. I was born into it, and I never got the impression Christopher thought I was special, that I was needed in some particular way. But he did have a special ability to read people. When Mona first became sick, I spent a lot of time on my own, wandering the property, the woods. I felt sorry for myself, something I knew was deeply selfish, but I couldn't help it. My mother's attention was focused on her, even more than normal, and Adrienne's, too. I couldn't even be in the same room as them; I could feel their agitation, their worry, like a vise. I hated it.

I remember wading in the creek, balancing on the wet stones. Christopher came up behind me, so still and quiet I didn't know he was there until he was standing right beside me. He crouched down and began to turn over the rocks and stones.

Look at that, he said, cupping a pickerel frog in his hand, its body olive green, splotched with black and brown. He motioned for me to hold out my hand and slid it onto my palm. It paused for a moment before leaping back into the creek below.

He placed his hand on my head, and I felt a warmth, an energy moving through me. My mother used to describe the sensation as a connection to the divine, and in that moment I thought I could feel it, too. He looked me straight in the eye, and it was like he was reading my thoughts.

You aren't jealous, Ophelia, he said. *You're scared.*

I shook my head, bit the inside of my cheek so hard I could taste iron.

You're a good sister to her, he said, with a conviction that made me believe it.

But where was I when she needed me the most?

I can't change the past, I remind myself, rolling over in my bed. All that matters is now. I can be here for her now.

CHAPTER NINETEEN

—

Someone is screaming.

I jolt up in bed, startled from sleep. My first thought is Lucy, but it's not Lucy. An adult, a woman, guttural and scraping, terrified.

Then silence.

Mona.

Theo is running up the stairs; he's by the side of my bed. His eyes dart back and forth, scanning for danger.

He thought it was me.

"What happened?" he asks, breathing hard. He looks from me to Lucy. Lucy will wake at the sound of a footstep anywhere in the house, but she sleeps through sirens, fire alarms, all signs of real danger. Her eyelids flicker but don't open. Theo takes a deep breath, fighting the flood of adrenaline coursing through him. "I thought . . ." He doesn't finish that sentence.

"I'll check on her," I say.

Theo shakes his head vehemently. "No," he says. "I'll go."

He doesn't say it, but he doesn't have to: What if someone has broken into our house? What if whoever hurt Mona knows she's here and has come for her?

"It's just us, Theo," I say, but I am shaking, too. "No one could have gotten past both of us and up those stairs."

"I'll find out," he says. He lifts the latch to the door.

"I'm coming, too," I say. Mona does not need a near stranger, a man, appearing in her room in the middle of the night.

She needs her sister.

Theo doesn't look happy, but he also doesn't put up a fight.

"Mona," I call out. "We're coming up."

I follow close behind Theo, grabbing on to the metal handle.

"Everything all right up here?" he calls out.

There's no response.

Dead. Gone. Missing, again.

"Mona?" I say.

Theo flips on the light.

Mona is sitting on her mattress, still, her arms wrapped around her legs. She doesn't meet our eyes.

"Was that you?" Theo asks. "What happened?"

"I just . . ." she says. "I thought I saw someone."

"You thought . . ." Theo steps in farther, scanning the room, the stacks of boxes, the radiator in the corner, casting its shadow. "Was someone up here?"

Mona shakes her head. A night terror. A vision. Mona, at six, sweat-drenched and shaking. *He's right there.*

"I can sit with you while you fall back asleep," I say. "If you want."

Theo stiffens. He doesn't like this idea, but he knows better than to say so.

Mona doesn't respond for a moment, but then nods, a small, quick movement. She blinks and rubs at her eye.

"Okay," I say. I look at Theo, *I've got this*, and he hesitates but then backs toward the stairs.

"I'll be right down there," he says. "If you need me."

He moves his hand toward the light switch, looks to me for permission. I nod, and he flips the switch before returning to the family room.

I sit on the foot of the air mattress. Mona lies down but, as my eyes adjust, I can see that her eyes are still open, fixed on the staircase like she's expecting someone.

"Are you okay?" I ask softly. "Is someone looking for you?"

She doesn't respond.

"It's okay," I say. "I'm right here. We're together now." I watch the stairs with her, although I don't know what I'm looking for. I listen to her breathing. Slowly, slowly it steadies, and then deepens. I wait until I am sure she is asleep, and then five minutes more, before returning downstairs to Lucy.

I glance at my phone to see the time. There are new notifications, more chatter on Reddit.

Clara has posted a new TikTok, and this one is about the fire.

CHAPTER TWENTY

—

I have tried to put what happened in Pittsburgh behind me. I have told myself I was a different person; that I was under so much stress; that it couldn't happen again.

The memory has always clung to me, though, the red patches of skin on my shoulder a constant reminder of the ways my mind can betray me.

I went to Pittsburgh for college. Until then, I struggled with formal schooling. I started middle school the fall after the disappearance, and it was miserable. An onslaught of people, voices echoing off metal lockers, sweat and Axe body spray and artificial watermelon and coconut. The way we would jam into the hallway—pushed up against one another, a human current—overwhelmed me. Everyone knew who I was, what had happened to me, what I had done to Clara with the raw chicken, a story that was exaggerated and stretched and twisted to fit the storyteller's need. I found a stuffed rabbit hanging by a noose in my locker one day—it had been stabbed with a pencil, too, for good measure, the stuffing spilling out—and that was it. My aunt pulled me out to homeschool me again, after I begged her. I refused to go back, and she homeschooled me all the way through high school.

But when it was time for college, she told me I should go.

"Go somewhere far away," she said. "It'll be different. A fresh start. You have so much potential."

Pittsburgh was as far as I was willing to go. And for a time, my aunt was right: It was better. I made a few friends, most of whom knew nothing about my past. I didn't start out lying, but I realized I needed to be more circumspect about what I shared after I got stoned in a floormate's dorm room, and he pulled out a copy of Christopher's writings, printed off the internet. *It's actually totally fascinating,* he told me. *I mean crazy, for sure, but still, like, interesting. All these people wandering around in darkness, asleep, and then someone finally turns on the light and they, like, don't want to see it.* I worked hard in class, did well. I talked to my aunt on the phone regularly, once or twice a week, and she told me she was so proud of me.

I know it's not easy, she'd say. *You're doing such a great job.*

But then, one day my senior year, she sent me a text:

Call me when you get a chance xx

It came through on the Friday before my winter exams, while I was pulling into my gravel driveway. My aunt and I hadn't spoken in two weeks—long but not unusual during finals period. I knew Anne didn't usually reach out first; she gave me space when I needed it and was there when I needed her.

I looked at the text again and felt a prickle of nerves. *It's fine,* I told myself, *just call her.*

I put the car into park in the small lot behind the house—a subdivided Victorian with terrible cell reception, metal lath in the plaster—and dialed her number. I rolled my head back against the headrest, looked out the window, waited for her to pick up. The lot was empty, except for a van I didn't recognize, old and dented. But there were always strange cars in the lot, friends of my first-floor neighbors, and so I didn't think much of it.

The phone rang again, and then I heard my aunt's voice.

"Lee!" she said, like this was an unexpected surprise. "I'm so glad you caught me!"

"I got your text," I said. "Is everything all right?"

"Oh, everything's fine," she said. "But I had a doctor's appointment this morning. They found a lump. It's probably nothing, but the girls wanted me to get checked out, make sure everything was okay."

"A lump," I repeated.

"It's fine," she said. "Nothing to worry about, probably. But they want to do some more tests. I wanted you to hear it from me, not, you know, secondhand."

Not from my cousins, she meant, not from Facebook. This was not nothing. This was, I knew from Anne, the same thing that had happened to my grandmother, at the same age. History repeating itself.

"They're just trying to rule things out. You know how doctors are. They like to be thorough."

"Sure," I said.

She changed the subject, asked about school, finals, when I was thinking about coming back for the holidays. I told her I could come back now, right away if she wanted, but she told me no, it was fine, Rachel and Peter were taking good care of her, and Clara, too, in her way. She'd see me soon. I told her I loved her, and she told me she loved me, too, that she'd keep me updated, and I stepped out of the car in a sort of daze, wandering through the empty Solo cups and crushed cigarette packs that littered the ground.

Fine, she said she'd be fine, and maybe that was true, but no one knew, not really. Not my aunt, not the doctors who treated her. I dug into my bag for my house keys, my fingers scraping against old wrappers and tissues and crumpled papers from class instead.

It turned out I didn't need them.

The front door was ajar, wedged open with a small rock. I nudged the rock out of the way with the toe of my shoe and let the door click shut behind me. *Probably the neighbors,* I told myself, *propping the door open for a friend without a key.* It wouldn't have crossed their minds that this was unsafe, that there was a reason the door locked automatically. They were young, and male, and living together. The world didn't hold the same threats for them.

I knocked on their apartment door, intending to ask them not to do it again. I knew they'd laugh at me after I left, roll their eyes, say I was overreacting, and I was ready for it. But when no one answered, a twinge of discomfort pulled in my chest. Why leave the door open if they weren't here? *Maybe they forgot,* I told myself. *Or it was the guys on the second floor.* A small thing, not worth dwelling on.

I climbed the stairs to the second-floor hallway. There were two apartments on this floor—one inhabited by engineering majors, who mostly studied and played video games and kept to themselves, the other unoccupied. The hallway smelled like dust and mildew and sweat, years of neglect. This house had probably once been a large family home—rose petals carved into the wood paneling, ornate vines on the brass finishes—but now the banisters were wobbly and precarious, spindles cracked and splintered. Only a third of the antique wall sconces worked, and so it was always dark, obscuring the threadbare patches of carpet, the soiled spots.

I knocked on the door to the engineering majors' apartment and waited. I listened for the rattle of digital gunfire, for shuffling footsteps, anything. But inside it was quiet. I heard a sniff behind me. A phlegmy cough.

A man I didn't recognize was standing on the stairs to the third floor, right by my door. Ropey muscles, a scraggly beard, the thick stench of cigarette smoke wafting off him. He was watching me, and when he saw I had noticed him he smiled, but it didn't feel friendly. I froze.

"You live here?" he asked.

Had he been standing there the whole time without me noticing him? Or—the possibility flashed in my head, sudden and unnerving—had he been inside my apartment? Had I caught him leaving?

"Do you need something?" I asked. I gripped the strap of my backpack tightly.

"Sorry," he said. His smile widened. His voice had a twang I couldn't place. "Didn't mean to scare you. Just doing some repairs."

"Oh," I said, thinking of the van in the lot. But the van had been nondescript: no logo, no phone number, nothing marking it as a work van. I stepped back, suddenly realizing how alone I was in this house.

"Your landlord didn't mention anything?"

"No. He didn't."

He reached his hand behind him, and I stepped back. He pulled out a screwdriver.

"I'll be done soon," he said. "You need to get past?"

"No," I said. I stepped back again. "I'm not . . . no."

He knew I was lying. He knew this was a change of course; that I had been going upstairs and now wasn't, that I was frightened. I knew better than to let people see I was vulnerable. I knew vulnerability could be viewed as an invitation, but I couldn't hide my fear. He shrugged, like it didn't matter to him one way or another, and I read something malicious in his expression. It looked, to me, like a smirk, pointed and mocking, like he was enjoying my panic. I took the stairs quickly, pushed through the front door and out onto the sidewalk, where it was bright, two bicycles rolling past, squirrels chasing each other up and down a black locust.

I called my landlord. He didn't pick up, and I knew he wouldn't call me back.

It's nothing, I told myself, *a repairman,* and in the sheen of the midday sun, it was hard to imagine anything else could be true. Even so, I couldn't bring myself to go back inside, not yet. I walked to a coffee shop and spent the next two hours there, until I was sure he'd be gone.

———

When I returned home, the front door was closed, just like it should have been. I turned the key and pushed. I stepped inside, and the fear returned. Music seeped out of my downstairs neighbors' apartment, a low, muffled beat. The smell of weed filled the hallway, along with something sour.

A repairman, I told myself. *That's all he was.* I grabbed my mail and climbed the steps, palming my key defensively. The sound of an engine revving and the exaggerated squeal of brakes filled the hall, the *pop pop pop* of digital gunfire. Everyone was home. *You're not alone this time*, I told myself. Even so, my stomach turned as I peered up my stairwell. Empty.

I put my key in the lock and then stopped and surveyed the stairwell, looked for some sign that something had been repaired. The lights were still out. The spindles still broken. The carpet still the same worn fabric.

You wouldn't necessarily see it, I reminded myself. *Maybe he was an HVAC guy. An electrician.* But what was he doing on my stairs? There were no air vents here, no outlets, no way of accessing wires or pipes behind the walls. Just old floral wallpaper, peeling up at the seams. A smattering of small nail-sized holes from a time when the residents cared enough to hang pictures.

He had no reason to be on the stairwell. He had been in my apartment. My landlord must have given him a key. I added this infraction to a running mental list. My landlord was used to college tenants who did not know or assert their rights and acted accordingly. I called him again, or tried to, but my phone cut out after the first ring, and he wouldn't have picked up anyway. I pocketed my phone and slid my key into the lock.

A repairman hired by the landlord, I repeated to myself. Frustrating; probably illegal; not a threat. But I couldn't stop thinking of his nondescript van, the rock used as a doorjamb, his malicious smile. I pictured the other possibility: a stranger, prying open the front door, creeping through our halls, trying each doorknob, trying mine.

It was locked, I told myself. *He couldn't have gotten in.*

But this house was old and falling apart, and so was this door, and maybe these locks weren't that hard to pick. I had never tried.

My door swung open. My apartment looked, as far as I could tell, the same as it had when I left: my clothes and papers littered across the couch, a pile of unwashed dishes undisturbed in the sink. But the air had a different quality to it. A disturbance, something not right.

You're imagining things, I told myself, but I couldn't shake the feeling. Something was off, wrong, and just because I couldn't pinpoint it didn't mean it wasn't there. A lingering scent of smoke or sweat too faint to fully register, the garbage can moved an inch to the right, something.

He's not here, I told myself, *and if he ever was he's gone now,* but I needed to confirm that was true. I searched the apartment to make sure I was really alone. I pulled out my phone, but the reception fluctuated between one bar and nothing, like always. *If I find someone,* I told myself, *I'll scream. My neighbors are home now. They'll hear me.*

I tugged on the door to the coat closet, which was old and warped and stuck in the frame. I tugged harder and it gave, swinging open. Nothing there except for coats, umbrellas, a box of knickknacks I had never unpacked. I checked behind doors and under my bed, any space large enough for a person, and a few that weren't—the cabinet under the sink, the trunk in my room holding sweaters and sweatshirts, the sliver of space behind the dresser.

I was alone.

I looped the apartment again, studying the floorboards, the baseboards, the doors. The light fixtures, the windows, the defunct intercom, anything that might show signs of interference or repair: a new bulb, a window that opened that hadn't before.

Nothing, but the feeling didn't go away.

Before I went to bed that night, I double-checked that my windows were latched, that my door was dead-bolted, that no one was lying in wait beneath my bed. I lay on my back and closed my eyes, but they fluttered open again at the house's creaks and groans, the radiators whistling, the second-floor neighbors cheering, laughing, a horn blaring outside. I turned onto my side and studied the wall's cracks and bulges, its patches of unpainted spackle.

The constellation of tiny pinpoint holes.

CHAPTER TWENTY-ONE

—

Lucy is in bed, and Mona is out somewhere—*I'll be back later,* she told me without giving any specifics, taking my house key—and so it is just me and Theo together, his arm draped over the back of the couch. He's made us daiquiris, the kind with lime and simple syrup and rum, which I used to love before Lucy was born. Now the rum goes straight to my head, but I appreciate the gesture, a reminder of our life when it was only the two of us.

"I've been thinking about Mona's situation," he says.

"What about it?" I ask, careful.

"I know a few organizations that work with battered women," he says. "We could set her up with some of them. Help her get back on her feet."

"What do you mean, back on her feet?"

"Just . . . you know, set her up with the resources she needs to get her life together. Therapy, a job, housing—they could help with all that."

"She has housing," I say, taking another sip of my daiquiri. "She lives here."

"Yeah, but that's not, like, a permanent solution."

"Neither is whatever housing she's going to get through an organization."

Theo gives me a look, like I'm being unreasonable.

"It's literally temporary housing, Theo. That's what you're talking about."

"She's living in our *attic*. In Lucy's room."

When I don't say anything, he asks: "How long do you see this lasting for?"

"I don't *know*," I say. "I'm not going to set a deadline. As long as she needs to be here."

Theo looks like he's about to say more, but he's interrupted by a rap at our door. We turn, and there is Niko, peeking his head into our family room.

"Everyone decent?" he says. He steps in, and Fey follows. Her attention flits from me to Theo; she obviously senses the tension in the air.

"We're not interrupting anything, are we?" she asks.

I hesitate, and Theo says: "No, not at all."

"Ooh, are those daiquiris?" Fey asks, spotting our drinks on the coffee table. "Could you make me one of those, too?"

Theo makes more drinks, and I usher Niko and Fey out back to avoid waking Lucy, my bare hands curled into fists in my coat sleeves. It's cold; we won't be able to use the patio much longer this year. Niko scrolls on his phone, and Fey takes a drag of her cigarette, her cheeks spotted red, and all I can think about is Theo's hypocrisy. If Niko and Fey were in need, he'd open our house up to them, no question. If his mother needed a place to stay, he'd be horrified if I said no. He probably wouldn't even think to ask.

"Okay," Fey says as Theo emerges from the kitchen, "important question for y'all. If you were going to pull off the perfect murder, how would you do it?"

"I'm a pacifist," Niko says, taking a sip of his drink and giving Theo a nod of appreciation.

"Oh, come on," Fey says.

"Fine, fine." Niko sets down his drink, leans back in his chair. "I'd go on the dark web and hire someone."

"You don't know how to get on the dark web," Theo says. Niko shrugs and grins like he's been caught.

"I work at a tech start-up," he says. "I could probably figure it out."

Family is the most important thing, Theo is always saying, but what he means is *his* family. When it's my sister in need, we need to tread carefully, keep some space. Foist her off on an impersonal organization and hope for the best.

"How about you, Fey?" Theo asks.

"Poison, of course," she says, crossing one leg over the other. "I'm a lady."

"Did everyone hear that?" Niko says, sweeping his finger from Theo to me. "If I ever drop dead, take note."

A muted thump from inside, the front door slamming closed. Fey and Niko turn to Theo, surprised.

"Lee's sister Mona is staying with us for a little while," Theo explains.

"Here? With you?" Fey shoots him a look that suggests they've already spoken about Mona, that Theo has shared his concerns with her, and I feel a twinge of discomfort.

"Yes," I say, at the same time Theo says: "Just for a little while."

"Have we met her before?" Niko asks. Niko is unfailingly considerate in social situations, the type of person who always notes small details about people, who will remember birthdays and anniversaries, who makes a point to ask about new jobs and family members and golf games.

"I don't think so," I say, as Theo shakes his head, *no.*

"Was she at your wedding?" Niko asks.

"She just moved back to the area," I say, like it's a response, and Niko, picking up on the tension, leans back in his chair.

"How's she settling in?"

"She—"

The glass door scrapes on its track. I turn and see Mona, backlit by the kitchen light. She smiles apologetically, like she's not sure if she should be here. She's wearing my sweater beneath her wool overcoat, which is fine. *What's mine is yours*, I told her, and I meant it. She must have seen it lying around.

"Your keys are on the secretary desk," she tells me, looking at Fey and Niko with some apprehension.

"Thanks," I say. "Mona, this is Fey and Niko. They went to law school with Theo."

"Mona," Fey says. She stands, drops the cigarette butt on the brick, holds out her hand. "*So* nice to meet you."

"*So* nice to meet you, too," Mona says. She mimics Fey's toothy smile, her tone almost mocking to my ear. Fey doesn't notice, or doesn't care.

"I hear you just moved to town," Niko says. "How are you liking Philly?"

Mona shrugs. There are only four seats, all taken, and so she lingers by the glass door, rubbing her arm.

"Let me get another chair from inside," Theo says, but Mona shakes her head. Niko half-stands, ready to offer Mona his seat.

"No, really," Mona says, waving her hand. "I won't be out here long. I just wanted to say hello."

"Well, it's great to meet you, Mona," Niko says. "Where did you move here from?"

"Oh, I lived all over," she says. "Lots of traveling."

"Remind me," says Theo. He's not looking at me, but the comment feels directed. "*Where* did you travel again?"

"Out west for a little while," she says. Fey holds up her pack of cigarettes, and Mona takes one. "And then back east, up and down the Appalachian Trail, that sort of thing."

I wonder if she's telling the truth. If that's the path they took.

"Where out west?" Theo asks.

"Oregon. California. Montana." Mona exhales, a puff of smoke. "All over, really."

"You know," Fey says, to Theo more than anyone else, placing her hand on his arm, "I've never been to California. Never. Isn't that crazy?"

"Wild," Mona says dryly. This time, Fey picks up on the tone.

"What do *you* do, Mona?" she asks. Her smile returns. "I hope you're not a lawyer. Too many of us already. Right, Lee?" She gives me a wink.

"In between jobs at the moment."

"Good for you," Fey says. The same tone she takes when asking about my maternity leave. "Taking some downtime."

"I wouldn't call it that," Mona says. "I'd call it being unemployed." Fey ignores the response, squeezes Theo's arm.

"You never told us your answer," she says. "If you were going to kill someone, how would you do it?"

"Oh, I don't know," Theo demurs.

"Oh, come on!" Fey says, her smile stretching. "You're the one with experience after all."

He holds up his hands, mock surprised. "Hey now."

"You work with *crim-in-als*," she says, drawing out each syllable, her southern twang less subdued than normal. "You must have some ideas."

"The only thing I've learned from my clients," Theo laughs, "is what not to do. Like, don't shoot the guy when a cop is right there watching you. Be mindful of security cameras. They're everywhere. Get rid of your gun; it's evidence. And for Christ's sake, turn your GPS off."

Fey nods, satisfied, and her head swivels toward Mona. "What about you?" she asks.

"What about me?" Mona replies, and I shift uncomfortably in my seat.

"If you were going to commit the perfect murder, what would you do?"

Mona looks down, silent, and for a moment I think she's not going to respond. She rocks her head from side to side.

"Well," she says finally, taking another drag of her cigarette. "I guess if I really wanted to kill someone without getting caught, I'd convince them to trust me. Get them to really love me, you know?" She looks at me, and my stomach flips. I see Christopher's eyes, the same ice blue as Lucy's. I will them away.

"And then?" Fey asks, goading.

"And then I'd convince them they wanted to do it themselves."

There is an uncomfortable silence. Mona drops her cigarette, stubs it out with her boot.

"Thank you for this," she says. "I'm going to bed."

She slides the glass door shut behind her, and Niko gives a low whistle. "Jeeee-sus," he says, taking a gulp of his drink. "That took a dark turn."

Fey's eyes are wide, her smile tight, like she's holding back laughter. "Well," she says. "That was illuminating. Lee, do you—"

"I'm going to bed, too," I say, pushing up from my chair. "Good night." I slide the door shut behind me before they can protest or feign apologies, saving everyone the trouble.

I pause at the top of the stairs. To the left is my room, Lucy asleep in her bassinet. To my right, the latched door to the third-floor staircase. The floorboards groan overhead. Mona is still awake.

I knock softly, lift the latch.

"Mona?" I half-whisper up the stairs. "Can I come up?"

There's a pause that lasts a second too long, and then the shuffle of feet.

"Of course," she says at last.

I climb the stairs. The third floor still feels like a storage space, but less so than it used to. Mona has wiped the dust from the blinds and fashioned curtains for herself out of old scarves she must have found in one of the boxes. There is a stack of books by her mattress, repurposed as a nightstand. On top is a pig-shaped lamp, with silver wings and a fringed light shade.

"Like it?" she asks. "Someone was just giving it away on the curb."

"We can do an IKEA run tomorrow," I say. "We'll get you some actual furniture."

"Oh, this is fine," Mona says, waving her hand. "I won't be here that long, anyway."

"You can stay as long as you want," I say. "Our home is your home."

"I'm not sure how your husband would feel about that."

She emphasizes "husband"; she has noticed that the tension hasn't gone away. I had hoped that was only obvious to me.

"He wants you here, too," I say, and Mona arches her eyebrows, glances toward the stairs. "He's under a lot of pressure at work right now. A really bad case."

"What's it about?" she asks, picking at her thumbnail.

"I don't know," I say. "He's been getting—not threats, exactly, but messages from one of the victims. It involves a young child. He doesn't like going into the details."

She looks at me.

"So the two of you don't talk about it?"

I shake my head, suddenly embarrassed. "No," I say. "Not . . . not really."

"Why not?"

"I think he wants to shield me from it."

"Do you want to be shielded?" Mona asks. There's something about her question that almost sounds like a challenge. I think about the life Mona has probably led, and how I must look to her now. Soft, protected. Naïve.

"No," I say.

"So ask him," Mona says. She sits cross-legged on her mattress, and I see a flash of her as a young girl, in my mother's bed, my mother's voice, *Mona needs to rest today.* Mona needed to rest so often. "If there's something you want to know, you should ask."

I feel a tug inside, the questions bubbling just under the surface:

Where were you? Where did you go? Why did you all leave me here alone? But I know that these questions are different, that asking them would change everything. Instead, I start around the edges, probing gently.

"Do you ever think about Josephine?" I ask. Our third room-mate, the one who left before the disappearance. "I used to think maybe someday I'd bump into her out in the world, but . . ."

I trail off, and Mona smiles faintly.

"Do you remember her?" I ask. "You were so young——"

"I remember," she says quickly. "What was it you used to call her?"

I'm not sure what she's asking.

"Just . . . Josephine," I say.

"Didn't she have a nickname?" Mona asks. "Something you used to call her?"

"I don't think so. Not that I remember."

"Hmm." She flops back onto her mattress, then rolls onto her side to face me, squints, like she's debating her next words.

"They're very close," she says, finally.

"Who?"

She raises her eyebrows at me, like it should be obvious, but I don't know what she's suggesting.

"Theo and Fey."

"Oh," I say, caught off guard. "They've been friends a long time. Since their first year of law school. Theo and Niko roomed together, and——"

"She touches him a lot."

"That's what she does."

"Not with you," Mona says. "Not with me."

"Well. With men," I say. "It's just how she is. I don't think it means anything."

"Have she and Theo ever been . . . involved?"

"Theo and *Fey*?" I say, like this question has never crossed my mind.

Mona raises her eyebrows again.

"No," I say, and I'm almost sure it's true. Fey and Niko have been together since law school orientation. Theo and Niko are like brothers. It's not possible.

"Never mind," Mona says. "Forget I said anything." She rolls onto her back again, returning her attention to the sloping ceiling. When I was pregnant with Lucy, I imagined we'd paint this ceiling sky-blue, sponge-paint it with clouds. I bought a bird-themed mobile for Lucy's crib, which is sitting in the closet, unused.

"Is Theo good to you?" Mona asks. "Is he a good husband?"

"Yes," I say. "He's a great husband." And it's true. There's been a disconnect between us ever since Lucy's birth, but that's normal. It happens to lots of people. We both care so much about Lucy, and the stakes are so high, and we don't always see things the same way. But we will find our way through, together.

I think about Theo bursting into tears at Lucy's birth. How afraid he looked when the nurse handed her to him, swaddled in her gauzy blanket. How awestruck.

"Are you happy?" she asks.

"I don't know how to answer that," I say. "Are *you* happy?"

"No," she says. She pulls her blanket over her. "But I think that's changing."

"Good," I say. "I'll let you get some sleep."

She nods, turns. "Good night," she says, and then something else, too. It's muffled, but I think she says *Fee-ah*, like she used to, like all the kids at Jacob's Hill used to, when Ophelia was too hard to pronounce.

"Good night, Mona," I say.

CHAPTER TWENTY-TWO

—

"Do you want to get out of the house for a little while?"
Mona moves around the kitchen like she's been here forever. She pulls two tea bags and two mugs out of the cabinet and sets the kettle on the burner. She bounces Lucy on her hip. Lucy presses her hand against Mona's cheek and laughs, enthralled by this new person, her aunt.

"Sure," I say. "Where do you want to go?"

"No," she says. "I mean *you*. You should take some time to yourself. I can watch Lu."

"That's okay," I say, but the offer is tempting. *Why not?* I think. *What's holding you back?* Now that Mona has come back to me: nothing. "Where would I even go?"

"Anywhere you want!" Mona says. She is animated, flinging out her free hand, and Lucy mimics her. "Go drink a coffee in peace! Bring a book! Live on the wild side!"

I laugh. "I can't ask you to do that."

"Why not?" Mona asks. "I'm staying in your house. Let me do *something* to help."

"I don't—"

"And besides," she says, "this way Lu and I will get to spend a little one-on-one time together. You'd like that, wouldn't you, Lu?"

I rack my brain for excuses, but none are forthcoming.

"It would be nice . . ." I say.

"So go!"

"Now?"

"Yes, now." Mona swings open the cabinet again, replaces my mug with a thermos. "I'm making this to-go. Take the whole morning! Go be a person again."

Doubt creeps in.

"I don't know how she'll do without me," I say. "Maybe we should start small. I could hang out upstairs, and you can get me if—"

"Absolutely not," Mona says. "You need to get out of the house. Otherwise, she'll know you're up there, and she really *will* be crying for you the whole time, and you'll be so focused on what's going on down here you won't be able to relax at all."

It's true.

"Okay," I say, surprising myself. And what surprises me even more is that it *does* feel okay. Mona loves Lucy. She's her aunt. It's fine—*fine*—to let other people help sometimes. That's what Theo is always telling me, and he's right.

Theo's voice echoes in my head: *Keep some distance between her and Lucy.* He'd be furious if he knew.

But he doesn't have to find out.

"I'll go to the coffee shop on the corner," I say.

"Go farther."

I laugh. "Let's start there. This is a big step for me." I give Lucy a kiss on the top of her head, and she does not even seem bothered to see me go.

"I don't want to see you back here before noon," Mona calls after me. "I'm serious."

I am light, like part of me is missing, like I somehow left an arm behind. Light, and off-balance, my muscles so used to compensating for

Lucy's weight on my right side. Without Lucy on my hip, or the stroller's thirty-five pounds of resistance, I move easily. I do not have to think about cracks and steps and brick sidewalks.

I am by myself.

It's not really the first time, of course. There were the trips around the block at Dr. Dana's insistence. Theo pulling a screaming Lucy from my hands, *go take a walk.* But it's the first time I haven't felt a tug toward home, a countdown in my mind, the burning question: *When can I go back?*

I feel fine. This feels right.

The coffee shop is small and bright, with a mint-green awning and a few wrought-iron tables and chairs out front. It was my favorite coffee shop before Lucy, but it is not particularly child-friendly and so I have not been here in a long time. Inside, the walls are painted a pale yellow, with local artists' paintings and photography hung in simple frames, prices written underneath. Scones and muffins and large fresh-baked cookies sit out on display; a philodendron's vines spill over the counter. A barista greets me and then turns her attention to unpacking boxes of tea bags, clearly in no rush, which is fine because, today, neither am I.

I stand by the counter, not bouncing and swaying, not worrying about blowouts or sudden crying fits or judgmental looks from other patrons. I give my order, pay calmly, wait. I find a table by the front window and sit with my latte in a real mug with a real plate and tiny spoon.

I look at my phone, and there is another email from Meghan Kessler: Hi again! Another message about "working together" to "tell my story."

I know how people like Meghan Kessler work. I've made the mistake of falling for this type of thing before: that reporter after Pittsburgh who pretended to be *sympathetic,* who just wanted to *hear my side.* Meghan has a story she wants to tell, but it's not my story, it's the best story she can get. She wants something that will attract attention, and *girl abandoned twenty years ago still doesn't know what happened* isn't it.

I put in my AirPods and load the second episode of the documentary, concerned there will be more about me. But this episode is focused on Christopher. Meghan mined old home videos, examined his writings, interviewed his former colleagues, his cousins on his dad's side, his second-grade teacher. He grew up in Drexel Hill, Meghan says, not far from the compound. His father was a police officer, his mother a parish secretary, though not especially religious herself. He was an unusual child, bright and idiosyncratic, with a heavy interest in religious iconography. His parents didn't know what to do with him. He grew up to be an engineer, and then abandoned that for philosophy, taking a post as an adjunct. He was worried, everyone agreed, about the coming millennium. He had a revelation, or a mental break. He spent years working on his treatise, or screed, or manifesto.

It's just a rip-off of Plato's cave, says one of his colleagues, *with some new-wave mumbo jumbo and paranoia about government tyranny mixed in. It's gotten more attention and analysis than it ever should have in the wake of his disappearance, and maybe that's what he was after all along. It certainly wasn't going to get that attention on its own merits.*

He was always a weird guy, a cousin says. *But, I don't know, maybe he was tapped into some part of the universe the rest of us aren't? He was into that spiritual energy stuff, laying on of hands and all that. Sort of far out for me, although I saw him do it once, for a neighbor whose arthritis was so bad she had trouble walking, and she could walk after that, so . . . I don't know. Weird stuff.*

Another one of my mother's small rebellions: medication, hidden in her nightstand. *Is it for Mona?* I asked her when I found it. Her face blanched, and she slammed the nightstand drawer shut. *Don't say a word,* she told me, squeezing my arm so tight it left a bruise. *Do you understand me? You cannot say a word.*

A text notification appears on my screen, from Theo.

How are my girls doing today?

My stomach churns with guilt. But Theo is wrong about Mona, and it's not fair of him to try to keep her and Lucy apart. Mona and Lucy love each other; it is good for Lucy to have another family bond. And it's good for me, too. A week ago, I couldn't leave Lucy alone for ten minutes, and now, because of Mona, I am at a coffee shop by myself.

This will be good for everyone in the long run, even if Theo can't see that yet.

We're good, I respond. Just out for a walk.

A part-truth.

There are Reddit threads on possible Christopher sightings, prompted by the most recent docuseries episode. I know I shouldn't read them—*all wishful thinking*, I tell myself, *none of it true*—but I click on them anyway.

> **ajollyswagman:** I was halfway through the second episode when I realized I had fucking SEEN this guy in Brazil a few years back. A friend and I were visiting Ibirapuera Park in São Paulo, and both of us noticed this long-haired white guy with four women all dressed in baggy brown dresses. He was leading them around like they were some sort of harem, and it was creepy as fuck.
>
> **dramallama8903:** what would christopher be doing in a metro park? sightseeing?
>
> **ajollyswagman:** Who knows, but it was real weird. I remember wondering at the time if I should step in and do something, but what, you know?

Someone else had spotted Christopher in Japan, at a Shinto shrine. A few posters had seen him in California, stalking around the Tenderloin or scavenging in a makeshift camp nestled into redwoods.

These "spottings" are all from years ago, I tell myself. *Distorted memories. They want to believe they saw something special, and so they're convincing themselves they did.* I am about to close out of the window when another post catches my eye.

> **pirateprincess5252:** I live outside Pittsburgh and there was this string of weird break-ins in my neighborhood a while back. The burglars never

took money or jewelry or anything valuable, just food and tools from workbenches, that kind of stuff. A few of my neighbors posted still shots of the burglars from their Ring footage, and I swear to god one of them was a dead-ringer for Christopher.

tyrantintraining: The Pittsburgh connection is interesting . . .

Tyrantintraining posts a link to the article about me written by the Pittsburgh reporter. Dramallama8903 follows up with a link to the Clara video. I set down my phone, my chest constricting. My latte has gone cold. A couple loudly fumbles their way into the chairs beside me, all bags and jackets, sprawling out. The pain in my temple is returning. I don't want to be here, alone, away from my child. Not anymore. I've been out long enough, a good first step. I am about to text Mona to let her know I'm coming back and realize, with a start, that I don't have any way to reach her, which means she doesn't have any way of reaching me. I left the house so quickly, I didn't even think about it. She doesn't have a phone.

All of my old, familiar fears come flooding back. What if something happened to Lucy while I was out? A fever, a fall, an apple swallowed the wrong way? What kind of mother leaves without some way to get in touch? How could I have been so thoughtless?

I rise from my chair quickly, the table wobbling, the mug clinking against its plate. *Calm down*, I remind myself. *They're probably fine. It probably doesn't matter.*

But I am already out the coffee shop door.

I turn the knob to the front door, and it pushes open, unlocked. I step inside. The wooden farm animals from Lucy's puzzle are scattered across the rug, next to board books and Lucy's turtle and a retro phone on wheels with eyes that dart back and forth. Lucy and Mona are nowhere to be seen.

"Hi!" I call out, too brightly. Maybe they're upstairs. "Back a little early!"

There is no response.

I step over a brown cow, a pink pig. *Don't panic,* I tell myself. *They have to be somewhere.*

But I know, in my heart, that's not true.

"Mona?" I call out again. "Lucy?"

Nothing.

Theo's words: *Be careful. You don't know anything about her.*

I run up the stairs. I know they will not be there—sound travels in this house; I'd hear them and they'd hear me—but I hold on to hope anyway. My door gapes open; the bassinet is empty. There is no one in the bathroom. I climb the stairs to Mona's room.

"Hello?" I call out. Her curtains are drawn, her bed made, her rucksack slouched against the wall.

Lucy is not here.

Lucy is not here, and Mona is not here, and how could I have let this happen?

Stop, I tell myself. *Calm down. Think.*

I return to the first floor to look for a note, a clue, anything. *Maybe they went for a walk,* I tell myself. But Lucy's stroller is in its normal place by the front door, and the straps of her carrier peak out from its basket. No note on the kitchen counter or stuck to the refrigerator door; only a pink plastic plate on the tray of Lucy's high chair, a crumb-covered tab of butter on its rim. Mona's tea from earlier, half-drunk.

"Mona?" I call out again, like she'll materialize from nowhere. *No no no.* "Lucy?"

Maybe they had to rush to the doctor's. The emergency room. Maybe there was no time to leave a note.

I left Lucy with someone I cannot get in touch with, who cannot get in touch with me. How could I have been so stupid, so thoughtless?

Breathe, I remind myself. *In and out, steady and deep.*

I think of the unlocked door, the bruises on Mona's face. What if whoever did that came looking for her? What if they found her, here with Lucy, alone?

I scan the first floor, try to reassure myself. There are no signs of a struggle. Nothing broken, nothing missing. A wad of cash sits out on the secretary desk by the front door, untouched. No blood.

I pull out my phone. It's early to call the police, but an hour from now might be too late. I dial 911, hear a ringtone.

The front door swings open.

It's Mona and Lucy, here, back, in front of me. Mona bounces Lucy on her hip, singing the second half to a song, *merrily, merrily, merrily, merrily*. A voice on the other end of my phone, *nine-one-one, what's*—I hang up, drop my hand to my side, stare at the two of them in disbelief.

Lucy has Mona's shirt collar in her fist. She is laughing—squealing—her two teeth showing.

They're here. They're back.

"You're home!" Mona says. She wags her finger at me in mock disapproval. "You weren't supposed to be back yet!"

"Where were you?" I ask. I don't mean to sound accusatory but can't help it. I am on edge, raw, all instincts firing.

"Just getting some fresh air."

"You didn't leave a note."

"I thought we'd be back before you," she says, tilting her head at me, *what is your problem*. "It's only ten-thirty."

"You left the door unlocked."

"Yeah, I don't have a key. We weren't far."

Mona's tone is sharp, defensive. She hands me Lucy and brushes past me to the kitchen. She has every right to be annoyed. She has done me a favor. She has been nothing but kind and helpful, and here I am giving her the third degree.

"I'm sorry," I say, following her. "I thought . . ."

I don't finish the sentence, but I don't need to. Mona understands. She looks back at me, twists her mouth.

"I should have left a note."

"We need to fix that key problem," I say, trying to lighten my voice.

"Oh, don't worry about it," she says. She turns to the fridge, rifles through it.

"No, really," I say. "You live here. You need your own key."

Lucy's weight in my arms is calming me. I was worked up over nothing. Lucy is here, and she is safe, and she and Mona were having a great time together until I got carried away. I'm letting Theo get to me. I'm letting his distrust color my view of my sister.

"How did the morning go?" I ask. Mona is slicing an apple from the fridge. She offers me some, then holds a slice out to Lucy.

"*So* well," she says. "We saw lots of doggies and made some new friends. Didn't we, Lu?"

"Friends?" I say.

"Oh, just some people at the park." She scrunches her face and then opens her eyes and mouth wide, a silly face for Lucy's benefit, but I have the nagging sensation that she's avoiding looking at me. I try to push it aside. I'm being paranoid again.

"Lucy doesn't usually like people."

"Really?" Mona says, still looking at Lucy. "Maybe you just needed to find the right ones. You did so good."

"Great," I say.

"Next time we're going to go down the *big* slide," she says, holding her hands apart for Lucy.

Next time. I take a breath.

"Thanks again," I say. "I really appreciate it."

"Of course," Mona says, finally meeting my eyes. "Any time."

CHAPTER TWENTY-THREE

—

The night after my aunt told me about the biopsy, I didn't sleep. I tossed and turned, running through the possibilities, my mind fixing on the most dire ones. When day broke and I pushed myself out of bed, my thoughts were murky, bumping against each other. The world felt out of focus, everything happening on a half-second delay. A sharp pain in my right temple.

I needed to get out of my apartment, I decided, needed to distract myself somehow. I'd go to the grocery store. I kept on my sweatpants, pulled my hair out of my face, threw on a coat and boots. It was a gray morning, snow from earlier that week still clumped in patches on the brown grass. I checked my phone and had reception again, but still no calls from my landlord confirming he had sent a repairman to my apartment, and nothing from my aunt.

It's going to take time, I told myself. *These tests and appointments and diagnoses, they all take time.*

The grocery store parking lot was clogged with cars and stray carts. Two SUVs backed up at the same time, nearly colliding. Horns blared, and I worried, for a moment, that there was going to be a confrontation. But the drivers stayed in their cars and maneuvered around each other, leaving the parking lot without coming to blows.

I stepped inside the store, and the sudden harshness of the lighting blurred my vision at the corners. I blinked to correct it. A tinny version of a song about Superman played over the speakers. A woman beside me wrested a cart free from the other grocery carts, wire jostling against wire. All around me, the squeak of wheels, the slip of wet shoes, the hum of conversation.

Coffee, I reminded myself. And a few things to eat over the next couple of days, just enough to last until I went home for the break: chicken salad, deli meat, a loaf of bread. Milk and cereal.

I pictured the man from yesterday in my kitchen, his boots on my tile floor, opening cabinets, the refrigerator door.

"Stop doing that," a woman shouted at her child. He jumped off the side of their cart, nearly backing into a pyramid of hot chocolate boxes. She grabbed him by the wrist. "If you can't behave . . ."

My phone buzzed, and I grabbed it, hoping it was Anne with an update, *false alarm, all good*, or my landlord with an explanation, *HVAC, sorry*, but instead it was my Information Systems professor, proposing a time for a review session.

Anne is going to be fine, I told myself. She was too good, too strong-willed, too optimistic not to be okay. *It's going to be nothing.* But if she was telling me already, it meant she thought it *was* something. It meant she was concerned.

I turned in to the cereal aisle, only half paying attention, and nearly collided with another cart. A toddler with a cowlick sat in the front seat, his legs banging against the metal frame.

"Sorry," I said instinctively, although I had stopped in time, hadn't actually hit them. The woman turned to face me, and my heart stopped.

Terese Taylor. From Jacob's Hill.

Her hair was cut to her shoulders and she had thickened out, looked healthier than before, but I still recognized her immediately. She recognized me, too, or I thought she did, her eyes widening before she caught herself and smiled neutrally, like you would at a stranger. She dropped a box of Cheerios in her cart, turned her attention back to the shelves.

"Terese?" I said.

She didn't respond, but the toddler turned toward me, like he recognized the name. Patchy red cheeks and white-blond hair. It brought me back to the residence, to Kai running down the hallway, shrieking with laughter.

"Terese," I said again, more insistent this time. "It's me. Ophelia." I stepped closer so she could see me more clearly, see my face. I had been twelve at the time of the disappearance, and it had been so long, but once she heard my name, saw my face, she should have known. She should have recognized me.

The toddler pounded his fists against the cart. I squeezed my eyes shut and opened them again. Kai would be twelve now, not still a baby, not this boy—

The woman pushed the cart down the aisle, her eyes still fixed on the cereal boxes, like I wasn't talking to her, like if she just pretended not to see me I'd go away.

"Terese," I said again. Her eyes flit back toward me, nervous this time, like she had been caught.

"Sorry," she said. "I think you have me confused—"

"Where are the others?" I asked. I knew my voice was too loud, but I wanted so desperately to have the answer, and here, I thought, was someone who knew, standing right in front of me. "Where did you all go?"

She shuffled backward, knocking a cereal box onto the floor with her elbow, and the boy—another son, I told myself, Kai's brother, maybe, he looked so much like him—burst into peals of familiar laughter. I pictured Kai, this age again, stirring leaves into mud puddles, holding out a stick for me to try. *Here, Fee-ah. Here.*

"Hi," I said to the boy, reaching out to brush his arm, like I had so many times before, and the woman jerked the cart back.

"Leave us alone," she said, harsher this time, and she pushed the boy away from me, down the aisle, the wheel on her cart loose, squeaking and rattling.

"I'm not going to tell anyone," I said. I followed her, grabbing the side of her cart so she had to look at me. "Please. I'll keep your secret. I just want to know where they are."

She pulled the boy upward, but he didn't want to go; he kicked his legs and his right sneaker caught in the seat.

"Where is my mother?" I asked. "Where is Mona?"

She pulled harder and her son came free, and now he wasn't laughing anymore, he was wailing, surprised and disoriented.

"Are they still with him? Are they with Christopher?"

She kept her head down, half-running for the door, leaving her cart full of groceries behind.

"Terese!" I called out, and a bulky teenaged store clerk stepped between us.

"Ma'am," he said, focused on me as the woman slipped out behind him. "Is everything okay here?"

Other patrons had gathered a safe distance away, watching. She was leaving, and no one was going to stop her.

"*Terese!*" I shouted again, but she was stepping through the sliding doors. And then I couldn't see her anymore, my time ticking down. I knew she must be weaving through the parking lot, buckling her son into his car seat. She was nervous. Maybe her son was resisting, maybe her hands were slipping.

"I need you to—"

"I know her," I said. I tried to push past him, to keep her in my sights. There still could be time—a minute, maybe two—before she put the car into drive, before she disappeared again into the ether. "You don't understand. I need to—"

"Ma'am," he said again. "You need to take your hands off me."

"Stop her," I said. "Someone needs to stop her," and when I tried to move forward, he grabbed my arms, and then there were others, a burly, ex-cop-looking man and a thin, balding one, and they were all telling me to *calm down* and using words like *assault*, even as they pinned my arms to my side, even as I called out for Terese, even though she was no longer there, having sped off back to god-knows-where, leaving no trace behind.

The police were called, of course. Standard operating procedure for that sort of "incident," for any "altercation" taking place on Giant Eagle premises. There was a report. No charges pressed, in the end, but a record created, another mark against me. I returned home without groceries. I lay on my bed, stared at the wall. Those pinholes really were everywhere, so small you'd look right over them if you weren't paying attention. I had never noticed them before, even though I had been in this house for over a year, and maybe that's because I hadn't been looking.

But maybe there was another explanation.

I squinted at one of the holes, looking for a lens inside, digging at the drywall with my index finger. It came up in dusty flakes beneath my nail, the hole widening.

The repairman who came but didn't repair anything, just smiled at me like he knew something.

Terese and her son, the look she gave me, like I wasn't supposed to see her.

They were watching.

They were still here, and they were nearby, and they were keeping track of me. After all this time.

I grabbed a roll of masking tape from the kitchen, ripped off a long strip and covered a cluster of holes. Scribbled over the gray tape with black permanent marker, to be safe. I ripped off another piece, and then another, and then another. I did the same in the stairwell, where they watched me come and go, the ripped pieces of tape zig-zagging across the wall, covering all the places a camera might be hiding.

If they wanted to see me, they'd have to come find me in person.

CHAPTER TWENTY-FOUR

—

Present day

Ever since Mona returned, I have been thinking about our mother. I have been trying to conjure her: her long braided hair, brown wisps falling around her face. Her sloped nose, her pointed chin. The raised veins that ran along the back of her hand, the freckle on the base of her thumb. Her smile, when she smiled at me.

I worry my image of her is faulty, that each time I have recalled her over the years I have added details, subtracted them, distorted her into something unreal. I worry I'm not seeing her at all anymore, just the faded outlines of a memory, colored in wrong.

Mona would know. There is so much I wish I could ask her, so much I want to know.

Soon, I tell myself. *When she's more comfortable.*

Mona has either slept in this morning, or she has been keeping herself busy in her room. She does not emerge from upstairs until Lucy's first nap. She's dressed in her own clothes, makeup applied thick enough to mostly cover the faded bruising. A small, flat travel wallet is visible beneath her jacket, until she zips it shut.

"I'm heading out," she says, short, matter-of-fact.

"Where are you going?" I ask. It's meant to be a friendly question, but her expression changes like I've crossed a line.

"I just need to take care of a few things," she says.

I need to tread carefully. I don't know what her life has looked like since she left Christopher and the others. I don't know what she's had to do to survive.

But I do know what it's like to have aspects of your life you'd rather forget. I can give her the space she needs.

"Okay," I say, smiling to show her it's fine. I am not going to push. "See you later."

The door clicks shut behind her, and a quiet falls over the house. The loop of rain from Lucy's sound machine drifts down the stairs. A steady *tap tap tap* from next door; our new neighbor must be hanging pictures.

I put on a daytime talk show for background noise and pull a laundry basket brimming with unfolded clothes onto the couch. It never ceases to amaze me how much additional laundry such a small person can create. I try, and fail, to fold Lucy's fitted blankets into neat squares, settling on a rough approximation of a rectangle. I roll up her onesies and leggings, all tiny, all meant for a much younger baby. I repeat Dr. Mann's less-than-reassuring words to myself: *She's probably just small.*

I picture my mother and Adrienne and Terese, pinning laundry to a clothesline behind the residence, our blankets that smelled like fresh air. *Come help, Ophelia.*

I look up, and Meghan Kessler is on my screen, smiling modestly in a light blue blazer and heels, chatting with the blond host.

But there is someone who knows what happened, isn't there? the host asks, crossing one leg over another. *What about the young girl who was left behind?*

Meghan nods, anticipating this question. *When the police questioned her after the disappearance, she claimed to have slept through the whole thing. And she's always stuck to that story.*

But you think that's what it is. A story.

Meghan arches her eyebrows, gives the host a knowing look. *I don't think she's lying. I think trauma can sometimes be hard to face head-on. So we build up fictions around it, stories that help us get through the day.*

The host bobs her head sympathetically. I grab the remote and turn the television off, but I've lost my focus. My mind buzzes, a pulse in my right temple.

There's nothing in my past that can hurt me, I remind myself. Not anymore, now that Mona is here, safe.

There's a knock at the door.

I open it, expecting Mona, back because she's forgotten her key, or a delivery person, dropping off an Amazon order. But instead, it's our new neighbor, Andi.

"Hi," she says, giving me a wide smile. "I'm trying to put together some furniture and could use an extra pair of hands. Any chance you could help? You don't need to *do* much of anything—I just need someone to hold a piece in place while I get the other side lined up."

I'm surprised, and it must show on my face because suddenly Andi is apologetic, backtracking.

"Sorry," she says. "I know it's an annoying ask, and you've probably got a lot going on . . ."

"Oh no," I say, waving my hands. "Don't apologize. It's just that Lucy is napping upstairs—"

"Oh yeah, of course."

"But the baby monitor's connected to my phone, so I can still see her."

Andi's rowhome is adjacent to ours; I'll never be more than twenty feet away, and I'll be able to see and hear Lucy at all times. I will be closer to her than I would be if we were on opposite sides of a suburban home. But this still feels like a step forward, something I would not have been able to do before Mona came back.

"*Thank* you," Andi says, her shoulders dropping in relief. "This new cabinet system is a pain in my ass."

We duck into her house, and I turn on the baby monitor app, the image of Lucy sleeping soundly in her crib coming through clearly on my screen. I turn the volume up to make sure I can hear her if she wakes.

"So what do you need me to do?"

The big furniture is all in place, mostly, except for the half-constructed cabinets. But everything else is still in boxes: banker boxes of books hanging over the edges of built-in bookshelves, a box of knickknacks and decorative bowls on the coffee table, more still sealed along the kitchen wall.

"We haven't made much progress," Andi says, showing me how to hold the wooden frame in place, and I shake my head, although it's true.

"You've got a lot going on," I say.

"That's part of it," Andi says. "But mostly I get so emotional looking at this stuff. I'll be doing fine going through our kitchen utensils—grater, fine, meat tenderizer, fine—and then I'll get to, like, a lobster mallet from our trip to the Cape and I'll be done."

"It's hard," I say, thinking of my own untouched box from my past on the third floor. After my aunt died, Rachel packed up what was left of my belongings and sent them here. *We can just get rid of it,* I told Theo when it showed up on our doorstep, and he laughed. *You're not at least curious? Your old pictures can't be that bad.*

"And I don't want Des to see me like that," she says. "It's not right."

Andi tightens the final cam lock nut, and my job is done. I check the monitor on my phone. Lucy is still sleeping soundly.

"What's Des into these days?" I ask, and she tells me about the books he's reading—"I can't keep up," she says—and about the pack of kids he hangs out with from Fairmount. "They're good kids," she says, and then gives it some thought. "Mostly. Well, I'm not sure about Caspian."

"Is there anything I can do to help with unpacking?" I ask, and she looks like she's about to protest, so I add: "I'm good at hanging things up." She gives in, and we work together, removing the packing paper from old picture frames, finding the right place for them. She tells me about the theater group Des has joined, how it's brought him out of his shell. She asks about Lucy, about the adjustment to mother-hood, about our favorite spots in the neighborhood, and it's easy, and for once I am able to keep myself in the moment, Jacob's Hill and the documentary and Theo all pushed aside, problems for another time.

"Shoot," she says, looking at the clock. "I need to jump on a Zoom call."

I'm surprised to see that forty-five minutes have gone by.

"Oh yeah," I say. "Lucy will be getting up soon, too."

"But can we do this again?" Andi asks. "Maybe with less furni-ture assembly and more alcohol?"

"Absolutely," I say, and I mean it.

I return home feeling good, Lucy still sleeping. My mind drifts to the box of items from my aunt's house, the one on the third floor, the one I've been avoiding. There are pictures of my mother inside, old photo albums from her childhood that my aunt gave to me.

Maybe I could finally handle it, after all.

I climb the stairs and walk cautiously past my room, careful not to wake Lucy. I reach for the latch on the door to the third floor but feel a twinge of uncertainty. This is our house, but it's Mona's room, at least for now.

I'm not prying, though, just looking for a box that belongs to me. I'll be in and out.

It's fine.

I lift the latch and the door swings open. A stale smell has re-placed the old dusty one. Mona has placed an ashtray by one of the dormer windows, cigarette butts beginning to collect. I take a closer look and see that Mona has carved through the layers of paint that sealed the window shut. I push up on the glass pane; it opens now.

It's her room, I tell myself, trying to shake the unease I feel about Mona smoking inside. And it's true, it is Mona's room, but it's also going to be Lucy's someday. The smoke is disgusting, seeping into everything, and it won't just go away when she leaves.

I will talk to her about this later. For now, I turn to the boxes, unstacking and rearranging until I find the one with my name written on it in Rachel's compact handwriting. I pick at the duct tape with my fingernail, get hold of the corner, peel it back. This tape is translucent, new-looking, incongruous with the brown packing tape that seals this box shut on the bottom.

Like someone has opened this box and then resealed it with new tape.

I picture Theo rifling through my things, seeing these pieces of my past.

Stop, I tell myself. If he opened the box, he didn't see anything meaningful or he would have said something.

I take a breath and open it myself.

Inside is an unorganized heap of items. Old spiral-bound notebooks. A T-shirt from Scoops, the ice cream place where I worked in the summers. An unframed diploma. I set them to the side.

Underneath are yellowed clippings of articles on Jacob's Hill. I kept them stuffed in the back of a drawer, hidden where my aunt wouldn't find them. I unfold them, the pages weak and tearing at the creases, scan the familiar words. A few include quotes from family members of the missing: Amy Price. Gregory Dunn. Elise Dagnelle.

Please, if you're out there, come home.

My stomach twists, and I place the article clippings beside the diploma. I reach farther in, my fingers brushing the hand-carved jewelry box my aunt gave me for my thirteenth birthday. I lift the lid, and inside is my mother's bracelet. I rub the silver chain between my fingers, blink back tears.

It's our secret, my mother told me. *Someone very important gave this to me, and now I'm giving it to you. I need you to hold on to this, okay, Ophelia? Will you do that for me?*

I place the box on the floor and pull out a photo album from my mother's childhood. In one picture, she's a teenager in a violet polyester dress, ready for prom. Anne stands beside her in fuchsia. In another, my mother is four or five, with too-long bangs, feeding a carrot to a pony. A bridesmaid at my great-aunt's wedding. A slouching preteen, reading in the corner. Eighteen and packing her Jetta for college, waving sheepishly at the camera.

No pictures from Jacob's Hill, of course. No pictures of the mother I knew.

An old Madonna cassette tape. *Your mother listened to this all the time,* my aunt told me. *I'm surprised it never broke.* For weeks after that, I listened to it all the time, too—play, rewind, play, rewind—until it dawned on me that it was something she had left behind. The mother I knew hadn't cared enough to bring it with her to Jacob's Hill, and so it couldn't have been that important to her, after all. I never listened to it again.

I put the tape back in the box and pull out my soft-covered notebook. Officer Leanne had mailed it to my aunt a few weeks after the disappearance—a sign they were done investigating, probably, although I didn't realize that at the time. She affixed a Post-it note to the front: *Thought you might want this back.* Someone had left grease stains on a few of the pages, flipping through with their grubby hands while eating a hoagie.

I jump at the sound of a door slamming, but it's just a car door outside. I relax, *not Mona,* but then feel a stab of guilt at my reaction. This is her room. I shouldn't be in here without her permission.

The box is too heavy and bulky to bring down the stairs, but I take the photo album and the bracelet and return everything else to its place. I restick the tape, turn toward the stairs, and my eyes catch on something shiny nestled in the blankets on Mona's mattress.

A small silver phone.

My stomach flips as I pick it up. There's a hairline scratch across its tiny screen, an old Nokia phone. It lights up, vibrates in my hand, a call from a number without a name attached. I drop it back onto the bed like I've been caught.

I feel a swell of guilt, replaced quickly by a surge of anger.

Mona told me she didn't have a phone.

A miscommunication, probably. Not a lie. I must have misunderstood.

But I replay our conversation on our first walk, and I am sure of what I heard. I asked her for her phone number, and she said she didn't have one. Unambiguous, no room for doubt.

And yet here it is, plain as day, a goddamned cellphone.

Theo's words, like a refrain: *How much do you know about her?*

She's told me so little since she's gotten here. I don't know where she goes during the day. I don't know who she sees. I don't know when she left our family, how long she's been on her own.

Stop, I tell myself. I have no idea what she's been through, but I know her life has been hard, and I don't want to make her relive anything she's not ready to relive. I know how painful that can be.

Lucy's howl pierces the air, loud, like I've missed her early cries.

My mind races. Too many thoughts, and they don't fit together, don't make sense. I leave the phone on the bed and go to Lucy, pull her from the bassinet.

"I'm here, sweet girl," I say. "I'm here."

Lucy hiccups, slowly recovering.

"What are we going to do this afternoon?" I ask her, trying to sound calm. "Do you want to see the big kids playing?"

I can get through the afternoon. Lucy and I can eat our lunch—a sandwich for me, cheese and toast and apple slices for Lucy—and then we can spend an hour or so at the playground, more if we stop at the dog park, too. If we keep moving, maybe I can keep myself distracted enough not to dwell on Mona's phone. I will ask her about it when she gets home, and she will have an explanation. It will be fine. I navigate the stairs carefully, holding Lucy tight to me, and, by the third step down, I notice there is something resting on the floor by our front door.

"Mail is here," I tell Lucy, setting her down beside her pillow. But it's not a stack of mail, just a single envelope.

Theo's name on the front. A photograph inside.

This time, though, it's not a picture of a young boy. It's a grainy picture of me and Lucy, taken from a distance. We're in Rittenhouse Square, sitting on our plaid picnic blanket, a water bottle and bag of food and Lucy's stuffed turtle beside us. I flip it over, and on the back there's a handwritten note: WHAT IF IT WAS YOUR FAMILY?

The pain in my temple returns. I take a picture, send it to Theo, with the message: You said this was going to stop.

Jesus, Theo writes in response. Okay, I'm handling it.

It's not enough. I think about Mona's words the other night: *If there's something you want to know, you should ask.*

You need to tell me what's going on, I write. Ellipses on Theo's end appear and disappear.

Okay, he writes back. Can we talk about this tonight?

Mona will be here tonight, I respond.

Another pause, and then: Right. I'm taking a lunch break soon. Meet me in Love Park?

Theo is already sitting on one of the benches when we arrive, two coffees beside him and a croissant for Lucy.

"What's going on?" I ask. He rolls his head back, takes a breath.

"It's related to the kid case," he says. I know this already. "The pictures are coming from a family member of the victims. I haven't wanted to go into detail because . . ." He looks up, trying to find the right words, and then looks from Lucy to me. "It's really heavy, Lee. It's a lot."

"Who is it?"

"I don't think she'd do anything to hurt you and Lucy."

"You don't think."

"She wouldn't," he corrects himself. "She's a good person. She's just—she's lost a lot."

I know how that can change a person. I know what even good people are capable of.

"Who is it, Theo?"

He purses his lips.

"I'm not a child. You don't have to protect me."

"I *do*," he says, and suddenly his tone is different, tinged with frustration. "I *do* have to protect you. Ever since Lucy was born . . . I don't know what's going *on* with you. You're different. Fragile. Walled off. Everything's a potential threat to Lucy, and I couldn't—I didn't want to add to that."

"You can talk to me," I say.

"Can I?" he asks, sharp.

"Yes," I say, sinking down onto the bench, beside him. "Theo, I want to hear what's going on."

"I don't know what's happening," he says. "With you . . . between us . . ."

"I want to handle this together," I say. "You can tell me what's happening."

He inhales, a slow, shaky breath.

"The woman's name is Jane Aberdeen," he says.

I nod, wait for him to continue.

"My client, Charlie Mazur, has been in and out of prison for years, but it's all been drug-related, burglary, that kind of thing. Nothing . . . nothing violent."

His eyes are glassy; he won't look straight at me.

"I got the last charges against him dropped. The police screwed up the chain of evidence, didn't have enough to make it stick. It was a really good result, and he was getting set up with services."

Lucy hits her fist against the side of the stroller, babbling a string of syllables. Theo gives her a quick smile, but then his mouth twitches. He taps the bench divider with his index finger.

"A week after the charges were dropped, he breaks into this house. He thought it was empty, or maybe he just wasn't thinking at all. He was probably looking for something he could grab fast, money sitting out, that kind of thing."

My stomach twists as I realize where this is going.

"The house wasn't empty," I say.

"No," he says, shaking his head. "There was a confrontation, and it turned violent. Jane was out of town when it happened. But the rest of her family . . ."

He blinks. I can tell he's remembering something: the crime scene photos, maybe, the blood-spattered house, the boy's small hands. The conversation with his client afterward, the rambling explanations, the incoherent excuses.

"Oh, Theo," I say.

"It was awful. Really, really awful."

I picture the woman returning home. Digging in her purse for her keys, inserting them into the lock. Opening the door.

"I love what I do," Theo says, his eyes meeting mine again. He's looking for revulsion, for horror, for judgment. "I help people. The criminal justice system is so fucked up, it's *so* broken, and my clients need me to help them through it to have anything resembling a fair shot. Not *even* a fair shot." He shakes his head. "But Jesus. This case."

He raps his finger against the bench divider again, and I place my hand on his.

"Jane wanted someone to blame, obviously, someone to pin her anger on. She found out about the dropped charges, and that was it. And I don't—I don't think I did anything *wrong*. I didn't do anything wrong. I was doing my job, and I don't mean that in a following-orders way. I was doing a job I think is *important*. I was doing it *well*."

I nod, hoping he knows I understand. He doesn't have to explain himself to me.

"But it was so brutal, and it happened right after Lucy was born," he says, glancing toward the stroller again. "I'd come home and look at her and see that boy. And every time we got one of those pictures . . ."

"I'm sorry," I say.

Theo squeezes my hand.

A tiny long-haired dog runs up to us, sniffing Lucy's stroller, and Lucy kicks her legs happily, until the owner tugs the dog away, apologizing profusely.

"I've been trying to handle the photographs discreetly," Theo says. "She's already been through so much, and I didn't want to make things worse by involving the police." He leans back against the bench grating. "But you're right. These photos affect you, too. If you want to do more. . . ."

I shake my head. For the first time in months, I feel like I have a grasp on the situation. I have information, the truth, and I can handle things. I can face this head-on.

"No," I say. "You're right. She's a grieving mother."

"If you change your mind," Theo says, "or if things escalate, we can switch course. If this is making you feel unsafe—"

"It's not," I say. "It doesn't."

"Okay," Theo says, studying me for signs of uncertainty.

"I'm glad you told me," I say. "I want to be a team. I want to handle things together."

"That's what I want, too." He looks out to where the long-haired dog is running, takes a sip of his coffee.

"What's Mona doing today?" he asks, and it sounds like he's making an effort. Suddenly, I see his hesitation about her in a whole new light. The reason Theo, who has always stressed the importance of second chances, who claims everyone deserves the benefit of the doubt, is now suddenly skeptical. Mona is a stranger with a past he doesn't understand. Of course he's wary.

"I'm not sure," I say. "She's out somewhere."

He nods carefully.

"Does she ever tell you where she's going?" he asks. "Or who she spends her time around?"

"No," I say. I think about Mona's phone again, and my stomach turns.

Theo's phone buzzes, and he looks at the screen, grimaces.

"I've got to get back," he says. He looks at me again. "You're okay?"

"Yes," I say, and I mean it. This feels like a step forward. He pulls me into a hug and kisses Lucy's near-bald head. Once he disappears into the city, I google Jane Aberdeen and Charlie Mazur. The first image result is a family portrait, taken at Independence Hall. Jane's husband is beside her, and, in front of her, the boy from the photographs, with a buzz cut and oversized grin. Her hands cross protectively over his chest.

Lucy looks at me from her stroller, her turtle clutched in her hands.

"All right, sweet girl," I say, fighting to keep my voice steady. "Time to go."

She is here, I remind myself, *and she is mine.*

The front door is unlocked, despite the fact I have told Mona we always lock it, even when inside. *It's just safer that way,* I explained sheepishly, and she gave me a look like I didn't know what danger was. But she agreed she would lock it, too, and now it's open.

A small thing, I tell myself, stepping inside. *Not a big deal.*

But my thoughts return to the cellphone.

Mona is back, sitting on our couch, flipping through a book she has taken off our shelves. "Need help?" she asks, rising.

"I've got it," I say, setting Lucy on the rug and turning back for the stroller, still outside. I've been doing this for a long time now. I have my system down; I can manage on my own.

I try to remember our conversation on our first walk together: I asked Mona for her phone number, and she said *I don't have one.* I'm almost positive those were her words, clear and unambiguous.

"Where were you two?" she asks, a question that is apparently fine when she asks it but too much when I do.

Because she's trying to start over, I remind myself. *Because she's trying to move on from a life she's not proud of. And all you're doing is going to baby music class.*

"We saw Theo," I say.

"Oh?" she asks, waiting for more.

"Yeah." I take off my jacket. "I took your advice and asked him about the case he's working on."

"And did he tell you?" She scoops Lucy off the floor, and my body tenses. I will myself to relax.

"He did," I say. "I think it was a relief for both of us."

"That's great," Mona says. She bounces Lucy, gives her a wide, open-mouthed smile, and Lucy responds in kind.

"Mona—" I start, and my chest constricts, like this is a mistake, like I'm going down the wrong path. I stop, but she's already giving me a quizzical look. She knows something isn't right. "Do you have a phone?"

She blinks, hesitates a moment too long, like she's debating what to say.

"I saw a phone," I say. "In your room."

"You went in my room?" she asks.

"Yeah, sorry," I say. "I just needed to get an old box from up there. I wasn't looking, or, I mean, I didn't *mean* to look. I just saw it. On your bed."

"You don't have to apologize," Mona says. She turns so I can't see her face and walks toward the kitchen, Lucy still in her arms. I can't tell if I'm imagining it, or if there's a tightness to her tone. "It's your house."

I follow her.

"But is it . . . is it your phone?"

"Yeah," she says, rifling through the cabinet for mugs.

"I thought you didn't have one."

"I didn't," she says, lighting the burner under the kettle. "It's new."

"Oh," I say. I sink into a kitchen chair, unsure whether to feel relieved or foolish.

"I figure if I'm going to get a job, I need a phone number," she continues, pulling tea bags out of the pantry. "It's one of the first things they ask on all the applications. And also . . ." She shifts Lucy onto the other hip and turns to look at me. "I saw how nervous you got when you came home yesterday and couldn't find us. Which—of course, it's a totally natural response. If I'm going to watch Lucy, we need a way to get in touch with each other."

A simple, reasonable explanation; I knew there would be one.

"Thank you," I say. "I mean it. And sorry. I didn't mean to, like, give you the third degree." I feel a twist of guilt. She got this phone for me—for Lucy—and I let myself get carried away with paranoia.

The side of her mouth quirks up.

"You have nothing to apologize for," she says. "You and Theo have been so kind taking me in."

"Of course," I say. "You're my sister. You're always welcome here."

The problem is that I know so little. It's so easy to second-guess when there's no context, no larger narrative to help make sense of things. If I knew more about where Mona and the others had gone, what their lives looked like, there would be fewer misunderstandings. I could help more.

Mona turns her attention back to the kettle, and I grab my phone from the other room.

"What's your number?" I ask.

She gives it to me, and I enter it as a contact.

"It's just a burner," she says. "For now."

"We can help with that," I say. "If the problem is expense . . ."

She shakes her head. "It's not just the cost. It's the paperwork. I don't, you know, exactly have everything in order."

"Maybe we could add you to our phone plan," I say.

"You don't have to."

"I'll look into it," I promise. She hands me my tea, and I watch her, try to see the little girl I remember in her half-smile, in her shuffling gait.

"Have you thought about . . ." I pause. What I'm about to say is not in my best interest, but it might be in Mona's. "Have you thought about talking to someone official? Like the police, someone like that?"

Mona's eyes widen. She does not like this suggestion.

"I just mean . . . it could help. You could get a Social Security number, that kind of thing."

"I don't want to do that," she says.

"I know," I say quickly. "I understand."

It's not true, though. I understand so little.

I think of Officer Leanne. I could talk to her—not about Mona's reappearance, of course, but about Jacob's Hill in general. Maybe new information has come out in recent years, or maybe there is old information that I was too young to understand when the disappearance happened. Maybe she can help me fill in some of the blanks.

"Hey," I say to Mona. "Do you think you could maybe watch Lucy again tomorrow? She had such a good time with you yesterday."

"Yeah, of course," Mona says, and this time she gives me a full smile. "Where are you going?"

"Just catching up with an old friend," I say.

Tomorrow, I'll see what Officer Leanne can tell me.

CHAPTER TWENTY-FIVE

—

I park outside the Strathhaven police station. In my memory, the building is massive, a fortress, but now I see it for what it is: a simple brick municipal building with a flagpole out front, not many windows.

You can do this, I tell myself, and I head inside.

There's a window in the entryway. Behind it sits an older receptionist, gray hair pulled back into a bun, glasses perched on the end of her nose. Next to the window, the heavy gray door I remember from childhood, locked. The receptionist looks up, leans forward.

"Can I help you?" she asks, her voice muffled by the glass.

"Yeah," I say, stepping forward. "I'm here to see Officer Leanne Paciullo."

"Leanne retired a few years ago." She smiles. "She wanted to spend more time with her grandkids."

"Oh," I say, caught off guard. "Well, could I—is there some way I can reach her?"

She tilts her head, assessing. "Can I ask what this is regarding?" Still friendly, but more guarded. I think of the photographs from Jane Aberdeen. Leanne was a police officer for multiple decades. Strathhaven is much quieter than the city, but she has probably had her fair share of run-ins.

"She helped me a long time ago," I say. I take out my ID and slide it through the cutout in the bottom of the window. "My married name is Ophelia Burton, but it used to be Ophelia Clayborne."

"Oh," the receptionist says, recognition dawning. "You know what, let me check on something."

She moves away from the window, pulls out her phone, and makes a call. I can no longer make out what she's saying through the glass, but I see her nodding her head, glancing back at me. I brace myself for a *no, sorry, we can't help you.*

"Leanne would love to see you," she says, returning to the window. She jots something on a piece of scrap paper and slides it to me along with my ID. "Here's her phone number and her address. She said she's home right now if you'd like to stop by. She's only a few blocks from here."

"Thank you," I say.

"Of course, honey," she tells me, and the way she says it, like I'm still a lost child, makes me wonder if she saw me come into the station that day twenty years ago.

Officer Leanne's house is past the elementary school, with its tall chain fence and blacktop full of children. Girls perch on monkey bars, their legs dangling; boys pelt each other with balls inside a wooden enclosure. There's a small girl with long, dark hair alone on one of the swings, and for a moment I see Mona as a child. The girl's head turns, a different, unfamiliar angle, and she jumps from the swing to find her friends, landing on sturdy legs, sprinting across the rubbery ground. My heart aches.

It's okay, I tell myself. *She's back. She came back.*

I turn onto a residential street full of Victorian houses. I check the mailbox numbers as they tick down: 65, 63, 61.

And finally, there it is: number 59. Leaves are heaped into neat piles by the curb, the last of the season. A child-sized tractor and scooter and bucket of chalk sit out on the driveway, next to a foldout camping chair. I walk up the front path nervously, unsure of what to expect. I ring the doorbell.

Leanne answers the door with a baby on her hip and a wide smile across her face.

"Lee," she says. "It's so good to see you. Come on in."

There are pictures everywhere. The first ones are older, Leanne's son Max. They show him growing into adulthood, and then having children of his own, and then their pictures begin to dominate the walls, a boy, a girl, and the baby Leanne is holding now.

"Are these your grandkids?" I ask.

"Sure are," Leanne says. "Benny, Anna, and this one here is Lincoln."

"They're beautiful," I say.

"Thank you." She gestures toward the kitchen table. I take a seat. "Do you have kids now?"

"A daughter." I show her a picture of Lucy, and she smiles.

"Wonderful," she says.

She makes us tea and pulls out a sleeve of cookies from the pantry. She asks what I'm doing, and she looks genuinely happy to hear about my job at the Academy, about Theo, about our life in Philadelphia. Max lived in the city for a while, too, she says, but he moved back here when Anna was born, and that's when she retired.

"Do you miss it?" I ask.

"Oh, sure, sometimes," she says. "But these rascals keep me pretty busy."

She looks at me, deciding whether to keep things pleasant or say what's on her mind.

"I've never stopped thinking about you," she says. "How have you been? Since . . ."

She doesn't finish the sentence. She doesn't have to.

"I've been fine," I say. "I've been doing much better."

"When you were in Pittsburgh—"

"It was stress," I say, cutting her off. "I was under a lot of stress, and I didn't handle it well. But I've gotten it under control."

A psychotic episode is what the doctors called it. I now know the woman I saw in the grocery store was not really Terese. I know the man in my apartment building was truly just a repairman, hired by my landlord who never notified his tenants of anything. But the idea of losing my aunt sent me into a tailspin, and I couldn't pull myself out of it.

"I'm happy to hear that," Leanne says, but she's looking at me with a police officer's skepticism, sizing me up.

"In fact," I say, "that's part of the reason I'm here. I'm in a much better place, and I want to understand what was happening. At Jacob's Hill."

"Lee," she says, leaning back in her chair. "We just don't know. There haven't been any new leads in a long time."

"I don't just mean the disappearance," I say. "I want to understand what life was like there. I have my own memories, but I was just a kid."

"We don't know that, either," Leanne says, gently. "Christopher was very secretive. Most of what we understand about the day-to-day life there was from you."

"But wasn't there . . . I don't know. Surveillance? Something?"

Leanne thinks about this and then leans forward, placing her arms on the table. "There was some surveillance before the disappearance, yes. If I'm remembering correctly, there was a point at which FBI agents had parked outside the compound to see who was coming and going."

"Were there recordings of us?" I ask. I remember Christopher's fears, *they're listening,* the magnets he buried around the property to interfere with their signals. Leanne purses her lips. My questions are making her uncomfortable.

"No. It never got that far."

"What about the other family members?" I ask. "Maybe they know something. Maybe some of them visited Jacob's Hill or spoke with their family before the disappearance."

Or maybe—although I do not say this to Leanne—their sisters and nephews and aunts have returned to them, too.

Leanne shakes her head. "Lee," she says.

"I just want to understand," I say. "If I could talk to them . . ."

As soon as the words come out of my mouth, I know it's true: I need to hear what they have to say. It was Anne's decision to keep me apart from them before. I went along with it, at her urging. She was worried it would be too much for me, or that they might be too unstable. She thought it safest to keep our distance, and maybe it was, back then. But that was a long time ago, and I am ready now.

And now, it's not just for me. It's for Mona, too.

"I'm not sure that's a good idea," Leanne says.

"It's not—it's not like before," I say. "This would be for healing."

My last conversation with Leanne had been in Pittsburgh, after I saw Terese in the grocery store. I called Leanne and asked if there had been any updates on the case. I must have sounded manic because she tried to shift the conversation to more personal questions—where was I, how was I doing—and I told her I was fine, better than fine. I was close to finding out where they were.

They're here, I said. *In Pittsburgh. I saw Terese Taylor.*

A pause, and then Leanne's voice, cautious: *Did you talk to her?*

She pretended not to recognize me, I said. *But it was her.*

There was a long, uncomfortable silence on the other end, and no indication Leanne was writing anything down: no keys clicking, no scratch of pen against paper. She didn't believe me. Instead of asking more about Terese, she asked if I was still in touch with my aunt, if I had talked to her about this.

She's had some recent medical issues, I said. *She's not well.*

Oh, Lee, she said. *I'm so sorry.*

"I wish I had stepped in sooner back then," Leanne says now. "I'm sorry I didn't . . . I'm sorry I didn't see where things were going."

"There's nothing you could have done," I say. "And I'm fine now. I'm good."

"You have support?" Leanne asks.

"Yes," I say. "I'm seeing a therapist." A part truth, to put her at ease. "Her name is Dr. Dana, and she's wonderful. She's actually the one who suggested I reach out to the other families. She thought maybe we could heal together. So if you know how to contact them . . ."

"I have some contact information," she says slowly. "I'm not sure how up-to-date it is. It's been a long time."

"That's okay," I say. "Anything helps. Even if you just have their names, I could—"

"I'm also not sure," she continues in the same cautious tone, "that everyone is going to want to talk about what happened." She pauses, like she's considering saying something else—*they're not going to want to talk to you*—but stops herself. "It's been a long time," she says instead. "The families may have found their own versions of closure, and if you contact them, without . . ."

"There is no closure," I say. "Not from something like this. Not without answers." *And I have answers now,* I want to say, *I can give them hope,* but I know this is not my place, and also not something Leanne would be open to hearing. She wouldn't be able to see past Terese and Pittsburgh and everything that happened before.

She nods, stirring her tea slowly. "Do you think," she says finally, "Dr. Dana might be willing to talk with me? Just a chat to get on the same page, and if she still thinks it would be helpful for you to talk with the other family members, maybe I can set something up."

"Of course," I say, my heart sinking. A dead end. "I'm sure she'd be happy to do that."

It's pouring when I return home, the rain falling in heavy sheets. I have no new information from my visit with Leanne, and shame-filled memories of Pittsburgh are swirling in my mind.

But maybe I don't need Leanne's help. I can find the family members on my own. I have three names to start: Amy Price, Gregory Dunn, and Elise Dagnelle, the three outspoken relatives, the ones mentioned in all the articles. I google them from the front seat of my car. Gregory lives in Connecticut, and Amy—or the Amy I'm looking for, anyway—does not show up in a quick search. But Elise

Dagnelle is in Ridley Park, just outside the city. She's a hairdresser at Elements Hair Salon, a place I can call. A place I can go.

Before I can overthink it, I tap the number on the screen.

"Elements," says a bored voice on the other end of the line.

"Hi," I say. "I'd like to book a haircut? With Elise? As soon as possible."

Some tapping, and then: "Elise is pretty booked up for the next few weeks. I can get you in with one of our other stylists, though, if you want something sooner."

"Oh no," I say. "That's okay. I can wait." She takes down my real phone number and a fake name—Sarah—and tells me she'll call me if anything opens up sooner.

I pocket my phone, my heart racing, and step out into the rain. I am still thinking of Pittsburgh as I walk the remaining block home. I swing open my front door to Lucy and Mona sitting on the kitchen floor, next to a large bin filled with oatmeal and plastic toys. "Old MacDonald" is playing over the speakers, and Mona is impersonating a duck, poorly, and Lucy is laughing.

This is what matters, I remind myself. *My family. Together.*

"Oh no!" Mona says when she sees me, breaking off mid-verse. "You're soaked!"

"It's gross out there," I say, hanging my coat.

"We weren't expecting you home so soon," Mona says. She gestures to the oats scattered across the floor. "Don't worry, I plan on cleaning this up."

I wave her off, *it's fine,* and then hear the rattle of a vibrating phone. Mona's phone is out, sitting on the secretary desk by the door. I grab it to bring it to her. Without thinking, I look at the screen.

A number, no name.

What are you going to do about the baby?

My body goes cold. I take steps toward them—Mona on the floor, Lucy leaning on her for support—but I am on autopilot, my mind buzzing. Mona's smile wavers when she sees my face, and I hand her the phone without meeting her eyes. She looks at the text, sniffs.

"What does that mean?" I ask.

Theo's words: *Keep some distance between her and Lucy.*

The baby. Is that referring to Lucy? And if so . . .

"Oh," she says. She's still looking at her phone, like she's trying to make sense of it, too. "I—"

"What does it mean, Mona?"

She finally looks up at me, and there are tears in her eyes, but I don't understand what's happening here. I'm trying to make sense of the words, what they signify.

"I didn't mean to keep it a secret."

"Keep *what* a secret?"

I grab Lucy, pull her against me. She arches her back, unhappy about the sudden interruption, the tightness of my grip. Mona startles, surprised, and then I see it dawning on her.

"This has nothing to do with Lucy," she says, trying to put me at ease, but it's not working. "It's me." She stands, and her hand goes to her belly. "I'm going to be a mother, too."

"You're . . ." My eyes drift involuntarily down, but I can't make out anything beneath her baggy sweatshirt.

"That's why I came to find you. The life I was leading . . . it was fine for me, but not if I'm bringing someone else into the world."

The life you were leading where? I want to ask. With Christopher and the others, somewhere off the grid? In and out of homeless shelters and motel rooms somewhere in the city? *What happened to you? What kind of life have you led?*

Instead, I tread carefully. "Do you know how far along you are?"

"Four months," she says. "Give or take."

I study her narrow wrists, her tiny frame. I'd never have guessed. But everything she wears is so loose, concealing.

"What's going on with the father?" I ask. I nod toward the phone in her hands. "Is that him?" She tenses, shutting down again, unable to answer.

"Sorry," I say. "I shouldn't—"

"I want to keep it," she interrupts, defensively, like I might try to talk her out of it. "I want to have this baby."

"I understand," I say. "And I'm here for you. I want to help."

"Thank you." She wipes her cheek with the back of her hand. "Because I don't think I can do this alone."

"You don't have to."

"I don't have a job." She sinks into one of the kitchen chairs, resting her forehead in her hand. "I don't have a place to live. I have no idea what I'm doing."

"You do have a place to live," I say. "You live here. And we can help you with all the rest."

"I can't keep imposing on you forever."

"You are not imposing," I say. I set Lucy in her high chair and hold out my arms, and Mona stands again, hugs me back, resting her head on my shoulder. Her heart is pounding, the knobs of her spine so pronounced beneath my hands.

"It's okay," I say. "We're going to figure this out. We'll figure it out together."

She composes herself, pulls back, takes in a ragged breath.

"Tea?" I ask.

"Yes," she says. "Please."

"Uncaffeinated?"

"I don't care."

I put the kettle on the stove and sit with Mona. Her hands are shaking. She's terrified.

"It's amazing," I say. "Becoming a mother. And frightening, and overwhelming, but it's incredible, too. And the way you are with Lucy—you're going to be a great mom. I can see it already."

Mona smiles, pulls at the short strands of her hair.

"Talking about it makes it feel real," she says.

"We should get you in to see a doctor."

"I don't have insurance."

"We'll get it." I think of the hours my aunt spent on the phone, the appointments, the paperwork, all just to establish I was a person, to get me an identity. "And Jacqueline is . . . Jacqueline, but she knows everyone in the city, and she does a lot of work with women who are in tough spots. She'll be able to help."

"You think she'd do that?"

"She offered at dinner, and I'm sure she meant it," I say. "She likes having a project. It's one of her better qualities."

Theo, too. Maybe this will help him come around. Mona is in need. She's trying to turn her life around. We can help her.

"Okay," she says. She nods, trying to convince herself.

"It's going to be fine," I say, squeezing her hand. "Better than fine." A baby. A cousin for Lucy.

"What if I can't do this?" she says.

"You can," I say. "We both can. We can do it together."

The rain keeps up all through the afternoon and into the evening, trapping us inside. Fey and Niko have brought over a board game, one with cards and tokens and a complicated set of rules, and Niko is trying to explain them to me and Mona as Theo mixes drinks in the kitchen. Mona's face is scrunched, disapproval Niko misreads as confusion.

"It sounds more complicated than it is," Niko says. "You'll figure it out as you go along."

Theo emerges from the kitchen with two Negronis and hands them to Niko and Fey.

"Ladies first," Niko says, passing his drink to Mona, and I am about to say something, provide her with an excuse, but she accepts the drink from him and takes a small sip.

"Delicious," she says, smiling approvingly at Theo. He ducks back into the kitchen and returns with three more drinks for Niko, himself, and me. *It was just a sip*, I tell myself. *Don't be judgmental.*

"Did you go somewhere today?" Theo asks, settling into the couch and draping an arm behind me.

I glance at Mona, who gives me a small shake of her head; she has not said anything.

"We were mostly around here," I say, cautiously. Theo frowns, glances toward the door.

"The car isn't out front."

"Oh," I say. "That's right. It's one block over, on Twenty-Fifth. We went out to Wissahickon this morning." A park on the outskirts of the city.

"Nice," Theo says, lifting his glass toward our guests, *cheers*. "How was it?"

"Good," I say, hoping he doesn't feel my discomfort.

"Lucy really seemed to enjoy being out in nature," Mona says, building on my lie.

"Those trails are so good for long runs," Fey says. She has been training for a half-marathon and loves to talk about it, but this evening I don't mind. "Theo, we've got to get you back out there."

Her hand on his arm.

"I think I'm on hiatus from long runs for the time being," Theo says, good-naturedly. "At least until work calms down and Lucy starts sleeping better."

"Work doesn't calm down," Fey says. "That's just a lie we tell ourselves. You have to make time for the things that matter to you."

"I know, I know," Theo says, sipping his drink and looking away, and I can't tell if I am imagining things or if there is something behind this banter, a hidden subtext. I think of Mona's suggestion the other night: *Have they ever been involved?*

I think of Theo's late nights.

Stop, I tell myself. I'm being paranoid, seeing things that aren't there. Niko appears unconcerned, responding to a text or email on his phone, and he'd notice, too, if things were off. Wouldn't he?

"I need a cig," Fey says, looking around the room. "Can someone keep me company?"

"Babe," Niko says, looking up from his phone. "It's pouring."

Fey lingers, and I feel another twinge of discomfort: Is she trying to get Theo alone? But Theo just cocks an eyebrow and says: "You'd run a lot faster if you cut that shit out, you know."

"I'll join you," Mona says, and a surprised smile tugs at the corners of Fey's mouth. "Can I bum one?"

"Of course," Fey says, and Mona follows her out the back door. She doesn't meet my eye, but neither does she appear embarrassed or apologetic. I think about her pregnancy, the baby, but try to push the thought aside. She's doing so much to get her life together. Who am I to judge?

"Have things at work gotten any better? With . . ." Niko asks, intentionally vague in case I don't know.

Theo squeezes my knee. "I think we're close to a plea deal. So it should be over soon, thank god."

Niko shakes his head. "I don't know how you do it, man," he says. "That's some real heavy shit."

"Someone has to," Theo says, shaking his head and taking a large sip of his drink. I lean into his side and he slides his arm down over my shoulder, squeezes back. "I'm looking forward to putting this one behind me, though."

The back door slides open, and Fey is laughing and Mona is smiling like they have a shared secret, and the smell of smoke wafts into the house behind them.

"Got your fix?" Theo asks, and Fey waves him off.

"Just getting to know your sister-in-law a little better," she says with a wink. She claps her hands together, turns to look at the rest of us. "Okay, let's play!"

CHAPTER TWENTY-SIX

Mona joins Lucy and me at the playground this morning, sitting with us on our plaid picnic blanket. Lucy has scooted to the edge and examines a blade of grass like she's trying to determine whether it's edible. Behind us, three little girls hop from tree stump to tree stump, singing a song they've invented themselves. Mona watches with what looks like a mix of interest and terror, and I can tell she's trying to picture herself in this life.

"Have you spent a lot of time around kids?" I ask, hoping this question does not cross a line. Mona shrugs, rocks her head from side to side.

"A little," she says, "but it's not the same."

"No," I agree. "It's not."

"I have a hard time wrapping my mind around what it will be like. To be responsible for someone like that."

"I don't think anyone can really understand it before they've experienced it," I say. But a part of my mind flashes to Mona, swaddled in a cotton blanket, Adrienne placing her in my arms.

"I can see her and Lucy playing together on those stumps someday," I say. Mona does not know for sure that she's having a girl, but she has a gut feeling, and so that's how we refer to the baby. "They're going to be lucky to have each other."

Mona smiles, but her eyes drift across the playground, like she's looking for someone. Lucy scoots toward Mona, and Mona's attention returns, a smile stretching across her face. They look so sweet together. Without even thinking, I lift my phone and take a picture.

"Don't," Mona says, her tone sharp.

"Oh," I say, dropping my phone back down. "Sorry, I just—"

"No, it's fine," she says, still on edge. "I just really don't like pictures."

"Sure," I say. I should have known better. "I should have asked." And then, changing the subject: "I have something for you."

"What is it?" she asks, her voice softening. We have already talked about the many things babies need—bassinets and blankets and bottle systems—and I told Mona she was welcome to any of Lucy's things. Lucy will have outgrown them by the time the baby arrives, and it will be nice to see them put to a new use.

"This one's for you," I say. I reach into my backpack until my fingers touch the cold metal chain, our mother's bracelet.

"Mom gave this to me for my twelfth birthday. Right before—"

I break off, unable to finish the thought.

I think your mother gave that to you for a reason, Anne told me once. We were in the kitchen, and I was sitting at the wooden table, fidgeting with the chain. *I gave it to her, and she gave it to you. She wanted us to find each other.*

My mother didn't plan on leaving me, I told her.

Oh no, Anne said. *I know. That's not what I meant.*

Now, I drop the bracelet into Mona's palm. She turns it over in her hands, examining the heart charm, the chain.

"I don't think it's especially nice or anything," I say. "But it was hers."

"I can't take this," Mona says. She holds it out for me, and I shake my head.

"Yes, you can," I say. I'm having trouble saying out loud what I've always believed about the bracelet: that it held a piece of our mother in it, that it was her way of protecting me, that it helped keep me safe out in the world, without her. Mona needs that protection now, too.

"You and Mom had a special relationship," I say instead. Mona, with one foot in this world and one foot in the next. Mona, the daughter our mother chose to take with her. "It's a gift for you and for the baby. You can give it to her when she's old enough."

She hesitates, and I think she's about to protest again, but then she folds her fingers around the silver chain, nods her head.

"Okay," she says softly. "Thank you."

My phone buzzes beside me. I look at the screen: a caller from Ridley Park. The hair salon. I answer.

"Hi, Sarah?" says the voice on the other end. I flush with embarrassment, but I don't think Mona is close enough to hear the fake name.

"Yeah," I say. "That's me."

"Elise just had a last-minute cancellation for this afternoon. If you're still interested."

"Oh," I say, looking toward Mona, who is mouthing *who is that.*

I pull the phone back. "Hair salon," I say. "They just had an appointment open up."

"Go!" she says, giving me a thumbs-up.

"It's kind of far."

"That's fine."

"Okay," I say to the receptionist. "I can do it. What time should I be there?"

I take an Uber to Ridley Park instead of driving myself. I feel a momentary twinge of panic on the highway when I realize this trip will show up on our credit card statement, but a single Uber charge will not stand out as unusual. And even if Theo does notice, I could be doing anything out here: visiting a playground with Lucy, picking apples at an orchard. I just have a guilty conscience, that's all. I have nothing to feel bad about. There is nothing wrong with leaving Lucy with her aunt.

We pass through sprawl and into wooded suburbs, thick patches of maples and oaks transporting me back. I think about what our lives will be like when Mona has her baby. I picture Lucy and her cousin in woods like these, watching for birds and foxes, walking barefooted in a creek bed. For once, I can see Lucy as a little girl, a ten-year-old in a tree house, a teenager at a campfire in the woods.

Maybe this is what we need. A fresh start, outside the city, somewhere more like this. Theo might be resistant to the idea at first—he loves the city, after all—but it's his pre-child life that he's really imagining when he says he wants to stay. He didn't grow up with the woods, so he doesn't understand how magical they can be. Mona and I could look out for each other, help each other, make sure nothing bad ever happens.

Just as suddenly as the woods started, they stop again, and we are on a long stretch of big-box stores and strip malls. Elements Hair Salon is in one of these, between a karate dojo and a medical testing site. The Uber driver drops me off, and I brace myself, walk inside. When I open the door, I'm hit with the chemical smell of bleach and hairspray. There are a few women working, all in black aprons and sneakers, chatting with their clients. I spot Elise immediately. She looks like Adrienne, so much so that grief ripples through me.

"I'm here to see Elise?" I say to the girl at the front desk.

"Sarah?" she asks, and I nod.

"Elise is just finishing up."

I sit on the low leather couch, flip through a copy of *Us Weekly*, pretend to look at the pictures. My hands are shaking. *Calm down*, I tell myself. *You're just here to talk.* She'll want to hear from me; she'll want to know that Mona has come back. Maybe she'll have her own good news to share, too.

"Sarah?"

Elise is smiling at me, ready to shake my hand. Close up I can see the lines on her face, the same lines Adrienne would have if she were still here. My heart jumps at the memory of her. I wonder if she's appeared to Elise in secret; if Elise knows the truth, too.

"What are we doing today?"

"I just need it cleaned up," I say as she pulls my hair out of its ponytail and hands me the elastic. "It's been a long time."

She nods, *not a problem.*

"I have a seven-month-old," I explain.

She smiles warmly. "I know how that goes."

She takes me back to the row of sinks, puts a towel over my shoulders, and asks me to lean back. Her hands are on my scalp, and I can't help but think of Adrienne's hands. Adrienne showed me how to braid, collecting the strands of hair, little by little, her fingers moving fast. *You should practice on your sister,* she told me. *It's easier on someone else.* When I tried to braid Mona's hair later that day, she howled and wrenched herself away.

Elise asks me to sit up, directs me to her seat. She brushes out my hair, studying the ends, a mess, I'm sure.

"You live around here?" she asks.

"In the city," I say without thinking.

"And you came all the way out here for a haircut?"

I freeze, swallow. "My sister lives out here," I say. "She's watching the baby."

"Nice to have family nearby." A throw-away comment. She combs a lock of my hair, snips off an inch.

"Are you from here?" I ask.

"Mm hmm," she says. Another lock, another inch. "All my life."

"Is your family around here, too?"

"They are."

"I think we might know someone in common," I say. She does not react to this. This is a town where lots of people know people in common. "Do you have a sister named Adrienne?"

She stops snipping for a moment but then resumes. "I did."

"She disappeared?"

She drops her hand, meets my eyes in the mirror. "Is this about the show?"

I shift in my seat. The hairstylist and client beside me stop chatting. They're listening now, too. The client gapes at me in the reflection of her mirror, her head half-full of foils. I catch her eye and she looks away.

"I—"

Elise realizes that others are watching, too, and she lowers her voice. "This is my place of work, do you understand that? This isn't some stupid game. My sister—"

"I know," I say. "This isn't about the documentary. I lost my family, too. Or I thought I did, but—"

"You had family members at Jacob's Hill?" Elise asks. She observes me skeptically; she doesn't believe me. "What were their names?"

"Sylvie Sorensen," I say. "And Mona."

"Jesus Christ," Elise says, softly at first, and then again, louder. She shakes her head, her expression changing from doubtful to angry. The hairstylist beside us sets down her scissors, like she might need to step in. "You're Ophelia?"

"I—"

"What did you do to them?" she asks, gripping her shears tightly.

I don't have much time. "They came back," I say. "Or Mona did—that's why I'm here. Maybe Adrienne—"

"What did you do?" she asks again, not listening.

"They're alive. They're okay. They're still out there. I came here because I thought maybe Adrienne had come back to see you. Mona came back to see me."

"Bullshit," she says. "I don't want to hear this."

"I thought you'd want to know," I say, grasping for words. "I thought maybe—maybe Mona wasn't the only one—"

"That's enough," Elise says. "I need you to get out of my chair."

I am already scrambling to un-Velcro the barber cape around my neck. I see the woman in the chair next to me grappling for her purse, pulling out her phone, and I hold up my arm, using the cape to block my face. I should have known this was a terrible idea. I didn't think this through.

"I know the truth about you," Elise says. "I saw the stories. I know what you did."

I jump down from the seat.

"I always knew you were hiding something," Elise continues. I try to step around her, but she blocks my way, not finished, her hand still holding the shears. "At first, I thought maybe you were hiding under a bed when he . . ." She breaks off. I can see now that the whole salon is watching. I can't shield myself from everyone.

"But then I saw those stories."

"I'm sorry," I mutter, eyes cast down at the floor. "I shouldn't have come here."

"I know you helped him. That's why you're still here and Adrienne is gone."

"I didn't." I'm able to push past now, but she turns, keeps shouting.

"Don't lie to me," she says. "Did you hide the bodies for him? Did you burn them? Is that what you did?"

I dodge around the gaping receptionist, through a cluster of women at the front door. I can't breathe.

"Where are they?" she shouts out the door after me. "You know where they are. What did you do with them?"

CHAPTER TWENTY-SEVEN

—

I have the Uber driver drop me off at a CVS near our house so I can purchase a pair of scissors. I even out my hair in a Starbucks bathroom with hesitant, uncertain snips. Pieces fall to the porcelain sink and I wipe them into my palm and throw them in the trash.

If my aunt were still here, she'd tell me that Elise's reaction was not really about me. *She's hurt and lashing out. She needs someone to blame.*

But my aunt isn't here anymore.

Outside, a helicopter hovers above me, the choppy beat of propellers echoing off the city buildings. I try to ignore my jangled nerves, try to focus, again, on the images that made me so happy just an hour ago: Lucy and her cousin playing hide-and-seek in the forest; Lucy and her cousin in a flower bed, holding long, writhing earthworms in their hands.

I swing the front door open.

Theo is in our kitchen. Home early.

"What the fuck, Lee."

He is here, and he is furious. He charges toward the front door, his face red, his jaw clenched. I step back instinctively, almost drop my keys.

"What are you doing here?" I ask.

It's the wrong question. He looks at me, incredulous.

"Where were you?"

"I had a—I was getting my hair cut."

"And you left Lucy here."

He almost spits out the words, his hands balled into fists.

"I left Lucy with Mona. Mona was watching her."

He rolls his head, stalks toward the kitchen and then back toward me, like he's trying to keep it together.

"It was just for a little while—"

"Jesus Christ, Lee."

"She's good with her, Theo."

My guilt gives way to indignation: Why *should* I apologize? Mona *is* good with Lucy, and I never agreed to keep them apart. It was an ultimatum, not a discussion.

"I told you to be careful around her." He's speaking slowly, with an artificial calmness, and I can see he is consciously trying to de-escalate. "I told you to keep her away from Lucy until we got to know her better. And then you move her into our house, without asking me, and now you're leaving *Lucy* with her? *Alone?*"

"Lucy loves her. Mona is her aunt. She—"

"She's *not* her aunt," Theo shouts, losing control, and I brace myself reflexively. He looks like he's surprised even himself, and he presses his lips together before talking again. "That woman is not your sister."

"What are you talking about?"

He looks at me for a moment, waiting for me to speak, and then shakes his head, disgusted, when I don't.

"You're still not going to tell me? After all this?"

My heart sinks. "Tell you what?"

"I know, Lee. I know what happened."

He looks at me expectantly, almost hopefully, like maybe there's still a way I could save this. Maybe I'll deny it, and it will all turn out to be a misunderstanding. Maybe I'll have an explanation, something that can turn this around.

Instead, I ask: "How?" and his face crumples.

"How could you keep something like this from me?" he asks. "We built a *life* together, Lee. We have a *child*. And it turns out I don't know a single fucking thing about you."

I don't have a response, so I ask again: "How did you find out?"

"I found out," Theo says, his voice rising again, "because there's a fucking *documentary* about you. The question isn't how I *found out*, it's how was I the last person in the *country* to know about it?"

"I didn't want you to see me differently," I say, barely able to get the words out. "When people find out, it—it eclipses everything else about me. I wanted to start over. I wanted to have a normal life with you."

"You never thought maybe you could give me more credit than that?" Theo says. "If you had just *told* me, we could have navigated this together."

I can see that he really believes that.

"I wasn't sure," I say softly. "You don't know what it's been like."

"You're right," he says. "I have no fucking clue what it's been like for you, because you never told me."

The house is unnaturally silent.

"Where is Lucy?" I ask.

"She's fine. She's with my mom."

"Where is Mona?"

"She's not Mona!" Theo shouts, his voice reverberating through the house. "I don't know who the fuck that woman is, but she's not your sister."

"She is—"

"Your sister is *dead*, Lee. Your sister and mother aren't estranged. They're dead."

"You don't know that."

"They've been gone for twenty years."

"They—"

"Christopher killed them. If they were alive, they would have shown up somewhere by now. *Someone* would have."

"Mona did," I say. "Mona came here. She sought me out."

"No, Lee." Theo is talking slowly again, like I'm a child. "That woman is not your sister. She's a grifter. She showed up at our house after hearing about you on TV. *That's* what happened."

"She knew things."

"The whole country knows things!" Theo rubs his hands down his face. "You didn't think the timing was the slightest bit suspicious?"

"Where is she?"

"I came home to ask you about . . ." He waves his hands. "All this. And then instead of finding you and Lucy here, I find Lucy with that woman, who . . . I told you, Lee. I told you from the very first day, there was something wrong with her. But you told me she was your sister, and I didn't think that was something you could be *wrong* about. I didn't know you hadn't seen your sister since she was *six* and *disappeared.*"

I can't breathe. The sharp pain in my temple has returned.

"What did you say to her?"

"I told her I knew," he says. "I told her I knew she wasn't Mona, that she was taking advantage of you. I said we'd do a DNA test. Press charges. That's all it took."

"No." The walls are closing in on me.

"She didn't even deny it, Lee. As soon as I mentioned a test, she packed her things and left."

"I don't understand," I say. "Why would she lie?"

"People lie all the time. About everything."

The words are barbed.

"She knew things that weren't in the documentary," I say.

"She was telling you what you wanted to hear," Theo says. "She's a con artist. That's what people like her do. They ask you questions, and they throw out bait and see if you take it, and if you don't they try something else."

"How did she know about the night terrors?"

"I have no idea what she did and didn't know and where she got it from," Theo says. "What I know is that a documentary comes out, *about you,* and then a woman shows up at our house—who you've never seen before—claiming to be your sister. She only parcels out information when she feels like it, because of 'trauma,' and as soon as someone calls her on her bullshit, she runs away. That's all I need to know."

I don't know how to respond. Theo is looking me up and down, like he's debating whether to say this next part. He must decide there's no point in holding back.

"I googled your real name."

"This is my real name."

"Your former name. Clayborne."

It hits me like a gut punch. He knows what happened in Pittsburgh. He knows what my mind is capable of.

"I want to see Lucy."

"You need to get help."

"Theo." I step toward him, and he steps away, around me.

"You need help, and I need to clear my head. I need some time to think. I just don't know what to think right now."

"Theo—" I say again, but he won't look at me anymore. He slams the door shut behind him.

CHAPTER TWENTY-EIGHT

—

Ten years earlier

At night in Pittsburgh, I could hear their voices in the static of my white noise machine, like whispered conversations at first, the hiss of my name emerging, and then more words, Christopher's voice, garbled and distorted. At first I didn't know what he was saying, but then it struck me. Of course.

Open your eyes, Ophelia. Open your eyes.

It's time to come home.

After the disappearance, I was a victim. After Pittsburgh, I was something else altogether.

I canvassed supermarkets and feed stores and hardware stores across the city. I showed an old picture of my mother—the one from her first and only year of college, the one where she was pregnant with me—to anyone who would look.

Have you seen her? I asked. *She'd be older now. Can you look closer?* But no one recognized her.

Look closer, I said. *Please.*

I imbued small things with an oversized importance, coincidences with weighty significance. I marked the stores where a cashier had responded to my questions with uncertainty rather than outright dismissal, taking these to be promising leads. I paid close attention to bus routes 27, 87, and 93 because those were the pages folded in my mother's book.

I interpreted an unfamiliar set of tire tracks in the slushy frost on my driveway one afternoon as something sinister, rather than what they almost certainly were: tracks from a delivery truck, from my landlord's car, from a workman's van.

This was ten days after finals week, and no one was supposed to be at our house. My neighbors had all gone home for winter break, and I didn't expect to see them again until mid-January, when spring semester began.

Maybe one of them came back for something, I told myself, but I didn't believe it.

What I thought—what I believed I knew at a cellular level—was that my family had been there. They were keeping tabs on me, trying to determine whether I was ready. Whether I could join them.

I bolted for the house, ran up the two flights of dingy stairs. The duct tape on the wall outside my apartment door had been torn off, the pinpoint holes once again visible. And I know now this was likely my landlord, annoyed by what he almost certainly viewed as "property destruction," never mind the broken spindles and light fixtures that escaped his attention year after year. But at the time, I thought there was only one explanation: My family had been there, and they wanted to see my comings and goings. The tape was interfering with their ability to surveil me.

Inside my apartment, everything was just as I had left it. Dishes piled high in my sink. Duct tape zigzagged the walls. Notepads covered my kitchen table, with lists of stores and dates and cashiers I had spoken with, along with notes about our conversation: *no, maybe, can't be sure.*

I tore the duct tape off the walls, addressed the pinpoint holes I was so sure contained cameras.

"I know you're watching. I'm ready now. Please."

I waited, but there was no response.

"I'm not closed anymore. I'm open. I'm ready."

They were silent, and I knew it was because they didn't believe me. These were just empty words. They needed proof I was ready to leave this world for a new one.

I tore a sheet from my notepad, and then another, and then another, crumpling them and throwing them across the kitchen tile. I emptied the recycling bin onto the floor, mostly cardboard and papers, uncorked a bottle of wine, soaked them with it.

It won't be easy, Christopher used to say. *We are weak creatures. We love the world too much.*

I unspooled long stretches of toilet paper, doused it in rubbing alcohol from under the sink.

"Are you watching?" I shouted, turning so they could see me from all angles. "I know you're watching. I'm ready. Come get me."

I lit a match.

PART THREE

—

RESISTANCE

CHAPTER TWENTY-NINE

—

The house is quiet, a constant reminder I am alone. It has never felt like this before, not even when Lucy was sleeping and Theo was at work. Then, there would be the shush of Lucy's sound machine, the possibility she might wake at any moment, the anticipation of Theo's return.

This is an empty quiet. A quiet that feels like it could stretch on forever.

This is a quiet I know too well.

I can't sleep. I stare at Lucy's empty bassinet, the shallow imprint on the foam pad, the pacifier resting against the netting. The clothing baskets on the floor, hastily emptied. I imagine Lucy in an unfamiliar room in Jacqueline's massive rowhouse crying out for me, and no one coming, no one soothing her, no one telling her: *Your mother loves you. She wants to be with you more than anything in the world.*

I run to the bathroom. My stomach is empty, but bile comes up, sour and acidic. I steady myself against the sink, splash water on my face. I can't go back into my empty bedroom.

Instead, I go upstairs.

All of Mona's things are gone, cleared out, like she was never here at all. Only the filmy smell of smoke lingers. Her rucksack is gone, the makeshift curtains taken down, the air mattress deflated and folded and returned to its box in the storage closet.

I've lost her again.

I see Mona, just a baby, Adrienne placing her gently in my arms. Her red, scrunched face so much like Lucy's. Mona, at six, her hair matted and knotty, her arms wrapped around my neck, small and light on my back. A ring of bruises climbing up them, blue and brown and green. Patches of red spots like pinpricks on her arms and legs.

The *drip drip drip* of water in the sink. The cold, wet stones, slimy under my feet. The water at my ankles, the empty forest. *Mom. Mona. Don't leave me here alone.*

She was back, for one unbelievable moment, and now she's gone. Because of Theo.

Anger floods me as I picture him storming into the house to confront me and finding Mona, instead, with Lucy. *Who the fuck are you, and what are you doing in our house?* He frightens her; she runs back to wherever she came from, to the life she was leading before.

I pace from one end of the attic room to the other, unable to stay still.

What life? I ask myself. *Where did she go?*

I know almost nothing about her.

I cross back to the dormer window, stare at the line Mona carved into the paint so that it would open. I picture her smoking in here, even though she knew this was supposed to be Lucy's bedroom, even though she was pregnant herself. But was she? She only told me she was pregnant when I confronted her with that strange text, on the phone she had claimed she didn't own. A cover-up, a story to change the subject. She told me so little about her life. Nothing about where she went during the day when she wasn't with us, who she saw, what she did.

Theo's words: *You didn't think the timing was the slightest bit suspicious?*

The documentary comes out, and my sister just so happens to find me in a coffee shop.

Luck, she said. A happy coincidence.

The pain in my right temple returns, and my chest constricts.

I picture an empty, cavernous space. A metal door.

I push the thought aside, picture Mona on the bench outside our house. Not Mona. Someone else—a stranger.

I wanted to believe her so badly, and so maybe I let myself. If I'm being honest, I didn't feel a tug of recognition that first day at the coffee shop when I saw her hand on Lucy's foot. I felt discomfort, fear. And I felt it again when I saw her waiting in front of our house.

A wave of nausea overtakes me, and I sprint down the stairs, making it to the bathroom just in time.

I go down to the family room, Theo's blankets still folded on the couch. I spread them out, lay my head on his pillow, which smells like his spiced soap. I close my eyes, certain I will not be able to sleep, but somehow, eventually, I do.

In my dreams, I hear my mother's voice.

Wake up, Ophelia. Wake up. It's time.

I am back at the residence, under sweat-damp sheets. My mother stands over me, holding Mona, half asleep, nuzzled into her shoulder.

It's time, Ophelia, she says again, soft and urgent.

I do not know if this is another drill, or if this time is the real thing. If it is the real thing, that means federal agents have started to gather at the perimeter of the property, armed. Ready for a fight. It means any noise or false step could end in bloodshed. I slip on my sweater, put on my boots, and wrap a cloth around them to hide the treads. A nervous energy pulses through the hallway, hushed whispers, the stale smell of sleep. Terese bounces Kai on her hip; he is red-faced and awake now, pushing to get down. Adrienne crosses and uncrosses her arms, her eyes flitting from us to the stairwell, waiting for Christopher's signal. My mother fusses with something in her pocket, adjusts Mona's weight. *We need to be ready at all times,* Christopher says. *We have to be prepared.*

The stairwell groans with footsteps, and my chest tightens: We're already too late. But it's Christopher, his expression somber, focused. He nods at Adrienne, and she waves us on, and we shuffle down the stairwell in silence, out the back of the residence and into the dark, and then into the woods.

We follow the same evacuation route every time. It's a path through the forest that only we know, unmarked by packed dirt or stones. It is not until we are deep in the woods that the first flashlight comes on, and then another, and another. We slip off our shoes and wade through the creek to avoid a trail.

Look what they did at Waco, Christopher tells us. *Look what they did at Ruby Ridge. You think that couldn't happen here?*

My mother and Mona are shadows in front of me. My foot slips on a moss-slicked stone, and I stumble, and my mother reaches back. I feel her hand on my arm.

This way, Ophelia.

We slip on our shoes again, back on solid ground, and walk deeper into the woods. When a branch cracks, the flashlights switch off again, all at once, and my heart pounds, and I am sure that if there is someone out there, they must be able to hear it, too. Mona wakes and begins to whimper, and my mother shushes her, and I reach up and place my hand on her back to help calm her.

It's okay, Mona, I say, *it's okay*, and my mother shushes me, too.

When the sound does not repeat itself, we push forward again, walking until we reach the same small clearing in the wood as always, a grassy knoll. On the real day, this will not be the final destination. It will be where we rest, where we gather supplies from a dugout in the knoll, the entrance covered with a corrugated metal slab and concealed with sod. I do not know what comes next. When we practice, this is where we always stop. There is a silence as we wait, until finally, Christopher speaks.

Not good enough, he says. *Not even close. If this were the real thing, they would have gotten us.*

Mona, cold and exhausted, begins to cry. I pull her into my lap and wrap my arms around her.

It's okay, I tell her, quietly, so no one else can hear. *It's okay.*

When I wake, my shirt sticks, damp, to my body, the sheets tangled around my legs. My breasts are sore; I have never gone this long without feeding Lucy. Sunlight shines into the room through the transom window. My phone rattles beside me. A text from Jacqueline with a photograph. Lucy is dressed in the taupe and gray that Jacqueline favors, too-fancy clothes from a too-fancy children's boutique. She is propped on Jacqueline's couch.

She had a good night last night and is doing well, Jacqueline writes. We had ricotta toast this morning, and we are about to go on an outing. She does not say where they are going. A safety precaution, probably. She does not want me showing up, making a scene, making things worse.

My daughter should be with me, I text back. You can't keep her away from me.

This isn't right. If I leave for Jacqueline's now, maybe I can intercept them before they leave for their "outing." For all Jacqueline's faults, she is a mother, too; she will understand. She will give me my daughter; she has to. I am slipping on my shoes when someone knocks on the front door, three quick raps.

I reach for the knob, my mind cycling through the possibilities.

Jacqueline with Lucy, recognizing the error of her ways.

Mona, returned, ready to explain herself.

I open the door, and it's Theo, looking like he slept about as well as I did.

"Can I come in?" he asks, like I'm a stranger, like this isn't his home, too.

I step aside and he enters, slipping off his shoes, looking everywhere but at me.

"I guess we have some talking to do," he says.

"I guess we do."

There is a long, uncomfortable stretch of silence.

"Do you want some coffee?" I ask, and at first he looks at me, incredulous, like this is an absurd suggestion, but then he softens.

"Yeah," he says. "That might help."

I start a pot, and the coffee drips slowly into the carafe.

"I keep turning this over in my head," he says, leaning against the counter. "And the problem is, I feel like I don't even know you."

"You do know me," I say, starting toward him. He flinches, and I step back.

"This wasn't just a lie," he says. "This goes to the core of who you are. I keep replaying all these conversations in my head, about your family, about your childhood, and it just . . . none of it was real? And then I think of everything else—your relationship with Lucy, your trust issues—and I realize how wrong I've been. About you. About all of it."

"I wanted to tell you," I say.

"So why didn't you?"

I sink down into the kitchen chair. The coffee maker chirps, and Theo pours a cup for both of us, the same old rhythm. He sits across from me, waits.

"It was so hard," I say. "Growing up like that."

"In the cult?" he asks.

"After the disappearance," I say. "As soon as anyone found out about it, it changed the way they saw me. I was a freak or a victim or both. It swamped everything else."

"I wouldn't have seen you that way," Theo says. "I don't see you that way."

"I didn't have friends growing up. Every once in a while, there would be someone who got *interested* in me, which is not the same thing."

Darla Pierce, with her green-tipped hair and charcoaled eyes, who wanted to do a séance to contact my family. The boy in college who had read Christopher's writings and wanted to talk to me about them.

"And then Pittsburgh happened, and it was like it confirmed something everyone else already knew. There was something wrong with me, and maybe there always had been."

"What actually happened in Pittsburgh?" Theo asks.

The words catch in my throat; I know how they will sound.

"I found out my aunt was sick, and it really threw me. I started seeing things. I thought my family had come back and they were watching me. I never . . . I never hurt anyone except myself. I would never do that. There wasn't anyone else in the house when I . . ."

Theo nods; he's seen the news articles.

"I was hospitalized, and treated, and when I finally got out, this reporter contacts me, pretending to be sympathetic, like she wants to hear my story. And then she writes this really fucked-up profile, suggesting I had somehow been involved in the disappearance. I was *twelve*. I was a child."

Theo reaches out for my hand. I give it to him.

"So I decided to start over. I changed my name, so the disappearance and the fire wouldn't be the first thing people saw if they googled me. I decided I was going to stop looking for my family. I made a promise to myself: I wasn't going to be that person anymore."

"You could have gone anywhere," Theo says. "But you stayed here."

"I don't know why," I say, although it's not completely true. There was a job opportunity that came up in Boston, but when I got the call, my whole body went cold. *What if they come looking,* I thought, *and I'm not here?*

"But that's why I didn't tell you," I say. "I didn't know how you'd respond, and I didn't want to think about that part of my life anymore. I wanted to move on. I thought I *had* moved on."

Theo nods, his eyes cast down at the table. He pulls his hand back.

"I hear you," he says. "And I can see how hard that must have been. But . . . we're *married*, Lee. We share a life together, and you kept this all from me. I don't know how I can trust you after this."

"You can," I say. "This is the truth. This is me."

He looks up, and his eyes are wet with tears. "How do I trust you with our *daughter*? How do I know you won't . . ."

"I would never do anything to hurt Lucy."

He blinks and shakes his head. "Lee, you already have. You did it as soon as you invited that stranger into our house."

"I didn't know."

His breath hitches. "I know," he says. "That's the problem."

"Theo," I say, and I am crying now, too. "You can't do this. You can't take her from me."

He cradles his head in his hands, and it is a long time—too long—before he looks up again. If Theo wants to take my daughter, there is nothing stopping him. He is a lawyer, with money, friends, a family support system. I am a former cult member with a history of mental illness.

"You need to go to therapy," he says at last, and my heart leaps with hope.

"I will," I say.

"I mean it," he says. "I know we've talked about this on and off since Lucy was born, and nothing's ever come of it, but you need to be in therapy *now*. We can get a recommendation from my mother."

"That's fine," I say, nodding. "I can do that."

"And I need to know where you and Lucy are at all times."

"Okay," I say.

"That means responding to my texts right away. And we can turn on Family Sharing on your phone so I can see where you are."

A second chance. I will do anything to get Lucy back. I pull out my phone, hand it over.

"And I need you to be *honest* with me, Lee. No more lying. No more secrets."

"I promise," I tell him. "You can trust me."

CHAPTER THIRTY

—

It is another Monday morning, and Lucy and I are sticking to our schedule. We are walking back from Mommy and Me, Amanda and Winnie a few feet ahead of us. Dr. Dana brought up the topic of autism today, and Amanda spent twenty minutes confirming Jackson was not displaying any red flags, which turned into twenty minutes of Amanda explaining how developmentally advanced Jackson is.

"I mean, I know it's early," I hear her saying now. "But is it *too* early, is what I'm worried about."

We exchange our goodbyes at Rittenhouse, and Lucy and I walk the remaining blocks by ourselves. Lucy is bundled in a padded one-piece suit with teddy-bear ears on its hood, her cheeks dappled red from the cold. Fall has given way to winter, the trees bare, early Christmas wreaths on a few of the doors. A text comes through from Andi: Drinks tonight? I respond with a thumbs-up. Theo is happy about my growing friendship with Andi, although I suspect a part of him wishes she seemed a little more stable herself. Lucy and I stop at a red light two blocks from our home, and I feel someone too close, a hand on my side. I jump, almost letting go of the stroller handle.

"Just me," Theo says from behind. Lucy's face lights up; she gives him a wide, gummy smile. "Pretty good timing!"

Theo has been coming home at lunch on the days I have therapy so he can watch Lucy and I can focus fully on my session.

"You want me to take her from here?" he asks.

"I still have a little time," I say.

"So take a few minutes to yourself," he says. "Get a coffee."

Until recently, I would have resisted, but these separations are getting easier. Theo was right about that, after all. Our conversations around my anxiety have changed now that he knows about my past. He's stopped pushing so hard. *Of course separation would be hard for you,* he said, after a late-night conversation about the disappearance, *of course,* and I nearly cried.

"I'm going to see Dr. Khatri," I tell Lucy. "I'll be back in one hour." Even if she doesn't understand, it helps.

"See you soon," Theo says, and the light turns green, and they're off.

There's a tastefully faded oriental rug on the wooden floor of Dr. Khatri's office, a mid-century-modern couch across from a leather chair, just the right number of potted plants. It feels lived-in but not cluttered, homey but not idiosyncratic. If you didn't know better, you could mistake it for someone's family room, straight out of a design catalog.

I know better.

Dr. Khatri sits on the chair and I sit on the couch. She's wearing a white silk blouse, slacks with a creased line in the front. Teal blue shoes with a pointy toe. Her hair, smooth and straight, is pulled into a low ponytail. It's no wonder Theo's mother likes her so much: This is a woman who has it together. She's probably only a few years older than I am, but a rising star in psychiatry. Or so I am told, anyway—by a website that lists the best Philadelphia-area mental health specialists, by online reviews, by Jacqueline, who knows her through conferences and the University of Pennsylvania alumni network.

I am not sure she is helping, just as I am not sure my moms' group is helping, but this is what Theo wants me to do, so I will do it. I have a debt to repay. I need to earn back his trust.

"How did you feel leaving Lucy with Theo this morning?" she asks.

"Good," I say. "Better."

So far, Dr. Khatri and I have talked about marriage, about motherhood, about how overwhelming it can be. About how that's normal, and how it's also normal to need help sometimes. Jacob's Hill has not come up, and until this very moment, I thought maybe she was waiting for me to broach the subject. Maybe there were rules in her particular brand of therapy—no raising a sensitive topic until invited to do so by the patient—and I could just avoid it forever.

But now she is tapping her pen against her notepad, her brow furrowed like she's turning over something in her mind. This is a look I've seen before.

"Do you want to talk about Mona?" she says, finally.

I smile wryly. "Which one?"

"You choose." She crosses one leg over the other, leans toward me on her forearms. Her shirt does not wrinkle or pucker.

"I'm Lucy's mother," I say. "My primary responsibility is keeping her safe, and I lost sight of that. I failed her."

"Let's not talk in terms of blame," Dr. Khatri says.

I take a deep breath and say the words I've said a dozen times since everything imploded. "The woman who came to our house . . . she said she was Mona, and I wanted so badly to believe her. I let that color what I saw and what I overlooked. I let her take advantage of me and my family."

This is the version of events that Theo believes, that Jacqueline believes, that I'm sure Dr. Khatri has been told. I do not know if it's the version of events I believe—there is still so much that doesn't add up—but there is no point in sharing my uncertainty here. Dr. Khatri will view it as a setback, not a genuine possibility.

"It was a wake-up call for me," I say. "I need help navigating this."

"And that's why we're here," Dr. Khatri says, nodding like I've said the right thing. "Are you comfortable talking about your child-hood?"

I know what I need to say to get through this: *I'm sorry. I'll do better. Please, show me the way.*

"Yes," I say, a *motivated* patient, a *compliant* patient. "I can do that."

I come home to Theo and Lucy reading a story on the couch. She's on his lap, so small against his chest, and he's doing voices for the different characters. A deep grumble for the bear; a high-pitched squeak for the rabbit. Lucy is enthralled. She loves this. She clearly enjoys being with Theo in a way she never did before—or maybe I just never gave them the opportunity to spend this kind of time to-gether.

I sit beside the two of them on the couch, my knee pressing against Theo's. His knee presses back.

We can do this. We can work our way through. We can rebuild our life together.

The story is over. The bear is not going to eat the rabbit, after all. Theo puts his arm around my shoulder, and I lean into him while Lucy turns the book over in her hands.

"Thank you," he says to me softly. *For keeping up with therapy,* he means. *For getting the help you need.* He kisses the top of my head, breathes in my hair. I can see the changes in him ever since I started seeing Dr. Khatri. It's like a weight has been lifted off his shoulders. I had attrib-uted all of his stress to work, blind to how much of it I was causing.

"I feel good about this," I say.

"Me too," he says. "Any plans for this afternoon?" He shifts Lucy to my lap and stands. He needs to get back to work before long.

"I might start sanding the floor upstairs during Lucy's nap," I say.

"Good for you. Sure you don't need any help?"

He's joking. He grew up in the city with contractors you call for that sort of thing. He is not handy.

"I think I've got this one," I say.

He buttons his jacket, grabs his computer bag from beside the door.

"I love you," he says, without the searching intensity I'd grown to expect. He knows who I am now, the real me.

He knows, and he's still here, and we're working through it.

This should be enough, I tell myself. *Let this be enough.*

I open the third-floor blinds to let in as much natural light as possible. There are circular stains on the shelf beneath the window, left by Mona's tea mug or water glass. *Not Mona,* I remind myself. The ashtray is gone, but a light dusting of ash remains. I can picture that woman, whoever she was, sitting here, smoking out the window, lost in her thoughts. Whatever they were.

What do we do about . . . her? I asked Theo, unsure of what even to call her, after we hashed out the conditions of his return. He ran his hands down his face, looked toward the ceiling.

We could file a police report, he said. *But . . .*

But she didn't actually take anything in the end.

But we know nothing about her, and the odds of the police tracking her down are infinitesimally small.

But the police report would be public record, and Meghan Kessler would get her hands on it.

And what would that public attention do to Theo's reputation?

And what would it do to my mental state?

So we do nothing, I said, the words sending a chill through my body.

Not nothing, Theo said. *We go to couples' counseling, and you go to therapy. We put this behind us. We don't let that imposter play a bigger role in our lives than she already has.*

I wipe off the ash with a damp washcloth. Time to get to work.

A week ago, I cleared out most of our old boxes. Some went down to the basement, others into the trash, others to the curb for our neighbors to pick through. And today, I'll start on the floor. The thick wooden boards, which vary in size, are cracked and splintered and likely original to the house. If Lucy is going to be crawling across them, they need to be refinished.

I turn back toward the room and for a moment I see Mona, vulnerable and shaking after a night terror, and I feel a stab of grief all over again.

Not Mona, I remind myself. *An imposter. A fraud.*

Theo has to know we are on the same page. He believes the woman was a fan of the documentary who took things too far, and so that's what I need to believe, too. She was obsessive; she learned about the disappearance and fixated on it; she wanted to insert herself into the drama. She took advantage of my vulnerability, of my need to believe that Mona was okay after all, of my willingness to respect her need for privacy.

If I express doubts, Theo will think I'm spiraling.

I need him to know I'm keeping it together.

I begin in the corner of the room on my hands and knees, shuffling backward with my wood filler and spackle. I work slowly, methodically, looking for dents and scrapes. It's important to have a project to do, something to keep my hands busy, something to occupy just enough of my mind.

An obsessive fan, I remind myself. The obvious explanation.

But there are two other possibilities that keep me up at night.

The first: The woman really was my sister. It's unlikely, I know. I remind myself of the strangeness with the phone, the coincidental timing of her reappearance. And if she was my sister, then why would the mere threat of a DNA test scare her away? But there were things she knew that couldn't have come from the documentary or the internet: Mona's nickname for me, the night terrors.

I crawl back farther, and I see a beam of light through one of the floorboards, a small hole. I put my eye to it, and there's Lucy, sleeping right below me. She takes a big, shuddering breath and rolls over onto her side.

The second: The woman was an imposter, but she was after something more sinister than fame or a role in a tragedy that doesn't really involve her.

She was after Lucy.

Theo has never acknowledged this possibility, but he doesn't know how close the woman and Lucy had become. He doesn't know the woman was the one pushing me to leave the house—*go, go farther, I don't want to see you back here before noon.* He doesn't know she claimed she was going to be a mother soon, too.

What are you going to do about the baby?

I can't let myself dwell on this possibility for too long. If it's true, it means I put Lucy in the care of someone who would do her harm. I can't have been that close to losing her.

She didn't take Lucy, I remind myself. *Nothing happened.*

I spackle over the hole, scrape off the excess with my knife. I reach the wall, cross to the other side, work my way back again. I find a discolored patch on the floor, a dark stain sunk into the porous surface. I dampen a cloth with hydrogen peroxide, press it into the spot, let it sit.

She's gone, and that's good, and the most likely explanation is that she was someone with a fixation who realized she was in over her head.

I know—I am more aware than most—that we don't always get answers. We don't get to fully understand what motivates the people around us; we don't get to have the whole story. Life is uncertain, and our perspective is so limited, so small.

And I know digging for answers could disrupt the delicate balance Theo and I have found.

I scoot back and a splinter catches on my leggings, tearing a small hole. Across the room, my phone buzzes. I pick it up and read the notification.

There's been another response to my Reddit post.

———

Ever since the woman left, I have been monitoring all references to the disappearance online—news articles, Reddit threads, tweets, and blog posts. I've pored through them for any references to me or Mona, for any sign of someone overly invested in the disappearance. If Theo is right, and the woman in our house was an obsessive fan, she should be here.

And if she's online posting about me, then at least I will know for sure who she was and I can accept it. I can move on.

But there has been no sign of her, nothing that has jumped out. Most of the chatter has been closely related to the content in new episodes of the docuseries. Reddit users have been discussing estranged family members of The Fifteen. Apparently I am not the only one who knows that Adrienne's sister is a hairdresser in Ridley Park. Someone suggested the possibility that Christopher reinvented himself as the leader of a different cult, "a la Osho," prompting a string of responses with photographs of other members of the prepping community, links to online manifestos, linguistic comparisons. But no posts from anyone claiming to be Mona, or bragging about fooling me. No one sharing personal information about me and Theo and Lucy. And she would be doing that, wouldn't she, if Theo were right?

So yesterday, I decided to try something new.

I have one photograph of the woman, the one I took at the park, with Lucy on her lap on the picnic blanket. It's not the best picture, but it's all I've got. I cropped it so that only the woman's face is visible—no Lucy, no obvious landmarks. I posted it to The Fifteen subreddit, with the question: Does anyone know this woman?

The first response was a question in return: How is this related to the disappearance?

I didn't respond. If the woman really is Mona, and she's hiding, I didn't want to out her. But if she's an imposter, I reasoned, the photograph might provoke a response from the woman herself, or someone else who knows her.

There were a few other immediate replies speculating about her connection to the disappearance, but without my participation, interest in the post cooled.

Until now.

There's a message from marcotheman, short and to the point.

I know her.

There are replies already. Details? Who is she? Is she actually connected to the case?

marcotheman: She used to work at the corner store by my old apartment in South Philly—I'd always see her outside taking smoke breaks. Idk if she's still there.

My heart leaps in my chest. I send marcotheman a direct message.

pleasehelp_throwaway: Are you sure it's the same person?
marcotheman: I mean, no? But they look pretty similar
pleasehelp_throwaway: Do you know her name?
marcotheman: No, never had a real conversation with her.
pleasehelp_throwaway: When was the last time you saw her?
marcotheman: A year ago? I moved and haven't really been back. She might still be there.
marcotheman: I thought she was kind of a bitch, tbh

I bristle, although I have no reason to defend her. She tried to tear my life apart.

pleasehelp_throwaway: What was the name of the corner store?
marcotheman: Anders Mini Mart

A real place. A real lead.

Thank you, I type back.

I should be happy about this information. This is what I wanted. Something tangible, actionable, a place I can go. I can confirm, once and for all, that Theo is right, that this woman is an obsessive fan, there's nothing more to it. I can quell my lingering doubt.

But there's a part of me that doesn't want that certainty, that wants to hang on to the possibility—however slight—that the woman really was Mona. If I go to the corner store and learn she was just a con artist, and I was just a mark, then I will have to face the reality that I have been duped, that in my desperation I overlooked a real threat to Lucy. All the possibilities—*Mona, not Mona*—collapsing into a single, inescapable truth.

And also: Theo can track my location with my phone, and I can't just leave it here. He'll notice if I'm not responding to his texts. If Theo finds out I'm still looking, he will be *concerned*, scared for me and for Lucy.

I'm not sure I can take that chance.

I slip my phone into my pocket and carefully descend the third-floor stairs. I open the door to my room, where Lucy is still sleeping, and watch the rise and fall of her breath.

Mona—the woman—is gone now. She's not coming back. I promised Theo I would let this go, and that's what I should be doing. We are rebuilding our life together; we are figuring out the way forward.

I need to focus on my future. I need to focus on Lucy. I can't let myself look back.

CHAPTER THIRTY-ONE

"All right," Jacqueline says, her gray-brown hair pulled back, her blue button-down rolled up at the sleeves. "Where do we begin?"

"You want to take that wall and I'll take this one?" I say.

Jacqueline does not see clients today, and so she is spending the day with me, helping me paint the third floor. *A fun project,* she called it when she suggested it, and even though I know what this really is—a way to keep an eye on me—I am grateful for the help. Plus, the alternative is Jacqueline grilling me over tea at our kitchen table, so this is a step up.

I pry open the first can of paint with a butter knife. The room is going to be robin's-egg blue, with gold-framed pictures of butterflies hanging on the walls, a plush pink rug spread across the wood floor. I pour the paint into two plastic trays, one for each of us.

"So," Jacqueline says, dabbing paint along the corners of the wall, "how are things going with Prisha?"

Dr. Khatri. Obviously, there are strings attached to this help.

"I thought sessions were supposed to be private," I say, trying to keep my voice light.

"Oh, of course," Jacqueline says. "I just wanted to make sure the two of you were clicking, that's all."

"We are," I say, and I hope I sound reassuring. "She seems like she knows what she's doing."

"One of the best," she says, turning to get more paint.

"And I do feel like it's helping," I say.

"Well," Jacqueline says, in a tone that suggests I haven't conveyed enough enthusiasm, or have said the wrong thing. "It's still early."

"I know." I paint the window frame, already thick from a century's worth of paint, running my brush over the discoloration from the woman's tea mug. *Gone*, like she was never here at all.

Who was she? I find myself thinking again. This time, though, there might be an answer, just across the city, waiting for me.

Jacqueline clears her throat and balances her brush on her paint tray. She's looking at me like she has something to say, and I brace myself.

"I hope you feel you can open up to her," she says finally.

"To who?" I ask, distracted.

"Prisha," Jacqueline reminds me.

"Right," I say. I need to push Mona out of my mind, need to focus on the task at hand. "I do. It's a safe space." That's the way Dr. Khatri refers to our sessions, and I hope parroting this phrase back to Jacqueline will be enough. But she gives me a look that suggests she isn't fooled before turning back to her wall, swiping a large X across it.

"You've been keeping what happened to your mother and sister a secret for a long time," she says. "And I understand that. But it's important to be able to face the past head-on. It's the only way we grow."

The *drip, drip, drip* in the kitchen sink.

"It's the only way we learn."

Keep up, Ophelia.

"Otherwise, we get stuck in the same old patterns."

My bare feet on the wet rocks, water soaking into the hem of my dress.

Hello? Where are you? Hello?

"I know," I say, willing myself to stop. "I know that."

"Sometimes we can *know* what's good for us, on a *conscious* level, but still have a hard time putting it into practice."

I picture Mona, not-Mona, standing outside a corner store in South Philly, her face framed with tendrils of smoke, holding all the answers. If I want them.

"I'm working on it."

Do I want them?

"Oh, I know, Ophelia. I can see that."

I have a good life here. I have Theo and Lucy, and they are my family now, and Theo thinks we are in agreement: The woman is a con artist, and it's not worth giving her any more of our attention and energy. I don't want to upset him any more than I already have.

"We all get stuck in cycles, though," Jacqueline continues. "Every single one of us. They're hard to break."

But really, deep down, I know that Theo is not the issue. It's me. I am scared of what I will discover if I find this woman: a con artist who saw immediately how weak I am; my sister, who left me again.

I've spent my whole life running from the past. I should know by now that hiding doesn't make it go away. It only leaves you unprepared when the past comes to reclaim you.

I can't hide anymore.

I clear my throat, check my phone, pretend to have received a text.

"Hmm," I say. "One of the women in my moms' group has an extra ticket to a musical performance this afternoon and wants to know if I can come along."

"Oh," Jacqueline says, her interest piqued. "Is it something at the Kimmel Center?"

Jacqueline likely has the Philadelphia Orchestra's performance schedule memorized, so this is dangerous territory.

"No," I say, "it's something in South Philly—sort of avant-garde, I think."

"How fantastic!" she says. "You should go."

"Are you sure?" I ask. "We made these plans—"

"Don't be silly," Jacqueline says. "We can paint anytime. You should go out with your friend."

I feel a small pang of guilt: Jacqueline really does want to help me, in her way. But this is an answer, a way forward. I will tell Theo I went to a show in South Philly, and Jacqueline will back up my story. Theo will be happy to hear I'm going out with friends; he won't question it.

"Thanks," I say. "I'll go when Lucy wakes up."

"Why don't you leave her here with me?"

"Oh no," I say, that old twinge of fear returning.

"You're going to take her with you?" Jacqueline asks. "To a performance?"

"It'll be fine," I say.

"Don't be ridiculous," Jacqueline says. "I'm happy to watch her. And I'm already here."

It will be okay, I tell myself. I have been leaving Lucy with Theo more and more—Dr. Khatri's orders—and I am getting better and better at the separation. It won't be for long; I'll go to Anders Mini Mart and then come right back. She'll probably be asleep for another hour, and I won't be that long.

"Are you sure?"

"Absolutely," Jacqueline says, beaming, clasping together her paint-spattered hands. "I would be *honored*."

Anders Mini Mart is at the corner of two streets lined with squat brick rowhomes, all with Eagles pennants and crucifixes in the windows. The storefront is bright blue, plastered in signs advertising lotto tickets and the ATM inside. A bright orange safety cone holds open the front door. I take a breath and step inside.

The store clerk behind the glass partition isn't the woman I'm looking for. She's in her early twenties, bored, swiping at her phone.

I nod at her, but she doesn't seem to notice me. I approach the counter, try again.

"Hi," I say. "I'm looking for someone. I think she works here? Or maybe used to work here?"

I pull up my picture of the woman on my phone, slide it through the partition. "Do you know her?"

A moment passes, but finally she sighs, sets her phone aside, squints at mine. I shift my weight nervously, waiting for a response, not sure what I am hoping to hear. None of the options are good.

"Don't think so," she says. She pushes the phone back. A dead end. I should have known this wasn't going to lead anywhere. Just an anonymous tip from someone online with no skin in the game, no reason to get things right.

"Okay," I say, adjusting myself to this new reality. "Thanks."

I tried, at least. I remind myself that's the important thing: I looked, and nothing came of it, but I'm not hiding my head under a rock anymore. I'm about to leave when an older man in a Phillies cap emerges from an unmarked door beside the ATM.

"Hey, Gerald," the girl behind the counter says. "This woman says she's looking for someone who used to work here."

"Oh yeah?" the man—Gerald—says. "Who?"

"This woman," I say, fumbling for my phone.

"I don't have my eyes right now," he says, patting his empty front pocket, but he takes my phone anyway, zooms in, squints.

"Maria?"

"Maria," I repeat.

"She's a thief," he says, and my heart sinks. "She take something from you, too?"

"Sort of," I say. "Did you catch her taking money from the till, or . . ."

"Credit card information. She put a card skimmer on my ATM. And god knows what else she was doing."

"Did you press charges?"

"Yeah, sure. Don't think anything came of it. But if she ever tries to step foot in this store again . . ."

"Do you know her full name?"

"Maria Salerno," he says.

"Any idea where she might be now?"

He squints at me, like he's not sure why I want this information, but then seems to decide he doesn't care. "No clue. She doesn't come around here anymore. But she used to drink at the tavern on Mifflin. The bartender there might have a better idea."

"Great," I say. "Thank you."

He shakes his head and gets back to work, checking the inventory. "Good luck," he says, like I'll need it.

Snyder's Tavern is a smoking-permitted bar, and the air is hazy inside, heavy with tobacco. There's an old-fashioned cigarette dispenser against the wall next to a jukebox. It's early still, but there are a couple of regulars at the bar, a table occupied in the back. I take my spot on a stool, lean my arms on the sticky counter, pull them back again.

"What can I get you?" the bartender asks. He's got a shaved head, muscular arms that fill out his black T-shirt. I ask for a pilsner and pull out my phone, searching for the name Gerald gave me. A few pictures come up, but none that look like the woman in our house.

The bartender sets down my glass on a coaster and is about to walk away when I ask: "Do you know Maria Salerno?"

"Maria." He smirks. "Yeah, but it's been a while."

"And thank fucking god for that," one of the regulars says, already drunk. He has floppy hair and a vein-streaked nose; he spends too much time here. The bartender gives him a wary look out of the corner of his eye.

"Why?" I ask, turning in my seat.

"She's a sociopath, that's why," the man says.

"Frank is just bitter because Maria never slept with him," says the man to his left. The bartender smirks again, and Frank explodes into drunken protests.

"What makes you say she's a sociopath?" I ask, trying to sound less nervous than I feel.

Frank remembers I'm here. He swivels back toward me, leans unsteadily on the counter.

"Have you heard of catfishing?"

"Sure," I say.

"That's what she did," he slurs.

"Frank," the bartender says.

"It's true!"

"It's not," says the man to his left, laughing.

"These poor saps alone in their basement think they've finally scored a model who's coming out to visit them soon, she's promised she will, but first she just needs to pay her mom's hospital bill." He laughs, steadies himself against the counter. "I mean, serves them right, I guess, for being so dumb."

"Oh, come on," says the man to his left, and Frank lifts his hands in protest.

"God's honest truth."

"Do you know where she is now?" I ask, and Frank gives me an exaggerated shrug.

"Probably off somewhere trying to convince the elderly she's their granddaughter and in trouble, needs ten thousand dollars for bail or some shit."

"Frank," the bartender says again as he dries off a pint glass with a dishrag.

"What? People do that shit."

"She hasn't been in here for a few months," the bartender tells me. "As far as I know."

"Maybe the consequences of her actions finally met up with her," Frank says, laughing to himself, and the other regular shakes his head in disapproval. My head feels light, and the pain in my temple is returning, maybe from the beer so early in the afternoon, or the cigarette smoke, or this conversation. I need to get out of here.

"Thanks," I say, leaving money on the counter, and as I'm leaving, Frank shouts after me, like it just occurred to him to ask:

"Who is she to you?"

I walk a few blocks before lowering myself onto a bench, cradle my forehead in my hands. Gerald didn't have his glasses, and Frank was a drunk, and so maybe it's all wrong. Maybe the woman was not Maria after all; maybe it's just one big terrible coincidence.

I look at my phone again, the results for Maria Salerno still on my screen. One is a website that promises all sorts of records: public, criminal, marriage, "and more." We have the answers to your questions, it says. I enter what I know: Maria Salerno, a woman between the ages of eighteen and thirty who lives in Philadelphia. It asks me for my name and email address, which I provide. Then it asks for my credit card information, a $28.05 charge.

It's not much—no more than I charge to my card on a regular basis buying purées and diapers for Lucy. But this would be a charge on our credit card statement from a website with a strange name, something that might catch Theo's eye. I can't let him know I'm still looking, even if the end result is that he was right all along.

I think about my options. I have another idea.

I open the website for the Philadelphia court system and search for Maria's name. Sure enough, she has been the defendant in multiple criminal cases. I click on the most recent one: *Commonwealth v. Salerno, Maria,* filed a little less than a year ago, case status: closed.

A gust of wind tears down the narrow street, and I pull my jacket tighter.

The judge listed is Judge Philip Haney.

The charges are for mail fraud, forgery, identity theft.

The defense attorney is Theodore Burton.

There is a moment when I don't feel anything at all. I read the words again, and again, trying to make sense of them.

This has to be some kind of mistake.

But every time I look at it, it's the same name, right there, staring back at me. Theodore Burton, Public Defender.

Theo knows this woman.

Theo represented this woman.

Theo is lying.

CHAPTER THIRTY-TWO

—

The public defenders' office is a white stone building not far from City Hall. I have visited the building many times, although not often since Lucy. Back in our pre-child days, Theo and I would meet up on our lunch breaks. We'd eat at Sister Cities or LOVE Park or—on cold and windy days like today—in Theo's office. He'd clear off space on his desk, which was always piled high with printouts and binders and case files.

Did one of those case files belong to Maria Salerno? Was it right there, sitting on his desk the whole time beneath a crinkled sandwich wrapper? How long has Theo known her? How long has he been lying to me?

Stop, I tell myself. *You don't know anything. Maybe there's an explanation.*

I can't think of one, though. The whole way over, I have tried to come up with ways this might just be a misunderstanding, a benign coincidence, something that will *all make sense* once we sit down and talk it over.

But there is no explaining this. Theo knew the woman who lived in our house, who took care of Lucy, who pretended to be my sister, from the moment she walked in our front door, and he said nothing. He made me think I was the crazy one.

I take out my phone and text him: I'm at your building. We need to talk.

No response.

I call. He does not pick up.

It's almost like he knows what's coming. I breathe, try to stay calm, try not to read too much into his silence. There is no reason for him to be ignoring me. This morning, we ate breakfast together and he kissed me on the cheek before leaving, just like always. This morning, we were fine. He's probably with a client, or in a meeting, or otherwise occupied.

"Lee?"

A lawyer I recognize from Theo's happy hours and work events—back when I used to attend those with him—is walking toward me on the sidewalk. Her name is Emily or Ellie, something that starts with an E.

"How's the baby?" she asks cheerfully. "Are you here to see Theo?"

"She's good," I say. "Yeah, we're supposed to get lunch together."

"Aww," she says. I follow her in, past security, up the elevator. I show her pictures of Lucy, and she shows me pictures of her kids—two and five, both boys, both handfuls, she says—and she swipes her fob and we walk through the office door.

"You know where you're going?" she asks.

"I do," I say.

Theo nominally shares an office with one of his colleagues, Logan, but Logan is almost never in the office, and today is no exception. Theo is somewhere else, too. The small, windowless room is empty. A motion-activated light flickers on when I step through the doorway. Theo's desk is covered in papers, like always, a stack of folders threatening to topple over next to his computer monitor.

Maybe he's at a hearing. Maybe I have some time.

I sit in his office chair, jiggle the mouse so the monitor springs to life, blinking on to a lock screen. There's information about Maria on this computer. Her entire case file, right there, if I can just figure out the password. I try a few different combinations—Lucy's birthday, Jacqueline's birthday—the screen shuddering each time, *incor-*

rect, incorrect, incorrect. Theo is required to change his work password once every few months, something he complains about because he can never remember his new one. *It's not actually more secure if everyone has to write all their passwords down on scraps of paper all the time,* he says. The answer is probably here somewhere, a new password written in the top margin of a notepad. I flip through the piles on the desk, lift them, feel behind the flat-screen monitor for a hidden Post-it note, slide open a drawer of hanging folders.

"Lee?"

Theo stands in the doorway, looking confused. He's wearing a suit jacket under his overcoat, so I was right about him having a hearing. Wrong about when he would return. He closes his door, hangs his jacket and coat on a hook.

"I saw your messages," he says. "Is everything all right?"

"Who is Maria Salerno?" I ask.

Theo's face does not betray any recognition. "Who?"

"The woman in our house. Maria Salerno. Who is she?"

He walks toward me, carefully, guarded. I stand, and he stops in his tracks. "Is that her name?" he asks. "Did you—"

"You *know* it's her name," I say.

He shakes his head. "Lee, I really don't know what you're talking about."

"*Maria,*" I say again, louder this time. "She was one of your *clients.*"

He takes another step closer, talks calmly, slowly. "I don't understand."

"I've been looking for her. For Mona. For the woman." This is coming out scattered, wrong. This isn't how this was supposed to go. "I posted her picture online, and someone recognized her. From South Philly. I went there and showed her picture around—"

"South Philly is a big area," Theo says.

"No," I say. "I know. I went to the corner store where they said they saw her."

"They?" he asks. "Who are you talking about?"

"I don't *know*," I say. "Someone online. Someone who used to live there."

"Okay," he says, his tone patronizing, like he's straining to understand. "This person on the internet recognized her, and then some person in a corner store."

"The owner," I say. "And then these men at a bar nearby, they knew her, too. They said she's a con artist."

"Okay," Theo says. He's nodding his head, processing. "That's good. This is good information. I told you. She was taking advantage of us."

"She's one of your *clients*, Theo," I say. "You *knew* her. You know her."

"I don't."

"I looked her up online. She has a criminal history. You were her lawyer."

He squeezes his eyes shut, blinks them open. He looks at the ground, the desk, everywhere but me.

"I thought things were getting better," he says. "I thought we were getting past this."

"Who is she?" I ask. "What was she doing in our house?"

"I don't *know*, Lee," he says, raising his voice for the first time. He catches himself. "I don't know any more than you do."

"But you represented her—"

"I represented a Maria Salerno," he says. "I guess, if that's what it says. I don't specifically remember her."

"You don't remember."

He runs his hands over his face. "Do you know how many cases I have? I have hundreds of clients a *year*. I don't remember all of them."

"Find her file."

"Lee."

"Where is it? On the computer? In some filing cabinet? It'll have her mug shot, right?"

"This is ridiculous."

"Find it."

Theo stalks out of his office, slamming the door shut behind him. My hands are shaking. I sink into his chair again, try to steady my nerves. On Theo's shelves, mixed in among the books on Pennsylvania court procedure and the criminal code, there are framed photographs of us. One from our wedding, formal, with Theo's mother, his aunts and uncles. Another from one of our early dates, the two of us on the Wissahickon trails, the frame hugging our faces, smiling and happy. Theo on our couch holding Lucy, swaddled and so small, only a few days old. He's looking at her like he's never seen anything like her.

The door opens. Theo is holding a large brown folder. He drops it down heavily on the desk. I stare at it.

"Maria Salerno," he says. His voice is cold, resigned. "There you go."

I flip it open. The first page is a rap sheet, and, sure enough, there is her mug shot. One picture of Maria head-on, one in profile. Her hair is long and dark in these pictures, her face more filled out, her cheekbones less defined. But it's her. I think. The same pointed nose, thin lips. Her smirk, like a challenge.

I look at Theo. "See?" I say.

He looks back at me in disbelief.

"Lee," he says. "That's not the woman you let into our house."

His words twist inside me.

"What do you mean?" I say. "Look at her."

"Lee."

"Theo, *look* at her."

"You need help." He looks like he's about to cry.

He's pretending, though. I'm sure of it. Whatever is happening here, he's not about to admit to it.

But his grief looks so genuine.

"I don't know where we go from here," he says. "I don't know what we're supposed to do."

No.

"You let a stranger into our house. You left Lucy alone with her."

No.

"And then you're telling me that you're getting better—that you're getting help—but meanwhile, you're running around the city because—because some person on the internet told you to? Listening to drunks at bars?"

No.

"And then this. I just don't know . . . You're not *seeing* things right, Lee. How can I trust you around Lucy when—"

He is crying. Silent, his shoulders shaking.

"Theo, I—"

"I don't know what to do. I don't know how to handle this. You need real help. You can't be around Lucy like this."

My world turns on its axis, and I realize the terrible mistake I've made. Lucy is not here; she is not with me.

She is with Theo's mother.

"You can't do this to me."

"I'm not doing anything to you," he says, his voice raised again. "I'm trying to protect my daughter."

"No," I say. I tear the picture of Maria from the folder, and push past Theo, who doesn't try to stop me. And of course he doesn't. He doesn't need to.

I've already lost her.

My house is empty.

Lucy is gone. Her clothes are gone, too, her books and toys hastily picked through. Her patchwork turtle still sits on our coffee table, its legs splayed. Jacqueline doesn't know how much Lucy loves that turtle, how much it means to her.

Lucy, my world.

Lucy, my everything.

I'm sorry. I'm sorry. I'm sorry.

CHAPTER THIRTY-THREE

—

I wake to silence. There is sunlight sneaking through the cracks around my blackout curtains; I have no idea what time it is. I must have passed out at some point last night, although I do not know how. My eyes are puffy, swollen from crying. I push myself out of bed and go downstairs to pump.

I will get Lucy back soon, I tell myself. *Today. I'll get her back today.*

I check my phone and see that it's eleven-thirty. I have a text from Theo:

> I made you an appointment with Dr. Khatri today. 4:00. This is non-negotiable.

That gives me the whole afternoon to figure out what the fuck is going on.

I set Maria's mugshot and Mona's picture on my phone side by side on my kitchen table, study them. I see differences, of course, but there are similarities, too—unmistakable, once you see them. The same person at different times in her life.

How did she pull it off? It's easy enough to explain how she knew about the disappearance and my identity. The documentary is everywhere, and she could have found out who I am and where I live online. She could have found out about my sister from the police reports.

But she knew details about my mother, too. She said I walked like our mother, that we held ourselves the same. *Because she knew that's what you wanted to hear,* I tell myself. *Not because it was true.* That simple statement had conjured so many memories: me lagging behind my mother and Mona on the dirt path, Mona resting her head against my mother's shoulder, my mother's hand reaching back for me. I had supplied those memories, not Maria. All she did was offer up vague suggestions and let me fill in the details myself.

And when she couldn't bluff her way through, she changed the topic. The night I brought up Josephine, and she wrongly suggested that Josephine might have had a nickname, she pivoted: *Theo and Fey, don't they seem a little too close? Haven't you ever wondered?*

The night terrors. She knew Mona had night terrors, or else she got very lucky when she faked one herself. How could she have had that information? But as soon as I pose the question to myself, I have the answer. I head down to our basement, where I've moved my box of things from my aunt's house. I peel back the mismatched tape and find what I'm looking for: my soft-covered journal. I flip through it.

The journal is a mix of drawings, poems, observations, and reports about my day. A few sketches of animals: a deer alert in the woods, a rabbit's face, with carefully detailed fur and whiskers.

Two girls in the woods, sitting side by side by a grassy knoll, a door at its center.

I flip to a drawing of a young girl with writing beneath it. The drawing isn't particularly good—just a twelve-year-old's doodle— but I can tell from the long dark hair it's supposed to be Mona. My pencil strokes left grooves in the page.

Mona had another dream last night, I wrote. *She woke me up screaming. I hate it. It's so scary.*

So there it is. My answer. I gave her everything without even realizing it.

I throw the journal back in the box and notice something else: the wooden jewelry box from my aunt. I open it, and the bracelet from my mother has been returned, nestled into the velvet lining.

She put it back.

Maybe she didn't want to take it. Maybe she knew how important it was to me.

Or, she put it back when she realized it had no monetary value.

I rub the chain beneath my thumb and index finger, slip the bracelet into my pocket. It doesn't matter why Maria returned it, whether she's a complete monster or one with a conscience. The only thing that matters to me now is Theo's role in all this.

And I'm prepared to rip our house apart to get that answer.

I climb the basement stairs and start on the first floor. I empty the drawers and cubbies of our secretary desk, tear through the coats in our front closet, rifle through the stacks of mail on our kitchen counter. I don't know exactly what it is I'm looking for. But if Theo and Maria were carrying on some kind of relationship in our house, there must be some sign of it here. A condom wrapper. A note one of them forgot to throw away.

I move to the second floor, search through our bedroom. The thought of the two of them in here makes me nauseous, my stomach turning as I stick my hand into the crack between the mattress and the headboard, check beneath the bed. Nothing. I turn to the closet next, and I feel a slurry of hope and dread as my eyes fix on something silver on the shelf: an old laptop of Theo's, one he never got around to discarding.

I take it down from the shelf, open it. The screen is black, dead.

I dig deeper into the closet, throwing old hats and scarves and Theo's childhood collection of baseball cards onto the floor. Finally, I find the cord, pushed back into the corner. I plug in the computer, tapping my leg anxiously as I wait.

It powers on.

There's a password to log on to the desktop, but I know it. *Delancey*, the street Theo grew up on, the same password he uses for everything other than bank accounts and work, with some small variations. I am not sure if he uses *delancey* or something more secure for his Gmail, but it doesn't matter because his password is saved and his inbox loads automatically.

Yes, I think. This is it; this is where the answers will be.

I search the inbox for Maria's name. There are results—mostly advertisements, a few email chains with a group of law school classmates, including a Maria Rottman. Nothing to or from or referencing Maria Salerno. I search for Mona: nothing. I search for Jacob's Hill and find an email to Theo dated the day everything imploded, from Riley Yost, a law school classmate I met at our wedding:

> hey theo, hope all's been good! i am on mat leave with baby 2 and have been going down some weird rabbit holes lol. was binge watching the fifteen and started looking at reddit threads and saw this—is that your wife??

My heart stops. So that's how he found out. That's why he came home angry.

No, I correct myself. *He knew before. He and Maria were working together somehow.*

But there are no other results for Jacob's Hill, nothing indicating he knew earlier. I open Instagram and Twitter, both of which automatically log on, too. I scroll through his DMs but find nothing notable: just a few memes shared with Niko, conversations with colleagues and arguments with classmates about Philadelphia's district attorney, jokes with high school friends. I turn to Messages, which captures all of Theo's incoming and outgoing text messages. Nothing remarkable shows up when I search for Maria, and nothing but a handful of logistical texts with Niko and Fey when I search for Mona. Yeah, Lee's sister Mona is here, too. No results at all for Jacob's Hill.

I type in the number for Maria's cellphone, hold my breath. Nothing.

He would have deleted all that, I tell myself. Anything incriminating— he wouldn't have let it sit there.

The absence of texts and emails doesn't mean he's innocent; it just means he's good at covering his tracks.

The alarm on my phone goes off, and I grab it, silence it, cradle my head between my hands.

Time to see Dr. Khatri.

"So," Dr. Khatri says. I run my fingernail along the grainline of the fabric on her couch. A small thread dangles at the seam of the cushion. I tug, feel it give.

"I'm not crazy," I say.

"No one is saying that." That's not true, though. Theo is saying that, and Dr. Khatri agrees with him, although she is pretending to be neutral, acting like she is willing to hear me out. *My trust is yours to lose,* she wants me to think, but I know better. People like me do not get the benefit of the doubt.

"I need to see Lucy." Lucy is with *him* right now, upset and confused, unsure of where I've gone. She thinks I've left her, and that's probably what he's telling her, not *I'm the one keeping your mother from you,* not *she loves you, she'll be back soon. She'd be here now if I'd only let her.*

"And we will work toward that. Together," Dr. Khatri promises. She leans forward, locks eyes with me. "Can you tell me what happened?"

"I found out who the woman was," I say. Already, an admission of dishonesty. All the time I was sitting here in her office, talking about *moving forward* and *putting the past behind me,* I was still looking for Mona. Dr. Khatri does not ask how I discovered the woman's identity. Maybe she already knows, or maybe it doesn't matter. She doesn't believe me, anyway. "She's someone Theo knows. One of his clients."

"I see," Dr. Khatri says. She's been fed this information already, prepped for what I'm about to say.

"I don't know why." I bite the inside of my cheek, try to hold myself together. "They were working together somehow, but I don't know what they were doing."

"Okay," Dr. Khatri said. She folds her hands together, nods, *I hear you but I don't believe you.*

"I have pictures," I say. "You can see for yourself. It's the same person."

I hand her the mugshot from my bag, pull up the picture of the woman on my phone. "See?"

She looks at them, her eyes darting from the mugshot to the phone and back again, and—against my better instincts—I feel a small glimmer of hope. *She'll see it,* I tell myself. *She'll see it, too.*

"Lee," she says.

"I know her hair is different," I say quickly, trying to explain. "And she's lost some weight."

Dr. Khatri nods again, *I hear you.*

"I'm not making this up," I say. "Other people recognized her, too. Someone online. Her old boss at the corner store."

She hands the mugshot and phone back. "These look like different people to me."

I push them toward her again. "Look closer," I say. "They're the same person. You just have to *look.*"

She takes them, but she looks at me instead. The time for listening is over. I have not convinced her.

"You've been through so much, Lee," she says, gentle, patronizing. "And at such a young age. You lost your sister, and now it feels like you're losing her all over again, and you *still* don't have answers. I think what's happening here is your mind is trying to help you out. It's trying to fill in the blanks for you, connect the dots, just like—"

"This is real," I say. "This isn't like Pittsburgh."

She leans back in her chair, considering.

"We need to talk about treatment options," she says. "I think we should start you on clozapine—"

"That's an antipsychotic."

"And we can monitor how you react."

"I'm not crazy."

"We may also want to consider inpatient treatment," she says. "Just for a short—"

"I'm not crazy," I say again. I stand, grab the mugshot and my phone from her.

"I know how hard this is," Dr. Khatri says, with her forced calmness. "I also know how important it is for you to see your daughter."

I grab my coat from the hook on the door. Dr. Khatri watches me from her perch with her neutral expression: the objective observer, above the fray. "If you want to move forward," she says, "this is the way."

I slam the door on my way out.

Outside, snow falls in large, sticky flakes. The sidewalk is crowded. People shuffle past each other in winter coats and thick scarves, hoods pulled up and faces barely visible.

I call Theo's cellphone. Again. It rings three times and goes to voicemail. Again.

"You have my child," I say to a voicemail inbox I know he'll never check. "You can't keep ignoring me."

But he can, because he is the one with Lucy and finances and a clean bill of mental health. Theo holds all the cards. He always has.

I look again at the pictures. I see the differences, of course, but I focus on the similarities: The set of her jaw. Her smirk.

Dr. Khatri didn't see them, I remind myself. *Dr. Khatri wants me committed.*

But Dr. Khatri wasn't really looking. Her mind was made up already; she saw what she wanted to see.

In fact, Dr. Khatri has never really been listening. She knew about the disappearance and Pittsburgh from the very beginning—from my intake forms, from the conversations with Jacqueline I'm sure she had. She had a picture of me in her mind before I ever stepped foot in her office. It gave shape and order to everything that came after.

And not only did Dr. Khatri know about my past, she's a friend of Jacqueline's. Of course she didn't see it.

She's been on their side this whole time.

This is the way the world works. It's always been stacked against me.

The wind picks up. My face stings, raw with the cold. I should go home, but I hate it there. All those empty rooms. The third floor, half painted, a blue X across the back wall. I reach into my bag and touch the velvet shell of Lucy's patchwork turtle. *She's still out there,* I remind myself. *You can still get her back. This is not like before.*

She is somewhere. I just need to get to her.

I clench and unclench my fists, try to center myself. I have legal rights as Lucy's mother. Theo can't keep her from me forever. The "right" thing to do would be to get a lawyer, to pursue this through the system.

But I know what will happen if I go that route. Theo will get a lawyer, too, and his lawyer will be better than mine. His will be someone he knows personally, someone who cares about him, someone expensive, someone Jacqueline will pay for. Most of our assets are under her control: funds locked up in trusts, shelled out at a trustee's discretion.

The judge will hear my history. He'll make up his mind right away. I know what a lawyer would say if I sought one out: *Usually courts favor mothers when it comes to custody, but in this case . . .*

I need to think. I need to do this a different way.

Where is Lucy now?

I call the number for Theo's office, and a receptionist picks up the phone.

"I need to talk to Theo Burton," I say. "This is his wife. Is he in the office?"

"He is," she says. "Just a second."

The phone clicks, and there is silence, and when the phone clicks again her voice comes back.

"Actually, he's out right now," she says. She sounds like she's just been reprimanded. "Would you like to leave a message?"

"That's okay," I say. "Thank you."

That's two new pieces of information: Theo is at his office, and his receptionist didn't know about our conflict before but does now.

Lucy isn't with Theo.

I call Jacqueline's office next. A receptionist picks up there, too, tells me she's currently with a patient.

Which means someone else has Lucy.

Not just someone else: Maria.

I start toward Jacqueline's rowhouse. I assume this is where Theo is staying, where he has taken our daughter. I picture her in there now, upset and confused, Maria stepping into my role. Theo's mistress, my replacement. Maybe that's been the plan all along.

I'm going to be a mother, too.

If Maria and Lucy are alone together at Jacqueline's house now, this is my chance.

I will take my daughter back. She is mine, and she belongs with me.

The city opens into Rittenhouse Square. Children run across the snow-covered grass in their puffy coats, arms propped out at their sides. If I still had Lucy, this is where we'd be this morning: Lucy perched on my lap, watching the older children roll snowballs in her quiet, thoughtful way. There are strollers everywhere. Babies in full-body suits, hoods pulled over knitted caps. Some the same age as Lucy, blinking in surprise at the snow.

This would have been Lucy's first time seeing snow.

It is *the first time she* is *seeing snow,* I remind myself. Lucy is still out there; she is just not with me.

She is with that other woman. That imposter.

But not for long. I am going to get her back, whatever it takes.

———

Jacqueline lives on a tree-lined street just off the park, full of towering four-story homes. They're all done up for the holidays: tasteful garland wrapped around iron railings, candles lit in windows. Small white lights twinkle from the window boxes. It looks like something out of a fairy tale, timeless and perfectly appointed, with the glaring exception of the house on the corner undergoing renovation. A rickety scaffolding blocks off a portion of the sidewalk, a pile of bricks and debris beneath it. It's a gut job: the house itself is being torn down and rebuilt, only the façade left standing. The workers have finished for the day; there's no one on the street except me.

Beneath Jacqueline's first-floor windows is a wrought-iron bench identical to our own. I think of Maria waiting on our bench the first day she introduced herself as Mona and my blood boils. How could a person be so heartless, so cruel? A sheet of ice coats the stone steps that lead to Jacqueline's front door. A wreath with a red bow hangs there, encircling her knocker, a lion with a ring through its teeth.

I knock three times, then wait.

It's quiet inside, but not an empty quiet. This quiet feels like someone hiding, frozen in place, trying not to make a noise. I picture Maria in Jacqueline's kitchen, one of Theo's intramural T-shirts hanging off her bony frame, motioning to Lucy, *shush.*

"I know you're in there, Maria," I shout. "I know you have Lucy."

Nothing.

I try the doorknob, but it's locked. A lockbox hangs from Jacqueline's railing. I spin the dials for the combination with cold, clumsy fingers, Theo's birthday, push the latch. No luck. They've changed it. They knew I was coming.

I bang on the door with my fist, so hard my hand aches.

"She's my daughter," I say. "She's *mine.* You can't take her from me."

I need to get inside.

I let Theo convince me *I* was the defective one, that I was a bad mother, that I was *bad for Lucy.* I let him convince me I was wrong—

and not just wrong, but losing my mind. I should have listened to my instincts. Theo and Maria are in this together. They're trying to edge me out.

First she took Mona's identity, and now she's trying to take mine.

"Lucy," I shout, louder this time so she can hear me, wherever she is. "It's me. It's Mom. I love you, and I'm coming for you. I'm going to get you back."

And then I hear it: Lucy's cry, muffled and soft, but unmistakable. Lucy, right there, inside, if I can just get past this door.

"She's my daughter, Maria," I shout. "You need to let me in."

I grip the railing, careful not to slip, return to the sidewalk to study the house. The front door, locked, the first-floor window, latched. The second-floor blinds rustle: Maria, watching. She thinks if she stays quiet, I'll go away.

She is wrong.

I am Lucy's mother, and I love my child, and they can't take her away from me.

I will not let Lucy grow up thinking I don't love her, that I didn't fight for her.

I stalk down the block toward the scaffolding. I pick up two bricks, rough and heavy in my hands.

I try the door knocker again.

"Maria," I say. "I don't want to have to break in, but I will. Please. Open the door."

No response.

"Maria, please," I say. "If Lucy is in there, I need you to move her to the second floor. I'm getting in there, whether you let me in or not."

I wait.

I take aim.

I throw.

The window shatters, and it's like the spell this block is under breaks. Lights flicker on in windows, eyes peer out of blinds. A few front doors crack open, careful, cautious. There's a cry from inside Jacqueline's house, loud and piercing.

"Lucy," I call out. "It's okay. I'm coming for you."

I climb onto the bench to reach the window, jagged shards of glass still clinging to the frame. I use the second brick to break them off, but I am not careful enough. I see the blood before I feel the cut. I block out the pain.

I hoist myself, ready to slide in through the opening when I'm hit by a smell like burnt hair. I see smoke, broken glass from a candle sprayed across the floor. I think of Lucy upstairs, hidden away on the second floor. Trapped.

"Fire!" I call out. "There's fire!"

The smoke alarms are blaring now. There's movement from the stairwell. A woman—not Maria, but Jacqueline's housekeeper, Alicia—is clutching Lucy tight in her arms. Sirens wail behind me.

"Help," I shout. "There's a fire."

I twist to lower myself, shifting my weight to my right hand. It's like a knife driven through my palm, and I falter, my feet losing purchase, and fall backward. My body twists, and I feel impact as my head hits the bench railing.

And then: Nothing.

PART FOUR

—

THE
ASCENT

CHAPTER THIRTY-FOUR

—

Lights flash, reflecting off the red brick. I am surrounded by people, medics, their hands on my arms. They are helping me up, ushering me into the back of the ambulance, a low bed, a tight space; they are shining a flashlight into my eyes. *What's your name*, they ask, *what do you remember.*

Smoke and Lucy and Alicia on the stairs. I twist myself around and they grab my arms, *no.*

"Where are they?" I ask. "Where's Lucy? Is she okay?"

"You've had a fall," says one of the medics. He's short and bulky, maybe only an inch taller than me but stronger. "We're going to get you checked out."

"Where is she?" I ask again, and it's not the right thing to say because his grip tightens. "Where is she?"

"Ma'am," he says, more forcefully this time. "I need you to calm down."

"She's my daughter," I say. "They stole her from me." The two men exchange looks and close the ambulance door.

—

I am handcuffed to an ER bed. There is a curtain separating me from the rest of the floor, a beeping monitor above me. No one will answer my questions. The nurses keep conversation short and to the point; they avert their eyes, frightened of me and embarrassed for me. Outside the curtain, I hear the scuff of sneakers, the rattle of a bed rolled across the floor. A heavy fog settles over me. I close my eyes, trying to will away the pain in my right temple.

The curtain loops squeak against the metal bar. I blink and there's Theo, disheveled, distraught.

"Jesus Christ, Lee," he says.

"Where is Lucy?" I ask, trying hard not to cry. "They won't tell me what happened to her. Where is she?"

"She's fine," he says, shaking his head. "She and Alicia are both fine."

"How could you do this to me?"

Theo drags his hands down his face.

"I can't do this," he says.

"You—"

"Do you understand what you've done?" His voice is low. "Do you know what could have happened if the police hadn't—"

The curtain rattles, and a nurse pokes her head in. "We're going to get her moved soon," she says to Theo, not to me. No one is talking to me.

"Moved where?" I ask. "What's happening?"

The nurse is filling out paperwork, eyes focused on some sort of checklist.

"Dr. Albertson will be here in a few minutes. She's just finishing up—"

"What's happening?" I say again.

"They're moving you to the third floor," Theo says, flat, controlled. "They're taking you in for psychiatric observation."

"No," I say. I try to sit up and my head throbs, metal scrapes against my wrist. "I'm not—"

"They're going to get you the help you need," Theo says. He sits in the seat by my bed, looking every bit the concerned husband. I want to tell the nurse to get him out of here, that he is the problem, not me, but no one will listen, not anymore. Theo is in total control.

"Do you need anything?" Theo asks me. "I can get some water, or . . ." I see the way the nurse is looking at him, with admiration, *still so caring after everything she's put him through.* Like he's a good, decent man.

"Go fuck yourself, Theo," I say, or maybe I just think the words, and then I close my eyes and give myself over to the fog.

My room is sparsely furnished: two twin beds, white sheets, dim lights. There's a spot next to the door where the gray paint is a lighter shade than the rest, an old hole that's been patched over. I picture a previous resident slamming her fist into the drywall, her head.

I was wrong I was wrong I was wrong.

There is a woman in the bed next to mine, but she has not said a word since I got here, not to me or anyone else. She has barely moved at all.

It wasn't her I missed my chance I fucked it up.

A cart rattles past in the hallway, the soft pad of footsteps on the vinyl flooring.

Alicia was with Lucy, not Maria. Theo has not started a new life with that woman, whoever she is. I had one chance to get Lucy, and now it's gone.

I know what happens now. I have been through this before. After the fire in Pittsburgh, after I was stabilized and the burns on my shoulder and back were treated, I spent ten days in the mental ward. There was a commitment hearing, and I was given an attorney but didn't see him until the hearing itself, where he received my file and gave it a cursory read-through.

It didn't take them long to decide.

One can't help but wonder, wrote the Pittsburgh reporter who pro-filed me after my institutionalization, what else Ophelia Clayborne inherited from her father. A shared instability, a disconnection from the world. A shared aim: to burn it all down.

Was Christopher my father? Maybe, although maybe my father was the sweet boy from my mother's freshman dorm, who wrote her songs and gave her his sweatshirt. But there is more than one way to belong to someone. Daughter, not daughter. Crazy, not crazy. Different somehow, not fit for this world.

Of course I'd end up here. This room even smells the same as the one in Pittsburgh: sharp and antiseptic, a chemical bite.

A woman raps on the open door and gives me a familiar, patronizing smile. "You're awake," she says. She's dressed in khakis and a polo shirt, like all the medical staff here. Street clothes, not scrubs, which could be too alarming. But her stethoscope and clipboard mark her as someone official.

Ophelia's story to the police never changed. She was asleep, she said. She didn't hear a thing. Those who have followed this case closely have long speculated that Ophelia was a witness to whatever transpired that night. She hid under a bed to survive. She watched, horrified, from a closet.

But what if she wasn't just an observer? What if she was a participant?

"I'm Paula," the woman says. "I'm one of the nurses here."

"I want to see my daughter," I say.

"What's your daughter's name?" Paula asks, friendly, like this is just chitchat.

"Lucy," I say.

"Lucy!" she repeats. "That's a pretty name. How old is Lucy?"

"Eight months," I say.

"Eight months," she repeats again, trying to build rapport. "Such a cute age."

I roll over to face the blank wall, dried drips in the paint. Paula is saying something about walking and talking, *and then, before you know it,* and I can hear her thumbing through my file. Her tone changes, slows, as she sees me through new eyes.

I am not getting anywhere close to Lucy for a long time.

I know how this looks. I know how I appear to the outside world.

But I also know this: I am right about Theo.

He is not the person he's pretending to be.

And no one sees it except me.

CHAPTER THIRTY-FIVE

—

Another day begins. I wake up, take a shower. I have a private bathroom attached to my room, so I only share the space with my roommate—whose name, I learned from the nurse, is Kerri—and Kerri rarely moves from her bed. It's an uncanny valley of a bathroom, almost the same as any other bathroom but not quite, safety-proofed to keep us from making any bad decisions. The shower curtain hangs on snaps, not rings, immediately detaching if you put too much weight on it. The metal peg on the wall can support the weight of a towel but nothing else; it snaps down if you put it to the test. Everything is tapered and smooth, no purchase for a makeshift noose.

I am engorged, sore, a constant reminder of what I've lost. We are not allowed breast pumps on this floor. But the hot water helps, and, in a few days, this last reminder of my connection to Lucy will be gone, too.

The nurses and therapists here pretend Lucy and I will be reunited once I am *well enough*. They tell me to keep Lucy in mind, as an incentive to get better. *For Lucy*, they say, when they want me to talk. *For Lucy*, they say, when they want me to take my medication.

I know better, though. I've lost Lucy, and she's not coming back.

Lucy, I'm sorry. I tried, and I failed.

I towel-dry my hair, get dressed. We can wear our own clothes as long as they do not have drawstrings or zippers or buttons, and Theo—the dutiful husband that he is—dropped off T-shirts and sweatpants for me. The nurses love him. They probably feel sorry for him, stuck with someone like me.

I have a group therapy session that begins in five minutes, and so I start down the hallway toward the meeting room, *early, a good patient,* past the common area with its round white tables bolted to the floor. A few of the other patients work quietly on a puzzle, bright orange and yellow sunflowers coming together in swirls.

I do not belong here, I remind myself. *This is not like before.*

But it doesn't matter that I don't belong here. What matters is how it looks, and I know it looks bad. I know how they see me.

I need to focus on the facts, keep them straight in my mind. A woman showed up at our house pretending to be my sister, but she was really a con artist named Maria Salerno. I was not the only one to see the resemblance between "Mona" and Maria. Only Theo and Dr. Khatri have claimed not to see it—Theo, who has reason to lie, and Dr. Khatri, who is biased against me.

To my left, one of the other patients is hunched over one of the shared telephones, speaking softly. A nurse standing nearby spots me. She looks away, too fast, whispers something to another nurse beside her.

"Her?" the other nurse asks, glancing in my direction. Everyone on the medical staff has at least heard about the docuseries, although they pretend to my face not to know.

Focus, I tell myself. Another fact I can be sure of: Maria Salerno is one of Theo's clients. It was right there on the court docket, public record. Theo must have recognized her as soon as she appeared at our house for dinner, but he pretended not to.

I step into the meeting room. The chairs are arranged in a circle, about half of them occupied. Our therapist, Harper, is already seated, rifling through papers to look busy. She is young, maybe twenty-four or twenty-five, and I get the strong impression she does not like this job.

Theo did not want Maria in our house. He didn't want her anywhere near us. *She's an addict,* he told me, trying to plant seeds of doubt. *I work with people like her all the time.* He told me not to see her with Lucy, which was tantamount to telling me not to see her at all. He was angry when she came to live in our home. Angry, and then resigned, and then furious the day she disappeared, a rage I've never seen in him before.

"Should we begin?" Harper asks, looking up from her paperwork. "Evie, how are you feeling this morning?"

Evie is the woman sitting beside Harper, pulling at the small hairs on her arms. "Fine," she says, her voice reedy and slight. "Adjusting."

If Theo didn't want the woman in our house, why didn't he say something? Why didn't he tell me who she really was?

"Let's talk a little about that adjustment."

Maria must have been holding something over him. *If you tell Lee the truth about me, I'll tell her the truth about you.*

Harper is talking about techniques for handling anxiety, a checklist straight out of some textbook. She tries to write something on the whiteboard with a dried-out marker but changes her mind.

I remember the question Theo posed to Maria when he "met" her: *Are you working now?* I understood it as a question about her employment, but he meant: *Are we a mark?*

The bruises on her face and arms appeared right after.

The woman next to me, with too-wide eyes and severely blond hair, is bouncing her leg, *tap tap tap,* full of nervous energy.

The last day Maria was in our house, Theo came home angry.

Tap tap tap, tap tap tap.

Theo came home angry, and then she disappeared.

Tap tap tap, so hard it rattles the chair, faster and louder and more persistent.

She disappeared, and so did all her things, just a dark stain on the wood floor left behind. The other regulars at her bar hadn't seen her: *Maybe the consequences of her actions finally met up with her.*

"This is bullshit," the foot-tapper says. Harper ignores her, her jaw tensing.

I told her we knew she wasn't Mona, Theo said. *That's all it took.*

A lie a lie a lie.

"What are we even doing here?" says the foot-tapper.

Where is Maria?

"You'll get your turn, Lynn," Harper says.

What did Theo do to her?

"Lee," Harper says, turning her attention to me. "Do you feel comfortable sharing why you're here?"

I am about to say no, pass, let someone else talk. Give Lynn her turn. Harper can't make me say anything, although it might get written up in my file that I'm being *uncooperative,* a *bad* patient, that I'm not making the effort.

I think about Lucy, alone, with him.

Hiding from the truth doesn't help. Hiding has only gotten me here.

"I grew up as part of a . . . group," I say. "We kept to ourselves, mostly, grew our own food, built our own community."

Everyone is listening, all eyes fixed on me. I bite the inside of my cheek, try to keep my focus.

"It was an unusual childhood, and I know, looking back, there were things happening I didn't understand. But the thing is . . ." I break off, almost emotional, compose myself. "Most of my memories are good memories. That was a happy time for me."

Lynn shifts in her seat, watching.

"That's what makes it so hard. That was my whole life, and it wasn't a bad life, and it's so hard to reconcile that with the rot underneath. I *can't* reconcile it."

Harper gives me a neutral smile, meant to convey sympathy, understanding. I focus my attention on the floor.

"I woke up one morning and they were all gone. They had left me behind, and they didn't tell me where they were going or what they were doing. I'm angry—so angry—that they left me, but more than that, I miss them. And ever since then, there have been times when my reality becomes disconnected. Not all the time, but sometimes. When I'm under a lot of stress."

Lynn half-snorts beside me, but Harper nods, encouraging.

"But that's not what's happening now," I say. "This is different. Someone found out about my past and took advantage of me. A woman pretended to be my sister. She needed a place to stay, and I let her into our house. I wanted—"

I break off, blink back tears.

"I just wanted it to be her so badly. I needed to know she was okay, that she had been okay this whole time, that I hadn't failed her."

I feel the weight of Mona on my lap. Her small hand on my arm, her face turned up to look at me. Her eyes, blue, not green like Maria's. Blue like Christopher's. *What are we doing here, Fee-ah?*

"You were just a child yourself," Harper says, trying for comforting.

"But this woman wasn't my sister. I think she had some kind of relationship with my husband. I think she was blackmailing him."

That's all it took, Theo said. *She packed her things and left.*

Lie.

"I think he did something to her," I say. "I think he did something really bad."

Harper's face contorts into a concerned frown.

"Does your husband make you feel unsafe, Lee?" she asks, leaning forward.

I shake my head. "That's not what I'm saying. The woman in our house was there one day and gone the next, and Theo was the last one to see her."

"Has he hurt you before?"

"He took my daughter," I say. "He put me in here."

"I see," Harper says.

"The woman's name is Maria Salerno," I say. "Someone should be doing something. I don't know if anyone is even looking for her."

"Do you want to talk about the separation from your daughter?" She's backtracking, her voice gentle. "That must be hard."

"No," I say. "I want to talk about this. Someone needs to *do* something."

But Harper is not listening to my claims. She is looking for the feelings beneath them, the disordered thinking at their core. Nothing I say will be taken at face value here. It is all part of my illness, a symptom to be treated.

I can talk and talk and talk and no one will listen, nothing will happen, nothing will change.

This was never going to end any other way.

At the end of our forty-five-minute session, Harper dismisses us. She packs her notebooks into her suede purse with exaggerated focus, avoiding eye contact as the patients leave, not wanting to encourage further conversation. Lynn lingers, staring at me like she wants to say something.

"What is it?" I ask. It comes out harsher than I mean for it to.

"I saw that documentary, too," she says. The side of her mouth twists. She thinks she's caught me in a lie.

"Yeah, well. That's my life."

"Uh-huh," she says, still smiling. "I watched the whole thing in two days. So fucked up."

"Yeah," I say. I turn toward the door, try to leave, but Lynn follows, still talking.

"It's crazy they never found the bodies," she says, like we're friends now, like this is a shared point of interest.

I shrug. "Maybe there weren't bodies to find."

"Oh, those people are dead," she says, and it takes every remaining ounce of self-restraint not to smack her across the face. *You don't belong here*, I remind myself. *Don't act like you do.*

But it's getting harder and harder all the time.

"Lee," Paula the nurse says, poking her head through the doorframe. "Your husband is here to see you." She says this like it's good news, like this is something that will cheer me up, and my knee-jerk reaction is to tell her I don't want to see him, but I think better of it.

"Okay," I say. "Thanks."

I follow her out to the common area, where Theo sits in a chair that's been weighted down with about forty pounds of sand, just enough that we can slide it across the floor but can't lift it over our heads.

"Hey," he says, standing, like he's about to give me a hug, but I flinch and he backs off. I sit across from him, cross my arms over my chest.

"How is Lucy?" I ask.

"She's good," he says. He shows me a picture of her, propped up on Jacqueline's wooden floor, wearing a headband with a floppy bow. He doesn't say: *She misses you.* He doesn't say: *She needs you, Lee. Come home.* He means: *She's doing fine without you. I'm not giving her back.* "How are you holding up?"

I lean forward. "I know you did something to her."

There is a momentary flash of panic across his face, and in that half-second I know I am right. But then he furrows his brow, readjusts his expression to gentle concern.

"Lucy is just fine," he says.

"Maria," I say. "I know."

Concern turns to pity.

"Lee," he says, gently.

"What was she holding over you?" I ask. "You knew who she was. Why did you let her into our house?"

"Lee, stop," Theo says, his voice low and tight.

"She didn't just *leave*, Theo," I say. "What did you do to her?"

He drags his hands over his face, rises from his chair. "I can't do this," he says. And then, loudly enough that Paula can hear, too: "I love you, and I'm here for you, but I can't do this right now."

"I know the truth, Theo," I say, but he's already leaving and doesn't turn around. It doesn't matter to him what I know or don't know. No one will listen to me, anyway.

Unlike Harper, our art therapist, Susan, has been at this a long time. There are easels set up for all of us, and she loops the room slowly, striking up gentle conversations with each of us about what we're working on and giving suggestions on technique if we ask for them.

I am not an artist. I am trying to draw the residence, where I lived for the first twelve years of my life, but as soon as I try to set it to paper the image eludes me. The number of windows, the color of the roofing tiles, the location of the vestibule.

"Are you drawing *Jacob's Hill*?" Lynn asks from beside me, emphasizing the last two words like this is a personal affront. I don't answer. I have been trying to avoid her, but she took the easel next to mine, and it was too late for me to move.

"What really happened to you?" she asks, leaning in closer. Susan begins to walk toward us, and Lynn straightens, returns her attention to her own painting.

"Do you think she was involved?" Lynn asks, her tone suddenly detached and neutral.

"Who?" I ask.

"The survivor."

The painting is all wrong: the church-red of the door, the shape of the annex. I rip off the paper to start something new.

"She was twelve," I say.

"Plenty old enough," Lynn says. "I've read everything— *everything*—and I think she must have been involved. How else does she survive? How else do you dispose of that many bodies?"

"They went somewhere else," I say. "They went off the grid."

"I don't buy it," Lynn says, and she begins rattling off facts and details she has gotten from Meghan Kessler and elsewhere—the jars of preserved food left in the root cellar, the clothes and shoes and Kai's small stuffed dog, all left in place. She talks on and on, but as soon as she mentions Meghan, I stop listening.

Meghan.

No one will listen to me, but everyone listens to Meghan. She has an audience, a voice, a pulpit, and she wants to tell my story.

Not your *story,* I remind myself. *She wants to tell* a *story. She's going to think you're crazy, just like everyone else.*

It will be Pittsburgh all over again. *Poor Ophelia Clayborne,* she'll say. *We thought she was a survivor, but Jacob's Hill claimed her, too, in the end.*

Maybe that's okay, though. Maybe it doesn't matter if I'm not presented well. I just need the story to reach someone who knows Maria, someone who will realize it's been too long since they've seen her. I need it to reach someone who cares about her, who will demand an investigation. An investigation will lead to Theo, and then Lucy will be safe, away from him.

"Have you read the manifesto?" Lynn asks. "Real Unabomber vibes."

There are so many places this plan could go wrong. Meghan might not use Maria's name, and, even if she does, I am not sure if Maria has anyone who will take notice. If someone does notice, I am not sure they will be the type of person the police will take seriously. There are so many unknowns, so much uncertainty.

"How does someone get sucked into that, you know? Who is *listening* to this guy?"

I have to do something. Theo is a monster, and he has my daughter.

"What are you working on today, Ophelia?" Susan asks, coming up behind us.

"I'd like to call someone," I tell her. "Family—my cousin. Can I access my phone to get her number?"

CHAPTER THIRTY-SIX

—

The morning Meghan comes to visit, I am nauseous, my stomach twisted into knots. From our short phone call, Meghan understands that she needs to pretend to be family. The hospital will keep her out if they realize she is a member of the press trying to extract a story. But all it will take is one person who has seen the docuseries, who realizes Meghan looks familiar, who puts the pieces together. The odds of this working suddenly seem vanishingly small and the risks uncomfortably high.

But at 10:05 A.M., Paula knocks on my door and informs me I have a visitor.

"Your cousin is here to see you," she says. There's no trace of recognition in her voice. I follow her out to the common room, sure she will feel my nervous energy radiating off me, or hear my heart drumming in my chest. But she seems unconcerned, and then there is Meghan, sitting at one of the round tables, rising from her seat when she spots me approaching.

"Ophelia," she says, smiling calmly, warmly, like we know each other. "It's so good to see you."

"How's your mom doing?" I ask, glancing at Paula, who is half-listening at the nurse's station, making sure the conversation is benign.

"Great," Meghan says, playing along. "She's thinking about you.

She wanted me to bring you something, but I wasn't allowed to bring anything in."

She gestures to the empty table in front of her. No recording device, of course, but also no pen and paper. She won't be taking notes, so I won't even have that as reassurance she'll get things right.

My eyes flit to her visitor's badge, *Meghan Bartos*. She notices.

"Kessler is my maiden name," she says, quietly enough that Paula won't hear. But Paula doesn't seem to be paying attention anymore, her focus on a table of patients playing Apples to Apples with a censored deck, their volume growing. Meghan's hair is pulled back into a ponytail, her face bare of any makeup. It's not enough to make her look like a different person entirely, but she also doesn't look like a reporter, here on a job. She looks like a regular person, a friend.

"So," she says, leaning in toward me. "I have so many questions for you, but I also know our time here is probably limited." She's good at making the right kind of eye contact, sustained but not aggressive, like someone who really wants to *listen*, someone who is really trying to *understand*. I'm sure she thinks of herself that way, too; it probably helps. "So why don't you take the lead. I know you said you have something you want to tell me."

"Okay," I say. I lower my voice. "But before I start, you should know this isn't about the disappearance. Or it is, but it's not about what happened that night. I don't know what happened that night. It's about something that happened after."

"That's fine," Meghan says. She must be disappointed, but she doesn't show it.

"I know this will probably turn me into a spectacle," I say.

"It won't," she assures me. A lie, but probably unintentional. Meghan does not think she turns anyone into a spectacle. "I want to give you a chance to tell your story. That's why I'm here."

I close my eyes. *This is for Lucy*, I remind myself. For Lucy, and for Maria's family, whoever and wherever they are, who must be out there, wondering: *Where is our daughter?*

I open my eyes and tell her everything.

CHAPTER THIRTY-SEVEN

—

At first, nothing happens. The days blur one into the next. I am sleeping, I am waking, I am sitting through another group therapy session, I am talking about suicidal ideation to Dr. Gresnik, a baby-faced man with shirts that always gape at the buttons: *No, of course not, never.*

I am thinking of Lucy. I am wondering if she's figured out how to catch a snowflake on her tongue, if she has any new songs she likes, if she's found a new favorite stuffed animal.

I am wondering how quickly my face will fade from her memory.

And then one morning Paula comes into our room to give Kerri her medication, and her voice has taken on a higher pitch.

"Good morning, ladies," she says, but she's avoiding my eyes and then staring for too long when she thinks I'm not paying attention. She lingers for longer than normal at Kerri's bedside, fidgeting with a clipboard, pretending to read the notes left by the nighttime staff.

I shower, dress, make my way to the common area. There are two young nurses at the nurses' station, jittery and alert, glancing in my direction and then away. One takes out her phone, and the other says *don't.* I shift uncomfortably in my chair, pretending to be distracted by the game show playing on the shared television.

Something has shifted. Something has changed.

I am about to go to my morning group session when Paula intercepts me, tells me that today I'll be talking one-on-one with Dr. Gresnik, instead.

"Why?" I ask. "Did I do something wrong?"

"Oh, no," Paula says, her face flushing. "No, you're fine. Just a change in schedule, that's all."

But Dr. Gresnik seems on edge, too. He clicks his retractable pen, his forehead pinched, sniffing at regular intervals.

"How are you feeling today, Lee?" he asks, the question he always leads with, a mood assessment, and I answer the same way I always do, *fine*. His face reddens like maybe I've said the wrong thing. He pauses and asks about suicidal ideation, like always, and I tell him no, my normal response.

"Let's talk about your relationship with your husband," he says, and I can feel that this is a test, that things could go one of two ways, and so I say the thing I know he wants to hear:

"Theo has been very supportive."

He sniffs again, leans back in his chair.

"You know," he says, "we limit patient contact to family and close friends for good reason."

"I know," I say, and I try to sound calm but my heart is pounding in my chest. Something has happened. Meghan has done something.

"If you aren't serious about your own recovery, then there's not much we can do for you."

"I know," I say again. "I'm serious."

There's a sheen to his forehead. He clicks his pen again twice, sets it down on his desk.

"Okay then," he says. "Any new side effects from the medication?"

The next time I am called into Dr. Gresnik's office, he tells me he has spoken with "the team," and they all believe I am no longer in need of involuntary inpatient treatment. I've been doing very well, hitting all my benchmarks. I am to continue treatment on an outpatient basis, of course, and there is a plan in place for that. But as of today, I am free to go. If I want to.

"Go where?" I ask.

He frowns. This is not a promising response.

"Home," he says.

And so now I am standing in the loading zone of one of the many buildings in the hospital complex, cars and bikes and people in scrubs rushing past. I'm holding my duffel bag full of sweatpants and T-shirts, along with the jeans and sweatshirt I wore when admitted. My backpack has been returned to me, too. Inside are diapers and wipes, a change of clothes for Lucy I never took out, her patchwork turtle. My phone. I power it on and am happy to see there is still a charge. I've missed messages from Andi. The earliest one suggests we meet up for drinks. The next, a few days later, is radically different in tone.

Holy shit, I saw the news. Are you okay??

I search for my name, and there are many results.

Meghan has written a story—*my* story, or a version of it, anyway—and it has spread like wildfire. She posted "Mona's" photograph and Maria's mugshot side by side and posed the question: Is this the same woman?

It is hard to know what to make of Ophelia Burton. I first met her in the common area of a hospital psychiatric ward. There were other patients in the room, too: a man shouting expletives, another counting the square tiles on the ceiling, a card game that nearly ended in a physical altercation. I braced myself for the worst. But when I saw Ophelia walking down the hall toward me, she looked like someone I might see at the park or at the grocery store, someone I might have gone to school with in another life. Someone I might have been friends with. She sat down across from me, clear-eyed and coherent.

"I don't belong here," she told me, and my first instinct was to agree with her.

But Ophelia has a troubled past. The only survivor of the disappearance at Jacob's Hill, she sometimes has difficulty separating truth from fantasy. She has a history of delusions and paranoid thinking. She once set fire to her own house, while in it, and was saved only because a neighbor walking by smelled smoke and acted fast.

Ophelia is troubled and unreliable, and that makes her vulnerable.

There are people in the world who will seek that out.

Meghan wrote that she didn't know what to make of my story about Maria and Theo, but it was clear that someone had worked their way into my life, taking advantage of my situation. Every time I look at these two pictures side by side, she writes, I see something different.

Do you see it? she asked her audience. And: Does anyone know this woman?

Her audience responded. There are long threads on Twitter and Reddit, some people calling me crazy, some objecting to the use of that term, others railing against my inhumane treatment.

lilyofthevalley82739: I wrote a letter to the hospital demanding her release. You can do the same—address and sample letter below.

soundofasparkplug: You can call them, too. Ask to talk to Marisa Vandergaard. She's one of the directors.

I stop reading and brace myself against a brick column. Is this what got me out? And what if I *hadn't* looked like someone Meghan might be friends with?

There is a helicopter above me, loud and close, setting down on the hospital landing pad. Two women in scrubs beside me talk loudly about a colleague they don't like, one of the doctors, *an asshole*. The automatic doors to the hospital open and close, and I'm hit with a gust of warm air. I have the sudden, irrational thought that at any moment someone might realize a mistake has been made, that I should still be in there, *where did she go,* and they'll come looking.

I need to get out of here.

I start walking. I cross an on-ramp to the highway, gridlocked cars below blaring their horns. I am on a bridge spanning the Schuylkill River, the sharp wind stinging my face, and I can see Center City spread out in front of me. Theo is out there somewhere, probably back at our rowhome, now that I am gone. He is out there, and he has Lucy.

A car drifts to the right, nearly clips a biker, close enough for the biker to slam his fist against the window.

I will find them. I will get Lucy back.

I walk the blocks to our house, the cold cutting through my layers. I climb our stone steps, try the doorknob, locked. I fumble with my key, but it doesn't fit.

Theo has had the locks changed.

I knock on the door, but there's no response, and I can feel there's no one inside. I sink onto the front steps and rest my forehead in my hands, when I hear a door swing open.

"Lee?"

It's Andi, on the neighboring steps, looking alarmed, and I see myself through her eyes. My puffy face, my duffel bag of clothes. She'll have read all the stories about me. She knows all the pieces of my past. I wipe my face with my hands, apologize.

"Oh, Lee," she says. "I've been so worried. Do you want to come in?"

She holds her door open, and I burst into tears.

Andi's house smells like banana bread, and, sure enough, there is a loaf and a half on her kitchen counter. I sit on her couch next to one of Des's discarded sweatshirts, a stack of books on the coffee table: *Dune, The Maze Runner*, a collection of stories by Isaac Asimov. A backpack slouches against the leg of a kitchen chair, homework spread across the table.

"He's listening to music in his room," Andi says, moving the backpack to a hook on the wall. "So don't worry, he couldn't care less about what we're talking about down here." She fixes me a cup of tea, sits on the other side of the couch, pulls one leg in.

"You don't have to tell me what's going on," she says. "But you can if you want to."

It all spills out of me: Maria's appearance on our doorstep, how she worked her way into our lives, her relationship with Theo, her sudden disappearance. I wait for Andi's expression to transform from gentle concern to alarm, confusion, judgment. It never does. I wait for her to tell me that I'm overreacting, that I'm imagining things, that I should be talking to a trained professional. Instead, she says:

"I have a security camera, you know."

I blink, surprised.

"It captures motion in front of your house in addition to mine. There's some way to adjust the settings to stop that, but, you know." She gestures around at her cluttered house. "I've never gotten around to it."

"So you have footage of Maria on there?" I ask.

"Maria, Theo. You. Anyone going in or out of your house."

"Can we check it?" I ask, and I allow myself to feel a flutter of hope for the first time.

"Yeah, of course," she says, pulling it up on her phone.

We scroll back to the day of the disappearance. There's footage of me and Maria and Lucy returning from the playground. I watch myself onscreen as I fiddle with the belt on Lucy's seat, pull her out of the stroller, kiss the top of her head. Another clip: me, alone, on my way to the hair salon to talk to Elise. Another, about an hour later: Theo, returning home. Even on the small phone screen, with Theo at the periphery of the footage, I can see how angry he looks: the set of his shoulders, the clenched fist, the aggressive way he stalks into the house.

For a moment, I allow myself to wonder what would have happened if I had been home instead of Maria.

Footage of an Amazon delivery person a half hour later; a clip of our neighbor and her Pomeranian walking past. But no footage of Maria leaving the house in a panic, carrying all her belongings with her. Nothing to support Theo's story that he confronted her and she fled.

"She never left the house," I say, staring at the screen.

"It's possible the camera just didn't pick it up," Andi says cautiously. "But it's pretty sensitive."

The next clip is Jacqueline, standing on our front steps, looking distraught, confused. Theo comes to the door holding Lucy, and the video ends. Another clip, ten minutes later: Theo leaving the house with a large suitcase. Another, five minutes after that: Theo leaving the house with Maria's rucksack.

Fifteen minutes later, I come home.

"What is this?" Andi asks, looking up at me. "What does this mean?"

"She never left," I say. "He killed her." The words stick in my throat. It was one thing to have the thought; it's another thing altogether to have it played out in front of me.

"We need to go to the police," Andi says, watching and rewatching the footage.

"They won't do anything."

"If they see this? Of course they will."

I shake my head. "It's just people coming and going. That's what they'll see. And Theo will use it against me." More evidence of my paranoia, my instability. I am not a person people take seriously. I am not someone people believe.

"Lee," Andi says gently. She's lowered her voice now, suddenly more conscious of Des above us. "There are people on your side. You know that, right? I don't know if you've seen the articles, but people care about your story. They care about you."

She's wrong. People are interested in my story, not in me. There's a difference. This kind of attention and support is ephemeral, fleeting. In a few days, when no new salacious details emerge, nothing to capture the public's heart and mind, I'll be forgotten. In a few weeks, when Theo is still free and I am seeking custody of Lucy, this will all be in the past. Theo will still be Theo, a lawyer with connections and resources, and I will still be his erratic wife who has lost it before, who might lose it again. *Who knows what she might do to herself,* Theo's lawyer will say. *Who knows what she might do to the baby.*

"I can't," I say. "I need more. Something definitive."

"You can," Andi says. "I'll go with you."

I shake my head, all nerves firing. I rise from the couch. "I need to talk to him."

"You can't do that."

Lazy footsteps cross the room above us. Des emerges on the stairs.

"Oh," he says, blinking in surprised recognition. "Hi." I wonder if he has seen the media attention, too, or if he's just startled to have a guest in his house. "Mom, what's for dinner?"

"Chicken meatballs. Don't make that face. You liked it last week." She turns to me. "Stay the night," she says. "We've got a guest room. You can get some sleep, and we can figure out what to do with the footage in the morning."

"What footage?" Des asked, his interest piqued.

"Nothing," Andi says.

A thought occurs to me. "Is the guest room on the third floor?"

Andi squints at me quizzically. "Yeah," she says, but before she can ask why, Des says again: "What kind of footage is it?"

"It's *nothing*, Desmond," she says. "Boring adult stuff. Don't worry about it."

"Okay," I say. "I just need to get a few things."

"You can't go back to your house."

"Why not?" Des asks.

"I won't," I say. "I'm going to CVS."

Andi looks at the front door like maybe she could block me from going.

"I need to pick up a prescription," I say. "That's all."

"Be careful," she says. "Come right back."

"I will," I say. "I promise."

And, of course, I mean it. I need access to that room.

It's night now: late enough that Andi will be asleep, and Des—if he's awake—will be preoccupied in his room, playing video games or listening to music with his headphones. Theo and Lucy will be sleeping now, too.

Andi's guest room has a door that leads out to a rear balcony, finished with teak benches and potted herbs, a view of the glowing skyline.

And that balcony abuts the roofing that juts out beneath our third-floor window. A window that used to be sealed shut with paint but isn't anymore, thanks to Maria and her smoking habit.

I climb over the low concrete wall that separates Andi's balcony from our roof, the shingles rough beneath my feet. I tread carefully, hopeful that if Theo hears anything above him he will chalk it up to squirrels, a possum.

I slide the box cutter I purchased at CVS out of my pocket and cut into the screen. The window scrapes on its tracks, and, once I've opened it enough that I'll fit through, I freeze, listen for movement inside. All I hear is the artificial sound of running water filling the space, Lucy's sound machine on full blast.

She's in here.

I climb through the open window. A nightlight switches on as it catches my movement, and I hold my breath, but Lucy doesn't stir. In the nightlight's glow, I can see the dim outlines of the room. Theo and his mother have finished painting it. They've decorated it for the little girl Lucy will grow into. A plush rabbit with floppy ears and long limbs sits on a tiny seat for a toddler, resting against a fuzzy pink pillow. Pictures of teddy bears doing ballet hang on the walls. Her diapers and swaddles are neatly stored in baskets on her dresser; the bird mobile floats above her crib. Doubt swells up in me: *What if Lucy is better off here?*

But then I see her, sleeping peacefully, her arms splayed out at her side. Her chest rises and falls, her eyelids twitch. I think about what Theo has done. My daughter belongs with me. It takes every ounce of my willpower not to grab her, to pull her against me, to climb back out of the window holding her in my arms and not look back.

No, I tell myself. If she cries and Theo wakes, it will all be over.

We need our car and the extra time this will buy us.

I creep down the stairs, careful to make as little noise as possible. Theo is sprawled across our bed, the sheets kicked to the side. He's wearing a Penn Law T-shirt, gray sweatpants. His mouth gapes open; he's sound asleep, oblivious. Theo is not afraid of the outside world creeping in. It has always been kind to him, always on his side.

For a moment, I can almost see Theo as a little boy, scrawny limbs, Batman sheets on his bed, Jacqueline tiptoeing into his room to turn off his dinosaur lamp. He rolls to his side, and I step back, but his eyes are still closed.

I see Theo in his Walnut Street apartment, at the beginning of our relationship, his first time living alone. Niko had recently abandoned him to move in with Fey, and so the apartment was an odd patchwork of furniture and appliances: a single chair, a blender but no coffee maker, two plates, one water glass, no lamps. We spent most of our time in his room, his bed a mattress on a box spring, sheets and no comforter. His face inches from mine on the pillow, earnest, lit by the sun coming through the blinds.

I pre-thread the zip ties I brought with me. I link them in a chain to the bedpost.

Theo, beside me on the bed at the hospital, looking at newborn Lucy with awe, touching her small hand carefully, with his index finger, like she might break.

I palm the box cutter and hold it to his throat.

"Theo," I say. His eyes blink open. "I'm home."

———

Theo slides his wrists into my makeshift handcuffs, never breaking eye contact.

"Lee," he says. "What are you doing?"

"I'm here for Lucy," I say. "She belongs with me."

"You don't want to do this."

"No," I say. "I don't. But you haven't left me many options, so."

My plan is to secure Theo well enough that Lucy and I have a full day's head start. We will take the car and drive for long enough to get out of Pennsylvania and through New Jersey. There will be Sophie Alerts, but likely limited to the tristate area. If we can get far enough away by the time Theo notifies the police, we will be okay. Once we get out of New Jersey, we'll abandon the car and strike out on foot or by train.

We will disappear.

"We can work through this together," Theo says, wincing as I tighten the zip ties.

This will be reported as a kidnapping. But not a stranger-in-the-night kidnapping, an aggrieved-parent kidnapping. The police will look but not that hard. A couple of days, maybe. We just need to get far enough that they don't find us in the next seventy-two hours.

"Lee," Theo says, trying to push up in bed but unable to move that far. "*Stop*. Think about what you're doing."

"Fuck you, Theo."

I am prepared. I packed some food to start us off—sun butter, dried fruit—and I know what to look for when we hit the woods. I know how to find water, how to purify it. I know what we can eat, what we can't. We can wait for the attention to cool, for interest to wane. We can make this work.

"This isn't you. I know this isn't really you."

I tighten the final zip tie, straighten to meet his eyes. "This *is* me. This is who I've always been, and I'm tired of pretending otherwise. I can't do it anymore."

I am a survivor. I am ready to do what it takes.

Theo realizes he's chosen a losing strategy, changes tack.

"This isn't going to work," he says with a forced calm.

I start toward Lucy's stairs.

"People know who you are," he says. "It'll be all over the news. They're going to find you right away."

I think of the morning of the disappearance: the scrape of a branch against my window, silence from the hallway, the shared bathroom. All of them, gone.

"No, they won't," I say.

"You'll need water, food. Supplies. More than you've got in there." He nods his head toward my backpack, bulging with only a fraction of what we need.

"My family did it with nothing," I say.

"Lee," he says, his voice lower now, almost gentle. "Your family wasn't trying to survive."

"You don't know that," I say.

"Just think about it, Lee," he says. "Think about what you're taking with you."

A flash of a memory: the nervous energy in the residence hallway, the trek through the woods. The grassy knoll.

"No."

"You're different from them, Lee," Theo says. "You're choosing life."

"No," I say again. "They left. They built a new home somewhere."

But as I say it, I see the corrugated metal, the small cavern-like room behind it. A glimpse inside: empty.

"This isn't the way, Lee," Theo says. "They'll find you and arrest you, and it will be a very long time before you see Lucy again. You know that. You know this won't work."

He's right. He's right and this is not the way forward because there is no way forward. There is no disappearing. This was never going to end smoothly, cleanly, without bloodshed.

I reach inside my backpack for my phone. I keep my hand low so

Theo can't see, open a voice memo and press record. I grab hold of the box cutter again and start toward him. He braces himself. Beneath his forced calm, he is terrified. I hold the box cutter to my wrist.

"Is this what you want?"

"Jesus, Lee," he says. "Don't do that."

"Is this it? Is this the way?"

I am my mother's daughter. The one she left behind.

"Lee," he says. He's repeating my name, like this will center me, bring me back, remind me who I am. But I know who I am. "Stop."

"I'm one of them, right? I'm a danger to Lucy. I let a stranger into our house—"

I push down.

"*Stop*," Theo says again. "Stop. You were right, Lee. You were right. I knew Maria."

I lift the pressure.

"You knew her," I say. "Who is she?"

"Let me go," Theo says, "and we can talk. We can talk this through. We can figure this out."

"Who is she?" I say, pressing down again, drawing blood.

"Stop," he says. "She was a client, okay? She was a client of mine. You were right. We had an affair and it got out of hand. It started when—it started when Lucy was a couple months old, and it was just—everything was so *hard* and nothing was getting better. We were barely talking, and you weren't leaving the house, and then all that stuff with Charlie Mazur and Jane Aberdeen happened. I was just—I was a *wreck*, Lee, and Maria was someone to talk to. I wasn't myself. I just needed—I don't know what I needed, and it was a mistake, and then I didn't know how to get out of it. I didn't mean for it to get to that point. I *love* you, Lee. I didn't mean for any of it."

He is crying, real tears, remorse and self-pity. He means this, or he thinks he does. He sees himself as the victim in this.

"So you knew the whole time," I say. My hand drops down to my side. "You knew she wasn't Mona."

"I *didn't* know that," he says, defensively. He tries to straighten himself, fighting against the restraints. "I didn't think you'd be *wrong* about who your own sister is. I didn't know how long it had been since you'd seen her. I didn't know about . . . everything that happened."

"But you knew her name was Maria."

"I knew she *went by* Maria. I knew she *went by* a lot of things. When she showed up at dinner, and you introduced her as Mona, I thought—I thought I had gotten really unlucky."

"Why would she do that?" I ask. "Why would she pretend to be my sister?"

"She was obsessed with me," Theo says. Even through his remorse and fear, his arrogance shines through. I can see how Theo must have basked in Maria's attention. His young, attractive client who needed his help. Who was so *grateful*. Who really *saw* him, Theo the hero, burdened by his commitment to justice and his unstable wife. "I don't know—it didn't last long between us. We only slept together a few times, and then I came to my senses. I told her how important my family was to me, that I needed to end things. I broke it off, but she wouldn't accept that."

I see Mona—Maria—at the coffee shop that first day, watching us, her hand on Lucy's foot.

"She must have looked you up," Theo says. "She knew how to—she knew how to find things on people. She knew how to use it to her advantage."

It wouldn't have been hard once the documentary came out, once there were threads on Reddit linking Lee Burton to Ophelia Clayborne.

"How could you let this happen?" I ask. "How could you—"

"I didn't know what to *do*. I told you to keep your distance. I told you I didn't want her in our house."

"Did you tell her to leave?"

"Of *course* I did," he says. "Of course."

"But she wouldn't go." I think again of Maria's bruises after our first dinner together, the man she wouldn't speak about.

"She said you wanted her here, and she was staying. And I thought she was your sister, so I couldn't—what was I supposed to do? She was crazy, Lee."

I flinch at the word, and then I realize all of Theo's references to Maria have been in the past tense.

"What happened?" I ask softly. "The day she left?"

Theo swallows, inhales a shaky breath, like maybe he's been waiting for this moment for a long time, desperate to get it off his chest.

"An old classmate sent me a post about the disappearance, with a message, *is this Lee?*, and, like, a laughing emoji. I didn't know what she was talking about. I started reading more and I realized that, Jesus, this *was* you, and this was why I had never met anyone from your family, and all the pieces started falling together. Maria wasn't really your sister, she was taking advantage. She saw a weakness, and she exploited it. She didn't care how much it hurt us. How much it hurt *you*."

He shifts in bed, uncomfortable from the ties.

"So I went home to talk to you about it. And instead of you, Maria was there, with Lucy. With our *daughter*, alone. I told her I knew everything. I thought that would be enough. I thought calling her out . . ."

"It didn't work," I say.

"She started taunting me. Saying I don't even know my own *wife*. Everyone knows, she said. My wife has been lying to me, this whole time, she's a lunatic, and everyone knows except me."

"I don't understand," I say. "What she wanted. If you weren't doing this together—"

Theo sniffs, his breath shaky again, and suddenly I do understand.

The text from an unlabeled number: *What are you going to do about the baby?*

It was from him. He must have a burner, a second phone he used to contact her, to cover his tracks.

"She really was pregnant," I say. "And it was yours."

"I told her to get an abortion," Theo says. "I told her I already *had* a family, and it wasn't her. It was a reality check, a scare, it reminded me of what really matters in my life. I thought she took care of it, that it was done, and then she shows up, months later—"

"And she works her way into our life," I say.

"She said . . ." Theo tears up again. "After I confronted her, she said she had this all figured out. A win-win for everyone. You get to think you have a sister again, that you're *helping* her, and I get to support her free and clear, without raising any questions about finances, or . . ." He blinks, steadying himself, and I can tell that this is a tipping point, that things could fall one way or another.

"She was a threat to our family," I say, trying to imbue the words with understanding. "She was trying to hurt us."

"*Yes,*" Theo says, his voice full of relief, grateful I understand. "She was going to take everything from us. If she came forward, I'd lose you, and Lucy, and my reputation, my job. And the alternative—"

"You were protecting us," I say.

"I was protecting us," Theo repeats. Always the savior. He really believes this about himself. He really doesn't think he was in the wrong.

"Where is she now, Theo?"

"I took care of her," he says. "She can't hurt us—she can't hurt you—anymore."

"You killed her."

His expression shifts, just slightly, a hint of doubt. "I was protecting our family. She was crazy, Lee. I didn't know what she might do—to you, to Lucy, to any of us."

"But especially you."

"Lee."

"Theo," I say. I wrap my fingers tightly around the box cutter again. I walk toward the bed, and he squirms, pulling at the zip ties, which hold tight. This time, I press the blade against his throat.

"You have a choice," I say. "You tell me where to find the phone you used to text her."

"Lee," he says. "Please."

"The phone, Theo," I say. "Or I'll handle this myself, right now. I know how to do it."

He swallows and winces, and then says, "It's under the couch. I cut into the bottom of it."

I pull the box cutter back and rush down the stairs. Sure enough, there it is, a slit in the black fabric, a bulge. The phone is on but locked, and I carry it upstairs. Theo lies still, but he's breathing heavily, and I can see the red indents where the plastic has cut into his skin.

"What's the password?"

"Lee, you don't—"

"Tell me your password."

He gives in, and I open his messages to find a long exchange with Maria. The early texts are mostly graphic: Theo telling her what he wants, Maria complying. A flurry of texts back and forth, then radio silence for two months. And then the texts start up again.

What the fuck are you doing?

I'm part of the family xx

A few days later:

What are you going to do about the baby?

There's a response from Maria an hour later, after our conversation about motherhood. We're keeping it, she says, and Theo responds: I won't let you do that.

I pocket his phone and turn off the recording on mine.

"Lee," Theo says. "You need to think about what you're doing here. We can figure this out together. It was a mistake, and I'm sorry, but we can move forward together. As a family. No more secrets."

"No more secrets," I repeat, my heart pounding. I palm the box cutter again.

"It's going to be okay," he says.

I tighten my grip.

"We can figure this out. Just let me go."

Upstairs, a high-pitched shriek.

"Don't do anything stupid."

Lucy.

"Lee."

Lucy needs me. She needs me alive and well and stable.

"*Lee.*"

She needs me here.

I let go of the box cutter and lift my phone instead. I dial 911.

"Lee, put down the phone."

"I need the police here," I say to the operator. "My husband killed someone."

CHAPTER THIRTY-EIGHT

—

ONE YEAR LATER

Theo is on trial.

The night I called the police exists as a blur in my mind. I got off the phone with the emergency dispatcher and called Meghan Kessler. It was too late at night, or too early in the morning. I left her a long, rambling message and sent her what I had: the recording of Theo's confession, screenshots of his text conversation with Maria, a description of the footage on Andi's camera.

I held Lucy close and breathed in her smell.

I love you, I told her. *I will always come back for you.*

I took her, half-asleep, to Andi's house, pounded on the front door. After the third round of knocks, Andi answered, confused and startled, surprised to see me outside and not upstairs. I handed her my daughter, told her the police were coming, asked her if she could take care of Lucy until we got this sorted.

Of course, she told me, taking Lucy into her arms. *Whatever you need.*

The two officers were both young, both clearly disturbed by the scene at our house. *She's not well,* Theo told them, like I knew he would. *She's trying to hurt me.* They took us both into the station, *so we can sort this out,* one said, exchanging looks with the other. They sat us in separate rooms. I do not know what kind of questions they asked Theo, but the ones they asked me dripped with judgment and doubt.

This woman, said the first officer, *you thought she was your sister.*

That's right, I said.

And now you think she was your husband's mistress, and she's missing.

Dead, I told him. *She's not missing; she's dead.*

But in the morning, everything changed. Meghan received my messages and blasted Theo's confession out into the world, posting it online for the public to consume and pick apart and assess. *Call the station,* she advised her fans, providing them with contact information for the local precinct, the names of the officers on the case. *Demand answers. Let them know you care. Ask them: What happened to Maria Salerno? Where is she now?*

Prodded along by the attention, the police began to investigate. It turned out Theo had not learned much from his clients' mistakes after all. None of the cameras on our block had captured Maria leaving the day of the disappearance, but several had shown Theo coming and going. Footage from a block away showed him loading the suitcase into the trunk of our car. He looked shell-shocked; he struggled with the bag's weight. Something was clearly *wrong.* But the camera caught other neighbors on the street at the same time, and they did not seem to notice. No one blinked an eye as Theo slammed our trunk shut, rested his hands against the lid, took in a steadying breath. They were not looking for a murderer, and so they did not see one.

The police pulled GPS data from Theo's devices, which showed two different Theos on the day of the disappearance. Theo's phone showed him traveling from our house to Jacqueline's around the same time Jacqueline picked up Lucy. He must have slipped the phone into the diaper bag, so it would look like he spent the rest of the afternoon with his mother, coming clean about our marital struggles and my mental state and discussing what to do. A good husband, a *concerned* husband, loyal and long-suffering.

And then there is the second Theo, the Theo who forgot he was still wearing his Apple Watch. This Theo went to Rittenhouse Hardware to purchase a shovel—which he bought with cash on camera—and then drove over the Betsy Ross Bridge into New Jersey, taking toll-free roads to the Pine Barrens, where he found a secluded spot in the woods.

Once they had that data, the police found Maria nearly right away, buried in a shallow grave.

So now I am here at the criminal courthouse, the same courthouse where Theo has stood beside his clients, ushering them through the large wooden doors into the courtrooms, whispering reassurance, strategy, explanations. Theo is in the courtroom, and when the doors swung open earlier I could see him sitting behind a wooden table beside his own team of attorneys. The gallery is full of Theo's friends and colleagues, interested onlookers, reporters and podcasters and other members of the media. Meghan is in there, along with a ruddy-faced intern who takes copious notes.

I am not allowed in.

The prosecutor—Yvette, a woman around my age who can't stand Theo and also seems to dislike me—told me this is because I am a witness. *That doesn't seem fair,* I told her, and she shrugged, *not my rule and not my problem.* It was to make sure I wasn't influenced by other testimony, she explained. Very normal.

Yvette seems nervous about putting me on the stand, but my testimony, she says, is an important piece of the story. Theo is not denying the affair, nor is he denying that he covered up Maria's death. He is claiming instead that her death was accidental, a fall—not a push—down our third-floor stairs. Theo found her body when he returned home, crumpled in a heap on the second-floor landing. He panicked. He knew how it would look. He made a mistake in judgment.

So we need you to explain that Theo had something to hide, Yvette told me, at a fast clip like always, like she had somewhere more important she needed to be. *We need to establish Maria was blackmailing him.* She warned me that the cross would be *difficult* and *personal,* and I got the strong impression this meant they were going to tear me apart.

They won't want to look like they're bullying you, she said, more to herself than to me. *That will help.*

That's fine, I told her, *I can handle it,* although as I wait here now for my name to be called, I'm not sure that's true. My truth is complicated. It's hard for me to pinpoint what I did and didn't know, what I really believed and what I wanted to believe, what I intentionally overlooked. It's the kind of truth that doesn't fare well in a court of law or under the microscope of public scrutiny.

I cross and uncross my legs, watching the steady current of lawyers in suits, anxious defendants, distraught families. The hallway is cavernous, sound bouncing off the marble walls and tiled floor. I notice my hands are shaking and grip the bench to steady them. There's a sudden rustle from behind the closed doors of Theo's courtroom, the sound of a hundred people standing and stretching at once. The doors swing open, and the crowd pours out, and out of nowhere there is the flash of cameras, the hum of questions, voices jostling against each other.

Yvette spots me and ushers me away from the crowd. Her co-counsel, a woman named Kayla, gives me a discreet thumbs-up.

"It went well in there today," Kayla tells me, when we're safely out of earshot.

"We'll put you on first thing tomorrow," Yvette says. "How are you feeling?"

"Fine," I say, because that's what she wants to hear. "I'm ready."

"How did it go?" Andi asks when she opens her front door. Des and Lucy are on the couch behind her. Des has converted one of his gym socks into a puppet, and Lucy is giggling, delighted.

"Kayla said it went well," I tell her. "I'm on tomorrow."

"You've got this," she says, ushering me back to the kitchen, and then: "Your cousin was all over social media today."

I cringe. I knew Clara was still giving commentary on the case, but I've successfully avoided those videos so far.

"No, no," Andi says, handing me a glass of water. "It's good news. She was getting dragged for some TikTok she made about the trial."

"Oh really?" I say.

"Yeah, your fans were calling her out for being a bully."

She says "fans" lightly, almost a joke, but I can't think of a better word to describe the group of people she means. It's an odd relationship, fervent and fragile. These are people who like the image of me, who are interested in the story that's being crafted inside the courtroom, without me.

"You want to stay for dinner?" Andi asks, and I shake my head.

"We should get back," I say. "I need to get some sleep tonight." I thank her and Des again, and pull Lucy close, and walk to our car for the drive home.

Andi and I are no longer next-door neighbors. I sold our rowhome a couple of months ago and bought a small house outside the city. There's a swing on the front porch, trees and a creek in the backyard. Theo was too much a part of our house in the city, memories of him in every room. Memories of Maria, too, tinged with shame and embarrassment and guilt, triggered every time I looked at the door to the third floor.

And, of course, there was our sudden notoriety following Meghan's story, heightened by the buildup to the trial. Strangers started lingering outside our front steps, watching for us, taking pictures. Our life was on display. It's less convenient to access our suburban house—and less tempting to visit, since it's not *the house where it all happened*—although I still tense whenever I spot a car parked on our street that looks out of place or an unfamiliar face walking by.

The proceeds from the sale of our city place are keeping us afloat for the time being, and I am sending out applications to museums and libraries located outside of Philly. I've gotten more initial interest than I expected, so maybe the notoriety isn't all bad.

When we reach our new house, I unbuckle Lucy from her car seat and grab a stack of mail from the mailbox. It's full of bills and advertisements and letters from individuals who are passionate about the trial, who have devotedly followed Meghan's coverage, who want to offer support, theories, claims, ideas. A letter from Gregory London in Elko, Nevada, who claims to have seen Christopher while on a spiritual retreat in the Mojave Desert. Another from Philippa Rove who thinks her next-door neighbor might be my mother. Very secretive, she wrote. Keeps to herself. A long, rambling missive from a Willa Basker, who believes she might have been Adrienne in a past life. She has vivid dreams, she said, describing them, and they bear no resemblance to the Jacob's Hill I remember.

They mostly mean well, unlike Maria, or if they don't mean well, they at least aren't actively trying to cause me harm. The people sending these letters tell themselves they're helping. They convince themselves this is information I want to have.

I turn on the television. "Of course she *knew*," says a blond woman with severely arched eyebrows. "A part of her must have *known*. How can you live in a house with your husband and his mistress and not *realize*? Not see what's going on?"

"So do you think she was in on it?" asks her interlocutor, a matronly brunette.

"I think it's certainly within the realm of possibility," the blond woman says. "I mean, this is her husband. Bringing his *mistress* into their *home*. She had to know more than she's letting on."

I know I am not really supposed to be watching this coverage. But I can't help myself; I need to know what's happening. Today, they're discussing the DNA test that showed Maria was, in fact, pregnant with Theo's child. They're discussing Maria's life, too. She was a runaway, on her own by the age of fourteen. She had to learn how to fend for herself, and so she did.

I can almost see some of myself in her, what might have happened to me if Anne hadn't stepped up or had let me push her away.

I watch, drawn into this story that doesn't really involve me anymore. Yvette told me some of these details during witness prep, but not everything. Maybe this was in part to avoid witness tampering, but I get the sense I am just not high on her priority list. I am a distraction, a complication.

A crucial, but unreliable, witness.

The trial resumes, and I am called to take the stand.

I take my seat in the witness box beside the judge. The courtroom is full, bodies jammed into each row of wooden benches. Theo won't meet my eye. He leans back, whispers something to one of his attorneys, who nods in response. Jacqueline sits two rows back, her face pinched. I try not to look directly at the jury, but I can feel their eyes picking me apart.

I spot Andi in one of the back rows. She gives me a reassuring smile. Des has Lucy this morning. He's taking her on a stroller walk not far from the courthouse.

Yvette is first to question me. She walks me through my experience of what happened: the documentary and Maria's appearance, her claim to be my sister. How she came to live with us. My ignorance of the affair. I try not to look at the jury, focus instead on getting my story right.

When Yvette is done, one of Theo's lawyers rises—the woman, Nadeen. Yvette told me she would probably be the one to cross-examine me so that the questions would appear less aggressive. Nadeen smiles at me for the jury's benefit, kind and respectful.

"Ophelia, you have a history of mental illness, don't you?" she asks, like she's sorry she has to do this.

"Yes," I say, like Yvette instructed me. Simple and straightforward, no equivocating, no elaborating unless asked to do so. My history is a fact about me, but it doesn't disqualify me as a witness. It doesn't mean I can't tell the truth.

She walks me through my past: my abandonment, my breakdown in Pittsburgh, my hospitalization, just as Yvette said she would.

"And so Maria finds you and claims to be your sister."

"That's right."

"Did you have doubts?"

I pause, and I'm prodded to answer the question.

"Some," I say. "Of course. But she said she was Mona, and I believed her."

"Why?"

I don't know how to answer.

"Did they share any distinctive physical traits?" Nadeen asks.

I picture Mona, at six, sitting on my lap on the cold dirt ground in the forest clearing. One of Christopher's drills, a month before the disappearance. The adults milled restlessly around us, waiting for instructions, for Christopher to say what comes next. *What are we doing, Fee-ah?* Mona asked, taking my hand in her small hand, crossing my fingers over each other and pulling them apart. The bruises—so many bruises—that covered her arms, and that rash, those tiny red pinpricks. I saw something like it again years later, visiting my aunt in the cancer ward, and quickly averted my eyes.

"Mona was so young when she disappeared," I say, just like I've rehearsed. "So there were some differences, of course, but a lot of changes happen between six and twenty-six."

Tired, and so easily winded, pushed to exhaustion by nothing at all. I think of Mona, bedridden for weeks at a time. I think of my aunt, toward the end.

We are going someplace special, I told Mona during that drill. *A community just like ours, but even better, with lots of other kids to play with. They know we're coming. They're waiting for us there.*

"But she didn't have any special knowledge that made you think she was your sister, did she? Information about your mother only she would know, that kind of thing?"

But what are we doing here? Mona asked, meaning the damp forest, the dugout.

"I didn't want to push her too hard," I say. "I didn't want to scare her away."

This is just the first stop, where we keep our supplies, I told her, and as I said it, a part of me believed it, too. *We've been storing up food to take with us. It's a long walk, and we don't want to show up empty-handed, right?*

"So this woman didn't share any distinctive physical features with your sister—and, in fact, you noticed some differences. And she couldn't give you any information about your mother or Jacob's Hill beyond what she learned from the documentary. But you're asking us to believe that you *really believed* this woman was Mona."

"I wanted her to be okay," I say. I wipe away tears, avoid looking at Yvette, sure she'll be disappointed. "I just wanted Mona to be okay."

On redirect, Yvette asks me about the many hours of therapy I've completed, my mental state today: *good, stable, lucid.*

"Do you still believe the woman in your house was Mona?"

"No," I say. "I was wrong. I wasn't seeing things clearly."

"Now Lee," she asks, shooting a knowing look at the jury, "did you know, when you asked Maria into your home, that she was having an affair with your husband?"

"No," I say. "Of course not."

"Would you knowingly invite your husband's mistress into your home?"

"No."

"Did you know that Maria was pregnant with Theo's child at the time of her death?"

"No."

"No further questions."

I am allowed back into the courtroom for closing arguments. Andi sits beside me, a welcome source of support. The prosecution's case is simple: Maria was blackmailing Theo; Theo snapped and killed her; he buried the body to cover it up. It's the story I believe, and I am a part of it—Yvette refers to *his wife and new baby* multiple times—but it also feels distant, like I'm observing it from the outside. This is the prosecution's story for the jury, for public consumption. It captures the facts the jury needs to convict. It doesn't convey what it was like to live it.

The story Theo's defense team tells is simple, too. Maria's fall was an accident. Theo was under a lot of stress and wasn't thinking straight. He knew how it would look; he is all too familiar with the criminal justice system, with the way the police build a case. He chose to bury the body to protect himself. A mistake, yes, a crime, true, but not murder. I stiffen when Theo's attorney mentions me, Theo's *mentally ill wife,* one of the sources of his stress. Andi squeezes my hand, and I am relieved that Lucy is with Des, not here.

The jury retires for deliberations, and we're told this may take a while. Andi stays by my side as we step out of the courtroom and back into the city, the sun glaring, too bright.

"Coffee?" she asks, and I nod. She texts Des, tells him where to find us, and we settle into a coffee shop a few blocks away from the courthouse. They're playing music, too loud, and my head is swimming, my temple pulsing.

"You okay?" Andi asks.

I blink back tears, try to pull myself together. I picture Theo walking free out of the courthouse, fighting for custody. Lucy, ripped from my arms again. Mona—the real Mona—at six, in a clearing in the woods.

"I can't imagine what this must be like," Andi says.

"What if I'm not good for Lucy?" I say.

Andi is taken aback by the question. She shakes her head, looks me over.

"Lee," she says, finally. "I see the way you are with Lucy. I see the way you've cared for her through"—she gestures with her hands—"all of this, and I cannot imagine a more stressful environment than this. You are a great mother, and I'm not just saying that. You are figuring this out."

"I couldn't save Mona," I say. "I didn't protect her."

Andi blinks, surprised—we have never spoken about the night of the disappearance—but then catches herself. She leans forward and squeezes my hand.

"You were a child yourself," she says.

My hands are trembling, and this time I can't stop the tears from falling.

"It wasn't your fault, Lee," Andi says. She scoots closer and puts her hand on my back, rubbing in small circles like my aunt used to do. "What happened to your family wasn't your fault."

"I don't know if I can do this alone," I say. I straighten myself, wipe beneath my eyes. Des backs through the coffee shop door, pulling the stroller along with him, and Andi waves him over.

"You aren't alone," she says. "We're here for you. It's going to be okay."

It's less than two hours later when the phone rattles on the table in front of us.

The jury is back.

CHAPTER THIRTY-NINE

—

There's a dirt path—or what used to be a dirt path, anyway—at the dead end of Cobbler's Road. The weedy overgrowth is matted down in two rows. I allow myself a momentary fantasy: the old white vans springing to life again, transporting my family to farmers markets and feed stores.

I know, of course, that's not possible. These tracks are from Meghan's team, barreling over the path to capture a few atmospheric shots of the old buildings, the quiet woods.

I park the car, pull Lucy from her car seat, strap her to my chest to keep her close. She still fits in the carrier, but just barely. It sags under her weight. The straps dig into my shoulders.

Guilty. The jury found Theo guilty.

I hear birdsong, and Lucy hears it, too, cranes her neck to see. The *cheer, cheer, cheer* of a cardinal, welcoming and familiar. The leaves form a canopy over the path, the branches interlocking, the air earthy and wet.

The jury announced the verdict, and the world slowed down, blurred at the edges. Andi pulled me into a hug, and I could see Theo's face in profile, surprised and disturbed, his lawyer leaning in toward him, to talk about options, probably, the possibility of appeal. I walked out of the courtroom, and I could hear the hum of reporters' voices, their questions overlapping, bouncing off one another, Meghan's voice behind me, *Lee, Lee, wait up.*

I pushed through the crowd to my car. I buckled Lucy in and closed the doors, shutting out the sound. I sat behind the steering wheel for a moment, debating, but I knew what I had to do. Instead of driving to our house, I took us here, to Jacob's Hill.

"This is where I grew up, sweet girl," I say, trying to keep my voice light, soft. "This used to be my home."

I can almost see Mona and my mother, walking ahead of me. My mother's hand reaching out, back, for me. I breathe in Lucy's hair, the baby smell now gone.

Through the leaves I see a yellow stone house with a red-tile roof, small windows spaced far apart to hold in the heat. The common house. Thick vines grow up its exterior now, the woods slowly taking it back. The front door is rotted through and half-missing, wooden panels splintered. The dirt path turns to stone.

I can feel the weight of Mona on my back, her thin arms wrapped around my neck. Sliding off, stooping down to examine the stones' rough edges as we worked together to build the path. *This one here.* The sticky stems of dandelions, the golden crowns in our hair.

My mother's voice: *My beautiful girls.*

Two daughters, one healthy and one so weak she often couldn't leave her bed. *Some people aren't made for this world,* my mother used to say. *My special girl, one foot in this world and one in the next.*

I walk along the stone path slowly, careful not to disturb it, up the steps to the front door. The doorknob turns in my hand, and what is left of the door groans open.

It's still here. The couches, now mildewed and torn, the cushions ripped apart by nesting animals. The grandfather clock, the hand stopped. The kitchen counters are covered in a thick sheet of dust and mouse droppings, a few handprints and streaks, empty bottles of beer and wine. Crumpled cigarette packs and condom wrappers litter the floor, left by teenagers who came here to spook themselves, to dare each other, to see who could handle it the longest.

I know what this house is to others: a strange place where strange people lived, who believed strange, silly things, who allowed themselves to be led like lambs to the slaughter. A place where a monster took hold.

But I don't see Christopher here. What I see are Mona's legs dangling from one of the wooden chairs, too short to touch the ground. What I feel is my mother's warmth as I leaned into her side on this couch, placed my hand on her stomach to feel Mona kick. *That's your sister,* she told me. *She's saying hello.* The deck of cards spread across the table, Adrienne's throaty laugh, Kai's shriek of giggles, River and Echo tussling beneath one of the tables, full of life.

This was my home. This was where my family lived.

But my family isn't here anymore. I know that.

I know where they are.

Lucy and I pass through the front door again, back onto the stone path, and then we veer off it, taking a route into the forest that isn't demarcated by stones or packed dirt. The forest has changed, the old markers grown over, but I know this route well.

This is the exit plan.

To the creek and through the water, upstream. Cold, just like it was then, my mother's firm grip on my hand, *keep walking, Ophelia.* Lucy kicks her legs, the weight of her heavy, the straps of the carrier digging in.

Out of the creek and deeper into the forest. I followed this same route the day of the disappearance, alone, farther and farther into the woods. *I'm coming. Wait for me.* Those missing hours, too hard to hold in my mind. I looked for them here. I knew the exit plan, had rehearsed it many times.

The forest is thick here, thorned branches scraping my arms. I hold up my hands to protect Lucy's face. We push through, keep walking until I see the knoll. Unremarkable, unless you know what you're looking for.

I know what I'm looking for.

I kneel down and scrape away the moss, and there it is: a metal door.

I think of Mona on my lap, her weight pressing against my chest, the story I told her. *This is where we keep supplies.*

A part of me believed it, but a part of me knew it wasn't true. A fairy tale to make us both feel better. Behind the corrugated metal door was an empty dugout, earthy and cavernous.

We weren't ever going anywhere else.

I had seen the medical vial in my mother's nightstand. *Is that for Mona,* I asked, since Mona had been unwell. Her panic, her fingers digging into my arm. It wasn't medicine, not really. She took it with us on our drills, rolled it in the palm of her hand.

The one thing missing from her nightstand.

My heart thrums in my chest. Lucy kicks her legs, and I place my hand on the cold metal.

It was exposed, just like this, on the day of the disappearance, the sod pushed to the side. I reached this spot in the woods, sure that this was where they would be, waiting for their orders, for Christopher's okay, for the pronouncement that we could go home, just another drill. But there was no one. The woods were silent, and the metal door was plainly visible, which it was never supposed to be. At the end of each drill, we packed down the sod so it wouldn't be discovered, so we wouldn't be found out.

They finished a drill, I told myself that day, *and now they're on their way back home, but they forgot to cover the door.*

And so I did it myself, packing down the sod with care, making sure it was covered. *When I get back to the residence,* I told myself, *they'll be there, happy to see me, happy to hear I corrected this mistake.*

This clearing in the woods: This is where they are. This is where they've always been.

I pull my phone from my pocket, ready to call the police, Leanne, someone who will open this door and find what lies beyond it. But I am deep in the woods, and there is no reception here. I stand and start back toward the creek, but after a few paces, I have reconsidered.

Here is what will happen if I call the police now: They will show up at the residence in their squad cars, bathing Jacob's Hill in red and blue. They will trample through the forest, bringing their crowbars; they will tear this door open. The police will not find my mother and Mona and the rest of them.

They will find the bodies they left behind.

I run my finger along the door's edges. Their gravestone. Their tomb.

After the bodies are found, the media will have a field day. Meghan Kessler will be overjoyed with the discovery, her docuseries coming to a neat and tidy conclusion. She'll take credit for having brought the missing pieces together. There will be media scrutiny. There will be jokes about shaved heads and comets and drinking the Kool-Aid.

My family will not just be a curiosity. They'll be a punch line.

I'm not ready for that. Not yet.

But I think of Adrienne's sister, Elise Dagnelle: She lost someone, too. Gregory Dunn lost his mother. Amy Price, a sister and two nephews. A part of them, always wondering.

I make up my mind. I will find the people who lost someone here before I do anything else. We can figure out how to protect and honor the ones we loved; we can decide, for ourselves, what the right thing is to do.

Lucy and I retrace our steps. Not far from the knoll, there are flowers blooming: bluebells and buttercups and a shock of golden forsythia. I pick them, hold them for Lucy to smell. We put together a makeshift bouquet.

"Your aunt Mona," I say to Lucy, "was a special person. One foot in this world and one foot in the next."

I see, in my mind's eye, my twelfth birthday. My mother's bracelet, bundled in fabric.

Our secret, she told me. A way for me to keep her close. A message to my aunt: *Take care of her. Please.* A message to me: *Anne is a person I love. This person will keep you safe.*

We do not get to know the thoughts of the people around us: not really, not fully, not ever. But here is what I choose to believe. My mother knew what was coming. She knew that this time, it was not a drill. Mona was not well, not strong enough to make it on her own in the world. Not strong enough to make it anywhere, maybe, and Christopher was never going to let her go.

My mother knew I could still be saved. She didn't abandon me. She wanted me to survive.

I lay the bouquet on the corrugated metal.

I wrap my arms around my daughter and she reaches up to touch my face.

Lucy, I am here for you. Always. We'll find our way through together.

I breathe her in, kiss the top of her head. "Okay, Lucy," I say. "Okay, my sweet girl. It's time to go home."

ACKNOWLEDGMENTS

—

Writing a second book is a much less private endeavor than writing a first book, and I am incredibly grateful for all the love, support, and encouragement I received along the way. First, a huge thank you to my agent, Julia Kenny, for your ideas and suggestions, and for shepherding me through this process, and to Arielle Datz and the Dunow, Carlson & Lerner team.

Thank you to my editor, Andrea Walker, for your enthusiasm and brilliant guidance, and to Naomi Goodheart, Madison Dettlinger, Vanessa DeJesus, Ted Allen, Carlos Beltran, and the rest of the team at Random House.

I am fortunate to have such an incredibly talented and supportive group of friends, both at home and within the writing community. To Kristen Bird, Jennifer Fawcett, Olivia Day Wallace, Emilya Naymark, Tammy Euliano, Julie Tollefson, Dave Wickenden, Steven Laine, Matthew Witten, Andrew Hallman, Iris Chamberlain, Josiah Child, and Jenny Kraft: Thank you for your keen eye, your insights, and your friendship.

Special thanks to Molly Booth for talking me through the day-to-day life of a public defender and Rick Meier for answering my questions on FBI investigations. Thanks also to Lucas Wujek for your guidance on preteen boy hairstyles and Katie Pinder for your southern dialect insights.

Thank you to my sister, Emma Wujek, who was not only an early reader but has also been a constant source of support, laughter, and wisdom throughout motherhood, and to K. J. Lawler, Ali Lawler, and Steve Wujek. I feel so lucky to be in this together.

Thank you to my parents, Mike and Janis Lawler, who have been reading my stories and encouraging me since I could pick up a pencil. Thanks, also, to my mom for being a great mother and nothing like Sylvie.

To Steve and Amy Buccola, thank you for your support and enthusiasm, and for being nothing like Jacqueline.

To Rhodes and Ada, thank you for being your wonderful selves, and to Vince: Thank you for everything.

The quote from Laura Johnston Kohl in the epigraph is from *Stories from Jonestown* by Leigh Fondakowski, a powerful collection of interviews with Jonestown survivors.

ABOUT THE AUTHOR

—

ALLISON BUCCOLA is an attorney and the author of *Catch Her When She Falls*. She lives outside Chicago with her husband and two children.

Instagram: @allisonbuccola

X: @allisonbuccola

ABOUT THE TYPE

—

This book was set in Baskerville, a typeface designed by John Baskerville (1706–75), an amateur printer and typefounder, and cut for him by John Handy in 1750. The type became popular again when the Lanston Monotype Corporation of London revived the classic roman face in 1923. The Mergenthaler Linotype Company in England and the United States cut a version of Baskerville in 1931, making it one of the most widely used typefaces today.